PRESERVATION

ALSO BY JOCK SERONG

Quota
The Rules of Backyard Cricket
On the Java Ridge

Jock Serong's first novel, *Quota*, won the 2015 Ned Kelly Award for Best First Fiction. *The Rules of Backyard Cricket* was shortlisted for the 2017 Victorian Premier's Award for Fiction, and was a finalist in the 2017 Mystery Writers of America Edgar Awards and in the 2017 Indie Book Awards. *On the Java Ridge* won the Colin Roderick Award in 2018 and was shortlisted for the 2018 Indies. Jock lives with his family on Victoria's surf coast.

@jockserong

JOCK SERONG
Preservation

TEXT PUBLISHING MELBOURNE AUSTRALIA

textpublishing.com.au
textpublishing.co.uk

The Text Publishing Company
Swann House, 22 William Street, Melbourne, Victoria 3000, Australia

The Text Publishing Company (UK) Ltd
130 Wood Street, London EC2V 6DL, United Kingdom

First published in 2018 by The Text Publishing Company

Cover design by W. H. Chong
Page design by Imogen Stubbs
Maps and symbols by Simon Barnard
Typeset in Adobe Caslon 12.5/17.5 by J & M Typesetting

Printed and bound in Australia by Griffin Press, an accredited ISO/NZS 1401:2004 Environmental Management System printer

ISBN: 9781925773125 (paperback)
ISBN: 9781925774030 (ebook)

A catalogue record for this book is available from the National Library of Australia

And I know that today, if I were to go to the deserted dune,
the same sky would pour down on me its cargo of breezes and stars.
These are lands of innocence.

ALBERT CAMUS
The Minotaur or The Stop in Oran

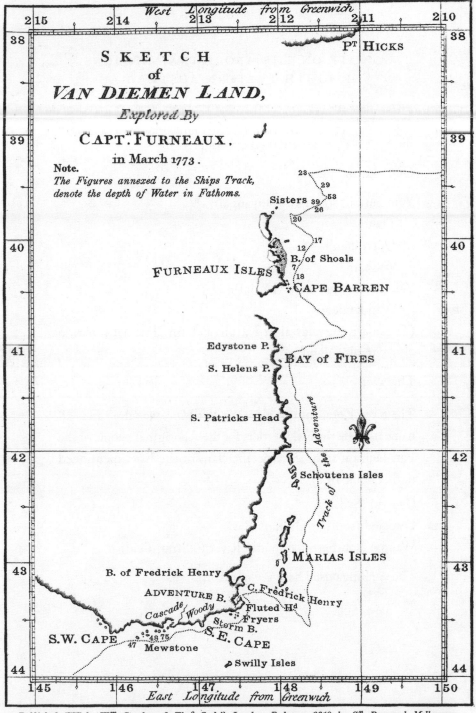

SKETCH
of
VAN DIEMEN LAND,
Explored By
CAPT. FURNEAUX.
in March 1773.

Note.
The Figures annexed to the Ships Track,
denote the depth of Water in Fathoms.

West Longitude from Greenwich

2 15   2 14   2 13   2 12   2 11   2 10

PT HICKS

Sisters

FURNEAUX ISLES

B. of Shoals

CAPE BARREN

Edystone P.

S. Helens P.

BAY of FIRES

S. Patricks Head

Track of the Adventure

Schoutens Isles

MARIAS ISLES

B. of Fredrick Henry

ADVENTURE B.

C. Fredrick Henry

Cascade Woody

Fluted Hd

Fryers

Storm B.

S.W. CAPE

48 75

47   Mewstone

S. E. CAPE

Swilly Isles

East Longitude from Greenwich

1 45   1 46   1 47   1 48   1 49   1 50

Published 1777, by Wm Strahan & Thos Cadell, London. Redrawn 2018, by Sn Barnard, Melbourne.

A NOTE ON THE ABORIGINAL NATIONS
OF SOUTH-EASTERN AUSTRALIA

The Aboriginal peoples encountered by the survivors from the *Sydney Cove* are marked opposite.

Gunaikurnai nation

Yuin nation, southern (Guyangal):
   Thaua
   Djirringanji
   Walbanja
Yuin nation, northern (Kurial):
   Wandandean
(These are the coastal or Katungal Yuin. The Yuin nation also extends inland.)

Tharawal

The term Eora, meaning *here* or *this place*, was the catch-all name used by the early settlers for the Aboriginal people of the Port Jackson area. The specific clans of the Eora mentioned in this book are:

Cadigal (Sydney)
Gweagal (southern Botany Bay)
Wangal (southern Paramatta River to Strathfield)

The spellings used here are not definitive.

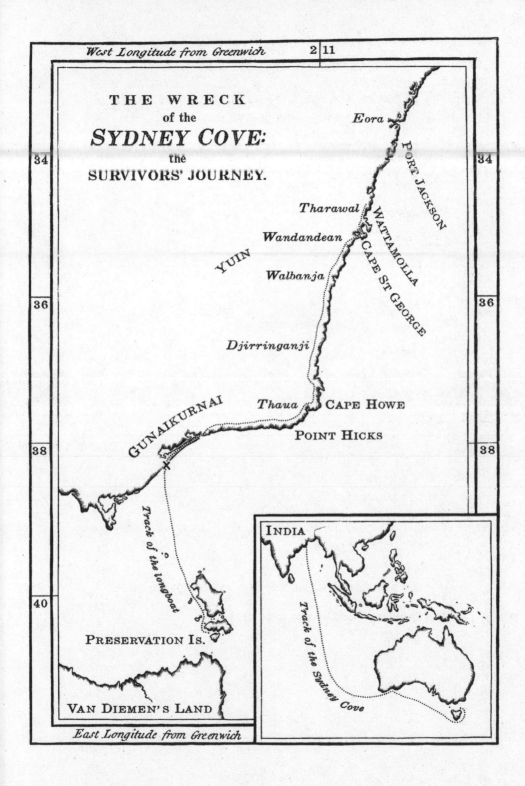

THE WRECK
of the
SYDNEY COVE:
the
SURVIVORS' JOURNEY.

West Longitude from Greenwich 2|11

34

36

38

40

Eora

PORT JACKSON

Tharawal

WATTAMOLLA

CAPE ST GEORGE

Wandandean

Walbanja

YUIN

Djirringanji

GUNAIKURNAI

Thaua

CAPE HOWE

POINT HICKS

Track of the longboat

PRESERVATION IS.

VAN DIEMEN'S LAND

INDIA

Track of the Sydney Cove

East Longitude from Greenwich

Author's Note

This book is a work of historical fiction.

It is based substantially on the story of the *Sydney Cove* shipwreck, which occurred near Preservation Island in Bass Strait in 1797. The version of that story that passes as 'history' is carried largely by the lost diary of a shipwrecked mariner, reproduced or perhaps paraphrased much later by a newspaper named the *Asiatic Mirror*. The diary extracts that appear in this novel are quoted verbatim from that source. There is precious little else in the archive to corroborate what William Clark wrote, let alone explain why he wrote it.

There are no signposts herein to tell the reader where they have lit upon 'history', and where the ramblings of my imagination. The difference between the two is a matter only of degree: some parts of this story are 'truer' than others. Where I have guessed, I have done so within the bounds of what I think the evidence makes possible. The errors, the biases and the affronts are entirely of my making.

History itself is fraught and frequently unreliable. The Djirringanji would have a different tale to tell about the day these bedraggled strangers wandered through their country. So would the Gunaikurnai, and the Wandandean, and many others, if only 'history' had turned its gaze to them.

Perhaps all of this is history, and none of it.

I

1

 The governor's quill stopped in its flow, as if it had struck some unseen obstacle.

'Tell me again, lieutenant. Carefully.' The nib hovered above the page, the hand suspended there, steady and waiting.

'A small fishing boat, excellency. It had been gone three days, working offshore from a bay to the south of here, about twenty miles distant. *Wattamulla*, sir. Native word.'

The quill waited. Governor Hunter's powdered hair caught the sun through the window behind him. The serene beauty of Sydney in autumn, laying its soft light on the bookshelves and the chairs.

'It was one of the deckhands that saw them. A Master Drummond. Early morning, on his watch. Three men, he thought they were natives at first as there wasn't much left of their clothing, and one's, ah…one's dark. They were making their way up the beach from south to north. The inlet there forms a pronounced indentation in the coast, but the beach is very short, I'm told. They were terribly distressed…'

The quill moved again, trailing blue words.

'…Crawling.'

'Yes,' came the governor. 'You said that before. Such a striking detail. Is there no doubt about that?'

'He was quite firm sir. Could see the tracks they'd made up the beach.'

'Go on.'

'Their condition was pitiable. They were hoarse, although not delirious in any way. They were taken on board and identified as a Mister William Clark, supercargo of a vessel named the *Sydney Cove*, three-masted country trader of three hundred tons displacement; his lascar manservant, name not disclosed, and a Mr Figge: a tea merchant travelling aboard the same vessel. She was bound for here as a speculative trading venture, having departed Calcutta last November and was app—'

'They named her after us? Let me guess. Rum?'

'It appears so, sir.'

'It makes me so…Did you know I've just had another still dismantled? Out near the Brickfields this time. They'll take the grain from their children's table if they have to. Part of me thinks these shipments are the lesser evil. I'm sorry, continue.'

'The vessel was beached, they say, after sustaining irreparable damage in a series of storms below Van Diemen's Land. The position of the wreck is a matter of considerable interest, excellency: north of Van Diemen's Land, yet south and west of any known position on the southern coast of New South Wales. If the estimate is correct, it supports those who maintain the existence of this strait that separates Van Diemen's Land.'

'You've notified Mr Bass?'

'Not yet, sir.'

The lieutenant watched as the governor made a note of this, then continued.

'They formed a party of seventeen, left thirty-two of their fellows on the island and departed in a longboat, having entertained hopes of sailing it to here and seeking rescue for the others and salvage of the cargo. Mr Clark holds a letter to this effect from the captain. A Scotsman, sir, Mr Hamilton. Addressed to you.'

He stepped forward and passed the envelope over the desk. The governor extended a hand to take it but the goose quill stayed where it was.

'Has this been seen by others?'

'No sir. It is unopened.'

'Very good. What else?'

'The longboat itself was wrecked on an exposed shore at about thirty-eight degrees latitude.'

'A second wreck?'

'Indeed. All of those aboard survived the incident and made the beach. Now, if these three are to be believed, excellency, they have travelled on foot from there. Around five hundred and fifty miles, through unknown territories, until they were rescued. And they would appear to have done this in a little over two months.'

'Your scepticism is noted, lieutenant.'

'Nine miles a day, sir. Forests, river crossings. Nine miles of it, *every* day and probably barefoot. And in spite of the natives.'

'Are you saying the natives represent help or hindrance?'

'I don't know. But the state these men are in speaks eloquently of their suffering. I am not suggesting they've confected their account. Only that...I don't understand it.'

'What is their condition now?'

'Unwell. Quite indisposed. Sores, insect bites. Some scurvy; underfed, of course. Sunburn. They have had at least one major skirmish with the natives: Clark has wounds through both palms—' He pointed to each palm in turn.

The governor smiled painfully: not a day passed without the bush testing his credulity.

'Stigmata?'

'Coincidence, I'm sure.'

'It's an odd way to be wounded. Do you say there is any… ritual aspect to that?'

'No. The other two were wounded also. But less seriously. Cuts and scrapes. Mr…Figge the tea merchant has a rather badly broken nose.' The lieutenant waited a moment as again the governor took up his quill and wrote. 'And there is this, sir. A journal, kept by Mr Clark.'

He handed the leather-bound notebook across the desk. The brown tanning was blotched with darker stains.

'You've read it?'

'Yes. It's very short, and as it wasn't addressed to anyone in particular I thought—'

'Of course.'

Governor Hunter opened the book and placed his fingertips where the cursive swirled over the first page. The headstrong sweeps of a hand marking posterity.

In the Year of Our Lord Seventeen Hundred and Ninety-Seven.

He began to leaf through the damaged pages, scanning here and there. They had been wet and then dry: they crackled in his fingers. He stopped, whistled softly, pulling the creases of his face.

'Did you see this? Clark made an inventory of the cargo.

China, tea…textiles, shoes…seven *thousand* gallons of rum.' He looked up, his pale eyes creased and hooded by long observation. 'Someone's going to be out of pocket. Where are these men now?'

'I have taken the precaution of separating them, sir. All three are accommodated in the guest quarters behind the main house. The doctor has been to see them and they are resting for now. But there is quite a clamour to have them tell their story publicly.'

'I can imagine. So; three remaining of, what did you say? Seventeen? What became of the others?'

'You will find when you read the journal, sir, that it's rather unclear. If you take it literally, two more of their number were left alive in the bush, only a day's walk south of where these three were found. I had the opportunity to ask Mr Clark about it: I thought he would insist that they be rescued quickly if they were left in peril.'

'Peril?'

'There had been conflict with the natives, he said.'

The older man's eyes narrowed. '*He said*. What did he not say?'

The lieutenant hesitated. 'There is discord among these men. Over what, I don't know. The fishermen said that when they found them on the beach they were divided: Clark was first into the boat with the other one, Figge, coming after him. *Scuttling*, sir, was the word they used. And the lascar after them. But with Mr Clark, it's difficult sir.' He grimaced.

'Speak your mind.'

'Listening to those fishermen, they thought it wasn't that Clark was leading Figge northward: it was more that he was trying to get away from him. The two things could look similar, I suppose.'

The governor stood and leaned over the sideboard nearest

the desk, pouring himself a glass of water from a decanter. He gestured vaguely with a second glass. The lieutenant declined with a smaller movement. 'Has anything specific been said about it?'

'No. The lascar keeps close to Clark, and he has no English. Clark and Figge have so far been kept apart. As you say sir, they have suffered a terrible ordeal.'

The governor returned to his seat. It creaked under him. He sighed and regarded his hands. 'Very well. Send the fishing boat back out with a detachment to see if the missing men can be located—we have names?'

'One's the chief mate, goes by Thompson, and the other one's the carpenter. I don't recall the name just now.'

'Good. And I think it just as well that you separated Clark and Figge. I will read these'—he gestured at the letter and the journal—'overnight and return them to you in the morning. As soon as these men are well enough to talk I want you to question them. I will deal with Bass and with Flinders and whoever else comes knocking in the meantime. If it all appears credible we'll need to arrange a rescue, of course.'

They watched each other in easy silence before the governor continued.

'Keep me informed, please. The salvage is going to be a debacle when the Corps get involved.'

'Thank you, sir.' The young man turned to take his leave.

'Joshua?'

The lieutenant turned back. His face was attentive, open and loyal, but his eyes were heavy with fatigue.

'How is she?'

'No change, sir. Thank you.'

2

Lieutenant Joshua Grayling came down the hill from Government House with the sun behind him and the convict maid at his side, slowing his pace to allow for her careful levelling of the tray. It had been four years since he first walked this path, and day by day a view had opened across the cove from up here on the hill; silver light scattered on blue. He loved the sight of it as any seafarer loved to behold the refuge of a harbour, and it eased his longing for home. Leith could produce no such light as this.

The view had emerged because the trees were coming down, fed into the fireplaces and sawmills of the colony. Neat houses appeared in rows and what had grown wild was rendered captive by tending hands. Not all the smoke was the natives' these days. Not all the shouting and the laughter were theirs, either.

Each season brought turned soil now, and the sounds of livestock. The ring of metal, unknown here through the ages, echoed in answer to the birds. Fishing boats stood by the warehouses at the water's edge, where Grayling remembered seeing only rock and saltbush in the past. The strange stepping shorebirds and the natives eyed each other down there in shared perplexity.

He stopped at the doorway of the guest quarters. With his boots on the mat, he studied the thread of steam rising from the teapot in the humid early morning air. The maid stood to his left with the tea service on a tray under her bosom, her face set in cold formality. Grayling had seen her papers. A year from her freedom and unable to make sense of what freedom might be: her and the unspeaking bush.

His right hand hung momentarily in the act of knocking. He had been so eager to begin, so consumed with curiosity, that he'd mapped no path for his questioning. Nor had he decided the most basic issue: whether he was assisting this man to tell his story or seeking to expose its flaws.

The voice from within, quiet but firm. 'Come in.'

It took his eyes a moment to find sense in the gloom. The light from the window caught the dust in a square beam that cut the middle space. It fell on the foot of the bed, the rough brown blanket crumpled there against the iron. The man was covered only by a sheet, though the room was cool. He lay still. He might, just briefly, have been dead.

He was tall: his feet rested on the footboard. The light shroud draped from the points of his body. He was emaciated, Christ-like to Grayling's eye; an impression heightened by his beard, full and uniformly brown. His hair fell away from his face in tangled locks of the same deep brown. Grayling thought perhaps the man was not so old as he'd imagined overnight, when his sleep was held at bay by thoughts of today's interview:

of speaking to a man who had passed so far beyond ordinary experience and returned.

Grayling motioned to the maid to place the tray on the bedside table. She did so and retreated silently, closing the door. The room was stark: a rug under the high bed, the small table with the tea on it set to the far side of the bed. An armchair by the small table. The sheet rose and fell with the man's chest, and that was all.

'Mr Figge? Lieutenant Grayling, sir. Personal aide to His Excellency Governor Hunter.' He stood with his hand extended, feet stiffly together. The man in the bed reorganised the shapes under the sheet, producing a hand. Grayling, surveying a face so swollen by sunburn that the eyes had been pinched almost shut, was surprised by the life in the grip.

'I trust you have been cared for?'

'Mm,' the man replied sleepily. 'I have. Thank you.'

The voice. More power in it than the punished body should have been able to produce. Honeyed as though it swelled from a blond timber instrument, but laced with an uncomfortable intimacy.

A silence tightened around them as Grayling studied the face on the pillow. The hair might have suggested the broad range of the man's age, but his features were inscrutable. His forehead and cheekbones bore the marks of suffering: the scratches and infected bites, the raw planes of purulent flesh. Grayling had seen similar effects on men stranded at sea, faces so racked by extremity that a boy of twenty might appear sixty. And more so here, for his nose was badly broken, an anvil of bone and whitened skin poking under his left eye, not quite breaking the skin. Tiny dark flakes of dried blood adhered to his face beneath the uppermost bristles of his moustache.

11

'I brought you tea. I heard you were in the trade.'

A minor smile pulled the cracked lips taut. 'I'm afraid my mouth is filled with…' He swallowed thickly. 'Ulcers. Might as well be hot water.'

'To be honest sir, around here you'd be lucky if there's any tea leaves in it anyway.'

The tiny smile again. Figge had turned his head to stare into the straight-edged beam of light. He spoke without looking back at Grayling, slurring a little.

'You have the others, then?'

'Oh, of course. Yes, yes. We have accommodated them elsewhere in town.'

'They are well?'

'I believe so. I am yet to meet them.'

Figge lifted himself up on the pillows with some considerable effort. He tried to reach across himself to lift the teapot; Grayling intervened, poured a cup and placed it in his hands. As the cup passed between them Grayling saw ripples in the tea from his own shaking hand. The liquid stilled when Figge took the cup.

Grayling sat in the armchair, his eye line now slightly lower than that of the man in the bed.

'Not too hot?' He heard his own forced joviality.

'No, it's wonderful. I'll be calling for the chamber pot after this, of course.' Figge made a face that mocked exasperation, but Grayling was taken by something else. The choice of words, the delicacy about it.

'Mr Figge, the governor is very interested in your story. As you know there has been so little exploration of the coast—indeed of anything beyond this settlement.' The eyes in the bed shifted his way, evaluating. Under the swelling they burned bright.

'What did you see out there?'

'I believe Clark wrote it all down,' he said eventually. 'Did he not?'

Grayling shifted in his chair and took a folder from the table where the tea service rested. 'I have his account and also the letter from Captain Hamilton that he carried. Both are extremely helpful but they are…brief. I would value some more detail from you.'

Grayling watched Figge take a deep sip from the teacup. 'I'm tired just now. My grasp of events may not be acute.'

'Yes, yes. Perhaps we could begin tomorrow. I could…I might read passages for you to comment upon. Would that be helpful?'

The man shifted under the sheet, craned his neck. 'You'd read it to me? The diary?'

'And the letter, if that helps you.'

'Never mind the letter, that won't detain us long. But the diary…' His sudden vigour opened a split in his lip; a bright red droplet appeared over the scarlet track of the old scab. He took up the teacup and drained the last of the tea, leaving a smear of blood on the china.

'Come back tomorrow morning,' he said, clearer now. His voice carried something softer than command. Persuasion. 'I may speak to you then.'

Grayling rose from the armchair.

'Oh, lieutenant?' The man was up on one elbow, smiling faintly. 'It was bohea.'

Grayling took a moment to understand. 'Ah! Yes, very good, Mr Figge. I believe it was.' He took up the tray and tucked the folder of documents under his arm. The room was still and silent again, but the unsettling presence of the man in the bed had lodged itself deep within him.

As he closed the door behind him, he imagined the man becoming inert without the human company that lit him. The eyes would go cold and dark and the voice would recede somewhere, into some silent depth beyond the reach of the virtuous. Or the sane.

In the space of ten minutes, the man in the bed had unnerved Joshua Grayling completely.

3

This, I must say, is a better fate than I'd expected. I am asked only to lie in bed and tell stories, and in return they'll bring me tea.

Well then, why not? I will bring him up the coast as we went. But judiciously. There are places I can take the good lieutenant, and places best left in darkness. One of those is Calcutta.

I do not recall bringing the jug down on the man, but that is the only explanation.

The handle is still in my hand. Fine china: a dynasty scene in blue, fragments here and there about us. His head is beside mine on a pillow that was recently white, the sharp edge of his broken skull not far from my nose. White chips of the jug are lodged in the deep cavity over his ear: he has china on his mind. The hair is glued in licks, his sticking dark blood now a bloom and splatters on the linen about us. Did I do this here? Or have I placed him here, and myself with him? I do not recall. Sometimes you wake thus, and no explanation is to be had.

I needed him undressed, of this I am sure, and yes—there are his clothes, neatly draped over the back of the chair. I lift the sheet and the planes of his naked back answer me.

His portmanteau, a nice piece, rests under the table.

I place a hand on his shoulder as I pass over to leave the bed and his skin is cool. Some hours have passed: the sun now lights the room in thin spears through the shutters. It falls on the heavy stone walls of the room: perhaps it was a cell in other times. There is something monastic, calm, about it. Standing bare in that gentle light the life returns to me and I will not rush it. I have some of this man's gore on my neck and cheek, leading me to think I must have been close to him when it happened. There is a little also on my left forearm. I am left-handed this time, it seems.

The portmanteau contains his clothes, some money and his papers. A letter of recommendation from his employer. I know already he is the right size: I studied this carefully when we met. I will dress in the clothes but first I must bathe, and the jug unfortunately contained the only water in the room. The gin bottle, I can see, is nearly full: missing only the small amount we poured ourselves. I take my previous day's drawers, slosh the gin onto them and wipe the blood from my skin. I am left smelling faintly medicinal.

By the time the *wallah* comes past in the corridor outside I have donned the dead man's fine britches, shirt and coat and taken a moment to use his oil in my hair.

I am John Figge, tea merchant, representing Sumpters of London.

And in that guise, by mid-morning I have found myself a desirable place to sit: on the platform of a cart, unhitched from its beast with the drawbar wedged in the low fork of a shady tree. Just high enough to cast an eye over everything.

Calcutta, the mighty stone ramparts of Fort William behind, arched windows squinting out at the Hooghly like the eyes of a sceptical merchant, one who counts and recounts each handful of coins. And on every square yard of ground between those walls and the river, the supplicant throng of Bengal: the ant-scatter activity of the byse caste, children darting underfoot, merchants and lascars hurrying between the pillars of the English society and the foresting masts of the waterfront.

Life abounds in this narrow strip of possibility, on the clogged streets and the chaotic boards of the quay. Ships berthed beam to beam, waiting to be engorged or disgorged. And out there—yes, just there, past the hulls of the country traders and under their slimy timbers—oozes the Hooghly, conveyer of half-dogs and raw timbers and human shit and ashes and the dreams of holy men upstream on the ghats. Between khaki and brown but paler than both, the discharge of a septic wound.

The clouds come and go and sometimes they descend and wander through the commerce, leaving dampness on the skin, but they make no difference to the unrelenting heat. It seeks to suffocate, gives no ground to the Englishmen. Look at them— dressed to a stubborn belief that they rule over the climate as well as the people. The sweat makes patches in the black of their frock coats and the dust sticks there, betraying their bodily torment. Heads puce above tight collars, they hector and bluster, one eye on the chap from Gloucester or Plymouth or Hull, one hand raised to cuff the boy who returned late with the tobacco.

The vessels are a miscellany: great schooners dominate the closer berths, brigs and snows and sloops further out, circled by insect clouds of coracles and dhows. Midstream in the river, the gunboats of the Company lie at anchor, glaring over all. A bridge to the north, a bridge to the south, and the heaving belly of Howrah on the other bank.

The rains finished two months ago, before my arrival here. But their legacy is everywhere, from the swelling of the river against the marshy banks to the putrid puddles in the street. At the far end of the wharf, children play on what appears to be a small grassy hill in the river. When I peer harder, it reveals itself to be an abandoned skiff filled with rice sacks that have burst open, the soaked grains sending forth a fine crop of lush green stems.

⁂

I am close to something now, with Figge to cloak myself in. A careful study of his papers and I have a good idea what I'm looking for.

A small man approaches and sits himself on the edge of the cart beside me. His slight body, his face and his hair mark him as Bengali, though his clothing is neither of their world nor mine. A long white tunic; a pair of sturdy leather sandals on his feet. Though I continue to study the wharf, I feel his eyes upon me.

By and by he begins to speak and I understand that he means to present himself as some sort of guide. He begins by describing the fort: *Its twelve-foot walls, sir. Thick I mean, not high.* Undeterred by my lack of reaction, he persists. *The moat is a most wonderful design. It can be flooded, and any hostile approach may be cut down most assuredly by enfilade fire.* Wedded to an inner script, he senses I am preoccupied but he prattles on about the botanical gardens and the great banyan tree.

Then he stops, watches me. Sees I am intent upon one vessel.

They were already working on it when I arrived at dawn, and it was the sense of urgency that caught my eye. The employment of large numbers of men, the queue of carts waiting to unload into it; the arguments, the shouted orders...All of it suggested that this modest little three-master of perhaps a hundred foot was the core of some vital commercial project.

My watching, which had begun in general interest, became focused upon this one ship. They had it empty at first, floating high at the wharf, and they rigged a block and tackle over the foremost yard so they could lower a great smoking ball of yellow brimstone into the hull cavity. The smoke seeped out the hatches, and here and there it would find a crooked seam or a split timber and a party would scurry to the place to apply tar.

So she leaks. This I noted.

When they had finished the fumigation, the men began working barrowloads of sand into the holds. The sand came from a small pile on the wharf, no higher than a man. They planned a cargo for her, then: something heavy. The slow pace of the loading told me there was an inner deck. There was some argument at that point, some protracted negotiation that stopped the work.

But now this little man sits here and, nearing noon, the operation has recommenced around the ship. We are watching together and he seeks to measure my thoughts by careful study (he will be another of the many who have failed in this). A cart arrives at the wharf's edge, then two more, carrying the dunnage: sticks and branches and fragments of thick bamboo stalks. Other carts arrive with heavy casks, two on each, and the oxen straining under short whips. There is much unnecessary yelling and waving around these carts: the work of men who have no work.

A cask comes down from the first cart. It stands briefly on the wharf and I can read the large crest they've singed into its side: *C&C*. There at last: Campbell and Clark, the minnow that seeks to take on the whale of the East India Company. Leisham's story comes back to me like he's standing there before me, gusting breaths of cheap gin into my face.

Six weeks ago, Leisham accosted me in a tavern in the deep recesses of this city, a node in a nest of veining alleys. He lurched over and barely managed to slur his own name before tipping himself a measure, uninvited, from my bottle. Sang for his supper, though, with the arresting claim that he worked for the most desperate man in the world. One William Clark, said Leisham. The unloved scion of a Scots trading house called Campbell and Clark, come to Calcutta to join the family concern and to prove himself in a conclave of flint-eyed Scottish merchants. Which he had done: the Chinese took him at mah-jong, the English at crown-and-anchor; he could not help himself with the local whores and, though he pranced about in the robes of respectability by day, the night had him firmly by the balls. Dissolute and impulsive, massively in debt, he had his fingers in the Campbell and Clark treasury within weeks.

Clark's fortunes came to a point of crisis, according to this Leisham. He didn't know what it was: whether he'd landed a great win at the tables, or whether his debts had compounded and he'd borrowed gigantically elsewhere to resolve them, but the net result was the same. Fatuous Mr Clark, despised by his family and deep in debt, took it upon himself to finance a speculative voyage of his own. A final roll of the dice that would pay out in complete vindication or utter ruin. There was rum involved—he could access that from the family's own distillery—and tea. Leisham had met the tea merchant already: a man named Figge.

And so, finally, here is Clark's speculative venture in the making. A crowd works to roll the branded cask over the gangway and into the hold. Another crowd runs forward with armfuls of the dunnage material. Somewhere in the gloom down there they will be packing it around the massive casks; any shifting of such great weights at sea would spell doom. A count of the pile on the wharf: three rows of ten, eight casks already below. I inquire of the little Bengali where one might send thirty-eight casks of wine, and he brightens at the prospect of helping.

Not wine, sir. Rum. You can see the crest of Campbell and Clark on each one. They have a distillery across the river at Howrah. Now the bright little man and his words hang in the foetid air while I measure their impact. Thirty-eight casks; two hundred gallons to the cask. A fortune. A bounty almost beyond calculation.

But I regret to say, sahib—my companion's face registers disappointment—*I do not know where they are bound.* He returns to chattering about architecture in hope of recovering this shortfall. *The colonnades are magnificent, and the porticoes gleam, sir, because of the use of chunam.*

The carts are lining up now: there is more to come. Madeira pipes, crates of porcelain, more crates marked as champagne and brandy. One such crate is placed too heavy on the deck and a great clattering of bottles sparks an argument.

The colonnades are magnificent, says my friend, and he says some other things. A procession of the low-caste men weaves slowly through the crowds, each bearing a pale lump on his back. I have to wait until the first one nears my position to make out what it is they carry: even then my mind protests the sense of it. For each man bears an animal skin—mostly calves, but some small pigs and even a deer, the heads gone and the necks rolled up and firmly stitched. Where the bones have come out of the limbs, those are sewn up also. They are water carriers, bent under the weight and trailing drips as they go. The pressure of the water inside the skins bulges the animals out to an approximation of their original shape. A bloated foetus; a headless goat with a knot securing the dark star of its anus, the bulbous limbs waving pathetically as the bearer's steps bounce the load. The swollen, splashing carcasses wending like some mad religious cavalcade through the ranks of the unbaptised.

There are men loading shoes in strapped bundles and piles of fine crockery into boxes of straw. The lascars in their turbans, loose cotton drawers and white jackets, preparing the rigging and washing those parts of the ship where the loading will allow them. Malabars, Malays, Hindoos, Gentoos, Persians. Only the smaller details in their dress to communicate the differences, and the differences are extinguished by sheer numbers. Human toil as insignificant as grain in the Company's mill. If a man could only see the scale of it, the mortality of others would cease to trouble him.

A terrified horse is led down into the smoky darkness, turns its desperate head back to the day. An eye huge with fear, a nostril, then gone. A buggy: a complete buggy, sprung below and canopied above, wheeled ridiculously over the gangway and in. Is it intended that the horse will one day draw the buggy?

Two larger men, Mahometans by the look, strain under the weight of a musical organ packed in a case, its pedals and elegant legs protruding beneath. As they set the thing on the deck of the little ship my gaze has narrowed to exclude all else in the world: no movement draws my eye nor sound my ear.

What travels on this boat is not the business of coastal trade. These are luxury goods, almost without exception. Such goods are not headed for Kerala. Not Gujarat nor Bombay. And who loads this finery onto a piss-leaky coastal trader in such a hurry?

It's Clark the Unloved Scion and his bloody great gamble all right, and it hasn't left port yet. No one paying heed, no one open-mouthed in astonishment as I am. Did this opportunity come to me alone of all men? What fates conspire to tempt me thus?

I stand abruptly and make for the wharf, leaving the tourman in my wake, still burbling about *the Great Tank of Calcutta, sahib*. Down the Esplanade Row, between the stalls and the lines of stacked provisions, around the remnants of the sand pile to the gunwales of the three-master. Out of breath when I get there, I stand a moment taking it all in: the swarming of the hands, the huddled conversations. You are going somewhere fateful, you lot.

I am thus transfixed when a man approaches. Shorter than me, now we're standing together, though most men are. Thick-built and rough from the years, and in the same clogged Brummy I remember, he asks me my business.

Leisham. He's forgotten me, of course, because he was blootered.

Good day to you sir, and forgive me the interruption. You see, I'm interested to know where this here ship might be headed, I tell him as bland as I can manage. *Int your fucking concern*, he replies. I sometimes think my eyes can cut a fellow from his impertinent line, because I see him now hesitating just a little: not sure, not sure. Then he stiffens again.

Why, where's the harm in such an inquiry? I offer. When do you sail?

Get your nosyarse face and have it gone from this wharf, he says.
Or I'll see to your query with a fuckin 'ook.

An odd empty second or two elapses before someone calls
to Leisham from the deck, needing him for something. It's in
turning and walking away from him that I pick up the very
detail I need.

Three boys slung from a bosun's chair over the stern. They're
prising away at something with jemmies, ripping it free with
timbery squeaks. A nameplate, ten feet long. One passes it up
to another on the deck, and on the battered length of carved
wood I see the name *Begum Shaw*. The second boy wields a
hammer and long nails, affixing the new nameplate, which is
held in place by the third while the hammering is done. The
lettering on the nameplate is picked out in fancy gilt: too fancy
for this lumbering old tub.

It takes me only an instant to see the two words on that
plate: *Sydney Cove*.

4

Grayling hurried from Figge's quarters to the small house nearby where the other two survivors had been placed. Walking the narrow path, he reflected on Figge's strange demeanour: the switches between listlessness and vigour; that extraordinary voice. The man was a lamp that flared in response to changes in the air.

At first, the Hamilton letter had made perfect sense to him; he'd read it the night before, squinting in the near dark. The captain's prose was crisp and direct. His ship was lost but the cargo had been salvaged and he sought rescue for his crew. No sentiment, no embellishment.

And there the cold logic ended. He had sent his supercargo, a family connection of the trading house, on the rescue mission rather than leave him to guard the cargo. Why? Why had he sent Clark?

And deeper than that, what duty did the colony owe to go

and retrieve the crew and cargo of a foreign vessel, a speculative business venture pursued in open violation of the governor's edict to stop drowning the place in rum? How many more of these ill-advised voyages had set out, and ended in undocumented disaster? Lost with all hands around the cliffs of Van Diemen's Land? Would the trading houses involved have reported their demise to the colony? Probably not. And the colony had no way of knowing they were coming.

Grayling was glad it was the governor, not he, who must decide whether a rescue should be mounted. It was morally right, of course, to save a stranded crew. But the retrieval of their corrupting cargo? It should be left to bleach in the sun.

The Eora were gathering in small groups under the trees on the slope between Government House and the township. Friendly greetings imitating Englishness in daylight; neither party under any illusion about what was going on after dark.

See the tall man here, a scarecrow hung on ancient bones. The natives hadn't looked like this when he arrived four years ago. Lean, yes; not gaunt. The man's feet were whited with dust from the path; he smiled and doffed an imaginary hat. Was he party to the outrages reported nightly by the settlers further out? Did he know the natives responsible? Did he seethe, under his grin, at the collective punishment meted out to the nearest and the slowest, regardless of anything they had actually done? Grayling tried to return the man's greeting in good humour, as was his way.

The house was one in a row, enclosed by neat pointed paling fences laced with tall geraniums. The door formed a face with the glazed windows, framed by a hairline of casuarina shingles, that gazed out over the sea. Looking towards Home, thought Grayling; perpetually checking for sails. The row and every house in it were simple and functional: straight lines sawed and hammered in defiance of a disordered world.

His knock was this time answered without reply by a short man, with the stem of a churchwarden pipe poking from his pudgy fist. His face plunged Grayling into gloom.

'Doctor Ewing.'

'Joshua.' Ewing lowered his eyes, shifted his bag from left hand to right. 'One's never idle in this profession.'

'So? How are they?'

'Oh, these two will be fine with rest. They've all got terrible… feet?' Upward inflection, as if it surprised him. 'I understand they've walked a great distance, but even that doesn't go all the way to explaining it. Deep lacerations, blisters. So forth.'

'The boy?'

'The lascar? Difficult to assess, given he speaks no English. On physical examination there's no significant wounds: just your bites, stings, abrasions. Distressed. I don't know. Something stirs him.'

Grayling wondered if the boy was troubled by his close proximity to his master, the supercargo Mr Clark.

'Perhaps he'll settle down,' Ewing continued. 'Now, Mr Clark on the other hand…Ah, forgive me, that was unintentional.' He smiled feebly. 'Mr Clark has those hand wounds in addition to everything else.'

'Yes, I heard about that.'

'Says the natives speared him.'

'Through *both* hands?'

'Indeed. Separately, but more or less simultaneously.'

Grayling tried again to imagine this, and again it eluded

him. The morning sun made shadows on the surgeon's face, under the heavy brows. The shadows looked like doubt.

'Do you think…? No, never mind. I will ask him myself.'

⊹

Even after the ravaged features of Figge, the sight of William Clark's face was a shock.

Like Figge he was severely sunburnt, and in addition to the overripe swelling and flayed patches there was bruising, his skin split like soft fruit over one eyebrow.

His hair had been brushed and oiled and his whiskers freshly shaved, revealing a deep gouge under one side of his chin. His hands rested on the bedclothes at his sides, bandaged like those of a pugilist.

There was a softness about his dark eyes, an almost childish vulnerability. Grayling concluded it was his lashes: the upper row long and dark, the lower ones thin, almost absent. He looked, Grayling thought, hard done by.

'Mr Clark.' By habit he advanced his hand, then swiftly retracted it.

The man looked over Grayling's shoulder, apparently to ascertain whether he had entered alone. He said nothing. Grayling introduced himself, taking refuge in formality. 'I have your journal,' he added. 'Thank you for your efforts in keeping it.'

'Yes, I…' Clark raised his bound hands. 'It dropped away, rather. Once this happened.' His speech was thick and slow, his accent familiar to Grayling: Edinburgh, not Glasgow. Voice younger than his pummelled face.

'May we talk, Mr Clark?'

Clark shrugged. 'We may try.'

'Just before the substantive matters,' Grayling looked around, then opened the folder as he had done in Figge's room. 'Where is the, your manservant?'

Clark nodded to indicate a door in the opposite wall. 'They have him in the next room.'

Grayling asked the manservant's name and Clark told him it was Srinivas; no surname that he knew of. He was a Bengali, Clark thought; he assumed so, only because he had met him in Calcutta. His age was oh, it was maybe fifteen, though Clark believed he always got it wrong with the lascars; someone had said so. Had they?

'Good.' Grayling let him mumble down to silence. 'Now, do you feel strong enough to discuss this?'

'I am quite well, thank you.'

'I'm grateful.' He smiled a smile that spoke of bland official-dom, though his heart was roiling. 'I wonder if the best starting point would be the voyage? I have Captain Hamilton's letter here to help us with our memories.'

William Clark watched the young lieutenant hold the letter up. Whether through injury or apathy, his head remained squarely in the middle of the pillow: he chose to engage his inquisitor by turning his eyes that way. The sidelong gaze made clear his mistrust. The wrapped hands remained by his sides; his hair in seaweed drifts over the pillow.

Slowly and reluctantly, his cracked mouth opened and the words walked themselves into the light.

5

We departed late from Calcutta. Early November, and the monsoon had ended many weeks before. My family's firm does not abide idleness, lieutenant, and especially not when the season for heading east offers such a brief opportunity for getting underway.

But finally we slipped down the Hooghly from Fort William. That putrid river carries all the sticks and broken baskets and rotting carrion of a civilisation in its mud, and stinks of it, too.

Six months ago, and my life is inverted.

I went to Calcutta armed only with a sense of duty. I don't care what you hear, no one goes there out of ambition. Both parents and four of my siblings called to their eternal rest, so it fell to me to consider the futures of the other eight. And of the family name, of course; the company. I am a nephew.

If I'd had my way in life I would have built some cosy business in Edinburgh, married at a suitable age and sunk my bones in an armchair when Providence allowed it. Life doesn't fall that way for all of us, does it, lieutenant? You look like you come from wealth, if I may say so. You'd be, what, twenty-five? I've got three years on you but in truth neither of us knows the world.

Within a year in Calcutta I had established myself. A place in the business and, as a consequence, in society. That society—the colonies are wretched places. The damned humidity, and the pretention with it! Off I'd go to their salons and I'd play my part, but by the time that first year was up I was done with it.

They wanted to send the *Sydney Cove*. The company wanted to send it because, as you would be aware, it has worked before. The livestock aboard, the china, the shoes, the fabrics, all of that was just a front for the rum. It was always about the rum, you understand?

Well, I imagine you do.

They own distilleries. *We* own distilleries, I am meant to say. If you can buy and sell land and ships and food here with the stuff, then making rum is simply another way of minting bullion. Oh, they knew the governor was set against it. They knew the state of this place, hooligans rioting at night, taking on the natives for sport. This Corps of yours; hah! Robber barons to a man. It is all just business, is it not? And while you might say it is a distasteful business to be in, if we did not take this opportunity, others would have. There is no room for wringing your hands in commerce, my uncles tell me. Because while you're at it, some other fellow will empty your pockets.

Anyway. The family knew there was a fortune in it. If that boat could have held one more gallon, believe me they would have shipped it, and to hell with the consequences. I am an ambitious man, but I saw it for what it was. The lust for profit had blinded them.

They bought a banged-up coastal trader, this bumbling old cow called the *Begum Shaw*. The crooks that offloaded her could scarce believe their luck. They caulked the hull, replaced some of the topsails, did this, did that and then they gave her a new identity before they sailed her back up the Hooghly.

Suddenly, she was the *Sydney Cove*.

A vanity name: that's the scale of the arrogance, lieutenant. Sending cargo that was never ordered—contraband, if you will, and naming the vessel to flatter the authorities.

But it was not just a ship that led us into disaster: it was people too, of course. Fifty-five of us: Hamilton and his crew, Figge and me, forty-four lascars. Hamilton was up to the task, just. Prone to bend under influence. I was supercargo under him, responsible for the company's loot. Chief mate Hugh Thompson, second mate Leisham—do you need me to spell that? All right. The carpenter was Kennedy. I shan't go through all of them.

The lascar, Srinivas, is assigned to me. His father was the *serang*. Attends...*attended* to his duties well enough. There is no doubt in my mind that his devotion waned over the course of our journey, as it did with all the lascars. The ones you retrieve, if ever you pluck them from Preservation, you should put them to the sternest inquiry.

The other man you have is the tea merchant, Figge. You will form your own assessment of him.

So the voyage. Unexceptional, until we turned east in the latitudes below forty degrees. Then the true character of that dreadful tub became apparent. Cranked over in the wind, the fittings would separate, or shear off. The sails tore, the stays parted. There were rats, worms, borers in the timbers and all of this I would have tolerated but for the one thing, the terminal thing. It leaked: a veritable colander. Started about a month out, as we were perhaps six hundred sea miles west of New Holland. We struck a gale from the south-east and suddenly the bilge is filling at six inches an hour. Now a gale like that, it's seasonal. *Not unexpected*—Hamilton's words. A ship constructed for these ordeals will groan and carry on, but it will prevail. But this thing, it was built for the river ports of India. It had no more business out on the open ocean than those natives outside have at your table, lieutenant.

So we're out there, horizons all round, the sea heaving and lurching, dreadful skies. Mr Thompson was able to isolate it: the boards had sprung under the starboard bow. For the love of God, if you're going to take the thing to sea would you not reinforce the bow? And it went on, and sickness followed. The lascars were down there knee-deep in seawater rafted with their own effluent, sloshing head-high. It went on and on and on, until we were weary of each other and our splattering guts and the damned ocean and the sky. It went on for the rest of December: the sea shouting like an idiot, sky just staring at us. There was some miserable attempt to roast up the salted pork for Christmas and I released a pipe of madeira to go with it but the lot of us were so wrung out that it ended in blows. I wasn't involved, of course, but you see the deterioration. Six short weeks and we're reduced to brawling and the flux.

We tried to fother the bow a couple of times without success: each time we got a sail over the side, the force of the sea would rip out its eyelets and we'd lose the thing. We had the lascars working the inside, neck-deep, jamming all manner of items into the gaps. The air below decks—I cannot describe. We nearly lost a couple of them, had to revive them on deck.

By the middle of January we're still out there somewhere off the west coast of the continent and this, you can imagine, should be the austral summer. Glorious soft dawns and hot days, south-easterly afternoons, that is what you'll hear people say. No such thing for us. The winds kept coming, and Hamilton said it was a year like no other. We fought the leaks until we were shipping about four inches every hour and the lascars were starting to fade. They'd been on those pumps for two or three weeks around the clock by then. It rips at their hands, their backs start to seize; you just don't get good work out of them.

Well, we came around the south-western extremity of the continent towards the end of January and the misfortune compounded: what should have been a steady south-easterly on the nose as we headed east was an endless sou'wester. Rain in sheets. And this in a vessel that was unworthy at best and downright dangerous the rest of the time. She wallowed like a pig before the wind and she carried all the rain. Some days I couldn't tell if we were sinking from above or below.

Hamilton was doing his best, I suppose, but the mood on board was descending into despondency. The low granite coast, all those isles as you round the cape, you saw them I'm sure. The cliffs after that, the endless miles of rock and nothing atop: those days were monotonous. And the nights! Gales pressing us against the cliffs, and the swell pressing the weight of the bilgewater through the boards so the hull was breathing through the hatches, and that great liquid mass of the rum in its casks down deep around the keel. Up every pitch and down every drop: casks hitting the hull, chains swinging and ballast shifting around. The bloody horse screaming. In the belly of every wave, this mad chorus of noise. She'd heave up again and the racket would reverse itself then start all over again.

The sails didn't have the strength to haul the nose up once it was down—she would spear deep into the troughs and everyone and everything would be doused in cold seawater. There were cattle packed below—cattle! And they bellowed in the night, water coming down on them through the hatches. It ran on your head in the cot, got its way through joins and bulkheads and left your feet clammy and trousers damp like you'd soiled yourself, and no prospect of drying out.

The cook made what he could of it but it wasn't much. The pork gone green, the drinking water brackish so your thirst mounted by the sip rather than abated. The lascars fainted and rolling half-dead in the passageways—no shirts, no shoes. I thought it an outrage at the time and my, how that changed.

All I wanted in the whole of creation was to get off that damned ship. But it went on and it went on until the heeling over swells was more than just the staggering of a poor-made ship. We were losing control of her. Figge took the captain aside and the next thing you know they're sending poor Leisham up the rigging to furl the topsail. Now you're a man of the sea, of course. You've seen such days and nights. Aside from my voyage from Leith to Calcutta, I had never been to sea and certainly in no way like this. It was evening, great clouds overhead and the wind so loud it carried off the orders. They sent lascars part-way up the yards to relay messages, but it was Leisham they sent all the way, poor devil, and it was bound to end badly. The only surprise was that he'd got the entire thing off its yard and managed to start his descent when he was brought undone.

He slipped, lieutenant. Just lost his footing, simple as that, and for a moment the grip of his hands kept him there but then the force of the downswing ripped him away and flung him—it is the only word I can use—flung him into the night. We never saw him again.

No prospect, of course, of bringing her round to investigate.

Nor launching the longboat, or the jolly. He'd improved the ship's performance, but that only raced us away from him faster. I suppose the ocean took him by its own means, and I pray it was quick.

No one spoke about it after he was gone. The grabbing and the slipping went on without pause. I thought at the time that I should never pass a longer night at sea, but shortly enough I would do so.

Next morning the wind died—as if it had taken what it wanted—and we limped on. The fires of the natives were here and there visible on the hummocks at night, their smoke in the day. It seemed impossible, peering up from the sea, to imagine humans up there. It was bleaker on the cliffs than on the sea itself, a vertical plunge from the flat edge of the land. Not a tree, not a hill. And the fires were *moving*, following our slow progress, it seemed. The same groups of savages, cannibals perhaps, creeping east beside us on steady ground. Making fires, watching, conspiring at who knew what. Sometimes it could be said with confidence that the fire meant a camp, a bright spark of orange and a string of smoke. But other times it formed a line and swept across a gully or followed a ridge, too long to be a campfire but…orderly. Marked by method.

Eventually we found the west coast of Van Diemen's Land and followed it south. Swung nor'-east around the foot of it with the topsails in rags, and somehow we made Maria Island on its east side. Hamilton had the other chart, you understand, Mr Furneaux's. So from there he was telling us it's a straight line nor'-nor'-east to Sydney.

The boat was slowly drowning itself, even then. Hamilton had us eighty miles off the coast and headed due north. I was asleep at the time. Middle of the night and we're hit by another front and it's on again, same as the other times only this time it's hitting us on the starboard stern quarter, from the south-east. Warmer wind, different ocean. Short, punching chop. Not the great marching lines of the roaring forties.

And Hamilton turns us west: makes the decision to run for shelter. The wind's a south-easter veering to a nor'-easter and as it gets to shrieking we're staring at a lee shore and gaining speed like we'll ram clean through the cliffs. Short swells dunt us left and right and the boat's bucking and swaying like some giant has the old cow by her left rear hock and he's tipping her on her ear, and thus it went for two hours.

Then there was a crack like a gunshot and a percussion through our feet and the ship spun on its heel and faced up into the wind. The ones who understood these things went below—they knew what it meant and they came back long-faced and said the bow, where we'd had all the trouble, had now collapsed. There was a sombre meeting: Hamilton and his mate, and Kennedy the carpenter, and Figge.

Pardon, sir? No, I have no idea what business a tea merchant had in such a discussion.

In any case, the leak was now beyond us: five feet of water in the hold, sloshing among the cargo. A small part of me thinks Hamilton was worried mainly for the human souls aboard: why else was I not consulted about the cargo at that point? If I was a company man I'd have insisted on more pumping, more repairs, and a stagger to Sydney. But as you may have guessed, I am not a company man.

It was determined that the pumps would not keep up and we must run her aground. The only decision left was where we could do so safely. By nightfall the water had reached the lower deck hatches and my cargo, along with most everything else, was submerged. It was a wretched night: a vigil on a dying ship. The getting cuffed and thrown by the sea, the acts of spite from within and without. I learned that night that men in extremity are a study in self-interest; the things they will do and say to save their hides. I craved some sign of the dawn, and when it came it was so jaundiced I wished for the dark again.

As the sun rose out of the east behind us, we'd tilted over so hard that it was no longer possible to stand unaided, and at times it was necessary to clamber up the slope of the deck. Below you could hear the livestock in their terror, immersed to their flanks in seawater and kicking at the hull. We should have ended their suffering, but we could see we might need them for sustenance.

Hamilton and Thompson were puzzling over the helm, attempting to sail a vessel that was lying on her side. What are the sail orders when the rigging drags in the sea? The lookout was in truth only ten yards aloft because the masts swept so low over the water. He called landfall. A shoal of sand and weed, and beyond it a small rocky islet. There was nothing left but to hope we didn't sink entirely before we got there. And it was close in the end, but we got in, between a cluster of the rocky islands—a mountainous one to our north and a flatter one to our south before the keel knifed a shoal and we halted.

Before us, perhaps eighty yards away, an island of boulder and sand. Beside us, a much smaller one, dome-shaped and entirely ringed by granite. No trees, just grasses and windblown scrub under cloud.

There the ship groaned and gave up. It died there and never moved again. For the first time in ninety-one days, we were utterly still.

Hamilton announced to those nearby that he believed we'd

entered a great firth. He was guessing, of course. We already knew we'd sailed into the gap in Furneaux's chart, and no one could have the slightest idea what the gap represented. More pressingly, we were still five hundred nautical miles short of Sydney. My mind turned to the obvious consequences of our foundering. The firm in Calcutta had no way of knowing we had failed to arrive at our destination. Sydney had never known we were coming. Deep in the clean white paper west of the known coast, we were far from any passing ship.

No one could know of our plight. There was no prospect of rescue. We had vanished from the face of the earth.

6

Charlotte Grayling knew the sounds of Joshua's arrival, habits in his movements he didn't know he had. She lay still and anticipated him—his voice, the small sounds of his breathing and the way his body carried the light.

One step on the bare boards of the verandah. One on the doormat he had fashioned from coiled rope. The latch, the swing of the door. Then his face, etched with the day but offering love or good humour. Such a boy he was, every day. She wanted to light the fire for him. To have something, anything, in the pot above the coals. But she was simply unable.

His eyes did not dart to the cold fireplace, not once. They homed in on her and she felt their love and concern. He sat on the edge of the bed, beside her shoulder. Not a tall man, not a heavy man. A man who stood upright because naval training had imprinted the posture on him, but who was less inclined to certainty than his stance suggested.

He asked her how she felt as he untied his boots and worked them off his feet. The soft light of evening and a solitary lamp glowed on his shoulders. How much pain was it reasonable to share?

'Oh, I'm fine.'

'Really?' He looked up. 'Don't tell me what I want to hear. Can you walk?'

An obvious thing to ask someone who was lying in a bed as daylight receded; but he meant the question another way. Her walking had been the single thing that divided them.

She didn't understand why she did it, knowing how it disquieted him; other than to say there was no child to rear, no parents to attend to. No occupation to her days, no threat or promise to spur her between his going in the morning and his returning at night. She was trapped in amber for him, here at the end of the world. As much as she loved to give him warmth and comfort, she was never going to be such a wife.

And so she had begun to walk. Not far at first: mere flirtations, it seemed. Longer ways to come home from the market; excuses to go and see traders further out. But these became furtive excursions into the bush, illicit in some unspoken way: undertaken for that very reason. She walked because she shouldn't. It was not *respectable* for an officer's wife to be seen on the sandstone country, scratched and sweating, hair flying. There were killers out there, the town said. Thieves of womanly virtue. They were as black as death and they moved without sound and they used the stones themselves for razors to lay open the white flesh of innocents. Pemulwuy was out there, and though she knew little of who he was, she knew what he represented. Pemulwuy was the darkness.

Walking was her act of defiance. Not against Joshua

particularly, but against his world that was now hers, and its insistence on fear. She felt he understood that it wasn't personal, but each time she did it she was testing his allegiances: to authority. To her.

'Not this morning,' she answered. Her legs had made the motions, but she couldn't coordinate them. They wouldn't talk to her.

'Ewing told me he came by.'

Ewing had indeed come by, muttering and smelling of brandy. His poultice this time had been ginger and beeswax, as ineffective as all the others.

Grayling frowned. 'He makes this great show that he knows what's happening, but I do not think he has any idea at all.'

'Don't be unkind to him, dear. He has greater responsibilities than some fainting woman in a bed.'

He reached over and stroked the hair from her face. 'May I see?'

She flinched a little as he reached around towards her left ear, the one furthest from where he sat on the edge of the bed, then inclined her head towards him. His touch was light over the swirl of her ear, the ringlet that hung just below her lobe that he often said was the most beautiful thing he'd seen. She had removed the combs she would normally wear, wanting her hair to fall and conceal the thing he sought: the large abscess that had formed just inside her hairline. She had found it with a mirror: it was angry and red, fading to a livid pink welt that contrasted against the cool pallor of her neck. The centre of the swelling was cratered, the crater circled by broken skin that had bled slightly. At the touch of his fingertip she grimaced.

'Have you been scratching at it again?' She could hear the way he schooled his voice to avoid reproach. The same thing

Ewing had asked her. She hadn't come to this by scratching her head. She wriggled slightly away from his inspection. But he took her face in his hands and looked into her eyes. Now she could smell his skin and feel the comforting pressure of his forearms, placed lightly on her chest. He was her refuge from this place when it overwhelmed her; but also her gaoler.

'What else? What else did he find?'

'Oh, there were things he found and things he didn't notice. He says my heart is going faster...' She laughed and fluttered her lashes his way. 'But he didn't ask about the rash.'

His smile faded. 'Would you show it to me, please?'

She rolled her eyes as he got up off the bed and drew the blanket back. She lifted her nightdress to her chest, knowing it shocked him. There, in a line across the end of her belly, below her navel where it met the hair, was the speckle of tiny pink dots, concentrated in the centre and spreading towards the points of her hips. She knew it was more livid than it had been that morning. It felt pricklish, raised like the trail left by a brush with a nettle. The rash puzzled them both, and Joshua had been unable to resist a connection to her wandering ways. *This is what happens when you go about like a native*, he had said. But even if there was some unknown form of stinging undergrowth out there, too much remained unanswered. It didn't explain the abscess behind her ear. And even allowing for her wanderings, how had she come into contact with such a plant down *there*?

'Enough, my darling. You're staring now.' She lowered her nightdress, returned the covers to their former position and mocked him with a prim look. 'Now tell me about these men.' She rolled onto a hip to face him, pulling the blanket further up under her chin. He sat down again beside her, worked down the buttons of his jacket and removed it.

'Well, the first one's Figge. Tall, grave-looking. His hair and beard are wild—'

'Of course they are, poor man.'

'Mm. And his nose, it's…smashed. I can't see Ewing getting it straightened out. I spoke to Ewing about him and he expects he will recover. In full health he'd be an impressive man; built very square. But his *eyes*. They were…' He sighed as if he had no words.

'They were what?'

'Ferocious. Bright.' He raised his hands helplessly. Charlotte knew from the look on his face that he was doubting himself. 'I suppose they've been places no man has ever been before…'

'The natives have.'

'Yes, yes, of course. Though I tell you, it feels like the natives are all here in town. You should see them around Government House this week.'

'You remind me. Boorigul has returned.'

'Really?' There was an edge of exasperation in his voice as he stood and peered around the doorway into the skillion. Charlotte couldn't move to follow his gaze, but she knew the girl was there in the shade, a dusting of light on her body. That aspect to her, the waiting for something. Her watchful eyes.

She had asked Boorigul to come in earlier in the day, had persuaded her to take the basket of washing and set about it. If Joshua had noticed the clothes hanging from the twine strung along the side of the house, it hadn't occurred to him that Charlotte was now incapable of churning the garments in the copper and thrashing them over the board. She should feel guiltier; but the aching back and the raw pink hands were more painful and ugly than the rash that had her confined to bed; the one they were so concerned about.

So Boorigul had done the work, bent indifferently naked over the steaming copper. Watching her, Charlotte wondered if it was how her own body would look to others, stooped over the same work. Short and softly rounded, Boorigul wore a circlet of dried grasses and a necklace of shells. Her body curved and swelled, and she stood without shame. When Charlotte saw her this way, the seams and constrictions of her own clothing were a small sadness. It seemed a practical way to go about it: no damp sleeves to contend with, and the sweat dried in the sun.

Boorigul's nakedness panicked her husband, she knew. He'd remarked awkwardly once that she might be cold, then shrunk from the comment as though he had imagined the air on her skin and it had been too much. Eora women crowded the hillside from Government House down to *tubowgully*, defiantly naked and in need of no one's shelter. It was impossible to live in the colony without becoming accustomed to it. But for Charlotte's husband, Boorigul's casual proximity to the house made the sight of her body altogether more alarming.

Their neighbours also hosted uninvited guests. They were a topic of idle conversation among the officers: the small boy who'd been brought into town by a detachment, the parents having been killed—she'd seen the despatches—*in an act of resistance*. The girl of marriageable age who had become a bored wife's project. The missionaries and their opaque motives.

Rarely were the visitors of full age. Older men and women, shadows in the grounds, sometimes wailed for their return. The householders shouted them back into the street. Like so much about the place, Charlotte could draw no bright, clear line to tell her which of the children sought refuge in the settlers' homes and which were held there against their families' will.

Boorigul had been coming to them since the previous winter: had appeared in the skillion one day sitting sodden and uncommunicative among the sacks of grain. There were rats out there, and other strange scurrying creatures that weren't rats but needed the same treatment. Charlotte had invited her inside. The girl refused to move, so she prepared a cot by the fire, laid blankets on it and turned the top one back invitingly. Still she had refused.

The refusals were not sullen or ungrateful, but were firm. Charlotte had resorted to bringing her food, which she accepted silently: eggs at breakfast time, a hank of mutton or *badagarang* in the evening. Cups of water, a cloth and a bucket in case she wished to bathe.

'What should we do?' Joshua was asking her now, as he climbed back onto the bed. Charlotte set great store by the sense they could find in their own conversation. Patiently opening and exploring a problem, venturing ideas, retracting them without pride when their logic failed under discussion. But was the girl a problem? Was there anything to solve? Joshua thought so.

He reached for structure and logic in everything. It was a difference between them that she found amusing. She was content to see the girl sheltered, fed occasionally, and tending to whatever other life she lived, wherever else, when she was not with them. Joshua worried for her safety: worried she would contract some illness out there in the cold. He said so now, but Charlotte laughed.

'She has lived in the cold, love. For years. And the heat, and the rain and the wind. She was doing it before the town came up. They all did. I believe they think our ways of dealing with the climate are inferior.'

'You haven't seen enough of the world,' Joshua said gently.

It seemed to her condescending. 'There's no way of living that surpasses our way.'

'Perhaps,' she said, and pulled the blanket under her chest to let him know she had shrugged. 'Listen.'

Outside they could hear an exchange of voices. Boorigul's soft whisper was only just audible; louder and more confident were the voices of older women, speaking rapidly in their language, peppered with fragments Charlotte could recognise as English: *lieutenant. Gub'nor. Missus.* The conversation sounded warm, reassuring. The old ones had come to check on her, to keep her company.

They were both silent while they listened. It had occurred to Grayling that he needed to make them food, and a fire. But he wanted to be near Charlotte.

'Tell me more about Mr Figge,' she said.

'Where was I?'

'His eyes, I think.'

'Oh, yes. Disconcerting: as if he knows your thoughts. Anyway, he wasn't ready to talk. Said we could start tomorrow.'

'What else? There's something else.'

'Probably nothing. Just, he became very animated when I told him I would read him Mr Clark's diary of the journey.'

'Surely you're not going to?'

She heard him let go an exasperated sigh. 'I know. But this is exactly what I'm saying—the offer just tumbled out of me because all I could think of was those eyes boring into me.'

'Why would you give Mr Figge a chance to corroborate what Mr Clark says? That journal, my love, it's your best comparison against Mr Clark's memory, and against Mr Figge's truthfulness. I'd be holding it close. But of course'—she lowered her eyes—'I'm sure you've thought of these things.'

Joshua had stood and moved to the pot above the fire. He glanced back sceptically at her. It was a game and both of them knew it. But she loved him too well to let an argument unfold. She smiled and he returned to the edge of the bed. Close to her, where she wanted him.

'Lie back and I'll tell you Clark's story,' he said. And, placing a hand on her brow, he began to relate the story, just as it was told to him.

7

I watched that space on the floorboards for many long minutes before I dared to move. Measured it with my eyes: seven feet, from the edge of the bed to the door. I could hear your voice in there, Mr Clark. Yours and the other man's, the naval man's. Him bumping you along, careful. You, stopping and flowing. Your truths, your half-truths and your silences. And your lies, Mr Clark. Let us be plain, your lies.

So I climbed off the cot. I have the strength, you know. Nobody checked because nobody thought to. I will always have this small advantage: check the Scotsman, check the Englishman. Never mind the Bengali. One may hear a great deal, may know and keep a great deal, when one is more or less invisible.

I inched my way across the floor. Plain, waxed boards, cool under my feet, your voices soft through the wall between us. Done in five short steps. Not a creak from the boards—bare feet are my handwriting—and I have an ear to the door. I want to hear you talk, Mr Clark. Maybe later, when you are done, I will take my turn to speak.

⸻⸻

I ask myself now, where did all the misfortunes start? Perhaps it was the day my father took me to see you. You sat in an office at Campbell and Clark's wharf, airs like a maharaja. A hundred yards downstream your family's terrible boat was already sucking in ooze from the river.

The office made you comfortable and it impressed the traders, I am sure. But it offered no welcome to small men such as my father and me. We could only approach such a door because my father was your manservant. No other lascar in the city of Calcutta would dare to knock.

The two *sipahees* at the door were low-caste men who knew my father. They stepped aside, we entered, and you bestowed an audience upon us. He had told me in advance to bow in a deep *salaam*, hand to forehead, before we said a word. You watched; your eyes gleamed at the sight. Then my father told you I was sixteen years old now—yes, a slight lad but a quick learner—and he wanted me to take over his role as your manservant. My father would still come to Sydney with the November voyage, but as the *serang* of the lascar crew, responsible to all and not just you. He believed it was time for me to learn the job.

The *punkah wallahs* worked the fans while my father spoke; the air barely moved. You heard him out but it was clear your heart was not in it. *Prasad*, you complained, *I am accustomed to your ways, and you to mine. Why must I start again?*

My father was accustomed to your ways: he carried them out in a china pot first thing in the morning. He knew this would be your line, and he rounded you easily. First, he said the *mistri*—the man who hired all of the company's labour—had approved the switch. This was not true, Mr Clark, I later found out. But you are too lazy for checking. Then he spoke of his standing among his fellow lascars, the forty-four of them who would be the backbone of the crew. He knew them all, from the *tindals* to the *topas*, the Mussulmen and the Hindus. Over the years he had come to know their families. Long before you arrived in Calcutta.

You were outfoxed. You cursed—peevishly—and told us to tell the captain, Mr Hamilton. Then you ordered us out of your office. So it was done: my father would sail as the *serang*, the man who stood between the lascars and the crew. He would calm them, keep them going, more so because he was not tied to you throughout the voyage.

You remember that day, I am sure. The moment of that decision. Perhaps, on the other side of the door now, you regret it.

The thing was cleared with Mr Hamilton, who cared little, other than it meant he gained a full-grown man among his crew instead of a boy. And we went home, my father and I, to tell my mother that it was done. Standing before her, my eyes were now level with hers where only months ago I had looked up at her. In its own sad way, it spoke of the need for me to go. She wept a little. It must hurt, I know, to send her only son away to sea. But I also knew it was my duty to follow my father: our family's long tradition. I had been on the river, around it, for years already; collecting scrap, running messages for the merchants and fighting other boys for a place among the lumpers.

There was no time to think of the losses, but my mother bore all of them.

⚜

Now I hear you telling the lieutenant about the voyage. Some of the truth; but only some.

You should speak of that evil man and how we all shrank from him. Even when he came on the day we sailed, late but not worried. He showed his papers. Ran his hand over the tea chests to make sure they were packed correctly. His long body, cruel hands. That voice, pouring English like a strange oil. And those eyes, I cannot think how to describe them but they were night-eyes. *I am Mr Figge*, he told us. *From Sumpters.* Speaking as though he knew and loved every man on board: he tousled my hair like he was some great ruler granting small kindnesses.

What sort of merchant, I wondered, wears trousers that reveal his ankles?

In the dull days across the ocean he spent his time in one cabin or the other, the door closed, talking endlessly—to you, to Mr Hamilton—about who knows what. I must take care here: he talked to both of you but never at the same time. As if he was feeding two animals that ate different food.

He talked like an expert about many things, never minded that the man listening might be backed against a bulkhead, nowhere to go. Perhaps he did not know how forceful he was. Perhaps he knew well and it amused him.

Sometimes I would ask my father about the strange man and he would speak firmly to me. *It is none of your concern*, he would say. *You are a bright and attentive boy but your imagination runs away with you. Leave it be. Attend to your duties.* And I tried to do so. But I could see changes over the long weeks at sea: his talks with you became more urgent. When we crossed the equator, before the gales, Mr Figge brought the second mate, Mr Leisham, into these talks. He looked scared, as you did.

Sometimes Mr Figge had you or him up against a door, or the masts, pointing his finger and speaking low and firm. He paid no mind to whether he was watched.

He *was* watched. By me, but I'm never seen. That one night I was clearing the remains of your meal from your room, out of view in the passage. Mr Figge was talking to Mr Leisham in that way I'd seen, pressing him. *Seven thousand gallons*, I heard him say. I knew he did not speak of the tea.

I felt no loyalty to you but I knew that did not matter. I brought you water, meals and messages, and of course I took away the chamber pot. These were my duties. As the ship heaved and wandered sideways I cleaned those meals off the walls, and off your coat and your blankets, when you threw up. You would sometimes forget it was me and go to my father for something: my father, who had known you long enough, would steer you back to me. *I am* scrang *now*, he would remind you. *It is the boy you seek*. And you would come looking for me.

Then the gales began and we thought they would never end. You told the navy man about Mr Leisham falling from the rigging, but you did not tell the detail: the moment that Mr Figge told the captain to send him up there. *There's no need to hand it*, Mr Hamilton said of the topsail. *It will soon enough tear itself free anyway.*

Send him, Mr Figge said: calm, very still. *Don't make me repeat myself.*

And those eyes took hold of the captain's and I saw he would not let go. So up went Mr Leisham. The masts were swinging, the tips eighty feet high, and by the time she rolled fully off one beam and onto the other, they drew an arc that might have been a hundred and fifty feet through the air, and Leisham inched his way up there with terror all over his face. Each time the roll switched to the other side the rigs'd throw over and he'd bear-hug whatever he'd been grabbing at that instant and this went on for so long, so long. And the miracle was, he got it done—he got all the way to the topsail yard while we watched him, whipping through the evening sky like a monkey aloft in a tree and he managed to hand it in: one furl off, two, three, and the more of it he tied onto the yard, the more it thrashed around him and the mounts and eyelets lashed him and the blows to his hands were breaking his knuckles, they must have been. He had his feet in the rat-lines, and he clung and he clung until his terrible death.

And the worst horror of it was watching Mr Figge standing there on the poop. Unbraced, legs apart, riding the swell. Mouth just slightly open, as for demons to pass back and forth. The worse our journey became—the leaking boat, the wretched weather—the less Mr Figge worried. He smiled wherever he went. Laughed, even.

You told of the storms well enough, Mr Clark, but you see them only through your eyes. You were dry enough most of the time, down aft and not often above decks. I brought you food to calm your belly. For us it was not the same. Our suffering led to fear, then panic. The captain had us in the bilge water, stuffing rags in the gaps, our skin like pastry, tearing on everything: corners, splinters, nails. But that pain was nothing beside being thrown about inside that small space in the dark, in every direction. The body would go slack for a moment after days of no sleep; the very moment the ship would toss you fully at a beam or the side of a cask. The whole great mass of the cargo was edged in by its own weight, and in the dark it threatened always to collapse.

Here and now, behind the door listening to you Mr Clark,

54

I feel my guts turn again at the memory. The smell in there: lamp oil and human waste, and something else—old seawater, or the pork. That water could come out of there only one way: by our labour. It is not the work of an Englishman nor a Scot to clear six feet of water from the hold. Such work falls to the lascars, since anyone can remember. The captain roared at us to man the pump on deck but cold and sickness had made us angry and at first we did not move. I say 'us' but in truth I was spared because I was your boy. I wonder now if my father foresaw all this. He led the men against the captain, saying no one could stand up straight out there in the wind and spray, let alone work the pump. I watched him stand up for the rest of them, with such skill that none could call it mutiny. I loved him and I admired him for that gentle strength. The other lascars looked to him too. Their *serang*, their protector.

The stand-off ended with an order that the men go below and bail with buckets, since they refused to stand on the deck in the frozen rain.

Twenty, thirty men went below then and began the bailing. Weak and moaning, staggering under the gallons. It was easy to slip, more so for those standing on the steps or working with their backs against the ribs of the hull. Sometimes they went under, coming up with the dreadful water in their mouths. Sometimes the waves rocked the ship so hard that the bilge-muck itself made waves that crashed from one side of the hold to the other. I saw their eyes in the dark, my father's too. I came to understand what he had done for me.

The bailing lowered the water level—as far as anyone could know when the water level kept moving. Over the long hours I often slipped away from you, Mr Clark, to see my father, but he had become a ghost. His eyes were empty and he showed no sign that he knew me. I brought him water, which he sipped only before handing it on. I could feel how much he wanted to drink it all, but he held firm: a great man, working in a hole. The others drank fast, till the water was gone. Any break in the work meant others had to work harder. And if the water rose again, we all knew the captain might send them back up to the pump.

Mr Kennedy, the carpenter, worked in the bow all this time. His curses and shouts reached the men bailing the hold, fuelling the fear that drove them. The ship was taking sly hits at him, catching him unawares. One moment he stood, the next he was on his back in the water. He swore like there were not enough curses in the world to fit his anger.

And you, Mr Clark, through all this you had me attending to you as though we were not part of the night, as though we stood on firm ground. You asked for pen and paper, for messages to and from the captain's cabin, tea and bread while you talked with Mr Figge. What could there be to talk about? I fought with the pot and the tiny cooking fire, the close work making me retch.

Even now I believe the men were ahead of the water, but just before dawn something changed. Mr Figge came to the doorway of your cabin and demanded you speak to the captain. The way he spoke, not the words, was enough to compel you. He was a tea merchant, which made him your customer, I imagine. But does that explain your shaking?

Only minutes later the captain ordered the lascars to the pumps once again. And no one would move. They stopped their bailing, my father too, and you could see the water rising again as they waited for someone to speak. It was my father, of course, who did.

No, he said, and only that.

I cannot have all of us perish because of the selfishness of a few, said the captain. He looked unsure whether my father understood him, but he did. *You leave me no choice*, the captain said next, and he walked off. I was standing near the two of them and I could see the faces looking up from the hold, hear their hard breathing over the slopping of the bilge water. My father looked as though he could not be moved. But the men around him, their eyes most of all, seemed broken.

The captain came back with Mr Thompson and Mr Kennedy, who had left the bow and wore drier clothes. You saw all of this, Mr Clark. You saw that they all carried pistols—not pointed but shown to us—and you could see Mr Figge coming along behind them, his right hand low. He stood behind the others but I too could see him in full, standing as I was off to the side. In his right hand he had a whip, a cruel-looking thing I had not known the vessel to carry.

I am ordering you directly to have these men attend the pump, the captain said to my father.

When nobody moved or spoke, Mr Figge pushed forward and used the whip, bringing it down through the hatch and into the hold where the men were. Then he reached in and took one—a boy whose name I never learned—and pulled him out by the hair. The boy screamed and tripped as he came up the steps, a clump of hair and some bloody flesh coming away in Mr Figge's hand. I saw him flick it back into the hold. Urgent words between the men, and they started to climb their way towards the hatch.

On deck they took their places at the pump brake, one by one bringing the great timber handle down, waiting for it to draw, then going again. No man could stand more than a quarter-hour of the work before he fell to the deck. Those who waited were lashed by the rain and the salt spray. The work would warm them, then break them all over again. Those who had just had their turn could not be roused to speak. My father went through these terrible hours along with them, trying not to show the pain. I cried for him as he suffered: I dreamed I was small again, so that he could shelter me.

Mr Figge walked among them without a thought for the weather, kicking here and punching there. Dull, heavy fists that splattered on wet skin and hair. Why, Mr Clark? Why was a tea merchant so keen to drive men beyond their endurance? You knew the answer then and you keep it now, buried in your half-told story.

The first to die was an old Bengali, locked onto the brake handle by cramp. His effort stopped. They took him down and he lay on the wet deck, a puddle of a man. No one thought much of it, for it was the way each man finished his turn. But he never moved. We stood around him, uncertain, then Mr Kennedy came up, took the man by his wet jacket and lifted him. He walked to the gunwale and threw him over.

There were sounds of horror. Kennedy took the pistol from his belt and pointed it directly at the men: first one, then another. He watched them down its barrel with the hammer back and high like a rearing snake. The work that was left in the men was nearly gone. And as it went, the price of pulling that trigger became lower.

So the work started again, and the next to fall was a boy who spat blood from the sores in his gums. The cramps knotted him, and he dropped hard onto his face with nothing to slow him. I do not think that killed him. It was more that the wick that burns within just failed. His eyes and mouth stayed open all the while, and it was the rain on his open eyes that told the rest of us he was gone. A boy, I said. No more than twelve.

That two men died working a pump may sound strange, looking back in daylight from a village under fair skies, but that is no reason for it to slip from your account, Mr Clark. Nor that three more died before the storm was over. Five of our number dead and no respect given them. No fire to cleanse them, tossed overboard like the night soil.

The last part of our voyage was as you told it. The patching of the leaks stopped the water, but that only delayed the fate that awaited us. They threw some cargo overboard, the things that were not so valuable. You saw, like me, that Mr Figge said nothing as the tea went over.

Then, when the ship came to rest on that shoal and we rowed ashore, none of us knew who we were anymore.

Broken light, I remember, and boulders: great domes and stacks, silver and white and grey and crowned with a curious orange dusting. Boulders with fierce faces, graceful ones, split and pocked ones. The one that looked to me like a woman swollen with child, waiting at one end of the beach with her lonely eyes on the sea.

Grasses shivered in the hollows between. Soft to the touch, it seemed, but no: the points pricked the fingertips. The colours and the hard grasses and the sharp edges of the dry weed high on the beach, they all said we had landed somewhere else, where the lives we all lived had nothing to offer us. You and I knew as little as each other, sir. Which for the first time made us equals.

I was luckier than most. I had shoes. And I had my father. He never made a fuss of me. He was the centre of many demands and I could see the weight of it on his face in that crowded jollyboat as we rowed to shore. But I felt his love like a cloak over me. As we spread on foot over the hummocks of that empty place, a mood came over the party that even the light of the sun on the white sand could not lift. Six men were gone: Leisham and the five of ours. But something else was gone too. The pistols, the whip—they had done their work. Now it was them and us.

8

When Grayling entered the guest quarters he was struck immediately by the smell, the thick tallowy reek of the doctor's ointments.

Figge lay apparently unmoved. His head a wild artefact on crisp linen, like a dog had leapt up and deposited it there. He rolled his eyes towards Grayling; some weather in the man had changed.

'I have tea coming, Mr Figge. Better stuff, I hope.'

'You are wanting to talk again, lieutenant?'

'Yes, that's my aim. I have an hour set aside so we can really—'

'You don't have the journal with you.'

'No I don't, I—'

'You said you'd bring it.' His voice slowed, like a waiting storm that drew power from the sea. *You said you would read it to me.*'

Grayling felt a surge of panic, rifling through words like 'reconsider' and 'on reflection', then stumbled on an escape route.

'The governor has instructed me to ask you for your account without the assistance of other sources. Just to make sure we have it…independently.' He tried smiling, reached out a hand to pat the man's shoulder. But Figge burst into movement, twisting up and sideways so that his wreck of a face was close to Grayling's and a gust of foul air connected them.

'You listen to me, *lieutenant*. I didn't survive two shipwrecks so you could play games with me. You understand? I didn't walk hundreds of miles through the bush so some preening halfwit could try out a *strategy* on me.' He shot out a hand and gripped the front of Grayling's waistcoat. His eyes bored into Grayling's. 'Do not attempt to toy with me. I am not a man you'd toy with.'

'I'm sorry Mr Figge, I…' Grayling found himself stammering. 'That was certainly not my intent.'

'And don't compound your idiocy by FUCKING LYING TO ME.' Spittle gathered in the corner of Figge's mouth, where the tiniest trace of a mad grin was forming. It was a performance. Grayling knew this, but it was no less frightening for that. 'Get out,' Figge spat. 'I shall consider at my leisure whether I wish to co-operate any further.'

Grayling turned on his heel, but before he had reached the door Figge called out. This time his voice was pleading. 'Oh forgive me, forgive me,' said the new voice. 'I have been through such terrible things. Sometimes I fear I do not know myself anymore.'

The lieutenant turned, his skin crawling. He looked at the fading light outside the window above the bed. He would play this game: see where it led. 'I must go anyway,' he said abruptly. 'I have a commitment.'

'I beg of you lieutenant, don't leave me. I am full of terrors.' Figge's eyes narrowed as another idea came to him. 'It's not duty, is it. This commitment of yours is personal, I think. You're worried.'

Grayling was suddenly flustered once more. He forced a smile.

'Tell me what it is.' Figge's tone, artfully laced with fellowship, invited him in. How did this man pass through tempers so swiftly? Grayling forced his revulsion down and stepped back towards the bed, even while he wondered why he did so.

'My wife is unwell. I must watch her closely at present.'

'The two of you came over with the governor on the *Reliance*. From England, I mean.'

'Scotland originally. Who told you that?'

'Oh, people talk. I am interested in people.' He made an airy gesture with one hand, the violence quite gone. 'So four years here, then. You must be close to him.'

'I had worked alongside His Excellency for some years before this.'

'The Corps will wear him down eventually, you must know that. What will you and your wife do then?'

'I don't think that is your concern, Mr Figge.'

The eyes, under the swelling, looked chastened. 'No, you're right, of course. I take it from your manner, lieutenant, that your wife is more than just unwell. What are her symptoms?'

Figge was gesturing at the seat beside the bed. Grayling resisted him. To ask of her symptoms was to invite a conversation about her body, the open stretches of her warm curving skin; the trespass upon that skin by this damned pestilence, whatever it was.

He felt the impertinence, keenly; but he was desperate.

He sighed. 'She has been getting worse for over a week now. She's a very—a very healthy woman, Mr Figge, but she has become weak and faint. Her legs will not obey her, they…I mean by that, she cannot stand. She has a rash over her abdomen and…'

No. Charlotte's health, her body, was not this man's concern.

'Go on. There is another thing.'

Damn him.

'A sore. An abscess, I suppose, on her head. Here.' He pointed to his own head, behind his ear. 'Like something bit her. But the swelling increases and it has been eight days.'

Figge was frowning, chewing his wild beard slightly into his mouth. 'Is she coughing?'

'No.'

'Feverish?'

'No.'

'Let me think about this, lieutenant. I am not medically trained, you understand, but I have some knowledge of the world.'

Grayling felt a wave of relief that Figge's reversal of the interrogation had ended. He thanked the man vaguely and turned again to go.

'I would be pleased to attend on her.'

The words were spoken evenly, neither hopeful nor dismissive, and they lodged like a hooked seed in Grayling. The man was not letting go.

'Good of you, sir,' Grayling fumbled. 'We shall see what unfolds.' He made it to the door but turned again, despite himself, to look at the figure in the bed. The eyes had never left him.

'Yes.' Those eyes were a hot brand on his flesh. 'You should go to her.'

9

Lovely of you to come, lieutenant. I hope I didn't frighten you, but the look on your face! I heard Hamilton's pomposity in your plummy mouth as you retreated. Fear not, I can weave through the obstacles in this little tale, even if you won't tell me what Clark's said or written. Whatever it is, it will only be constipated by formality. He saw what I saw and felt the things I felt, but on the page the dreary bastard will suck the life out of them.

The boy doesn't speak. Clark can't write. The story in its greatest form lives in me. And here it starts: with the early light and the new day breathing soft upon me. I am seated away from the others, on a boulder in a clearing. More boulders stretch beyond, great towering piles of granite that thrust towards the rumbling sky. Nearer in, they are fringed with great hummocks of grass. The tussocks caused me pain last night, bulging here and there into my resting bones.

But what fills the world is the birds. It is them that make the grunts and yarks and other complaints I hear, sounds that might have issued from a barn full of unfed livestock. Birds of an ordinary size, sooty black, short of tail and clumsy afoot, wandering like drunks over these clumps of grass, peering into holes then honking apologies when they find inside not the mate they seek but some other irritable tenant.

There are other birds about: gulls and skuas overhead, and lumbering fat grey geese along the back of the beach. Someone found a penguin in a crevasse between two boulders. But these sooty ones are by far the most numerous. As my eyes adjust I find there are dozens, hundreds of them, all doing this same thing: waddle and stagger, inquire at the mouth of a hole then blunder onwards.

We have made camp, the lot of us, atop a giant colony of these dundering imbeciles, and as the men set their feet upon the ground they trip and stumble among the burrows. Swearing at each other, swearing at the birds. I should join them. I should be up and about in vigorous pursuit of our salvation.

But I like to observe.

This circular flat with its bird warrens and its hard, spiky grasses is home to forty-nine souls: ten of us Englishmen and Scots, and thirty-nine lascars, many of them huddled around a fire, though it is not cold. They're burning broken planks because fire makes sense of the world.

The ship lies just across the little beach and a short stretch of water, swamped to her gunwales and still in full sail as though she intends to continue on underwater. In her dying moments she righted herself somehow, and thus her bow faces us squarely. It lends her a nobility she doesn't deserve, the old heifer.

By sun-up we've six or eight of the dimwitted birds on a fire, necks wrung and roughly plucked. Hamilton didn't get wet last night and he's there in his fine trousers and his jacket, making speeches. *The ship is lost*, he declares, like that's a revelation when she sits there on the bank, awash in the leftover chop from last night and groaning like a beast in labour.

The bird flesh is greasy and it stinks but I've had worse. It comes away in strips from the bones, and the muscle differs little from the sinew. The guts are bitter, fishy and dark. The teeth can work through these bones, but the powdery remains in the molars are the least pleasant part. I do not forget a bird, and I have seen these ones in the north, way north in the Arctic Circle. I cannot fathom how they would be here too, but it is them, I have no doubt. The clumsy shape, more beak than tail. I wonder how the living feel as they watch me devour the dead. I suppose they are too stupid to make the association.

Hamilton, barely brighter than the birds, is still talking. He has a plan of sorts. We are to use the jollyboat to retrieve everything from the ship and bring it to the beach. We are to load a barren rock, maybe a mile long, with the baubles and trinkets of faraway civilisation: plates and shoes and spices and a horse and cow and for the love of Christ Himself a musical organ. What pretty mischief: we are making a tiny England.

There is the other thing: the thing lodged deeper in me than all that trivial finery: the barrel storage of seven thousand gallons of rum. What's surer than the sunset is that these fools will break it open and gorge themselves to a rolling stupor. And a revelation it will be if that stupor is at all discernible from their intellects when sober. We were headed for a colony where rum is money. The carcass of the *Sydney Cove* holds a fortune in liquid form, enough that a man could buy his own mountain and never work again, and this mob would guzzle the lot.

The bird is reduced to skeleton and I toss it at some of its former comrades, bumbling about on the sand in pompous clamour. Beyond them are the seals, piled one atop the other all over the boulders, and I count fifty of them just within the curve of this bay. In the dying hours of the *Sydney Cove*'s voyage I saw perhaps a thousand. Blubber and fur: a bounty more valuable even than the rum, and more lasting. There is a fortune to be made out of what I know: that a ship lies broken here, laden with riches. That an industry could be got underway, clubbing these stupid beasts and skinning them.

The boulders around me are glittering in the morning sun. *Untold riches*, they sing, *for the man who lives to see Sydney*.

Hamilton is talking about the longboat, but as I am not one of his crew he cannot address me with any authority. I lie here, indifferent to his fine words, while the others must sit upright and listen attentively.

The longboat. He wants the longboat repaired of the damage it has sustained in the wreck, then modified and reinforced for a long journey. He is forcing himself to devise a practical course, but the despair in his heart is transparent to all. We are placed most exquisitely in the hands of Fate. A boulder island north of Van Diemen's Land and south of New South Wales. A place where no ship goes. Where no man, possibly not even the Savage, has yet placed a foot in the entire history of God's creation.

⸻

I stand—dust myself off, because Figge would do so—and turn my attention to Hamilton. He wants a well dug. It's late summer here, no surface water anywhere. They go to it with the only spade from the *Sydney Cove*, choosing a hollow between two stacks of granite, and eventually strike water at seven feet. Horrible stuff.

I walk away from the men at their labours and head towards the western side of the island through a range of large granite domes. Winding in and out among them, over gravelly sand and feeble topsoil, I come across one of the lascars, the *cassub*, squatted to shit between two stunted bushes.

I stop to watch him and he protests mildly, but he has his trousers around his ankles and his hands bracing his knees: he can hardly shoo me off. Standing to the east of him, it occurs to me that the smell of the shit is wafting my way. The wind is blowing west.

This is an interesting development. Hamilton, of course, sailed us directly into the gap in the Furneaux chart: the blank paper in the long coastline that stretches from the southern tip of Van Diemen's Land all the way north-east to Sydney. Furneaux lost his way about there: the pencil left the page for a crucial few hundred miles. Now that we are in Furneaux's gap, the larger question looms: what exactly is in it?

A short herb grows beside the squatting man. Silver-blue and sprouting vigorously from pure sand. I tear a little of the foliage and bite into it. It tastes of salt, mildly herbaceous. The shitter is watching me dolefully so I push him with a foot. He topples sweetly into his own dung and it makes a thick orange-brown print on his thigh.

I move past him and on to a low range of the giant boulders, eyes drawn to the sea again. Looking west. The onshore wind has streaked the white foam out there and as it pushes at me two thoughts occur almost simultaneously: I am looking westward and seeing water—so where has the coastline gone? And there is *swell*, not just chop, moving across that water towards me.

This is no estuary. There is a long fetch of open sea out there.

This enigma stays with me over several more days as the lascars busy themselves retrieving the *Sydney Cove*'s cargo. The weather is fine: the longboat is dragged up onto the beach and braced by heavy timbers, sourced among those already breaking free of the ship's corpse. Kennedy works shirtless in the sun, sawing, nailing, planing: straking her sides and fortifying her guts for a long voyage.

For us, waiting, it's a diet of rice and bird. Nobody will starve here. At least, not for some time. On occasion we have dined on the enormous grey geese that wander the island. They scare easily, but they only take flight after much awkward lumbering. In between there is a moment of opportunity. The heavy flesh on them roasts well. The Javanese are trying to eat the big conical limpets from the boulders. But they are tough as hell, and no amount of pounding on the rocks or boiling in seawater will soften their fibres. I tried the rubbery flesh—once. The taste is of wharf posts at low tide. Better to bait a hook with the damned limpets than to try eating them.

There are cumbersome dark fish of various kinds among the rocks, including a thin one with sandpaper skin and a sharp horn on top of its head. On the sand, the men fishing have found another creature altogether: a long, slender flat-fish that appears more like a reptile. When brought to the surface it carries the colours of the seafloor in perfect mimicry, complete with the speckles, but these soon fade to a dull brown. A row of sharp spines lies flat against its back, flaring only when it is subjected to the indignity of capture. These ones eat well, comparable to a good English cod. When I see one brought in I make sure to seat myself by the lucky angler and remind him of my position as client.

These are the most fortunate days of our odyssey. I walk and think and take such small advantages as I can. On the beach at the southern end of the island, a round boulder stands topped with a smaller one, looking like some fat old harpy who's tumbled onto her arse in a stupor. The sky is huge and never quite empty: if it's not clouds racing past it's birds of countless sorts. The oily dark ones we've been eating are the most plentiful but there are gulls both large and small, and just occasionally a white eagle, its broad wings backswept to a handful of flight feathers extending like fingers that grip the air. I watch it draw its circles above us, the beak with the tip curved for taking out eyes, and I wonder, are we merely meat to it? Meat that unhelpfully moves about but soon enough will lie soft in the grass for the talons to plough?

When the inevitable happens and the thirsty Lothians break into the rum, it is me who goes to Hamilton and points out the other little island just to our south-west where, perhaps, he might want to isolate the intoxicants. Logic would say Clark should be protecting his investment, not me, but I am not concerned who perceives my plans in motion.

After another two days' work the men have ferried the grog across the water. I later observe them—not the lascars: grog doesn't seem to light their fancy—gazing sadly out towards the faraway casks, neatly stacked along the foreshore above the tide line. I would feel some sympathy for the dumb oafs who have lost their one means of release. But they cannot apprehend the true value of those casks.

Hamilton has named our island Preservation—for its dubious role in our survival. I was mildly surprised that he avoided eponymy, but perhaps he didn't want his good name associated with this debacle. During one of our murmured conversations I suggest to him that he call the other little island Figge's Isle, in sly honour of the poor sod who bequeathed me his trousers. Hamilton replies that islands should be named more practically, and human names should only be chosen from among the deceased. He has me there: as long as I walk and draw breath, Figge remains alive. And with characteristic lack of imagination, he settles upon Rum Island.

Rum and Preservation. What a pair.

10

She hated the days when she couldn't get out of the place.

She hated the monotony, the great weight of time that pressed on the roof and made the windows knock. She hated watching the light and feeling it burgeon, then decay, like life itself. She would have said that she hated to cook and to clean and to wash; to conform to the air of authority that pervaded every home. But right now she would have given anything to throw her body at a task and to puff the stray hair from her face as she raised an unseemly sweat.

Because the bed was worse than anything. The helplessness of it, the waiting. Domestic work she could tolerate. It contributed something to their lives. But this lying around! She was too weak for rage: if not, she would have stormed out and plunged headlong into the forest.

She held her visions of the forested world deep inside, used them to fortify herself against the hours. The powerful smell of the secret, enveloping trees and their straying edges of bark; the long twigs that whipped and draped over the sandstone; caves and ledges and trickles of cold water arranged in complex symmetries that beckoned her to believe all of this was intentional display. That beholding eyes, even hers, were the only thing required to complete the perfection. She had begun to think the bush spoke at a different pitch and that, although she couldn't hear it, her body mourned its absence when the house enclosed her. Perhaps she was going mad. Perhaps it was the sickness.

In the afternoon she caught herself waiting for him, imagined him there and close to her, *closer* to her, above and inside her and breathing hard by her cheek and in her ear, taking her hair in his hands and rocking against a sea or the stars or the wind perhaps, some gale over the shores that rushed life into the trees. She imagined the times when it was the two of them and the land outside whispered spirits through their tiny house and sent them raptures she could not explain: then she would drive her fingers into the ropes of his back and gorge upon the good fortune of him, that back of his unmarked and strong and arching in perfect beautiful agony for *her*. In those moments, when she knew him so completely, she could see past their lives into some other place where they still existed together; yet in slivers of those same instants she did not know him at all, for his eyes would fade from passion to an immeasurable distance. As if oceans separated him from her; oceans they had made together.

It infuriated her, the waiting for him, but there was nothing else to do. She had tried reading but her head hurt. She dozed occasionally but only woke up dry-mouthed and dizzy. She threw back the covers when the irritation overwhelmed her but her legs refused to swing over the edge of the bed.

By the time Joshua came home she was worse than she had

been all day. She'd thrown up in the tin bucket he'd left her, and could not summon the means to get up and rinse it. She could hear him pause at the skillion as he came past the well. The room would stink, but she could do nothing. He showed no sign of noticing the smell when he entered. He stepped swiftly across the room and laid a hand on her forehead, watching her with eyes full of worry. He murmured that she was a sweet girl, and she raised a smile in response. He looked left, back towards the skillion.

'Boorigul's gone again,' he said. She nodded. She didn't want to discuss that. He took the bucket away without comment.

She watched him go through the same procedure as he had each evening since the illness appeared, his way of resisting futility. He went to the pot over the coals to bring her soup, and she allowed herself a smile at the sight of his back. He placed the bowl carefully on the lap table he had fashioned for her. When she sat up she felt cold air on her shoulders. The night had a chill about it that was new, and the dark had crept forward earlier.

'It's good,' Charlotte murmured between sips.

'The kitchen said it's made from kangaroo tail.'

She feigned disgust. 'Can't we just imagine it's beef?' But she sipped again and saw how it filled him with relief. 'What stirs out there in the colony?' she asked, mock-serious.

'Army worms. Twice as bad as yesterday, all over the maize and the vines. Don't know what did it—maybe the damp morning.'

'The place is attacking itself.'

'Mm. Attacking us.'

Joshua sat on the edge of the bed in his underwear and she dropped a hand on the small of his back as he waited for her to finish the food. She ate against her will, to ease his concern.

When she was done, he took the little table with the bowl on it and deposited it by the door. He returned to the bed and she reached an arm out so that his head rested on the slope of her chest, just beneath her shoulder. Her fingers found his hair and traced light strokes through it.

She found that she was fighting back tears. Everything, *everything* was at risk. She must defeat this, whatever it was, or she would leave him condemned to the town and the vagrant howling of men unmoored. He was holding her tightly now in the tangle of warm body and bedclothes, as if he sensed her terror.

Once again, she coaxed him into conversation, to shift them both from the unstable ground of her welfare, and drew from him the details of the discussion with Figge. He explained the unnerving offer the man had made, to attend on her and—had he understood correctly? To offer some cure?

She waited without a word until he was finished. 'He's unsettled you,' she said.

He nodded reluctantly. 'I can't define what it is. I know I don't want him near you.'

'Do you think…' She paused. 'Do you think there is some great scheme in him?'

'What do you mean?'

'A plan of some kind…I can't see how any of it could benefit him. He's a tea merchant with cargo onboard the ship. It's in his interest that the ship makes it to Sydney and the tea sells.'

'No. I cannot see a scheme to it. But he's *revelling* in this somehow.'

'What about the coast, the way these two described it? You say it runs south of here, this line that goes all the way down to the very end of Van Diemen's Land.' She drew it with the tip of one finger down his thigh and he stretched, cat-like, at the pleasure of it. 'But it is interrupted—' she lifted the finger. 'There is a part of the coast that nobody has charted?'

'Yes. Furneaux missed about two hundred miles. He sketched some islands, but west and north of them is a mystery.'

'And that's where the ship is?'

'Somewhere. Or it's in among those islands.'

'But further in? Further to the *west*, where Furneaux—'

'Drew nothing? That is one possibility.'

'Very well.' She was animated now, clutching his arm. 'But why would a captain send his vessel in there? I know you would want to shelter from the weather that was damaging the ship, but if it was already in distress, why would you push into that uncharted place?'

'Maybe they had no control over it.'

'Maybe. Surely nobody would do so *intentionally*.'

The word hung between them, the idea of someone's deliberate plotting; a capricious god-hand in the chaos.

Charlotte watched Joshua lean forward to extinguish the candle with a short breath. The darkness settled over them and she felt the warmth of him and wondered painfully for how much longer their bodies could share comfort this way. The darkness gave her the courage to form the words.

'You know, I'm not getting any better…'

He did not answer.

'We need to be realistic, Joshua. If I should…'

He had found her lips with his fingers, stopping her. 'There's plenty we haven't tried.'

Outside a cold blue moonlight made shadows from the unfamiliar trees. Somewhere near the house, an owl piped a soft vigil.

They both knew what had not been tried.

11

 The following morning, Grayling returned to Clark's quarters, his mind crowded with contradictions.

He found the doctor beside Clark's bed, a basin on the bedclothes. He was carefully washing the hand wounds. Grayling watched, transfixed by the water trickling through his palms and into the dish, tinted and flecked. Ewing peered over his smooth white fingers as they tended the edges of the wounds. He did not look up. Grayling was aware now of another man, seated in an armchair on the far side of the bed. The man had his hat placed neatly on the floor beside the chair, but he nodded his head deferentially when Grayling looked his way.

'Who is this?'

Ewing answered him. 'This man is William Martin, lieutenant. An assistant surgeon with some interest in my work here with Mr Clark. But he has...other interests, don't you Mr Martin?'

Martin stood. He extended his hand enthusiastically.

'Lieutenant, I have not taken the liberty of speaking with Mr Clark here until you arrived.' He looked both to Grayling and to Clark as he spoke. 'I work with Mr George Bass, sir.'

'The surgeon.'

'Yes,' Martin smiled. 'We also have an interest, as you might know, in the coast hereabouts. Mr Bass is at sea right now on the *Enterprise*, but I thought I should take the opportunity to hear Mr Clark's tale.'

Grayling looked at him blankly.

'It concerns a section of the coast that has greatly exercised our minds.'

'This supposed sea passage north of Van Diemen's Land?'

'Precisely.' The easy confidence marked him more as salesman than navigator.

Grayling looked at the doctor. 'Doctor Ewing, have you been sharing these discussions outside this room?'

If Ewing was shocked at the accusation, he didn't show it. 'Not at all, lieutenant.'

Clark watched the exchange without interest.

'I see.' Grayling thought for a moment. 'You understand, Mr Martin, that what transpires in here is confidential.'

'But of course. The same can be said of our interest in this.'

'Very well. Observe without comment, please. Mr Clark's condition is still very delicate. Which brings me to you, good sir.' Grayling patted the bedclothes somewhere near Clark's knee. Clark glared at the hand and Grayling withdrew it. 'Are you improving, Mr Clark?'

The wounds on his face were darker and drier now, the inflammation slowly easing.

'Somewhat. Mostly now it is *irritation*.' He looked from Martin back to Grayling. 'You have my journal with you again.

Is it the handwriting you're struggling with?'

Grayling was much too interested to be deterred by Clark's show of reluctance, or by the presence of Martin, the opportunist. He drew a chair close to the bed, while Martin returned to his on the far side. The doctor packed his implements and left.

'It is the longboat journey, Mr Clark. Your journal, of course, doesn't commence until the overland journey begins. Would you kindly tell me how the longboat came to grief?'

⚓

The wind blew consistently through February, though it was warm and mostly dry. My responsibility on the company's behalf was to watch over the cargo, but that aside, I was little occupied.

The longboat, as you know, was slipped on the beach at the southern end of Preservation. Mr Kennedy had added two runs of straking planks so the sides were higher, less likely to admit any waves. After about two weeks the captain set about crewing it. He'd made a decision that it was he who should stay with the wreck and the cargo, though I am the supercargo and all of the bailed goods are my responsibility. I don't say it was the wrong decision: only that it might not appear conventional.

The longboat had no name. Just an open hull, no shelter, under the command of the chief mate, Mr Thompson. He is—or he *was*—a reasonable fellow, though much in the way of all ships' mates he was abrupt. We took the carpenter, Mr Kennedy, because such a voyage demands repairs from time to time, and having worked on it for two weeks he knew the vessel best.

Yes, we took Mr Figge. Well, lieutenant, you would have to ask *him* why. I imagine he would say that being a trader he was in a good position to assist with a salvage claim.

Like? 'Like' is not a word that comes into it. You stagger through the bush with a man and it is dark and light and wet and dry and you are hungry and sore. There is no place for notions of friendship. If you asked me did I admire his bravery or tenacity or skill, I would answer no. None of those things.

No, I do not wish to speak further of him.

So. It was Thompson and Kennedy and Mr Figge and me. There were a dozen lascars, along with my manservant Srinivas… yes, the boy in the next room.

I do not know their names, other than one was the boy's father, Prasad. He was their *serang.* Why do you want their names? Heavens, I wonder at times where this questioning is going.

At any rate, the letter you have in your hand, addressed to Governor Hunter, was written by the captain. I saw him write it, in case that is also animating your suspicions. I have not read it because I am not in the habit of reading that which is not addressed to me, but I understand that it explains the ordeal of the storms and the wreck and the island, that it gives an inventory of the cargo, which I could have supplied you in any event, and that it asks for a merchant or government vessel to render assistance and deliver the crew to Sydney.

We departed the island on February twenty-seventh, my twenty-eighth birthday, as it happens. You will want to know what we had with us, no doubt. We had latitude, through the use of the *Sydney Cove*'s sextant; given we were planning to follow the coast north we had little need of longitude. There was one small mizzen sail rigged up because we believed we'd be sailing downwind most of the way, and two sets of oars.

The longboat had no keel to speak of. We thought this was

to our advantage. It would enable us to get into river mouths and such, and we could break up the voyage that way. Two weeks, we expected. And why, I ask you now, lying here in this state, why did we have any such confidence? Providence had turned its back on us already, many times. Why would our shallow-keeled tub with its flimsy sail find its way up that coast in a fortnight? Without incident?

I'm not.

I am quite all right. The sooner I get through this, the sooner you'll leave me alone, that's why.

We stopped once on the northern coast of a long island that ran south to north. All granite boulders, like Preservation, but forming a great mountain at its southern end. Made a fire, ate some of the large grey geese that frequent those islands. I felt the weight of our responsibility heavily there. Thompson had command of the boat, but it was incumbent upon each of us to ensure the boat made it to Sydney: if it did not, then not only were we seventeen lost, but the remaining thirty-two on Preservation would be lost too.

But misfortune has tarred us, as you know, lieutenant. There was only a day or so between that stop on the north-running island and the abrupt end of our voyage. Out in a wide stretch of sea dotted at first with rocky isles and then wide open, we sailed the longboat and we rowed it sometimes, or the lascars did. Towards sunset we felt a luffing breeze from the south-east and it built during the evening after dusk.

Just on dark the sky changed. The early stars went out and the wind picked up sharp. There was worry among us at this turn of the sea's mood. We set watches for the night: there were enough of us on board that it was an easy schedule and the lascar boy and I slept briefly before they woke us to keep watch.

It was the two of us and Mr Figge, the rest insensible, and I woke to find we were following a low coast now. Very close, running east, not north, and the waves were sharp under us, rushing foam at our beam. Darkness out there, shrubs on low dunes and some native fires. Mr Figge had the helm. Neither he nor I are sailors but he appeared capable, just bracing the boat against the wind and adjusting sidelong over the waves that passed under us. I gave him no further thought. I was engaged in calculations of various kinds: the speed we were making and the likely distance to Sydney. When misfortune struck, it came from nowhere at all.

I do not know what went wrong with Mr Figge's handling of the craft—you would have to ask him—but without warning we plunged nose-first into the trough of a large wave and the bowsprit caught in the sea and we went end-over. One moment I was slumped there on the edge of sleep and the next I was in the water and the longboat was capsized. The provisions and equipment were floating around us, though fortunately some of it had been stowed in oilskins.

I see it now, their heads in the water. I hear men coughing, calling out to one another. It was not terribly cold, but panic seized us nonetheless. The lascars—Mussulman and Hindu alike—they are prone to band together in any extremity and so they gathered themselves in undisguised self-interest and took hold of one another. The boy Srinivas, of course, found his father and clung to him in defiance of his duty, refusing to separate from him despite my entreaties. I called to them all to get themselves on the windward side of the upturned vessel so that it would not roll onto them. One of the others, Kennedy I think, had busied himself cutting away the shrouds lest we became entrapped. But no one was tangled, and every man was able to find himself something to hold onto.

I will bring you into my confidence for just a moment, lieutenant.

Two days into my twenty-ninth year, a time for consolidation. Family, titles, positions. You have a wife, no doubt? Ambitions and responsibilities? Me, I was floating on my back in the night, looking up at the clouds and here and there the stars behind them, taking stock. An orphan, a neophyte in the family firm and in the shortest month of the calendar I'd managed to shipwreck myself twice. I hope you'll understand if I...

No, no. Enough.

Being flipped in the surf at night must be as bad a result as you could wish upon a man but for once, luck was with us. I was floated and bobbed and rolled by the breakers for long enough that I started to shiver. Then my feet struck sand beneath me and I realised Providence had delivered us into the shallows. The first glimmer of good fortune since we slipped the fucking hawsers—excuse me, lieutenant.

The longboat was gone but we still had many of our stores and we had lost not a single man. One by one the rest staggered ashore. I counted off the crew and the lascars counted themselves. There were no injuries. For some time we stood there in the darkness, just able to make out the shape of our boat as the waves set about dismantling it before our eyes.

At such a point, strangely, one hungers for activity. But there was nothing anyone could do. Men wandered off to find refuge, to make fire and dry themselves. I took the boy and we made for the hummocks of sand at the rear of the beach, found a hollow under the overhanging scrub and slept a few hours, damp and restless.

At daybreak we could see we had made landfall in the middle

of a vast, flat beach that stretched beyond sight to the south-west and the north-east. Large pieces of the boat were washing in the shallows. Behind us were unending dunes; before us, a horizon entirely devoid of anything: not a reef, not an island and, most wretchedly of all, not a sail. It was hard to imagine an emptier world, but our minds were already filling it with terrors.

There were unspoken questions about authority now that we were walkers, not sailors. Nothing was clear anymore and survival was all.

By the time the sun rose we were burning the timbers of the longboat.

12

Clark had turned himself onto one side, facing away from the lieutenant. It was unclear to Grayling whether this was a response to his physical straits or a sign that he had finished speaking. In either event, there seemed little value in pressing on, and he had much to cross-reference with Figge. He made a note to check Clark's estimates of latitude so that he could update the charts for the governor.

Outside, the sun was high over the settlement, dappled in those places where trees remained. He watched the natives in the clusters of their endless conversation. This was what they did, he figured. They sat and they talked. Their tendrils of smoke were a fixture in the lanes and in the bush. In place of finery they wore string. Were they discussing the settlers, the growing predicament they represented? Or something else entirely, a thing they had been discussing since before anyone arrived? If that was so, how long had the discussion been going on? There was a great precipice, a gulf behind the arrival of the fleets: like trying to think of eternity but without the comfort of God's presence.

He followed the path to Figge's door, knocked and was called in by that voice of his, imperious, but textured like night-blue satin. To his surprise, the merchant was sitting up in the armchair, though still with an invalid's air. He made no attempt to rise but offered his hand in greeting. The grip was firmer now.

'You look well.' Even as he smiled and said it, Grayling tried to understand why he felt worried that this man was regaining his strength. It should be unalloyed good news that a man who had staggered in from months in the bush was now recovering and would soon become a contributing member of the colony.

'I have taken a short walk this morning,' Figge smiled. The eyes, like lamps.

'Excellent news, sir. Feel up to talking?'

'Most certainly.'

'I have spoken to Mr Clark about the longboat journey just now, and he has painted a very vivid picture for me—a spectacular misfortune, I must say.' Grayling sat himself on the wooden chair and opened the folio he was carrying. He removed the sheets of paper on which he had made notes of Clark's tale, and began to read them to the man in the armchair.

He tried to maintain a slow pace and watched Figge every time he reached the end of a paragraph, or turned a page. The silence was such that he expected at any moment to find him dozing, but the eyes continued to burn attentively.

Grayling was making small choices in the narrative, thinking about what he wanted to share with Figge and what he wanted to hear from him without prompting. The choices came at him like potholes in a road, often too late to be avoided. He reached the part of the story where Clark had explained to him about the midnight watch in the south-easter, the one taken by him and the boy and Figge. At the mention of it, Figge shuffled himself slightly higher in the chair and rested his elbows on its arms. He steepled his fingers in front of his chin, but again did not speak.

Instinctively, Grayling skipped over the reflections Clark had made about the hopelessness of his situation, about his career. He'd taken careful notes of the man's words, but he saw no relevance in what Figge thought about such things. They were, after all, the survivors of a shipwreck and that was the matter at hand.

And then he had finished. Figge hadn't moved, hadn't commented. Grayling looked up from the pages and into those eyes, pushing against a reluctance to see them.

'Sir, do you take issue with any of that?'

'Take *issue* with it? Why would I do any such thing?' He smiled generously. 'No tea today?'

'I'm afraid I rushed out. I can have some ordered and brought over if you would like.'

Figge waved a dismissive hand. 'It's fine. And enough of this "sir" business. You mustn't address me so formally. We could be brothers, we're so near in age.' The tip of his tongue protruded just slightly, to probe at a crack in his lower lip. That way he had; that way of giving disjointed answers, out of sequence. Grayling was beginning to understand that it was deliberate: intended to unsettle.

'Have you thought further about my offer?'

Grayling knew precisely what was meant by this, but chose to feint. 'I'm sorry? Offer?'

'To attend upon your wife. I can help, you know.' The eyes, fixed on him.

'That won't be necessary, thank you,' Grayling hurried.

Figge's eyes never left his, but the smile returned. 'As you please,' he purred. 'And never mind the tea. It was more about drinking it with you. Joshua.'

13

Sleep had taken her far from the room and the bed and the known world, to a cold brook that slid over shifting gravel in a peculiar light, quietly dripping leaves, and she did not trust her feet to guide her. The light was like a taste or a smell and it would not leave her, even as the room reappeared and Joshua was standing there.

Rather than disturb her, he had made himself busy. She watched him light candles, revive the small fire that he'd set burning that morning. She willed herself back into the room and away from that cold sticking gloom, though she could not find the words to greet him. He found the plates of fish that had been delivered by a girl from the governor's staff earlier in the day, some time when Charlotte was at odds with time. She knew she had been thrashing when the girl arrived; hair wild, the covers back and the nightdress bunched around her hips as she fought the choking grip of her delirium. She pleaded with her eyes that her body had been taken over, but it must only have made it worse. The girl had stood transfixed in horror, set the plates on the table and fled.

They were Charlotte's own plates, the plain earthenware kind they wouldn't serve to visitors. Had the *Sydney Cove* arrived safely, they might have been tempted to buy export china. The other officers' wives would have elbowed each other in their rush. She stared at the plates and her thoughts cleared, as the sleep lifted like fog.

Sacrifices. Charlotte had never uttered a word about the material expectations she might have had as the wife of a naval officer. She walked her endless loops, down to the wharves, along the ridges and through the laneways that loosely defined the township. The talk of dangers, of a vengeful Pemulwuy out there somewhere, caused her no concern at all. Nor did she ever look homeward: this was a choice. She wore self-possession as reassurance for him: she wanted only his companionship. When he was not there to give it she walked, alone.

He placed his loose pile of notes down on the table and she watched him stare at it. She had thought this business of his, the shipwreck, would be straightforward. Nothing about it should cause him misgivings, yet he sighed as his eyes turned from the notes to her.

When the food was warm he poured two bowls and came to her. His pained expression upset her all over again. Every bright and memorable thing in her life here radiated from him.

'Soup,' he whispered. 'Sit up.'

He waited for her to do so but she didn't move.

'What is it?'

'I'm not for moving.'

'What do you mean?'

'Can't. Just take the pillows and prop me up will you please?'

'How long have you been like this?' Joshua was horrified by the slump of her body, but she made a faint sound that she had intended to be a laugh.

'Not long, dear boy. Excellency sent one of the maids over. She has attended to my—' She looked down coyly, and gathered breath to speak again. 'But no feeling, hmm…legs. Gone. Suppose we assume's…not coming back.'

He ran a hand through his hair, scratched at his scalp in helpless anger. 'Did Ewing come by?'

'Mm. Tried a poultice on my head this time.' She rolled her head slightly so he could see the wad of bandages behind her ear.

'He's guessing, the fool! He's just tossing coins now. What of the rash?'

'Still there. Little redder, maybe. I do wish the man didn't have to keep probing around down there.'

He reached in and slid an arm under her back, lifted her and placed two more pillows under her. She sensed his fingers tracing the knobs of her spine as he eased her down again. He seemed about to withdraw the arm but instead reached the other arm over her chest and held her tightly.

Every day for two weeks she had deteriorated steadily, and he'd made it clear he believed the land had done it. Some malignancy at the heart of it, something the natives had called down upon her, was one of his theories. Never since they were children had she heard him pass cruel judgment on anyone. He was scrupulously fair by nature, but his judgment went haywire at the slightest threat to her.

He was clinging now, his arms uncomfortably tight around her, and she felt a tiny convulsion in him. He was trying not to cry, and he would not lift his head.

She ended his torment by speaking first. 'So, come on. What have the men told you today?' She waited while he gathered himself and sat upright.

'Clark told me about the longboat journey, the second wreck.'

She dwelled on this, closed her eyes. 'Seventeen on it, including these three men, Figge and Clark and the boy?'

'Yes.'

'Fourteen missing. Dear me.'

'Not till later. All of the seventeen got off the boat alive. It's the walk that's odd.'

'Some other side to this, isn't there. Have you asked the boy?'

'No. He's a Bengali lad. Would never have had a day of formal tuition in his life. He might be able to name the topgallant yard and such...' He wiped his eyes awkwardly with a sleeve. 'But these people don't speak the King's English, darling.'

'Very well. And you're having to'—a yawn overtook her—'compare the accounts of these two, Mr Figge and Mr Clark. Have they differed so far?'

'Not in any profound sense. But—'

'But what?'

'It's a small thing. Mr Clark told me about the three of them being on watch together on the longboat in the middle of the night. Everyone else asleep or at least not paying attention. Just the three of them out there in the dark, sitting up. Now Clark says the breeze got up, the sea got up, but he never put it more emphatically than that. He never said it was a storm, or that the swell became monstrous or anything of that sort. He just noted that the wind speed increased and that there was chop coming across them. And you'd say, I suppose, well, he's a sailor, he's bound to talk in those terms. But he's not, you see: he's a supercargo. A civilian, in charge of the goods on board, with no more seagoing experience than you have. And such a person, if the conditions had turned significantly, would speak of the terror. You see? Maybe an old hand would use terms like "chop" and "breeze" and the like, but not this man. If it was strong enough to capsize the longboat, wouldn't he have described it more…dramatically? At any rate, he was vivid enough about the trials of the *Sydney Cove*.'

She had felt her eyes closing as he spoke, but they opened when the rhythm of his speech stopped. 'What does it take to capsize a longboat?'

'Well, this boat would be almost a small ketch. It's not a dinghy. I don't know, maybe thirty feet long? Not much of a keel, but they modified it to deal with heavy seas because they knew what they were in for.'

'And if the seas weren't enough to capsize it…'

'Someone has intervened.'

They sat in silence a moment. He was holding her afloat in consciousness by talking; if he stopped, she feared the thread would break and she would slip somewhere beyond his reach.

'I'd taken detailed notes when Clark was speaking. I read that part to Figge and he just sat there smiling. Smug: there might have been feathers in the corners of his mouth.'

'Figge was at the helm,' she said softly.

'Yes.'

'Could've struck something. A reef.'

'They would have said so. Clark just says they flipped, and Figge, the helmsman, doesn't say anything.' He studied her face.

'But how could it be in anyone's interests to scuttle the long-boat?' She frowned and rubbed at her temple. Her shoulders tensed as a wave of pain passed through her.

He sighed. 'I don't know. It can't be, can it? You have to

assume they were all trying to attain Sydney in that longboat. But it just *nags* at me. Those men were found in circumstances that suggest serious discord. Yet the diary says nothing of it, and nor are they saying anything. I must go back and start reading through the diary with Mr Clark. If there's a fault line, it will appear.'

Her face was turned towards him and she tried to maintain her smile but it faded slowly. She let the sleep take her. Even if it would mean the silent curling brook and the gloom, the faint glow of neither moon nor sun but something else. He was here now. The last she saw of his eyes they were locked on hers, filled with pain and concern.

14

❁ It irks me to describe that night. It revealed clearly for
the first time the inadequacies of Clark and the rest of
my travelling companions.

In the early evening, so long and golden, we allowed the little
sail to take us north-east, standing off against a mere breath
of wind from the south-east. I don't mind admitting I was in
irritable humour: destined for Sydney, yes; but with all manner of
hangers-on, and only my leverage over Clark to make advantage.
Any chance of success hinged upon me walking into Sydney
alone. And I could not be caving skulls. Not in these numbers.

The lascars were in agreeable mood, talking among themselves, adding power with the oars when the breeze dropped.
Two of their number prepared food, tearing strips from the oily
black birds we had collected on Preservation and handing them
among us. The parts of the fowl that others wouldn't touch
made my share so much the greater.

In a cleared space in the bow, they brought out provisions that had survived the slow death of our ship: biscuit, salt pork and other morsels. But as we finished this light repast, I began to notice the change coming over the sky. Not the build-up of a storm, but an unmistakable altering of mood and a thin line of feathery cloud gathered on the eastern horizon. The light sickened in the west, until the very character of the sky had turned sour. The land out to port was near enough to look like sanctuary should the night turn ugly. Someone, some fool, spoke of this: *we could land her and sleep on the coast.*

We arranged ourselves into two-hour watches, three on, fourteen off. By these numbers, there would in theory be enough sleep, but it was hard for us to come by. Some of them tried to make space that would allow for slumber, arms tucked in their jackets, chins against chests, though they ended up slumped against each other like drunks. An optimistic few decided upon the well: curled down there like cats, till the first of the larger chops tipped seawater in and they found themselves aslosh in a puddle of muck. None had noticed the change in the weather.

To avoid unnecessary intercourse with these dullards, I reviewed my plans with eyes closed, tucked centrally near the stern, where the boat did not move about so much. The ship was where it should be, more or less. There is no ideal place to hide a hundred feet of busted-arse country trader. But I could scarce believe my luck in having led Hamilton to an island behind an island in a strait that no navigator has ever put on a chart. The ship and its wealth were safe for now. The thirty-two could not leave: I had imprisoned them without need of a single sentry. There was one way out, and so long as I was in the longboat, I controlled it.

Wet slapping commenced on the starboard stern. The sea was rising.

Clark, though. Clark appeared to have had a crisis of conscience. Unfortunate. He avoided my eyes and busied himself with the duties one would expect of a supercargo—how fortunate that no one expects any duties of a tea merchant. His complicity in our little endeavour was absolute: if he were to denounce me, I would as readily denounce him. And there was not a witness in the hemisphere to what I had done with dear old Figge: not even Clark knew. My identity, my credentials, were beyond question.

He'd seen what happened to Leisham. Now he understood the fog between things that go wrong and outcomes fully intended—and the potential that lies therein. So what were his options as I looked at him there? To stay true to the course, trusting that I would do what was necessary to further our scheme.

I knew then I must watch over him. And he knew, in the instants when his eyes darted helplessly to mine, that he could not waver.

⁂

I must have dozed, because next I knew there was a lascar tapping fearfully at my foot, waking me for my watch. No more than a boy, this one, smooth jaw and the blue-black hair thick and luxuriant. Like the others he had no coat, no shoes and no English. No sooner had he woken me than he compressed himself in the well and did not move again.

I watched as the bodies resumed their repose after the brief interruption of the watch change. The chief mate, Thompson, asleep at the foot of the mast where he affected to ply his little expertise as a seafarer. The carpenter, dumb brute that he was, snoring like he'd just rolled off a whore. Only one of the lascars remained alert: the one who was manservant to Clark.

And Clark was awake too. The wind was strengthening, the sail creaking against its stays as the wind put weight in it. In the darkness it receded upwards in a pregnant billow, Clark's eyes down there, two lengths of a body away.

'You're awake then Clarkey,' I said to him, and 'Don't call me Clarkey' he muttered back, adding *fuckin Sassenach* for good measure.

'They're all asleep,' I said to him. 'Just you and your portable arse there.' Nodding to the lascar boy he had.

'Aye,' he growled. 'So?'

'Just want you to know, Mr Clark,' I said over the wind, 'that this would be a poor time to have a change of heart. If that's what you're thinking.'

'Not thinking anything. Mind for yourself and I'll do likewise.'

'Look around you, Clarkey. All of 'em sleeping peacefully.' The wind knocked the boat aheel as I said this. 'None of 'em can come to Sydney. You understand?' He looked pained. More than pained: like he'd eaten a hornet. Scares a man to hear another talk like that. The boat was twisting through diagonal seas now, lifting a little higher, falling a little deeper. 'Fifteen souls, Clarkey. Lot of work. Will you take your share?'

I could see the horror in his face, the augur of complicity twisting in his gut. Greed I can understand. I can even respect it. But greed without a corresponding adoption of the moral burden? Well, no. That will never do. Clark must stain his conscience with as much or as little of this affair as I.

They all slept on around him, and of the boy it was hard to tell but his little garden was walled by silence. In the distance the glow outlined the dune behind the beach not far away, the breaking surf mere yards off our port side as we followed the coast.

All along the dark swell of the hillside were the tiny speckles of the natives' fires, like the last living embers in a darkened hearth. These we had seen on the west coast of New Holland, and again in the south as we approached Van Diemen's Land, even on its grimmest escarpments. Occasional flits of movement, the tiniest echo of a voice that might be no more than a seabird, or might be a fellow human across the water. But we had seen nothing of the kind around Preservation. Not a curl of smoke by day, not an ember at night. They were gone from that bouldered landscape, and not by our hand. Further proof that I had landed our ship in a place beyond the reach of all meddlers, whether pink or brown.

The fires on this coast were a reminder of the thing we knew instinctively: any overland journey would necessitate us dealing with the natives. At that stage they were a code to us, a cipher. For the lummoxes snoozing around me, the natives represented everything that was confounding about New Holland. Like the trees we came to know, that shed bark but keep leaves, these were occupants of an inverted world—wily and calibrated to a different understanding. And later we learned that this was why they drew violence from Englishmen's hearts. Not only did they speak a different language but they thought a different thought.

I had no advantage at sea, but I knew I would have the advantage on land. If it came to violence the natives would do us easily, and only the cunning would escape it. Those people watching us behind their fires could be the agents of my triumph.

I was an arm's length from the tiller. The swell had gathered more power from the persistent wind, and soon its bashing and heaving would wake them all. The opportunity provided by this fortuitous watch—me, him and the boy lascar—would soon pass.

The sea would take a few, the natives the rest.

Slupslup, the greedy water on the stern. Clark stared bitterly out to sea, as though the answer awaited him there. And maybe it did. I had a hand on the tiller and he hadn't seen. Drew it into my armpit so we slewed to port, degree by degree. With my other hand I could reach the line that controlled the sail and I took in a few feet of that so the sail tightened and we gained speed. More angle, more speed, and Clark hadn't noticed a thing. His boy was asleep. High on the next wave I'd got her squared to the swells, pointing straight at the coast.

She ran down the face of the cresting wave and it was so simple from there. More pressure on the line and the sail quivered with the force in it. The longboat surged forward and drove itself in, nose down and ploughing into the green water at the base of the wave. The bowsprit went in like the stem of a mosquito and I could barely contain a laugh, to think I'd stung the ocean into slapping us.

Clark suddenly twigged but he was too late. The weight of the wave behind us, and the stopping force of the buried nose—it was inevitable now. I was sprung high into the air at the stern, the wind a-swirl round my face and hair and men awoke, screamed and clung as they found themselves standing vertical. For only an instant, however.

Thereafter we inverted completely and all was water and sound.

15

 I wrote these things down so I wouldn't have to answer your tedious questions, lieutenant.

No. I cannot fathom the cause. Mr Figge had the tiller.

Then? Then the morning came. We sat in a line on the beach watching the longboat break up. There was a discussion that started and faltered several times about whether we should build up the fire to try to signal someone. But the hard fact of the matter was that we were nowhere. We were only slightly less nowhere than where the *Sydney Cove* herself was. The conversation would wander over that topic for a while, then die. Mr Figge was the only one adamant about anything: that we must get up and walk north.

The other option that was raised—I think it was Mr Kennedy raised it—was that we could try to fish the boat out of the surf, repair it again and sail it back whence we had come, to Preservation. I cannot for the life of me imagine what this would have achieved—other than to ensure the deaths not only of ourselves but of all involved. As much as I dreaded the prospect of walking to Sydney, which we believed to be more than five hundred miles distant, there was no reasonable alternative.

We watched the birds diving for fish in this emptiness and the words were nothing.

I studied the lascars more closely now. They were the majority of us: what if they no longer shared our purpose? What if they turned mutinous? You hear of it. They looked to the *serang* for leadership—wizened old fellow, slow in all things but with a kind of stoicism about him. Nearly among those who lost their lives at the pumps, which demonstrated that they do reach an age where you are better to leave them behind. Lascars have a feeble grasp of hierarchy: they will readily follow such an old peasant, one who barely says a word. They have no interest in seeking out and following the authoritarian. Plentiful and cheap they may be, but they are the softest parts in the machine and liable to fatigue in a way that cogs and wheels do not. One must guard against failure at the weakest link.

The old boy held them together, I will credit him that. Even there on the beach, they sat with their legs crossed, waiting on his every utterance, Mussulman and Hindu alike. The boy lived in a state of fealty to his father as much as to me. Which is why my fear was rising: if the thirteen of them acted in some form of concert, if he exhorted them to do so, then our numbers, and by 'us' I mean Mr Figge, Kennedy, Thompson and me, would be insufficient to resist them.

And to whom did it fall, lieutenant, to be the old man's opposite number? Kennedy was a craftsman but otherwise a simpleton. All the acumen of a tree nail. Thompson was a brute and a man no one would follow. And Mr Figge? You must be forming your own ideas about him by now. He wore this air of insouciance, as though our trials were none of his concern. He seemed the least interested in leadership and yet, by some trick of his demeanour, the most confident of survival. It is for that reason, maybe, that I did seek out his counsel from time to time.

Let me tell you what we had—it is in my nature to construct inventories. We had rice. We had a couple of tomahawks, some knives, a pot for cooking, some bolts of heavy cloth, and tins for carrying water. Mr Figge had a tinderbox. We had a musket and two pistols, some ammunition for these, and a pair of small swords. When we loaded the boat I believed the combination of these weapons would enable us to bring down game—seabirds, as we initially hoped—in order to feed ourselves. In this, it turned out, I was profoundly mistaken.

We were wearing the clothes we were wrecked in. The first time, I mean. Well, what do you think, man? No one had been able to salvage a sea chest of their belongings. We were in shirts and breeks, perfectly fine in that weather as long as we were dry and moving about. Crossing rivers, or in the early mornings, the cold was a problem. Kennedy and Thompson had hats, but neither Mr Figge nor I had been able to save ours in the sea.

The four of us wore goatskin straights on our feet. As you would know, lieutenant, these are ideal for moving about the ship but they are a poor protection when traipsing in the bush. The choice was an invidious one: either tackle the bush, where the straights would be inadequate, or walk the beach, where each footfall would further abrade them until they broke apart and fell away. The lascars had been barefoot all along, and within a week we would be as well, turning our toenails to horns and splinters. Extraordinary how the pain of damaged feet compounds other miseries.

Kennedy had retrieved his wood saw and a hammer and chisel from a box in the bow of the longboat. Having lost everything in the world, his complaint was that they would rust on him.

And the only other items I can think of, lieutenant, are a pencil and the journal which you have in your possession. Again, a duty thrust upon me. It wasn't my book, nor my pencil. I offered the items to Mr Figge. I said to him that I would have to lead the party in all things, and that it might be a fair division of labour if he took responsibility for recording our exploits in the journal. He gave every appearance of being an educated man. But he flatly refused. *I have no regard for posterity,* he told me.

Kennedy collected the timbers that had washed ashore. He lay two sections of the boom parallel and braced a frame between them to create a sort of wide ladder, the rungs made fast with mitres and rebates. He carved handles into the ends of the booms, then lined the underneath with cuts of sailcloth and a section of the hull's copper sheathing so it would glide over the sand. And thus he had created a sled, onto which we loaded our belongings. I assigned the lascars to dog it: their faces were sceptical as they each picked up the handle-ends and considered the task.

We drew away from the landing place, the sled leaving a smooth track in the untouched sand.

I looked back only once.

There was the carcass of the longboat, a furlong off the beach, ribs poking from the yellowy waters of the sandbank. A small shark was nosing into it, drawn by the stink of us. Its back was a dull military grey, but the tips of its fin and tail glowed a queer olivine in the sunlight.

II

16

By the time a week was done we had fallen into a rhythm. We were following a vast beach, seemingly endless, stretching resolutely east as though it would take us into the heart of the rising sun. There was no feature, nothing at all, to break up the stretch of the horizon. Only sand and the blue arc of the sea and the line of the commencing sky. No visible islands, no reefs, not a headland or a sandbank and rarely even a bird.

There being no other qualified candidate, I knew it to be my responsibility to take care of navigation. Mr Figge had made his indifference clear, neither Thompson nor Kennedy had any understanding of such matters, and the lascars are of course preconditioned to follow. Sydney lay north, not east, but I had considered this—the *Sydney Cove* had pressed deeply westward, meaning that we must have been recovering that same ground by walking east. It seemed logical that eventually the coast must turn northward.

The beach was narrow, despite its heroic length. At times we despatched a lascar to walk inland: they reported the same each time. There were lakes in there, swamps, but the way seemed impassable. I had myself ventured to the top of the dunes to look inland, and that was what I too had seen: a deep depression in the land, many miles wide, its low places spotted with lakes. Beyond it, steep rises that may have been the foothills of a greater mountain range. Forested, mostly: tall eucalypts that receded in the faraway hills until they turned grey-blue. But in the places that were bare of trees there lay meadows of unknown pasture. Some providential hand had divided the countryside into stands of eucalypts and tracts of meadow, resembling the ordered work of a cropper—but never square, never fenced. The lakes and waterways prevented us traversing it, but otherwise it looked to be agreeable country.

We had been lulled by the beach into thinking there was not much alive around us, that the place existed in windblown suspension. But the view over that dune put an end to any such belief. The abundance in the wetlands was extraordinary: birds I recognised, such as pelicans, grebes, ducks and cormorants; and some, like the black swan, that mocked familiar forms. There must be food for all of them: fish or shrimp sustaining them all, and I was heartened. The dwindling supply of rice would not spell our end. We could go on eating what was around us, if we could work out how.

The vegetation up on the dunes was rude and unfamiliar. Thick shrubs, growing on both faces of the sandy slope and all the way down to the beach. Their leaves were leathery and dark, with serrated edges like a carpenter's saw. But what was remarkable about them was the flowers: just like a chimney sweep's brush, only these were a most pleasing yellow. These shrubs were by far the most abundant living thing on those dunes. Aside from them, saltbush maybe. Some spiky grasses. That coast is a wasteland.

Onward, eastward, the sled trailing behind. Into the sun in the morning, casting long shadows ahead of ourselves in the afternoons. The mornings were cold, I might've said, but the sun had strength during the day. The Europeans among us felt its sting, though whether the sun had any effect on the lascars I could not tell. They walked together, clustered at the rear. The boy I would keep with me whenever I could. Still I was having to domesticate him to his duties, keep him from the simpering closeness to his father. Kennedy and Thompson were inseparable, grumbling about the lascars, about the walk itself. At each stop they were the hardest to move, at each meal the greediest.

I walked at the head of our little group most of the time, Mr Figge mostly content to amble off at a slight remove. The lascars fell behind with the sled. Complaining, I suppose, though one never knows for certain what their patois is about.

Figge had one pistol. Thompson had insisted on having the other—for what reason I do not know. I had relented only because I was fairly sure the seawater had rendered them useless. The musket was soon thrown away on account of its great weight.

A walk of this length along any beach, as you can imagine, lieutenant, takes the mind through states of intense concentration, meditative calm, and sometimes into close study of what seems ephemeral. For hours on end I would examine the things passing under my feet. It was a clean beach, littered only with little white bones, very light and shaped like hulls. Dwelling upon its pristine state led me to conclude that what happened to our little longboat was exceptional: this was not a wild coast. There was simply not the flotsam to indicate bursts of temper in this sea: just the meandering tracks of seabirds and small fragments of pink and white shells (though no amount of searching would reveal the source of these, which we thought might be food).

I cast back to my brothers and sisters; the dead, the living. Matters between us that seemed so important had been reduced to triviality by my distance from them. The only way to survive such privations is to harden, to cast sentiment aside. But I hear their voices, even now talking to you, and I heard them clear as the wind on that beach. They were not kind. I—

No, no. Never mind.

We would eat at dawn and at dusk, stopping through the day to pick tentatively at whatever we could find. We had very little water, and would begin our day by wringing moisture off the grasses and into our parched mouths. We discovered that for our evening meal we could steam the rice in a bed of torn greenery with just a little of our water. It was…edible.

We struck the first river mouth within a few days—you might have the date there in the journal. My theory, based on the frequency of the river crossings and the foothills we could see in the distance, is that there must have been a substantial mountain range somewhere further inland that was depositing all this water at the coast. The first one was no great obstacle: it had split and forked across several sandbars so that we were able to wade it. Nor did it flow very fast: I surmise that we were crossing it at the end of the dry season. The lascars took the sled on their shoulders and were able to carry the provisions clear.

But the river mouths further on, of which there were several crossing that beach, presented us with more difficulty. At these, we were forced to stop and make camp, walk the bank inland in search of a place to ford, and if we could not find one, then resign ourselves to the making of a raft. Each time, Kennedy would bellyache about the labour involved and how it all fell to him. Yet he took great pleasure in being the only one with the necessary skills. We began to take the sled apart and to refashion it so that it gradually became a raft. I sent the lascars into the heathland, where they would fell hardwoods with the tomahawk and drag the logs back. My God, they were slow: infuriatingly so. Each time, we were camped by the river for several days, waiting upon the log gathering and Kennedy's carpentry. Kennedy would lap the logs together and fashion heavy pegs where lapping wouldn't do. He was most ingenious in this work, but even then, our results were mixed: the first few times we tried rafting we all ended up in the water. The damned things would come apart under pressure or just sink. Fortunately, these early disasters—Ha! More shipwrecks!—only happened at places where the water was low enough that we could wade out of trouble.

We lost boat timbers this way, and we replaced them with forest timbers. And so, with distance, we shed the last traces of our seafaring selves. The shipwreck was smeared all the way from Preservation halfway up this beach and, eventually, was gone altogether: a made-up cart-raft had taken its place.

The flats around the edges of these estuaries were populated by thousands of tiny white crabs. They massed on the hard sand, creating the illusion from afar that the ground had turned liquid and was flowing. The overburden of their holes, dotted everywhere on the sandbanks, revealed their positions, and it was just a matter of being quick enough of hand and foot to sweep them into a shirt or onto a sheet of calico. The lascars thought this a fine game—they were quicker than us. Thompson tried the same thing and wound up flat on his face in the wet sand.

The spectacle reduced one of the Bengalis to helpless laughter, and he wore the first mate's fist in his mouth. At first, we fussed a great deal about cracking the crabs open and cooking them. But we found that we lost too much of the nourishment in doing that, so we simply ate them raw and crunched our way through the shell. We were sick the first few times we tried it. After that, our guts hardened to the sea-taste and the digestion of fragments.

Mr Figge, being taller, was not so fast with the crabs, but nor was he fussy. He would eat them just as readily as he'd eat a gull or gnaw at something that turned up in the tide-line. A man of curious appetites, to say the least.

17

Mr Clark, I've heard every word of yours, here with my back against the door. Now I see that you intend to hide as much as you tell.

The doctor visits once each day. A hand on my forehead; a cloth on my wounds if he can be bothered. His concern is for you, and that is fair. My suffering is nothing compared to yours. I am tired, still footsore, but able to walk out of here if I choose. But to where? My father is gone. What is there in the world outside for me? My employment with you, but where does that stand now? There are no guarantees about what you may require in the future. This town holds no promise for me. Indeed, it holds great danger.

Each time the doctor visits, I make faint and sorry-eyed. He probably knows it's an act but I don't care. He smells of grog and his cures are ridiculous. As soon as he leaves, I'm back to the door to hear you, Mr Clark, weaving your coarse net of a tale for the lieutenant. My goodness, the things you have forgotten.

Like the testing of the gun. When we sat there on the beach in the sun, slapping at those huge biting flies. You saw him check the flintlock and frown as he looked through the breech, muttering about it being ruined by the saltwater. Wasn't it you, Mr Clark, who told him the gun was finely made and would survive it?

Because he took the gun and loaded it then, primed it, snapped it shut. *I tell you it is inoperable*, he said. And then he took young Devesh by the ear and hauled him up, laughing at the lad's pain. He moved so quick: pressed the muzzle against the poor boy's forehead and said *I hope you are wrong, Mr Clark, because if you are right then this will be on your conscience.* And he pulled the trigger.

Jai sita ram, there was no more than a fizzle of smoke from the pan—the round failed. The boy had wet down his leg and Mr Figge threw him to the ground, laughing.

And why have you not spoken of those first days with the natives? We all felt the bush moving around us: not just trees in the wind but thumps and snorts and barks. Small game, mostly, but not always. We saw a fine yellow dog one day, tall as a pariah dog but lighter. Kangaroos—we had heard about them. But until the time I was looking down as one of them took off in fear of us, and I heard the heavy thumps, it was a frightening, mysterious sound.

So there were sounds that we knew through seeing their makers. But then there were others: brushes and whispers so faint they suggested the land itself was talking to us. We discussed it among ourselves. We were being watched, it seemed; followed, even. You gentlemen did not talk of it, but you must have thought it. All of us knew there were natives on these shores. The signs were clear: the old fireplaces, the faraway smoke.

On our third day of walking we saw footprints on the beach. Adult footprints, coming out of the bush and passing down to where the sea washed the sand flat. They ended there, then started again nearby and returned to the tree-line. The prints were close together: someone walking slowly. None of us had gone ahead: there was no possibility that the prints were ours. Why, after three days of watching us in secret, might the walker now be so open?

It was a message. These people who could melt into the shadows with such ease, they must be deliberate about the leaving of footprints.

Within days we were seeing the cooling remains of fires, a burning tree with a strange object at its foot—an animal trap, we thought, made of fine string and bark. As we moved along that mighty, endless beach, a great crowd of watchers was all the time edging away, allowing us room.

These thoughts rested uneasy in me during the day. Then, on the fourth night of our walk, I woke for no reason at all from thick sleep, pressed against the bodies of the others—as was our habit to keep warm. There was no movement around me, only snoring. My face was turned upwards and I should have seen the thin trees and the bright moon. But that is not what I saw.

I saw the shape of a man.

A man standing above me, looking down at me, his face in shadow so I had no idea whether it showed friendship. It was a head and shoulders, dark against the sky. I could not say how I knew, but it was clear he was not one of us.

Perhaps the shock made me move. The sleeper next to me jumped awake but already the man was gone without a sound. He was there, then he was not.

For the next few days I tried to put it behind me. I told my father: in his kindly way he said I was sleeping poorly, as we all were, and that it was most likely some vision from my dreams. I tried to accept this. But it did not ease my heart like other things he said. I think now that he knew the man had been there.

⁂

The second time it was late afternoon and I had gone out in search of food. I had one of the short swords, and no idea what I would do with it.

I crossed the mouth of a creek, and then another. Clear water, sand and pebbles on the bottom. The creeks never flowed simple and straight to the sea: their path always curled through the land, much like mine now: a sandbank here, holes and reefs there.

I was wasting time, swinging the weapon at sticks. The bushes turned hollow, led me deeper, away from the camp and the beach. It was a path, I see now, but at the time I did not notice. The branches made an archway ahead of me, a frame for the dim light, and then a man was there.

I felt no fear. The ground had produced a man before me and it was no surprise. What came over me was a flood of relief that a fellow human lived here. Here, where all was uncertain. Did tigers roam the night? Was the water poisonous to drink? Was the earth infested with things that slid and crawled, and might they bore into my body and burst into hideous eggs and worms? We knew the place only as a sketch on a page, a crooked line between land and sea. The map was silent about what lay within. But this, a man with divine light in his eyes, the sun on his chest: this said to me that human warmth was here, even here.

He was neither hostile nor welcoming. Only, perhaps, as curious as I.

I watched him, as the air quivered between us, for a sign to say which way this would turn. A small twitch from his long fingers; darker than mine on their backs, pink like the Englishmen's beneath. A slow step forward, shinbone leading, and I felt his easy balance on the ground. No sound. Fingers of his right hand feeling the air and only now could I see the spears in his left, and both of us were making decisions.

His was made: he lowered the spears to the ground, those fingers still reaching my way. Two heavy birds moved overhead without interest in us: black ones with a white fan on their tails, almost crows but not. I dropped the sword. I would have smiled too—I think we both knew what a spectacle I'd make trying to wield that thing—but it occurred to me that to show teeth might not be a mark of friendship. I was thinking faster than the heartbeats of the birds.

He parted the branches that half-hid him the same way I might move through a crowd, my thoughts elsewhere than the things in my path. His eyes never left me. And now he stood before me: tall, slender—not ribs and points like us and the Englishmen but taut and firm, bigger than me but lighter on the ground. His nakedness mocked the rags that hung from me.

And then he was speaking and his voice was no different from mine. Lower perhaps; more like yours, Mr Clark, but these were the voice and the eyes and the body of a fellow man.

The words of course I did not know. I caught some of them, rolled them about in my mouth, but they told me nothing. I felt them for their tone and decided they were no threat. Now he was sweeping that right hand behind his hip, low down, and tilting his head over his shoulder.

I followed, guessing that was what he asked of me. Over fallen timber he jumped silently, gripped and moved on while

119

I slipped and fell keeping up. Then we came down into a gully and I heard voices. Once again, the words a mystery but this time voices of men, women and children. Laughter, argument, a baby's cry—all of it rose with an orange glow through the bush. I smelled wood smoke, saw moving shadows against the leaves high above. I was tired, stumbling, but he led me on. No words; just the pull of his moving body.

Then the trees without warning let go their grip on me and I had burst upon a crowd.

For a moment they terrified me. All talk stopped and every eye had me. Their stares were nothing like the gaze of the first man. Mostly they sat, knees by their elbows, except for those few who were a moment ago—before the arrival of the strangest man they had ever seen—fixed upon some task or other.

My new friend spoke to them. He had authority, it seemed, because they listened closely. And as I watched them talk, about me I suppose, I understood clearly that this was no chance meeting. I had been watched: *we* had been watched. This time and place had been chosen. It seemed a good thing they hadn't dragged in one of the Scots.

The people moved in around me, bending to inspect. Words passed between them, none directed to me. Bengali, I found myself saying. *Bengali*, and they were trying it too. *Bengali*, and I almost laughed, for what was a Bengali doing here? The first one in all of time to stand here, and I'd forgotten to use my own name. But they were testing *Bengali*—they found shapes in the word like the edges of a stone. Then the man who found me, the senior one, said a word in answer.

Kurnai.

Another man called the others back away from me, stepped forward and placed a hand upon my head, left it there as he turned to the others. A point had been made. As if he said, *See, he is flesh like the rest of you.* And, bolder now, they came forward again, their hands upon me everywhere but mostly upon the garments, what was left of them, tugging and testing but stopping short of tearing them. A woman had my left hand, placed it against her own, matching the fingers, and I saw that part of her last finger was missing. A mishap of some kind, I thought.

A man handled my poor cock, testing it on its hinges and shifting the balls with his other hand. The sores on them burned at the touch.

Faces came close to mine and gentle fingers took my chin, pulled it down. Eyes searched my mouth like someone buying livestock. I wondered what they thought to find in there— stored food? But they closed the mouth again with a sort of easy laughter, as if a problem had been solved. I watched the laughter, watched the men. Every one of them had a tooth knocked out: the same tooth.

My thoughts ran loose: this was all so much, but the two things came together: the feeling of my skin and the looking for this missing tooth. They knew I was not one of them, yet they checked for that mark. They knew I was walking their land and yet they felt for proof I was flesh. Firmly now I had it: they did not think me a sailor, for nothing about me told of a connection to a ship. Nor did they think me a lost wanderer from other lands. They thought me a ghost.

I laughed; they laughed too. I could see, I could understand that when we thought of them as spirits in the forest, all along they thought the same.

Hands on my shoulders, making me sit. I worried that my long time away might cause the men—Mr Figge, that is—to go on without me. But the natives seemed to know this. There were looks back in the direction I had come from, hands moving to say *you are fine*. A handful of meat was pressed into my palm, soft and damp. An old man with a beard pointing long to his stomach made hands towards his own mouth that I should eat.

They waited until I'd consumed the whole piece. They held their discussion, their other business. Smoke lifted from a deserted fire while they watched me. Children clung to their mothers but watched me too. Those mothers rolled string against their hips, or worked at bowls of grain, but their eyes never left me.

When the meat was finished they seemed to ease: by the fire they were in fine mood, teasing and sharing stories that were made of looks and sweeping hands. The tiny ways of friendship that looked so similar across the world. I saw a woman place a hand on another's knee as she whispered in her ear and they both burst out laughing. How could they touch and hear and pass secrets, just as we do? Who taught us all the same?

18

In her twisting sleep she had screwed to one side of the mattress, head slung over the edge, a lip and an eyelid hanging slack. She had dribbled on the floor below: through the fierce pain of opening her eyes it was the first thing she noticed.

Joshua had come home at some stage: she didn't remember it. He was talking, or making sounds anyway, small and distant. He approached and coaxed her head back onto the pillow. The movement woke her more fully: she focused on his eyes. A new agony gripped her and squeezed her face into a grimace. She fought it; levelled her expression.

The talking again. '—Lord, Charlotte. Has Ewing been? How long have you been—'

'…'s worse.' She pushed the words out, thick and obscenely soft. 'Don't think…supper, 'f you…'

The pain was worse behind her ear. She lifted an arm with difficulty and felt there with her fingertips. The swelling had grown; it radiated heat. Her fingers did not recognise the scalp as a land they knew.

'What has happened with the numbness?'

She waved a heavy hand at the sheets across her legs, a point near her hipbone. 'About here, I—' She tapped the skin on her upper thigh, shrugged. 'Rash…' Touching the inside of her other arm, the curve of her neck.

She drew a breath, swallowed and concentrated on the words. 'Gov'nor's man brought gin from His Exc'ncy.' The square bottle stood on the table. 'Worried about you.'

'About *me*?' Grayling couldn't help the edge of sarcasm. 'Ewing's given up, hasn't he?'

She worked her shoulders into a small shrug.

'Well we can't do *nothing*! This is insupportable!'

'Shh. Tried praying. I'm not much…'

'*Praying*? There's no God here, Charlotte!' He clutched at his hair in frustration. 'He's watching the other side of the earth where all the bloody people are.'

'Please…please.' She extended a hand towards him. 'Sit down. Tell me…the day. Thought about what you told me…'

He sat beside her, swung his feet onto the bed. She closed her eyes to hold on to the pleasure of his voice but he did not begin.

'Please.'

She looked again. His jaw was clenched as he waited for his anger to subside.

He took a breath. 'I spoke only to Clark today. I had other things to do. He was telling me about the start of their walk.'

She reached for his hand and ran a thumb over his knuckles, wishing it could be like any other night; that they could cling to small pleasures.

'They…ah, they sailed north from where the *Sydney Cove*

124

was wrecked and they struck land—that's the second wreck, I mean—somewhere west of the coastline hereabouts. You see, from Sydney, the coast drops straight southward, and the coast of Van Diemen's Land is the same. North–south. But at some point, it must veer sharply to the west. It's quite odd—Clark insists they were walking straight east for the first couple of weeks. No doubt Mr Bass will head out there directly upon his return and try to resolve the whole question. Anyway, Clark was more talkative today, thank God. He was telling me about their decision to walk for help, rather than waiting there.'

"S right isn't it? No rescue out there.' She was pleased to see he was warming to the conversation.

'Yes, but what interests me more is the politics of the decision: Mr Kennedy, the carpenter, was in favour of going back to Preservation Island. Mr Clark and Mr Figge wanted to press on. And who's here now? Clark and Figge. No Kennedy.'

'You're saying…?' Her head rang so hard with pain that she feared only a seizure could end the pressure.

'I don't know.' He was focused somewhere else in the room, hadn't seen her wince. 'But at the least it's reasonable to assume there was an alliance between these two, even though Clark is refusing to discuss Figge. It's like, like they've had a falling out. Just a silent lascar between them.'

'A mutiny?' she mumbled. 'Some…want to press on, some want to go back?'

'And maybe even a third group who just want to stay there, build a shelter and wait for help.'

She wanted his voice. She wanted more from him so it wouldn't be just her and the pain. 'Who led them? Mr Clark?'

'He says he did. The structures that applied at sea had no currency on land, of course. He says Figge was no help, Kennedy and Thompson weren't up to it, and the lascars had their own senior man who they listened to.'

'Who was that?'

'The boy's father. A Hindu man named Prasad.'

'Hmm.' She bit her lip, pressed her eyes shut.

'Clark was talking today about them just following this long beach for weeks, crossing river mouths from time to time, but no danger of any kind, really. I think we've covered about three weeks of the walk, taking us up to late March, and there's been no deaths, not even any contact with the natives. It seems they'd worked out how to eat and drink, at least a little.'

She picked at a loose thread in the blanket. 'And the boy?'

'I've told you—he can't offer anything. I have to work this out through the accounts of the other two.'

'No. Who *cares* for him? No parents here, no—'

'He is of an age where he can make his own way in the world. Plenty such as him are already at sea.'

'Does Mr Clark visit him?'

'The lad is in the room adjacent. He probably waits on Mr Clark if he's well enough.'

She thought about the story and for a while the words were all there was, and the storm in her body had abated. She spoke again, quietly. Placing the words with great care.

'Here...' she sighed. 'One thing to land here among people who love you. Quite another to do it alone.'

19

When Grayling reached the guest house the next morning, he found Figge's long form folded into a wicker chair on the front verandah. His wild hair had been swept back and tied, though he had not clipped his beard and it remained a prophet's tangle.

Doctor Ewing sat on a small stool in front of him, with Figge's outstretched left leg settled on his lap.

Grayling took up a chair beside him and placed the journal and the letter in the leather folio on the ground between his feet. For a moment they both looked out at the garden in silence. Small, bright blue wrens darted about on the ground, tails flagging as they picked at unseen grit.

'I see you brought the journal,' Figge said brightly.

'Mm. There are a couple of passages I thought I might check with you.'

'I can tell you, without you having to read me anything, that

Clark is not to be trusted.' Figge had turned towards Grayling, one eyebrow arched.

'That's not what I meant,' Grayling replied. 'It was merely…a couple of his descriptions. I wondered what you would make of them.'

Figge snorted in derision, and then smiled as though the unpleasant topic had never come up. 'You have the porcupines here too,' he said after a while. 'I saw one daundering round the garden. The dog was most put out.'

Ewing had a pair of circular spectacles perched on the end of his veiny nose and the man's foot in his hands. Grayling peered over the moving knuckles and saw the doctor was removing the great toenail with a pair of tweezers. He had it lifted and was tugging gently to one side. The nail was blackened, its leading edge chipped and scored. The skin wasn't giving it up easily, but Figge seemed unconcerned.

'Are they feeding you well, sir?' Grayling asked.

'Splendidly, yes. Where are you up to with our stories?' Grayling noted the plural. How many stories were there?

'Mr Clark was kind enough to describe your walk over the very long beach that stretches eastward from where you made landfall.'

'Ah yes,' Figge smiled fondly, as though recalling a childhood memory. 'Goodness me. Monotonous.'

'I want to read you his account of that walk. Is now a good time?' Grayling looked down at the toe. Ewing had lifted the nail back so that the new pink skin underneath was exposed. He was teasing the nail in various directions but it refused to yield.

'Oh, of course.' Figge still showed no sign of discomfort at the operation on his foot. 'Please.'

Grayling read the account Clark had given him the previous day. Figge smiled at various points, even laughed once or twice, but did not interrupt. When he had finished, Grayling asked him his opinion of the story.

'Yes, most comprehensive,' Figge replied. Not for the first time, Grayling had the sense of a man mimicking refined manners. He decided to take a small risk. 'You've not once asked after Mr Clark's welfare, sir. Is it not a matter that concerns you?'

'Haven't I?' Figge raised his eyebrows, approximating surprise. 'How is he, then?'

'Oh, he's coming along.' Grayling picked up his folder, opened it and took up a pencil.

'What about the lascar boy?'

Grayling watched him as he asked this. The air of a casual thought. 'I'm told he's receiving medical care, although there's little wrong with him as far as I know.'

'Oh.'

'As you're aware, he has nothing to say.'

'Quite.'

'Perhaps it would be useful if you took up the story from where Clark left off?'

Figge heaved a long sigh. The doctor exchanged his tweezers for a pair of pliers, muttered *one two three* and ripped forcefully. The nail came away and he held it up in modest triumph. Figge hadn't moved. He took it from the doctor, examined it closer to his eyes. It was thick and curled, more like a shaving from a hoof. Figge put the nail between his front teeth and nipped at it. His lower teeth worked at scraping the little shreds of bloodied flesh on its underside.

'Let me see then, Mr Grayling. I will do my best.'

'The first thing to note is that the beach did eventually end.

'We came to a point where Clark and his boy probably wished for its return: what followed was rock-hopping over boulder points and some wasteful wandering in and out of small bays. A great sweep of dunes rose to the inland of us: nothing grew on them, you understand. Not a blade of glass. *Nothing.* If the great mass of New Holland led with its westward edge into the Indian Ocean, then perhaps it trailed its eastward edge in its lee, this smudge of sand fading into the ocean behind.

'What can I tell you about? A meal; I remember a meal. Up to then, meat had been hard to come by because the others were so fixed in their thinking: they could kill and ingest only that which they already recognised as edible. For myself, I was far less concerned: if the thing had muscle on it, then it was going to sustain me. They spent pointless hours throwing rocks at crows in the hope they could bring one down, and never did.

'We were sitting around a fire in front of the dunes, just on dark. The others were eating the eggs of a swan that one of the lascars had managed to scare off its nest in the wetlands behind the dunes. I was roasting a badger, just a dark mass in the coals, its little claws upraised like a flipped ottoman.

'Where the edge of the dune beside us had broken away there was a gigantic mound of shells. All of them were those striped snail shells: not land snails, but the ones from the rock pools. We were discussing, Clark and Thompson and I, how the mounds had come to be created. Thompson figured some seabird was nesting there and would bring the snails from the sea and feast upon them. Now this was an attractive argument at first, given the sea was only a hundred yards away, but there was ash all through the pile. Did the birds make a fire and sit round it roasting snails? And why was it a pile at all? Birds don't care.

'I put to Thompson that this was the remains of natives' feasts over many generations. He scoffed at me. I suggested there were many tons of shell in the pile, and that either this was a Herculean bird that lifted them all, or he had to be suggesting that there were teams of birds working together. He said that was right: they were co-operating. I could see his anger building and I must say it amused me. I asked him whether he had observed, anywhere on our walk so far, teams of large birds working in concert to carry snails.

'And that was it from him. He leapt to his feet and a fight broke out, one to which I could contribute very little for all of my laughter. And you know how it is when you're in that position, lieutenant, and you're laughing? It made me weak, and it fuelled him all the more. He was trying to hit me and I was giving him the odd one back and I'd split open his eyebrow and all of a sudden, the old lascar man speaks up and he says: *The boy has met them.*

'Well, you can imagine that put a stop to the fisticuffs. The old man pulled his boy upright and he stood there all slender and angelic, a most winsome creature. Everyone listened now and the old man said the boy met them in the bush and was taken into their camp. They are called *Kurnai*, he told us, and they are kindly disposed.

'It appeared to me that all the lascars knew of this because there was no consternation among them when it was announced. We, on the other hand, were astonished. Why hadn't we been told? Were these natives going to appear again? Why were we eating crabs and fucking smelly badgers if there were people who could feed us? The exchange quickly rose to anger again.

'Now I am not a man to take umbrage, but it was a little perplexing that the lascars had kept this to themselves. It surprised me not at all when Kennedy stood up and grabbed the old man by the throat and demanded that he summon the natives immediately. It was precipitous, though: you don't manhandle the *serang* unless you're prepared to deal with insurrection. Even if you're nowhere near a boat.

'The old man protested that the matter was beyond his control. *They are watching us anyway*, he said. And I suppose that tallied with what I had felt all along; the eyes among the trees.

'So a new scuffle broke out, but this one odder than the first: the lascars were emboldened now they were no longer at sea, and furious to see their *serang* treated thus. Nonetheless they were physically smaller than us, and after a fusillade of swatting and cuffing it was over. The boy would be sent back out to bring them to us, and some sort of parley would be concluded.

'The next day the boy went with his father, under instruction to make contact with the natives and encourage them to meet with us. For us, it was a long day of waiting, and it was hard not to query whether they'd seceded out there, never to return. Nothing happened, hour upon hour. Mr Clark grew angry because we had lost a fine day for walking. Then a column of smoke appeared inland, apparently some signal from the natives that our approach was under consideration. The smoke threaded straight into the sky, veering neither left nor right, so still were the conditions; thus reinforcing Clark's point. While we were playing at diplomacy, we were losing momentum.

'In the late afternoon, as we variously slept and sat awaiting their return, we heard the sound of movement through the bush towards us. The old man appeared first out of the trees, followed by his son, and then came the natives, all of them men. I sensed, lieutenant, that they had some awareness of, shall I say, stagecraft: they strode forward one by one, naked but adorned in paint on their bodies and faces. Strong men, carrying no weapons and looking entirely at ease. They were graceful, lieutenant. Warriors. It saddens me to say it, but nothing like the broken wretches you see outside.

'Clark's journal? I thought that was all secret now. Which part...here? Very well. *The natives on this part of the coast appear strong and muscular, with heads rather large in proportion to their bodies.* I'm not sure about the heads, but yes, the rest of it.

'Where? This?...*they are daubed with blubber or shark oil, which is their principal article of food. This frequent application of rancid grease to their heads and bodies renders their approach exceedingly offensive.* Clark and his sensibilities. It wasn't something I noticed. It was ostrich oil, anyway.

'Show me. Ah...*Upon the whole, they present the most hideous and disgusting figures that savage life can possibly afford.*

'Really? That's the only reason you brought the journal here, to ask me that?

'Maybe the difference is not in them, lieutenant. Maybe it is the difference between Clark and me. One sees what one desires to see. A smell might remind you of home or it might turn your guts. Same smell.

'Yes. In any event, there was a discussion, seated on the ground. Several of theirs were the spokesmen, and they addressed themselves to the boy and his father. No doubt that was due to their earlier familiarity, but it irritated Clark no end. There was an exchange of gifts: we gave them some of our short bolts of calico and they gave us food. Have you ever eaten carrots when they are still very fine and tender, lieutenant? Eaten them raw, I mean? That is what these tubers were like: paler, still with the dirt on them, but delightfully sweet. They carried them in animal skins, and they ate them with us as though that was important to them. They made a great fuss of our clothes, lifting them, then watching our eyes as though they were concerned they were hurting us. I believe they were unsure whether the clothes were part of our bodies.

'We were able to show them, by drawing in the earth with a pointed stick, that we were going north. I did not detect any sense that they understood what Sydney was or why it might matter to us, but they certainly grasped the notion that we intended to continue up the coast. To our drawing they added an important feature: they drew a river to the north of us and then a line across it. I took them to mean this river was the end of their territory: either they did not know what lay beyond it or they were not kindly disposed towards those who lived on the other side.

'We left after an hour or two on the basis that they bid us *adieu*, but that we would see them again. All very civil. In fact, more than civil—I would say that we were firm friends by the end of it.'

⧚

'Firm friends?' Grayling compelled himself to stare deeply into those eyes. 'So why did these people later spear Mr Clark?'

Figge laughed, revealing a graveyard of tumbled brown teeth.

'You're assuming they were the same people. And you're assuming Clark didn't deserve it.'

'What are you telling me, Mr Figge?'

'All in good time, sir. Don't be rushing us.'

'I will thank you not to play games with me, *sir*.'

Figge paused, seemed to reconsider the direction of their

conversation. 'You're tired, lieutenant. You look wearier than I do, and I've had quite a journey. What ails you?'

'This is not the purpose of our discussion. My...'

'Your wife. Your wife ails you, because she herself ails.'

'My wife is unwell, Mr Figge. I have told you that.' This infernal man. He had found a window left open somewhere and was climbing into his soul.

'Has she worsened?'

Grayling hesitated. 'Yes. She is very poorly.'

'Still no movement in her legs?'

'The paralysis has grown worse, and she is becoming delirious.'

'Why are we sitting here talking about the past, lieutenant? I say again, I can help her. You are a civilised man: you're observing an unnecessary degree of restraint. You only need to relent.'

Grayling felt the dread swimming in him like nausea. There was a line he did not want to cross, the one that demarcated professional duty and personal anguish. But this was a torment more exquisite than that simple conflict. Figge's battered face, even as he watched Grayling—expectantly now—was a sea of crossing currents: kindness and compassion and empathy, rippling the surface of darker waters through which he could see the half-lit backs of malevolent creatures, large and slowly circling.

20

I've waited behind the door, wearing a shine on the boards.

I've come through your room, excusing myself, in countless false expeditions to the outhouse.

But the lieutenant has not come today, Mr Clark. Perhaps he has gone to Him for the continuation of the tale. Perhaps He is already claiming credit for the meeting with the Kurnai.

I have been thinking back to the whale country, Mr Clark. You should tell that next—when the walking became something more than weeks of sand and eastward march.

The spells of beach then point, beach then point, began to tilt north-east, and finally we reached a right angle in the coast, pressed tight between the sea boulders and the great forbidding forest. The few times we tried to push deep into the trees, we found that they went on and on into the land, so endless and frightening that we stopped trying. Around that time Mr Figge muttered to you, *This feels like testing the extent of death itself.*

The day before we met this turning of the coast we passed two islands; the first just a rise of boulders a thousand yards off the beach, capped in green and circled as always by the birds. The second was much greater: it rose from the sea after we had crossed another sandy bay, four miles from one sand spit to the other. I was trailing behind my father over those miles, watching the rise and fall of his feet and the sand stuck to the blood on them. His shoulders, narrow and bent by years and miles. A faraway memory of being perched up there, complaining, I suppose, as he carried me through the crowds of Chowringhee. The wonderful smell of him from up there, him and the day. Serious smells, not easily understood. *You are an intelligent child*, he would tell me as I clung to his hair, *a bright and attentive boy*. Now he was an old man, the respect of others replacing his failing strength. And I was not yet a man of any kind.

At the end of that bay, the end of my thoughts, we reached the second island, larger but closer to the shore. It was hot: we walked towards the back of the beach, seeking a place to lie in the shade and maybe find water, and it was in one of the dune shadows that we found the canoes.

They were as long as two men, narrow and made from large sheets of bark, tied at both ends with twine that seemed also to be made from bark. There were sticks crossed inside them like bones for support, and they were clean enough of sand that we knew they were in use. They could only have belonged to the Kurnai, and something about them felt familiar. Not that I had seen their canoes before: I hadn't. No, more that it was the same as the night at their camp, the way those people filled the land, and the land filled them.

Do you remember, Mr Clark, looking out at the island and seeing the houses there? The little domes in twos and threes?

I thought then: not only do they have the run of the land, the miles that might stretch between one man and another, but they put homes where they want them for the seasons. To be rich, I had thought until then, was a walled palace. But now I wondered if being rich meant not needing the wall.

The going was flat and easy then, only the one creek crossing, a stream the colour of tea that crossed the beach no deeper than our shins. By night we had reached a round point made mostly of dunes. On one side of it we looked south. On the other, we looked east. Mr Clark said we had reached the very corner of the continent: Cape Howe, named after one of their admirals.

As had become our way, we lay down and drew hopeful piles of leaves over ourselves against the night's chill. In this we were never successful: shivering came as snoring did, like it or not. That night I was curled beside my father, surrounded by the other Bengali men. The Mussulmen rested further out. But past their sleeping bodies, across the ground, I saw his eyes glittering in the dark, fixed on me like those of a watchful beast.

He may call himself Figge, and you may accept it as his name, but that is just some word. It's a sign on a door to an empty room, and the wind blows through it.

I feared it that night and it came to pass. He was waiting for a chance.

21

Joshua Grayling rushed from the guest quarters to his home on Bridge Street, hours ahead of the schedule that ruled his days and ashamed that he'd spent so much time listening to the strangers and their tales when his responsibility lay at his wife's bedside. He hurried down the track, over the open slope that three years ago had been cloaked in forest. Head down, thoughts scattered by panic, he was unaware of the gentle late autumn sun and the birds and the shadowing trees. He made no effort at conversation with the men beside him.

He entered alone, leaving the other two on the narrow verandah. His eyes locked on the bed. She was there, moving fitfully, her skin slicked with a greasy pallor. Her murmuring belonged neither to sleep nor consciousness. He shook her, called her name and she lit up with recognition.

'You're early, father…Bible. I'm…Papists.'

'Charlotte!'

She screamed as he shook her again, then slumped in his arms, glass-eyed. A tiny murmur escaped her.

'Charlotte, I have Mr Figge with me. I want him to see you.'

'Figge? Is he truly that?'

'Mr Figge, the tea merchant. And Doctor Ewing. You have to sit up.'

He hauled at her armpits until he had raised her slightly onto the pillows, but was unable to prop her in a sitting position. Each time he tried, she fell to one side or the other. He kept his arms around her ribs, his head steadying hers, and yelled at the doorway. Ewing ran into the room alone, carrying his leather bag. When he reached the bed, he took some of Charlotte's weight by holding an arm. Grayling continued to look towards the door.

'What's Figge doing?'

'Lighting a pipe, last I saw.'

'What? *Figge!*'

The voice snaked in from outside, calm and pleasant. 'Yes?'

'What are you doing? I thought—'

Figge's face appeared around the doorframe, hair swinging below his jaw. 'You thought?'

'I thought you had agreed to assist!'

Figge looked confused for a moment. 'But lieutenant, we haven't discussed my terms.' He did indeed have a pipe in his hand. He drew comfortably on it now.

'I have her,' muttered Ewing. 'Go and talk to him.' The doctor laid Charlotte straight again on the pillows and Grayling looked over her before crossing the room to step outside. Figge was reclining on the timber bench beside the doorway with his legs crossed. He looked up and patted the bench beside him: summoning a child who must be gently chastised.

'What are you doing?' Grayling demanded. 'You said you would examine her!'

'I know. I did. But I will need certain guarantees from you first.'

'*Guarantees?* I don't know how you are accustomed to dealing with people, Mr Figge, but that is not how I do things.'

'Oh please, lieutenant. It's how the whole place does things, isn't it?'

Grayling paced in front of the recumbent Figge, through his clouds of fragrant smoke. His first impulse was to slam the door on the man and tell Ewing to do his best; but he'd seen Ewing's best.

He pointed at Figge. Withdrew the hand, resumed pacing. Figge watched in quiet amusement.

'What is it you want?'

'Very little, really. I want a berth on the rescue voyage that goes to Preservation.'

Grayling could not think of a reason that this would be a bad idea. Figge might recognise landmarks. He would have knowledge of the cargo and…surely there were other advantages.

'Fine.' Even as he said it, he was at a loss to know why he was being drawn into this charade.

'*And*—' Figge raised a hand, and a conspirator's smile. 'I'd like a uniform.'

'What?'

'A uniform. For the voyage. Some braid…epaulettes. A pretty one, lieutenant. You could arrange that, I'm sure.'

'You have no *commission*, Figge. What on earth do you want with a uniform?'

'Oh, I don't know. Theatre? Pomp.'

'For God's sake. All right…yes.'

'Excellent.' Figge made his way slowly off the bench and tapped the pipe out on a rock in the garden. Grayling watched him with mounting fury.

'Hurry up!'

'Yes, yes. There is no rush.' Pocketing the pipe, he stood to his full height, pushed closely past Grayling so that his bulk overshadowed him, then strode into the room. When Charlotte caught sight of him she cowered into the bedclothes, breath shuddering with sobs. Even in a clean set of borrowed clothes he projected ferocity: the eyes and the wild beard drew the attention towards the awful wreck of the nose.

Grayling reached the bedside and stroked his wife's hair, taking strands and threading them behind her ear. His fingers touched the lump as he did so, terrifying him anew. Figge moved forward without seeking permission and reached between Grayling and his wife. The lieutenant withdrew, and suddenly Figge had his hands on her body, turning her onto her front. She had gone limp.

'This ear?'

'Yes.' Grayling stepped helplessly back from the bedside. He could still smell the smoke on Figge. Ewing was standing by, peering over Figge's shoulder. In his suit and spectacles, the bag clutched at his waist, he only made Figge look more dangerous.

Figge had a hand on Charlotte's neck; his long, spatulate fingers reaching all the way around it. The breath caught in Grayling's throat as he stared at them. They were not the fingers of a tea merchant. Figge swept the hair away from where the swelling was, then bent to examine what he had uncovered. Grayling wanted so desperately for him to find and purge the malignancy that had latched upon his wife, and just as fervently he did not want the man's hands on her. But they were surprisingly light: a kind of clinical ease infused his every movement.

'Yes,' he muttered to himself as he probed. ''Tis there.'

He had two fingers placed either side of the abscess, pulling away from each other to stretch it, then pressing inwards to squeeze it. A little blood and pus came from the centre of the swelling. He looked around Charlotte's jaw to ensure her mouth was still clear.

'Doctor? You have a clean piece of cloth?'

Ewing hastily placed the bag on the ground and rummaged through it, producing a length of muslin.

'And a blade?'

The doctor's face registered alarm. 'What are you planning to do, sir? Are you qualified in any way to do this? Lieutenant, I—'

'Give him what he seeks, doctor. You've had your opportunity.'

The doctor fumbled through the bag again and produced a scalpel. Figge took it in his right hand and held the wadded cloth against Charlotte's ear with the left. He drew the scalpel across the crest of the boil and quickly pressed the cloth over it. When he lifted it, the cloth was blotted with a putrid discharge that was now oozing from the incision. He blotted again.

'Give me little forceps,' he muttered. Ewing did not move but stood stunned as he watched the dabbing and the bleeding.

'Comport yourself, Doctor Ewing. I need to, very finely… those tweezers from this morning. Now, please.' The honeyed voice, under careful control. He extended his hand towards the doctor, palm upwards. Once more the doctor delved in his bag and found the requested item. Figge mopped several more times before he removed the wad of cloth and stretched the incision open again.

'Lieutenant, would you mind moving out of the light?'

Grayling shifted slightly to his left, unwilling to be an inch further from his wife than was necessary. His shadow moved away as Figge worked into the wound with the tweezers, wiping them once or twice on the cloth. Charlotte did not once move, nor react to any of this. In a fleeting instant of white-hot terror, Grayling believed her spirit had given up and was gone from her body.

The tweezers emerged again and this time Figge stood. He held them up as Grayling moved closer. Between their tips was a small creature the size and shape of a sesame seed. It was a dark golden colour with thick stumpy legs and an abdomen that was huge in relation to its size, dimpled like a broad bean. It disgusted Grayling.

'This thing came from in…from under her skin?'

'Yes,' Figge replied, still peering at it as it wriggled in the grip of the tweezers. 'I don't know what they are—some little spider, most likely. A burrowing kind. They cause paralysis.'

'How did you know this?' asked Ewing.

'I had one on me in the bush. It was near my arsehole—pardon. Very uncomfortable. The natives cut it out for me. It was when you said, lieutenant, that your wife had lost the power in her legs that I understood. The paralysis climbs the body.'

Grayling watched as Figge's hand flexed on the tweezers. The creature burst.

'How much longer would—'

'Days.' The tall man moved closer to the lieutenant, fixed him with cold eyes. 'I saved her, lieutenant.' He raised the soiled tweezers to eye level between them, then drew them towards his mouth. For one horrifying moment Grayling thought he was going to lick them. But he grinned as he spoke: '*I* did this. You understand?'

Figge bent and dropped the scalpel and the tweezers into Ewing's bag. 'And you, doctor—see to cleaning up that wound. She should be perfectly fine in the morning.' He turned to Grayling. 'I look forward to your confirmation of the terms we discussed.'

The eyes bored into Joshua Grayling. He cursed himself for having given in to this bully. A decision formed without thought. 'There will be no such terms,' he snapped. 'Now get out, I beg of you.' He was shaking. Figge stood briefly in the doorway, wiping his hands on the thighs of the borrowed trousers. Grayling and the doctor stared back at him. Charlotte was still face down but beginning to moan under the wad of cloth that Grayling held over the wound.

'Very well. I shall take myself back to my quarters,' Figge said evenly. He looked back at Charlotte, who still had not moved. The sheet was pulled down on her back, exposing a shoulder and one limp arm. Ewing held the gauze against her head.

Figge smiled faintly as if a passing thought had occurred to him.

'Don't ever get her in the family way, lieutenant. I felt those hips, friend. A good-sized infant will kill her—I guarantee it.'

22

There was a morning when the sun shone so perfectly over everything, and you sent my father ahead to lead a party searching for water. He was gone the whole day, along with those men. The sea was calm, the waves lit silver from behind. Gannets dived at unseen bait. The surf pounded itself into a fine mist that hung in the air and further out, the blue of the ocean was smeared with green where the wind had begun to whip.

You, Mr Clark, were locked in some argument with Mr Thompson and had no need for me. I walked for most of the day alone, sometimes in company with one or two of the Bengalis, each of us too tired to talk. I lost myself in my own thoughts, small things rendered clear and sharp.

I saw a moth hidden perfectly against the bark of a tree. I heard the squeaking of our feet in the sand. When our way led into the bush I heard birds that sang in loud peeps in the gullies. Returning to the beach, I felt the ocean's soft rushes on the shore, so different to its angry crashing on the southern coast where the ship was lost.

We crossed three river mouths that day and the wind sighed from each as though the land was breathing. As we moved slow across the beach between the second and third, Mr Figge came alongside me. He had waited for the moment, I know. The lascars were scattered along the warm rocks we were crossing; some behind, some in front. My father was away and you were deep in discussion with the mate.

He was smiling at the sun, then at me. I made sure to look straight ahead.

'Good morning my young friend,' he said. Nothing in the words to fear, nothing in the manner but a man simply saying hello. From another man you might say the voice was lovely. But it stirred cold fear in me. I nodded to show I had heard him, but did not speak.

'You understand me. You have English, I believe, and it is perfectly good. Do you know you talk in your sleep? *In English*?' He laughed.

I walked on, trying to show him nothing. He must have aimed to trick me. My parents had never told me I talked in my sleep. But was this world so different that I had betrayed myself without knowing it?

'It is a wise strategy to separate yourself from the world of these men. They want to assume your ignorance, so you give them what they expect. Clever boy.' He watched me closely. 'I think this ruse of yours will fail, however. People get tired. They make mistakes. I think you will make a mistake. Do you have another plan after that? When it is revealed that you understood all along?'

Our feet crunched into a new stretch of beach, his footfalls heavy and widely spaced, mine fainter and faster between. Again I made an empty face and prayed that it would hold, as the animal eyes searched. The smile around his mouth did not belong with the eyes: it was bright and open like a child's. I thought then that I had never known such evil. I knew nothing.

'The problem with disguises, with these false versions of yourself,' he continued, 'is that one day there comes an intersection: a person who knew you before, a place you've already been. I myself have been other people, you see. The world is big enough to accommodate them all. But one must be vigilant. If you live through this, people will know your name. They will recognise you—the boy who survived the disaster of the *Sydney Cove*. Can you remain the endearing mute boy in the face of all that attention, lad?'

He laughed a little, then fell silent. The beach ended at a rock pile. A path began there—other feet had worked around this problem—then we came into an open forest where the lower part of every tree was burnt. The middle of each held the leaves, and the tops were bare.

Still Mr Figge stayed close to me. Still he had not spoken. Two heavy branches overhead rubbed together, a sound like human pain. Then for a long time the only sounds were our crunching steps, the hissing of the wind through the hard, dry leaves and the distant roar of the ocean. The birds had stopped calling.

I thought about the days of tricking money from the travellers at the river. My desire to be among the boys who could do it, who could flash a glinting coin, the ones with the careless confidence. And the handful of times I tried it, Mr Clark, it worked. Trip a man over by colliding with his knees, help him up and clear his pockets in the process. Or have him hand over his own money with a tearful story of a dying sister.

You're no different, I thought. *Slow and cocksure. I will have your fucking coin.*

Careless confidence. I looked straight into those eyes I feared and hated, and I smirked. I spent every coin I'd ever liberated in the markets; I summoned every ounce of the swagger I saw in the biggest of the riverbank thieves and I poured it all into that sneer. And it took him, for a heartbeat or two. He looked confused at the show of defiance. Then he threw his head back and laughed.

'Very good, lad. *Very* good. You've removed any trace of doubt that you understand me; but really, marvellous effort.' He walked in silence for a few minutes, staying close by, until his laughter had faded away. Then he began to speak again, more thoughtfully.

'Do you think,' he asked, as much to the birds as to me, 'you have already passed over the place where you will die? After all, nearly everyone will die in a place they have already been. They cannot know if it is the highway, or the river or their own bed. But one such place will be the last they ever see, and although they see it every day, they do not know its sad significance. But look at us—walking almost certainly to our deaths, and it will without doubt be on a stretch of ground we have never seen. Transported from this world to another, through a portal we are yet to experience.

'And that death, it seems likely, will be at the hands of an agent we do not anticipate. Maybe one of the natives. Or a wild animal—do you think we know of all the beasts here by now? I think not. But maybe it will be one of us, that last person we see. Like the familiar sideboard in the corner of the invalid's chamber…ah! It is you!' He pointed at some of the men walking nearby. 'Or you, or you.

'Interesting, isn't it, that this lot believe they will go to one God. Have a, hmm, a *meeting* man to man. About the *sins*. You'—he pointed a teacher's finger my way—'you believe you will answer to many gods. But these people out there, your Kurnai, they've made a god of their landscape. You understand? *None of it isn't God.*'

He seemed to dwell on this for a time, deep in thought but never letting me away. Then he said:

'The fascinating thing is the way the world repeats itself. I have been wrecked before, boy. Fifteen years ago. Pondoland coast, on the Cape. Terrible thing. She was an Indiaman, the *Grosvenor*, and the tragedy almost exactly prefigured ours. A hundred and fifty on her, and laden with wealth. How does such a thing happen? Happen *twice*? I was fourteen—that would be your age, near enough?' He looked at me intently but I did not react, and he continued talking. 'We were cast upon the rocks and the survivors regrouped on the shore. It was decided we must walk. Fierce tribesmen in the bush. *Bush* is an African word, did you know that? Of course not'—he winked—'you can't understand me, let alone the Africans.

'Six weeks we marched, and only eighteen of us made it to Cape Town. How do you suppose all those people died, my friend? Exposure? Attacks by the savages? Well, perhaps. That was certainly what the authorities were told.' He snapped off a branch so we could pass under it. 'One survives and is reborn. What an interesting discussion this would be, wouldn't it? If only you understood me...'

The afternoon's gold light came down now, in sparks and haze through the trunks: the land caught in a sigh.

'You remember the badger sow I caught the other day?' he went on. 'They're not like our badgers, these ones; it had a second cunt.' He stared at me intently, seeking a reaction. 'Aye! Two cunts—who would've thought? And the strangest thing: after I dispatched it with the rock, I carried it along…bloody heavy it was…and as the carcass cooled an infant stuck its head out of the other cunt. Just appeared there! It seems they carry their young that way, tucked up in there.'

He placed a hand lightly on my chest now, stopping me. He began to mutter in his excitement. 'Now this is today's lesson. The parent might provide that refuge, inside itself. Cosy in there, aye, but the parent died. All parents die. And the body cools and the unknowing child emerges, wondering why the world went cold.'

His eyes, his teeth. He was leaning close, staring unfocused. For all the world I knew I must not react.

'I ate the parent; well, you know that. But I, ah…' He licked his lips and smiled. 'I spent some time on the child.'

Then the walking again; for the walking never ended. The dying sun made evening shadows in our footprints and still he wore me close. We came up off the beach: more open rocks, some with small round pebbles trapped in them. Us in the grip of the land. I ached inside and I wanted only an answer from the rocks. Had the natives found a way to trap those pebbles? Could it be that they talked to the rocks, and if that were so—could they keep a terrible man from his designs?

23

Charlotte Grayling left the house early this time, with nothing in her hands.

Other times she had taken a basket, a pannikin of water, a heel of bread. But the heart of the matter was to increase the feeling, each swing of her hands a reminder of her vulnerability.

She hadn't walked since the time she'd fallen ill. Part of the misery of her sickness was the inability to do this: to be freed of the constraints of the tiny house, the unspoken judgments of the neighbours. They were officers' wives too—they watched, they saw and they kept count. To hell with them: now her strength was back and her body would resist the urge no longer.

She waited until her husband had gone, headed to Government House in his small cloud of purpose, then she slipped out in the opposite direction, making her way down the lane with a nod to the Cadigal men sitting close by a fence in the shade of a tree that belonged to no one in particular but to them all along. It was something Joshua never understood about the walking: far from slipping into some bottomless void in the land, she was watched everywhere she went. The men by the fence could describe her every movement in the bush, just as the neighbours could report on her domestic routine.

It was early enough that the settlers had no interest in a white woman making her way towards the edge of town. Only the convicts were about: mucking out the night filth, saddling horses. The smells that defined the place, the wood smoke and baking and the waste of humans and livestock, had not yet risen with the sun. There would be no heat to escape today, no need for urgency in the early hours.

She watched her boots. She watched the skirts about her knees. The ground: earth and small grasses, stones passing under. Each yard still familiar, she strode harder. The last cottage, the one that belonged to the broken man with his ticket of leave and cloudy eyes. Russick, who had turned down the offer of land on account of his ulcered legs and was near enough to blind now.

Open country now, cleared in anticipation of the township's growth, but abandoned while fear of Pemulwuy's fighters gripped them all. No one wanted to risk provoking him by pushing the settlement further into the bush. Not yet.

She knew the path that ran from the end of the street, the one the convicts had cut with their picks. She had no way of knowing whether the Eora had made the path in response to the making of the street—a furtive way in and out of the English world—or whether the path had always been there and the street was its clumsy tracing. From there, the land sloped up, the scrub touched her shoulders and brushed her cheek. The delicate perfume of the wildflowers, slaughter and tar receding. Up more, and she was breathing harder. The path snaked on

153

past a boulder, a tangle of roots. *Is this how they felt?*

Voices in the trees. The demented chatter and song of the birds, challenge and seduction shouted over each other like the drunks. And higher than the birds, the sea air breathing over the canopy, making it shudder and murmur. The leaves of the giant eucalypts tapped each other on their hard edges, the touches in their millions collecting into a great sigh, and as the wind slowed from each gust the sigh disintegrated again into the singular, hard touches of the leaves.

The sweat was beading on her forehead, slipping in her armpits and gathering in the small of her back. She worked harder, pushing with her hands on her knees when the ground rose steeper before her, until there was a clear stretch ahead. She closed her eyes, willed herself to keep them shut, and extended her fingers so the soft ends of the foliage traced over them. She counted eight steps before her trust faltered and she opened her eyes. She could have kept going. She chided herself, walked faster. It was still a path, though nothing behind her spoke of civilisation anymore. The bush had closed around her.

It felt like this.

To not know shelter. To search for water, food, comradeship. To be occupied only by the body's needs must be akin somehow to the absence of want. If the body needed to drink from a stream she could oblige it on her hands and knees. If it needed relief she would hang her hands over the low branch right there and *piss*. To have had that word and never uttered it, to speak it to the empty bush. The times she had heard it used among the men and had bowed to the necessity to smile it away. She had burst upon a native woman on one such walk, squatting and engaged thus. The woman had barked some admonition at her and laughed loudly. Being seen: it was as harmless to her as having been overheard using the word.

Fuck. The crowding trees absorbed the sound, so she said it louder. Loud enough this time that it rang in the gully. The bush did not react and the profane thrill sparked again in her. The path was fading and now descended into deeper glades. Water dripped somewhere nearby and the birds were different here; no longer shouting but speaking in brief melodies that echoed between the tall trunks. A great protruding burl glowered over her from the nearest trunk, a face carved in a keystone. She sat, felt the damp soaking through her skirts, and removed her boots and stockings. When she stood again the clammy ground oozed between her toes. *Out here, like this. This is how it felt.*

She lifted the skirts a little, hefted them in her hands. Twigs and bark and moving insects among the folds, hems heavy with dirt and moisture. She was lost now. She knew it. There was no clear way of knowing where the ocean lay, where the sun would track towards evening. Down here, under the mysterious shroud of the moving branches, she was lost.

She was a child again, had wandered into a forbidden room and could feast her eyes on the adult things, might imminently be caught. The wave through her body again, the coursing tide that unfocused her eyes and carried both desire and repletion. She had lost herself. She closed her eyes and let the sweep of it overwhelm her, surrendered to it vaulting down through her hands and over the delicate pads of her fingertips.

She placed her fingers over her eyes and spun a full circle, then another and another. When she removed her hands she had to steady herself against a tree. Now the bush had closed around her. Now it held her in unspeaking embrace, only sounds and sensations. Now it offered no clue to the way home.

By the time her husband returned in the evening, Charlotte had drawn a cask of water, removed her clothes and washed them, and had made a passable stew from the odd things the store would give her.

He came through the door with the cares of the day graven in his face. She wanted immediately to take him and hold him, feel his familiar warmth. But he only grunted as he took a chair and began to remove his boots. When he was done, and with her standing expectantly across the table from him, he sighed and spread both hands on the rough timber surface.

'Dark in here,' he muttered, and fumbled with the tinder box to light a candle.

'I'll get the lamp,' she replied, measuring him silently for some sign of his mood. Now more than ever she must be the woman she had left waiting at the near edge of the forest.

'You washed your dress.'

She had her back turned, reaching for the lamp as she heard him say it. She looked around and laughed. 'I do wash our clothes occasionally, Joshua.'

'No.' He fixed her with a look of specific query in his eyes. 'You washed the dress you were wearing when I left this morning.'

'I was brushing the fireplace out and I got soot on it.' She tried the laugh again, faltered and blushed.

'Your boots by the door,' he continued. 'They've been scrubbed. Why would you scrub your boots if you got soot on your dress?'

She looked at him helplessly, her mouth slightly open as she waited for inspiration to arrive.

'Scratches on your forearms.' He was looking down now,

speaking quietly. 'Please don't lie to me in addition to…whatever it is you do.'

A tear formed on one eyelid and it infuriated her.

'You're walking again, aren't you?' He glared at her, suddenly a stranger. 'Did they have to go and get you again? Or did the natives bring you in?'

'I found my way.'

'Why are you *doing* this to me?' he demanded. 'What is it I'm not providing to you? Is it my, my physical affection?'

His awkwardness tore at her heart. It was not that, of course. He loved her whenever she pleased, and she felt his love as a barrier against the chaos beyond their walls. But no amount of love could guide him to the strangest depths in her. The years were telling her now: they were not coming closer to exploring this terrain. *I might not be like you*, she had thought back in Leith, *but I do love you*. The landscape offered occasional temptations to burst free, to run at the thickets or throw herself into a rock pool and shiver the walk home. But in those offerings it drew her away from him, and into itself.

'It is nothing,' she said eventually. 'There is nothing I could want for.' She pulled out a chair opposite him and sat down, reaching across the table to take his hands in hers. 'I cannot explain to you why I do it because I do not know myself.'

He exploded from the table, sending the chair tumbling. 'You *do* know why! You must—you get up in the morning, you watch me leave and you *plan* it, damn you. You wait for your chance and you go out there, and you cover your tracks afterwards. You endanger yourself and then you deceive me. Why can't you just—'

'—make house like the other women?'

'Now you see fit to *mock* me?' His rage was building to a

157

fearful height now and it scared her. 'You nearly killed yourself with your last escapade. I had to bring that…that man into our home because of it. Is that it? You want the faith healer back here again with his…with his *hands*—?'

'Please do not be this way.' She was weeping now, reaching again for his hands though he kept them away from her. 'Please my love. I won't…I'll never do it again.'

He sighed at this. Some of the anger seemed to leave him. But she knew in her heart it wasn't true.

24

The whale country. I don't know if I can call it that.

The days with my father, numbered by then. The coast running north and folded green hills and trees that hid the light.

Eighteen miles a day and you were barefoot like us by now, Mr Clark, tripping over scatters of cannonball stones, small and round enough to move underfoot. Birds we never saw on the highest branches, hundreds of feet above, their sound, both whip and whistle, ringing through the bush.

We came upon a cut in the slope behind the beach where the land opened like a wound and the trees stopped and all was rock and gravel, twenty yards wide. The gentlemen argued over what it was: some said it was made by God; you, Mr Clark, said it was no more than a natural fold in the land. A Javanese man said it was made by the natives and that it was a quarry. He said it quiet, not wanting to upset the gentlemen after the business with the snail shells, but he would not be shaken from his view.

Nearby I watched a fat badger sipping from a pool of water that had collected in a rock hollow, her broad head reflected in the water's surface. She stopped drinking, looked up at me, steady and slow. The rippling water around her snout became still, and for an instant the badger and her soft dark eyes were a sign of hidden tenderness in the land.

Although it was open country, it changed before our eyes. Tiny bushes came only to our shins, then we were crashing through head-high thickets with sheets of papery bark, and cursing and cracking through twigs that clawed at our eyes. Then the land would open up again, and all pain would pass and the heath was covered in pink and red flowers like animal paws, and others like brightly coloured spiders or exploding fireworks.

The lascars were weak—we all were weak. The gentlemen rained blows on us in their confusion and fear, kicking sometimes, and we simply endured until the attacker—whether Mr Kennedy or Mr Thompson, with his round red face and his pig's eyes, became tired. But Mr Figge never showed strain: he'd laugh his hard, rattling laugh, so different from his speech, that bore no warmth for anyone else. For a man with a voice like a strung instrument, he had a laugh that tore the nerves.

⁂

The sea rocks were streaked with dark reds and greys and even a dull yellow, so they looked to hungry men like lumps of raw fatty meat.

The natives here stayed wide of us, shy again. It was only ever the men, unarmed but watching. The small trees, thicker here, made a deep shade that tricked the eye. The watchers knew the shade and they used it to appear and disappear. We talked about it, in close. My father felt that the natives understood our northward aim and were waiting at points ahead of us. The paths appeared under our feet, and they led us to the watching men and on past them.

You were full of talk at night, Mr Clark. About the river mouths we had been crossing, so fine they would one day be the sites of great cities. The hills that fall to them, the plains beyond. *The trading houses will be here*, you said. *The mills there and the administration there*. The unclear edges between reeds and shallow pools would be no more, you claimed, *when firmly defined by sea-walls*.

Once I was certain you were done with me—feeding you, preparing your writing materials—I would return to my father and listen to him talk softly in the thick silence of the bush. *You must attend to Mr Clark at all times*, he reminded me one such night. *Much of what we value is scattered now. When all breaks down, the only thing you will have to hold onto is your duty*. I asked him what he meant by this but he only continued. *Do not be one of those base men who panics and resorts to his own interest*.

I said if all else was chaos, I would remain true to him: my father. *I am old*, he said. *You are a bright and attentive boy. There is much before you and this test may be the making of you. You must cleave to duty*.

Within moments I could hear he was asleep. I was disturbed now, and wide awake. Out there in the night our people slept. They were tired, some of them injured, hanging in the unclear space between anger and open mutiny. Nothing was true any longer: they were neither sailors nor employees nor even allies. Only walkers, greater in number but smaller in size. And unarmed: the last shreds of authority had meant that the gentlemen carried the weapons. Perhaps that mattered less than it might have. The guns were ruined as far as we knew, and as for the knives and tomahawks—well, the ground out there was covered with weapons. A rock, a knot of timber: any such would kill if used in stealth.

The morning after that conversation, there was another beach, cut by a river: this one narrow but deep. Again you pressed your authority and sent the man named Mohan in to test the depth. That teapot tint of the water meant there was no knowing what he would find: he quickly disappeared up to his waist and then was afloat, and it was all he could do to stop himself being carried off through the river mouth and out into the ocean. He came ashore cursing and hard of breath.

While the gentlemen sat and rested, some more of our men scouted inland, to find that the river stayed deep and became even wider. So again, once again, the making of a raft. There was nothing left by now of our floating sled. The work was slow, felling and chipping logs with the tomahawk, Mr Kennedy pleased as always to have a turn at giving orders.

As we worked, an old native man came to us, the same scars across his chest, knobbed and stretched with age. It was less of a shock now: some of our party did not even look up from their work. He marched up bold to my father, thinking him our leader. He pointed at the river, his fingers making the water, and said a word several times: *Nadgi.* Then he indicated higher with his chin, over the water to the forest on the other side. *Guyangal.*

He stood tall, swept his arm low across the northern sky as though he wanted to take in everything ahead of us. *Yuin,* he cried, to no one in particular. Then he came in closer: sharing something small but significant. He dotted his hands over the nearby landscape, smiling. At a hill, at the nearby sea, at the forest itself. *Thaua,* he said. There was a confidence in him about these things, he spoke the words with strength. But the men gave voice to their confusion with sneers.

For it was not clear whether he spoke of a place or a person, or even a group of people. You offered the man some pieces of calico, but he wanted nothing to do with trinkets and with a great sigh, he turned his back on us.

When the raft was made we crossed the river mouth. As soon as we'd done so and taken our belongings onto the sand, another man came forth, this one younger and stronger. I cannot say how, but he was not the same kind of man we had just left on the opposite bank.

In this man's smile also, a tooth was gone, but a different one. He wore no paint on his face; I could not say if he had marks on his chest, for he wore a splendid coat of dark grey fur streaked with black. Opossum fur, I saw when he came closer, turned in so the skins faced out and the deep, soft fur was on his body. I longed to feel the way he must have felt in there. Mr Figge had killed an opossum three nights before, wringing its neck as it strayed too close to his food. He cut it open and we ate everything out of it, pulling with our fingers inside the bag of fur. When we were done, we threw the hide into the fire. Stupid.

The man called towards the trees on the riverbank. One by one, people came from behind them, and for the first time there were women and children. All naked but for small things, like the cords around their waists. They made their way across the sand flats at the river mouth, smiling with their hands out to touch us.

Perhaps it is as well that nobody has asked me to talk of those days, because I do not know what I would say about the feeling that came over me. I saw in their hands, in their eyes, the chance that I could be anybody to these people: not just Srinivas the lascar, or the servant, or the son of Prasad. Not a Bengali, or even a sailor or a boy. I could be *anybody*, as they could to me.

Two of the women came forward with woven bags containing oysters still wet from the rocks. There were no such shells near us; they must have come from further upriver, or from other waters. We fell upon them with great hunger, as the natives smiled. They brought us tea as well, a strong brew that smelled of aniseed and felt bright inside. *Warraburra*, said one, gesturing at the steaming bowl, for he knew how good it was.

When we had finished the meal, children came forward to collect the oyster shells. The man in the opossum cloak sat next to my father, who placed a hand on his knee and said the word we had heard from the old man on the other bank. *Guyangal*.

The man's eyes lit with great pride. He placed his hand on his chest and repeated the word, and the other one, *Thaua*, back to my father. Then he swept an arm around all of the people there and said it again.

You were keen to make it known we were walking north: they pointed into the bush and drew maps in the sand that made clear we should walk inland, but you corrected them each time. This went on for some time—each time you insisted they would turn to each other and talk with serious faces, then nod together. Then they would point inland again. It tested your patience. You sighed, turned to the others and stood up to show it was time we left. The meeting ended with the man in the cloak appointed as our guide, and we set off, the senior man and his two friends at the front, pointing out things they thought important.

The flies moved lazy over our skin, stopping at the places where we were cut. I would forget them, only to find them crowded at some sore like beasts at a waterhole. Under our feet passed ashy streaks of burnt ground, tiny shoots coming through.

The Mussulman Mohan fell in beside me.

How do you feel? I asked him, as he was among the oldest of us.

I hadn't seen him smile in days. *I am all right*, he said. *My mouth hurts.*

I reached for his mouth—*may I?*—and he opened it and pulled his lips back. There were cruel sores all along the gums, some around his few teeth, showing their crumbled roots. I looked down, shamed by my pity for him. His shins were crossed with scratches from the stiff twigs, like all of ours were, but then I saw his feet. This ground tore the ends off every man's toes, but his looked like some animal had tried to eat them, all blood and torn skin. Small clouds of eager flies tried to settle as he walked.

The women came out this time, he said, puffing a little.

It took me a moment to understand. *Ah yes*, I said to him.

I think they mean friendship. As I didn't answer he went on. *These are not the—what did you call them?—the Kurnai. We have crossed a border and been passed to these Thaua people.*

If he was right and the natives were not just 'natives' but all sorts of different people, and we were being passed between them, then much else was possible. Word of our progress—and our misdeeds—would travel ahead of us. And the other thing: our efforts to learn any language, or follow any custom, must start anew each time we crossed a river and found ourselves among new people.

We had eaten little that day, had made do with sucking at flowers as we had seen our guides doing. They showed us shoots and berries that were good to eat. There was a small white berry that grew in great numbers and had a seed in it. It tasted much like a crisp apple, but the Thaua men laughed and made clear we should not eat too many of them, making great gushes with their hands at their backsides. We understood perfectly.

When the dark came we were too tired to make a fire. One by one we lay down where we had been standing as the Thaua disappeared into the bush. They attached no importance to goodbyes.

Early the next morning Mr Clark was up and busy with his journal. It was, he told us, the thirtieth day of March, just over seven weeks since the ship ran aground.

We crossed a small river on foot as the morning lit up. We came under thick smoke from the burning grasses for eight miles or so over the shallow growth on the hills. Eyes stinging, we came to a larger stream. This time we Bengalis were sent in to test its depth: we were down to the depth of our heads within yards of the shore.

Mr Kennedy took out his tools and we were sent for logs: the slow work of raft-making began again. But this time days of waiting and working were saved by the return of our Thaua friends. They had brought with them two younger ones, around my age. They watched the work, bent with their hands on their knees, then waved to us to stop. Mr Kennedy looked angry.

The Thaua men stepped into the heavy bush behind the riverbank where the tall tree-ferns made shade and moss, moving expertly over the wet ground. In minutes they had each found the head of a long, fallen trunk. These, I could see, were chosen, and not just any timber. Each had been cut down and each was slender and straight.

They pulled one free of the scrub and stood it on its end, as tall as the river was wide. Moving up to a small rock that stood higher on the bank, they let the trunk fall. It landed perfectly on matching rocks on the other side. A bridge, fixed at both ends by piers of rock. Back they went into the bush to repeat their steps, and when they had done it three times, they'd laid the three trunks as straight as rails next to each other. Two heavy boulders wedged them at either end so they wouldn't roll, and over we went, jumping from the logs in high spirits when the crossing was done. Even you, sir, managed to swallow your scorn for a moment. Mr Figge looked amused, but then he always did: amused and interested. So much of life was a bug in a jar to him.

The men took up their bridge and stored it on our side of the river. I thought them to be good men: they treated each other well in their work. They stayed with us as we pressed north into the evening, the heath turning to forest now and the forest to rainforest, thick with drips and shudders. Four miles of hard going under great thickets of ferns and palms, then a fork in the trail, and we were forced to bow our heads to pass under branches. The undersides had been cut back. Some of the cuts were old, and the bark had grown over the knots. The work must have gone back generations. The path led deeper among ancient things, and the trunks beside me were worn smooth. I let my hand fall on them as I passed and found it followed the same shine on those trunks.

Just on dark, the path opened into a clearing, as when I was first taken in by the Kurnai. Again the sound of gathered voices, but this time a great many more. Slices of it through the trees, colour and movement. And then out and down a short hill into a place where we stood in wonder. Understanding for the first time.

Of course we were watched, I thought. Of course there was such certainty, so much understanding in everything they did. For there in front of us was a village of perhaps fifty or sixty houses, set apart from each other with space between. Fireplaces and stacked grain. The trees around the edge of the place marked with symbols, so clear they could have been ship's ensigns. There were people moving about dressed in opossum cloaks or simple animal skins. One coat I saw was like the fur of a cat, dark and covered in perfect white spots. Mothers carried fat babies. Children played. Men reclined together and talked. Families sat around their evening meal, dogs waiting beside them in hope of scraps. But it was the houses that stopped me.

I studied the ones closest by, a cluster of them built the same way: framed in bones. Huge ribs had been dug into the earth on their heavy ball-end, and they speared high into the centre of a circle as they narrowed. Whales, one of the Javanese said. Where the bones met they were tied off with something that looked as strong as the best cordage on a frigate, and the spaces between bones were thatched with sticks and grasses, reeds and other things. The very best pair of ribs at each house had been kept to frame the doorway, the door itself a sheet of soft bark.

The families that belonged to these houses ate from bark sheets, but their food came from clay vessels, charred around their sides like they had been fired. Their water was poured from tied-up animal skins that made me think of the water-boys of the Hooghly. These were people who wanted for nothing. It was us who came to do the begging.

There was singing, dancing, heavy sticks driving rhythm and men who barked and yelped. As we sat and watched, the old people checked my body for wounds with their soft hands on my arms and legs. They washed the sores they found with oil, smeared thick grease on the worst of them. I didn't see my father during all this but I later learned he was well cared for.

He, and the old Mussulman, Mohan. And I am sure you too, Mr Clark.

We had come more than a hundred miles on foot already, you told us that night. But you had no map to confirm it. You wrote our progress in your journal by the firelight, checking the brass dials we had saved for you from the dying longboat. The natives watched with interest, sensing that in some way you were consulting their universe. *How far to go?* we asked, because we knew it to be the real question. You guessed four hundred miles.

That night I was taken into a hut to sleep, and the earth under my head smelled of other people. The ground and the sweat of a living body. I slept alone, neither on duty for you nor beside my father. The first night I ever spent on my own terms.

A hundred miles, and we had not lost a man. Not a hand had been raised against the natives. The only hands raised were between us.

⁂

In the morning I woke in the knots of a dream I could not separate from thoughts of the evening before.

The Thaua were running about in great excitement. Children took me by the hand and pointed to the sea. Other children had hold of my countrymen and my father. I saw you, Mr Clark, being pulled to your feet and hurried on. At first I feared some disaster, but there was a look of great excitement on every face, and they were using a single word, over and over. *Garuwa!* they cried, and it whipped them ever higher.

I followed where I was taken, along with the others, down new paths over a large, low hill where we could see the sea. The whole of the village was with us, led by one old man with a most wonderful silver beard. They honoured him as they went, jumping about him and calling him *guman*.

I watched the others in secret as they were hurried down the same path. Mr Kennedy and Mr Thompson, reluctant again, complaining as they went. You wanted your pride, Mr Clark: the keeper of our records, hugging your journal and your bag of brass instruments to your chest. And Mr Figge, enjoying the scene too much for words, his huge paws resting on the heads of the children and in his eyes some hideous thought on a low fire. I cast him from my mind, so much did I want to keep hold of the joy around me.

Down the hill, faster and faster until I feared my feet would fail me, and then we burst out of the scrub at the edge of the beach and onto the open flat sands. In front of us was a wide circle of bay, surrounded by hills like the one we'd come down. Most of the Thaua were already there on the sand. They were looking out to sea, looking at the great, tall fins of killer whales working the glassy surface not far from shore.

There were three of the huge fish there, fins taller than the men pointing at them, circling and circling. The wide tails broke the surface and smacked it, and between the three fins there was a stirring in the water. The movement of something very large. The reflections on the surface swirled away and now the thing was clear: a whale calf, caught in the herding of the killers; rolling, twisting but trapped where they could have it easy. All four of the animals spouted seawater: from the killers this was a fierce jet, but the calf's was ragged and airy. And with every loop, they drove it closer to the beach.

Some of the younger men had waded into the water, taking care not to get too close to the great fish in their struggle. A stray fin, a blow from the mighty tails would crush a man's bones. But the Thaua shouted and laughed, sometimes at each other, sometimes at the whales. The sunlight appeared now, from where the sun worked its way through the trees on top of the ridge behind us. These blankets of light fell on the moving animals, gleamed on their backs, and they fell on the young men also, finding the ripples of their bodies.

Eyes turned, among all this, to the beach. Two strong timbers had been driven into the sand, about forty yards apart. Between them ran the old bearded man—shouting and dancing, waving his arms in the direction of the whales, somehow urging the animals towards shore.

The killers were ramming the calf now. It bellowed its lost hope, broke the surface with its giant head, pleading for the old man to dream something else. A flash of its eye, then gone. They slammed it again: its tail rose and fell in the beautiful sun, perfect white beneath. Impact, shudder, a rush of bloody froth. The old man thrashed on the sand, digging clumps with his feet, head back and roaring, sweat shining on his back and the flying sand sticking to it.

His pace grew ever more urgent. He bent now, throwing handfuls of air from the sky to the ground. Birds made loops over the sea, then arrowed into it one after the other, as if he had told them to. The crowd was parting, some to see the killing in the shallows, some the old man. But he was tied to a giant force: he knew nothing of what was around him.

I knew this was their matter, not mine, but my heart cried out for the whale. The killers were baring their teeth as they plunged into the suffering head, and the gusts from its spout were pink now with bloodied air. The three killers turned away from the whale, knowing it was past escape. They took themselves further out from the beach and I waited with dread for them to turn. And so they turned, gaining speed as they came. A great roar came up from the crowd on the beach: they hammered my ears with their shouts and clapping and in those moments as the killers closed in I was no longer passing through but staked to the day. The dancing bodies, the fierce will of the animals, the sand and sky: none of it paid heed to me. The moment only demanded that I see.

The whale had rolled side on to the beach and now they struck it at full speed, forcing another gust of dying breath. They struck it so hard it slid up onto the sand and the men closed in with their spears, launching them one after another into the soft flanks. Streaks of blood ran from each buried spear and from the comb that lined the downward corner of its great mouth.

I looked back to the old man. He had sat in the place where he'd been dancing, around him all the stirred sand. His head was down, chest rising and falling, forgotten by the crowd.

The calf was helpless on the wet sand. Its tail curled upwards as though terrible agony clenched its belly. Once they could see the spears had done their work, the men removed them with a twist to get the barb away clean. They came round the seaward side to roll it further out of the water. The sand, clinging in great wet clumps to its skin, slid down as it rolled. The whale was perhaps twenty foot long and all of their effort would move it no more than a few feet. There it rested: upside down, white belly offered to the sun.

The men slapped the hide of the whale and made approving sounds to one another. Although its carcass was higher than the tallest of them, a boy had somehow climbed up on the far side and now ran along it—a woman who might have been his mother roared at him and down he came—and now the men closed in around the mouth. I could see that they had tools:

short axes like ours but made with a stone head. They chopped away at the comb, cutting and pulling until it all came away like a wet sail. This was taken to the women with great ceremony. The men now heaved open the great mouth and stood it that way using the spears. The first few shafts bent under the weight of the jaw, until more were put in to spread the load.

From where I stood I could see only some of this. A man climbed inside the mouth, a job I would not have taken for any amount of money. The killers were still cruising just off the beach, and I thought I understood. They were the *wallahs* awaiting their coin. The whale's capsized eye reflected the circling fins in sorrow and confusion.

And this is how all of us are taken down.

Mr Figge had moved in beside the men who were working on the whale's mouth, and I saw him lift the knife he carried: the largest of the ones we had saved from the longboat. He passed it to the men: they examined it, then cheered and patted his back and passed the knife into the mouth, to the man in there, working in the half dark. Their voices rose, Mr Figge made a sound like *Ho!* and they all reached in, pulling out a huge slab of soft meat: the tongue of the whale.

They struggled with it: it slid from their hands every time they tried to lift. Others arrived with cut branches and they slid these under the tongue, rolling it onto them so they were able to pick up the ends and carry the meat like a *tikathee*. They walked like this, into the water and up to their waists, and I felt the river again and the dogs of the dusty city just quick, before they rolled the tongue off the timbers and into the water. It floated there, the pink thing with no shape, trailing its sinews.

The fins came in to the offering. The heads and bodies of the killers appeared, their patches of black and white. They fell upon the tongue like mad dogs, no heed to each other or the natives. For a moment their power boiled the water and the work of their teeth bloodied it.

But then the surface was still and all was done. The women led their children back up the hill and the men prepared themselves for the long work of butchering.

25

'How are your hands?'

Grayling stood framed in the doorway of Clark's small house, having found it open. The flies were gone now; the season was at an end. People were leaving their houses open to air the smells that the summer heat had trapped.

The lascar boy stood beside Clark's bed, lifting him forward to wash his back with a wet towel. The door between their two rooms was open. Clark held his hands up feebly. Both were still bandaged.

'May I?' On receiving a small nod of assent, Grayling walked in. Propelled by some opposite force, the boy finished his work, draped a blanket over Clark's shoulders and left the room.

'Improving, thank you.' Again, that wariness. 'Are you wanting to question me further?'

Grayling attempted a smile. 'Well, we're still a long way short of Sydney.' Receiving no response, he continued. 'When we left off a couple of days ago, you were telling me about the walk along the beaches towards the east. I then took up the story with Mr Figge and he was able to describe the point of land where the coast swung north. He told me of your meeting with the natives he called the'—Grayling checked his notes—'the Kurnai people, and then he said that you got to a river and that was the end of their lands.'

'That's his assumption,' Clark answered gruffly. 'I saw no clear evidence of the beginnings and ends of lands, or whether they even had borders. Once we crossed that river, the *Nadgee* they called it, I heard all sorts of names being tossed…' He was racked momentarily by powerful coughing. 'Tossed about. *Yuin, Guyangal, Thaua*…' His hands rose and fell with exasperation.

'Mmm. Mr Figge mentioned that you were unimpressed with them.'

'There wasn't a great deal to be impressed with. Hospitable enough, but I saw no evidence of modern society among them. They could be subdued without incident, I believe, in the course of opening the land. They seemed to gravitate towards the lascars, which I think tells you all you need to know.'

Grayling dwelled a moment on that comment. He felt that its obvious meaning was not the intended one. 'Did they not respect you, Mr Clark?'

Clark regarded him sullenly. 'Insofar as they were capable of any intercourse with us, lieutenant, they directed it to the boy's father, the *serang*.'

'And Mr Figge encouraged them in that practice?'

'Mr Figge does not abide authority, if that's what you're asking.'

'Was he undermining you?'

'What sort of question is that? We were trying to survive, lieutenant.'

Grayling waited. He had annoyed Clark, raised his blood. That was no bad thing.

'Can I ask you one more thing, while I am making a nuisance of myself? Then I will return to listening quietly to your tale.' He didn't wait for Clark's response. 'On the island, on Preservation I mean, what measures did you see Mr Figge take to secure his cargo?'

'The tea, you mean?'

'Yes, he's a tea merchant—what did he do about the tea?'

'I—I don't remember.' Clark seemed puzzled. 'None, I don't suppose. Some of it was jettisoned when we were trying to lighten the ship. At the end, you know. And once we were established on the island Captain Hamilton ordered the crew to unload as much of it as they could manage. Mr Figge seemed content with that, as far as I recall.'

'Did he request that it be taken over to the other island, to Rum Island, so that it was out of the way?'

'I would be fairly sure he did not. People don't gorge themselves on tea, you know. What are you trying to establish, lieutenant?'

'Oh, nothing at all, sir.' Grayling laughed, looking to retreat as gently as he could. 'Sometimes I become preoccupied with foolish details. Now let me get you going with the story again. There is this excerpt I hoped you might elaborate upon:

> 'April 2nd.—Travelled 8 miles this forenoon. In the mid-morning we were most agreeably surprised by meeting five of the natives, our old friends, who received us in a very amicable manner, and kindly treated us with some shellfish, which formed a very acceptable meal, as our small pittance of rice was nearly expended. After this little repast we proceeded 6 miles further and halted.

'So these "old friends" were the Kurnai?'

'No, these were the Thaua. We had the shellfish. The ear-shells, you know them? Spiral, like a flat snail, very tough flesh. *Gurun*, they called it. And they had killed a whale and we had eaten some of that with them, though the men found the flesh hard to keep down.'

'They killed a *whale*? Do they have boats?'

'No.' Clark shrugged. 'There was…' He appeared to change his mind about something. 'They just speared it on the beach.'

'Remarkable.' Grayling wrote this detail down, scratching a hard asterisk into the page to remind him to come back. 'Then there was this, the following day:

> '*3rd.—Had a fatiguing march over very high bluffs, sharp rocks…interspersed with stumps of trees and other sharp substances, by which our feet were so much bruised and wounded that some of the party remained lame for some time afterwards; and to aggravate our sufferings we were now living upon a quarter of a pint of dry rice per diem. As we got out of this harassing thicket we missed two of our unhappy fellow-travellers. At 4 p.m. we provided ourselves a lodging for the night, having walked, or rather crawled, 10 miles, over the ground above described.*

'What do you mean you "missed" them, sir?'

'They just…it was Thompson and Kennedy. They got themselves lost because they sat down to tend to their feet and we moved off, not realising they weren't with us. An easy mistake to make.'

> '*4th.—Waited for our missing companions until 12 o'clock, when, to our great joy, they made their appearance; we then proceeded on our journey…*

'A full night and morning you say they were gone. That seems…surprising.'

'And you, lieutenant, seem hell-bent on cross-examining me. Once you are lost in that country, the situation compounds itself every passing minute. The way you should go looks like the way you've already been. The surface is rock, as I wrote, so you don't leave footprints.'

'Couldn't they merely have called out?'

'Nobody was much spirited for calling by this point.'

⁂

I can hear this lieutenant closing in on you, Mr Clark. He will come to the truths I cannot speak, and I pray only that he reaches them before anyone else is harmed. *Our missing companions*! I wish I had known how you would slant this tale in the journal—I would have left when I had the chance.

Yes, they had sat down to rest their feet—not that their feet were any worse than anyone else's.

What kept them, at first, was the girl. We had all seen her, though she tried to avoid our eyes. She was naked, just some strings and such about her, and although she might have been younger than me, she was grown as a woman.

The last finger of her left hand was gone: something I had noticed before, and only on the girls. I remember my eyes fell on the back of her thighs, the most perfect thing I had ever seen. The sun on them, the long curve of a soft surface, taut when she moved: hard muscle under skin that glowed. I was drawn to her, but at least I fought myself. When she looked back over her shoulder in our direction I saw the face of a girl, not a woman, and I felt shamed by my own body. Her eyes were kind and so pretty, and I fancied she was on an errand—for her mother maybe—though I had no good reason to think it. She stood on the rock shelf above the water, looking into the rock pools. And those pig-men, Mr Kennedy and Mr Thompson: they stared at her, hungry.

The girl dived in. She was gone a long time beneath the surface, then she came out with her hair laid down wet and her hands full of the *gurun* shells. She did it again and again. The times she stood full out of the water, the drips spilling and running over her breasts and her belly: still now my body pulls tight at the memory of it.

You were right—we did get up to move off. It seemed the wise thing to do, with all the men now looking at her. If she had noticed us, she did not show it. But those two vultures, they moved straight towards her. And I watched you, Mr Clark, and I saw the decision you made as you watched the thirteen of us: our fury at what was about to happen. You drew out the short sword. Raised it in challenge—not to them but to us—and ordered us to move on.

As you pushed me forward I looked back once. The girl had seen them now; there was fear in her kind eyes. A warning she'd been given now turning to truth.

The last I heard as I dragged my feet up the hill and into the bush was her scream, and then the splash. And I tried to believe as I walked on that the splash was her escape: her refuge in the arms of the sea.

You walked us as far as we could stand, Mr Clark, and we collapsed many miles from where we had left those men to their deed. The same as always: the hope of cover under dead branches and leaves, the turning and aching on the hard ground. But when the sun rose and we opened our weary eyes, a party of Thaua men stood there. In the early weeks we'd posted a watch, before the marching overtook us, but even had we kept up our watches, these men would not have been seen. They were not there: and then they were. They carried their weapons. Not raised, but there to see. No one needed to ask why they had come. Mr Kennedy and Mr Thompson were with them, eyes on the ground. The word you used later: *hostages*, though no one had a hand on them.

You started talking, Mr Clark, as though the matter was yours to control. *Now listen here, good fellows. Which of you is in charge?* Again, as before, they ignored you, and they spoke to my father. Fast and sharp, razor-words in flakes like the heads on the *cannadiul* spears. You gave up when you saw they would not listen to you. Besides, the time for you to seek respect had passed back at the rock pool.

Six hours it took us, begging and apologising for those wicked men. The loss of all the calico we had left, and the short sword and two of the knives. And when they finally handed the pig-men back to us unharmed, the Thaua's faces showed us only disgust. The shared feast was in the past now. Their guiding down secret ways, their shelter and their trust—ashes.

Nobody could bear to ask what the men had done, nor learn the state of the girl. At some stage it became clear Mr Figge had formed a view. At a moment during the afternoon's walk he took Mr Kennedy by the neck without a word and dragged him to the ground. He screamed for mercy but none was shown. No one moved to protect him; no one felt any kinship for him at all as Mr Figge drove his fists into that mean old head again and again until the blood was no longer coming from wounds you could see, but the face itself was one broken fruit and still he was hitting him. And each blow brought a small grunt of effort from Mr Figge, flecks of splattered blood getting in his eyes, but other than that he was silent and calm as a man chopping wood.

After a time, he dropped Mr Kennedy to the ground and stood tall again, a little out of breath, and he frowned at one fist and pulled a tooth from his knuckle and flicked it at the man's face. Then he lifted him by his throat and examined his eyes a moment. Once satisfied he was still alive, he dropped him to the earth. Mr Thompson watched all of this in silence, for if one thing could be said for certain, it was that his time would come, too. It was the dark genius of Mr Figge that none could tell when.

It wasn't long after that—the fifth of April, you said—that we came upon the wide, sandy bay: four miles of it, a river at its southern end and another to its north. The southern one we knew we could ford easy enough. We had no way of knowing this river meant we would leave the Guyangal, or the ones who called themselves Thaua, but there was a change of some kind. Their men came to see us off—I would say to farewell us, but there was no fondness in it.

They examined Mr Kennedy's beaten face and nodded. One of them took hold of Mr Thompson with a look that said *why is this one unmarked?* They were calm, careful. They took my father's hands and pointed across the river, told him that what lay there was *Djirringanji*. Once again, I did not know if this *Djirringanji* was a people or a place, or if there was no difference for our hosts. They were still using that word, *Yuin*, like it was a great nation of some kind, and these other words for people like *Thaua* and *Djirringanji* lived within it somehow, as we Bengalis were Indians too. My father listened patiently, and muttered his thanks.

We made to gather our things and ford the river, but the men bade us wait and stepped into the shallows with their spears up. Two of them walked easy, eyes on the shadows of the trees. One who had waded deeper coiled himself like a spring and let fly at the surface. The spear stuck, then moved away upright as if walking off. The man darted after it, taking hold of the shaft as a strong tail whipped the water. He grabbed hold of the tail and pulled it behind him as he walked out of the river and onto the shallow slope of the sandbank. Then he lifted out a fine shark, about four feet long. It thrashed its head at the spear and at the arm that held it but the tip had gone deep.

How had this beast had been patrolling around us as we stood knee deep, without us ever being aware of it? We are blind men here.

A fire was made. We sat, and the shark was sliced clean along its frame into belts of pearl-coloured flesh. The Thaua men roasted these on sticks and handed each to the Bengali men. Taking their food at the hands of the Bengalis did nothing for the mood of the gentlemen.

I remember the sorrow of that meal, Mr Clark. The shame of it. We saw your shame that day, even if you hide it now from the lieutenant. The offering of the shark meat said *never come back here*.

⁃⁞⁃

Grayling wanted to give Clark more room, allow him to expand his tale. He was about to resume his questioning when the faintest of sounds caught his attention. A mere brush, the squeak of one floorboard beyond the door.

The boy. He placed the observation to one side, focused on Clark.

'You say the Guyangal country—or this, you said, Thaua

country—ended at a river, Mr Clark? That seems to be the way your journal has it.'

'A river, yes. Shallow enough; and we were fortunate to catch a shark in the shallows. We'd eaten that, so we were well fortified. Let me see…a short rocky headland on the far side of the river and we found ourselves out in the sunshine on this bonny curve of beach, dolphins in great numbers just beyond the breakers. The going was better along the beach. You can imagine, lieutenant: warm sun, the sand flat and hard and the wind soft. You feel as though you could walk forever. The only one struggling was Mr Kennedy, who was at that time quite unwell and had to be assisted along his way.

'The second river crossing, the one at the northern end of the bay, gave us more trouble, and Mr Kennedy being indisposed, we resolved to go inland in preference to building another of our rafts. The walk took us over hills covered in yellow daisies, and though the river frustrated us, we'd eaten well and were moving over good ground. Much like the haughs, you remember?

'My concern as we lay down that night was to keep the party together: there were rumblings among the lascars that I neither understood nor cared to investigate. It is the way of their people that something is always the matter: on shipboard they are known to be malcontents, which is why a good captain always keeps them occupied.

'Of course they'd suffered, lieutenant. We'd all suffered; there was no room for special sympathies.

'Mr Figge was developing an infection in the back of his hand which was limiting his ability to assist with the ordinary tasks like preparing food. Though I shouldn't say that: he never did anyway. He usually ate by himself, ripping away at small animals he'd captured along the walk, apparently indifferent to their size or shape. Nothing about the food seemed to trouble him: he would devour it noisily and lick it from his hands, whether raw or cooked; untroubled by any distinction between meat and offal. You will see, he's retained the most weight of all of us. I watched him eating this way one particular night: he had a medium-sized animal a little like a cat, but spotted. I watched him cracking small bones in his jaw and pulling gristle from his teeth and I wondered, had his manners dropped away so sharp in just a few weeks? If he'd always been this way, there must have been consternation when he dined with the tea people.

'A certain wariness grew in us, for we had gone three days by now without seeing a native. The last lot, the Thaua; they were friendly enough but I saw no reason to be confident that would continue. They were capricious. There was no doubt that our greatest peril lay in the whims of these people. The lascars havered away and gave these people new names every time we crossed a major river, but their essential nature never changed. No more than it does here, I dare say. We were in discord about how to deal with them, lieutenant. Let me be blunt with you. We'd tried ingratiating ourselves, giving out trinkets, and it had won us some favour. But we were low on all of our supplies now, almost bereft of functioning weapons.'

'There was no immediate threat posed, was there?'

'We'd had no trouble up to this point, I grant you. But the case remained for constant vigilance. Some of them were in favour of just going along as we were—the trinkets, the acting as though we were a circus sideshow: all the touching and laughing and poking and pulling they engaged in. I'm a Scotsman, lieutenant, like you, and frankly it's tiresome to be prodded by savages.

'Thompson and Kennedy wanted to meet them with force,

185

which was just preposterous. We knew there were hordes of them out there. We didn't even know if our guns worked, and we would've perished in an instant if we'd relied on the blade or two we had left. The natives had spears. They had throwing sticks, tomahawks. We were exhausted anyway. Not Figge, of course.'

'What do you mean?'

'He kept his health, as I said. Probably the only one who could've put up a fight.'

Grayling's face creased in confusion. He opened the battered book on his lap and turned carefully through the pages until he found the passage he wanted. Clark watched this calmly, knowing what Grayling sought.

'Mr Clark, you say in your journal that a couple of days after this—you were still inland, I believe—you did indeed come into some sort of conflict? I, err, I'm referring to this:

> '8th.—Bent our way towards the beach this morning, and travelled along about 9 miles, when we were stopped by our old impediment, a river, at which we were obliged to wait until low water before we could cross. We had scarcely surmounted this difficulty when a greater danger stared us in the face, for here we were met by about fifty armed natives. Having never before seen so large a body collected, it is natural to conclude that we were much alarmed. However, we resolved to put the best appearance on the matter, and to betray no symptoms of fear. In consequence of the steps we took, and after some preliminary signs and gestures on both sides, we came to some understanding, and the natives were apparently amicable in their designs. We presented them with a few yards of calico, for they would not be satisfied with small

stripes, and, indeed, we were glad to get rid of them at
any expence, for their looks and demeanour were not
such as to invite greater intimacy.

Clark had listened with a hand over his chin, reflecting on the words he had written in extremity, read back to him now in the safety of a quiet room.

'I am not easily frightened, lieutenant. But these savages are quick between moods.'

⚜

Go on, tell them, Mr Clark. Tell them what the matter was. That these people, the Djirringanji, had learnt through their own means about the type of men we had brought among them. That they were not going to allow you and Mr Figge and the other two passage without bond of their good conduct.

They stood like the trees on the ridge above us: one, then three, then a dozen, twenty, fifty. Staring down at us with scorn on their faces. Is it possible, Mr Clark, that we were not some kind of gods among these people, but clumsy flesh and no tools? Dying on our feet in a land where these people lived at ease?

The men on the ridge came down and it felt like we would be tried, that was how my father saw it. *They are calling upon us to justify ourselves*, he said to me, quiet.

They had weapons: long, thin spears aimed at some point between the ground and our hearts, which said they could be moved either way. The sun picked out the chips of shell they had glued to the barbs and I imagined them breaking off inside me, lodging like curses. They also held the spear-throwing sticks they called *wumeras*—clacking and sliding, soft in their ready hands.

Just a movement now could fill the air with missiles.

They waited and let us weaken further in our fear. Then

they sent their senior men forward, older men with anger in their eyes that sparked and flamed into a burst of yelling and pointing. Fixed upon Kennedy and Thompson. Of course.

Your calming gestures, Mr Clark, smiling like a man selling a lame mare. I'd not yet seen such an act from you, and nor had Mr Figge, for he burst into unhelpful laughter. The Djirringanji did not know how to take this. They watched you, watched Mr Figge, and began their shouting again.

My father stepped forward, and for just a moment I felt his age, felt the strain in the movement. But he rose because he was the *serang*: his authority had survived the wrecks and he carried it in the bush, as much as Mr Thompson or Mr Clark had lost theirs. Perhaps it was this that the Djirringanji sensed, for their mood changed as they watched him. He was a still spot in the moving, whispering crowd: when he sat and looked up, the leaders of the Djirringanji sat too. By slowly drawing on the ground, he was able to show them that we wished to walk north, and that we were all friends. To play out this last point, he got up and embraced me, then Mr Kennedy and Mr Thompson and Mr Figge; finally even you, Mr Clark—wooden as a board.

The Djirringanji spoke to each other and my father waited with his eyes down. We knew he had calmed them. The most senior man raised a hand and waved his agreement, though he did not offer friendship.

Such a moment for you, Mr Clark, to make a gift of some lengths of cloth. The old man spoke to those behind him and one came forward with a kangaroo's tail, stepping past you to present it to my father.

The bolts of calico lay there at the old man's feet and he looked at them, then looked at you as if to say, *Get this rubbish away from me*. He did not move a finger to pick them up.

26

'Is the packing making a difference?'

Clark was sitting up in his bed again, a book face-down on his lap. An irritable breeze was harassing the town, whipping leaves and dust through the sash window on the far side of the room. Grayling crossed by the foot of the bed and closed the window as the stray leaves swirled at his feet.

Clark regarded his bandaged hands, turned them over front and back like misplaced parcels. 'No, lieutenant, it is not. I fear the holes will not fill.' He remained in mournful contemplation for a moment. 'How is your wife coming along?'

Grayling was surprised by the inquiry. 'Very well, thank you sir. It is remarkable how quickly her health returned after Mr—after the parasite was removed.'

Clark looked furtively towards the door. 'You will say it is not my concern. But you should not let that man anywhere near your wife. I am pleased she is recovered, but…'

'But what?'

'Never place yourself in his debt.'

Grayling forced a smile. 'She is well, Mr Clark, I am grateful for that. Now come—we have much to discuss. Would you care to take some sun today? I feel we should be making the most of it before the season turns.'

Clark hauled himself from the bed, his expression still wary, and Grayling took him gently by the elbow.

'How are your feet? Are you up to this?'

'Yes, yes. Fine.' Clark pushed the damaged feet into a pair of slippers and they made their way, arm in arm, through the door of the cabin and out into the light. The front of the house was in the lee of the wind; a pool of still air collected on the verandah.

'So,' Grayling began. 'It seems that by the eleventh of April, you'd reached this large loch, and I take it from your account that you had a couple of native men accompanying you.'

'Aye, different people again. They spoke to us at great length; hand signals and so on. *Walbanja*, they said.'

'That's the tribe?'

'I suppose so. They were still saying *Guyangal* also. You can't distinguish. They called the lake *wallaga*. And they took us up a little hill so that we could look over it, because you see in the centre of the thing was this island that was shaped perfectly like a duck. Climbed a damned hill—in our state—to be shown an island shaped like a duck. This is why you can never quite take them seriously. But the island, anyway, they called it '*umbarra*': that's 'island'. Or 'duck', I don't know. But I, yes.'

'You what, Mr Clark?'

'I suddenly felt this terrible keening for home.' The wind toyed with the strands of Clark's hair, and the age that the ordeal had added to him suddenly fell away. Grayling realised it was the first time he'd felt truly sorry for him.

'Why?'

'*Umbarra*, I suppose. I heard it as "umbrel-la". And the duck, so absurd, and I just thought of the glens and the lochs back home. There's precious little here that reminds you of anything familiar.'

'No, I suppose that's right. These Walbanja people, were they friendly or hostile?'

'Friendly, in their way. They found us a meal of mussels. Didn't sit well in every man's belly. We were having trouble keeping food down by then, and mussels can be disagreeable at the best of times. But, hm. Hungry, so we took the chance.'

'The Walbanja weren't to know that, I imagine.'

'No, but nor can you discount their potential for treachery. The ones who guided us, even camped with us—there were occasions when they greeted others who just appeared, and then you'd find that those ones had spears hidden in the grass. They'd come up very agreeable but they had other options if needed, you understand.'

'Did the guiding assist you? I imagine their intimacy with the coast must have been helpful.'

Clark appeared momentarily puzzled. 'The odd thing was, they didn't go straight up the coast.'

'But they knew where *you* were trying to go?'

'I assume they did: we gave them every indication. They looked north and they said *kuru*. This was an interesting aspect, lieutenant. There were very difficult hills to our west throughout those early days of April, and sometimes they crowded all the way in to the coast. These natives, the Walbanja, they didn't necessarily follow the shoreline. Sometimes they took us deep inland. We followed a river valley at one stage, far into the hills until we were all quite cold. There was discussion among us about whether we were being led into a trap, or if they were simply entertaining themselves at our expense.'

'Why would they bother to do such a thing?'

'As I said, lieutenant, one must reckon with their duplicity. *Wadbilliga*. Had I written that down?'

Grayling checked the journal, sun bright on the pages. 'No, you hadn't.'

'That was the place they led us through. Bastard country, hard on the feet. Thick growth that tore at us for days.'

A detachment was being assembled down the hill, a cluster of brightly coloured uniforms and glinting metal. A sergeant shouting orders, children circling as close as they dared to watch the spectacle and pack horses draped with chains for their quarry. Grayling normally knew who was being sent out, and in pursuit of whom. This one he had no idea about. He concluded it was the Corps, pursuing their own ends. He turned again to Clark.

'These others that would visit while you were being guided: did you find that unnerving?'

'Sometimes, aye. The business with the hiding of spears and the like. Unpredictable. The best we could do was to make ourselves the objects of humour. Funny faces, singing songs… but you can only go so far in making a man like Mr Figge appear harmless. I believe they had their private views about him.'

Again, his veiled references to Figge. Grayling made a note of it. 'What about the lascars? What would they have thought of these natives?'

'They appeared to view them favourably, and I believe the

lascars felt warmly towards the natives.' Clark stood abruptly and winced as his feet took his weight. He turned back towards the house. Grayling took this as an indication that the discussion was over.

'Aye,' Clark finished. 'Turned out to be mistaken, of course.'

27

There's no finer feeling than strength returning. Food prepared for you; the caress of clean sheets.

I imagine Clark still mopes about, grieving for his failed fortune and nursing those ridiculous paws of his. His lascar boy I have not seen, though I believe they keep him near to Clark. His whereabouts may become a matter of some importance to me. Depending how things turn out.

I can walk the township now, chop a little wood: *thock thock*. I talk to the natives, morose crowd that they are. I sit on the verandah in the mornings and take in the sun, listen to the birds. My celebrity precedes me down these rutted streets: a swept hat, a short burst of applause or a blushing curtsey. As far as the barracks are concerned, I am neither in custody nor, I suspect, entirely free to go. But that is the way of the whole place—ask a convict whether they are imprisoned and they will answer, *That, sir, is the riddle.* They come back voluntarily when they bolt, men who've found the ghost of themselves somewhere in the night, in the trees. Begging to have the irons back on.

⚓

Through early April with the coast insisting north, Clark mumbles one day out of his prognostications that we'd be around two hundred miles from Sydney. Covering an average of eight miles a day, perhaps allowing for a slowing as fatigue worsens us, we might be only a month from our destination. He knows and I know that our project has become pressing.

We're stopped by a lake: low country, easier going but a vicious-looking range of hills in the background. A couple of the natives are walking with us: three times these men have materialised as we stood at the edge of a river. They have names for each of them that sound like the honks of rutting animals. *Nurooma. Morooya.* They move us upstream or down, because invariably we've selected the wrong point at which to cross. This knowledge they share unguardedly and with evident pride. My imbecile shipmates scoff and grumble each time they are relocated, but they know the worth of it by now.

Once placed at the appropriate crossing, the natives indicate with the usual choreography that they want us to wait, and then scurry off into the bush, returning with a canoe they'd dry-docked somewhere nearby. These are beautiful craft; perhaps even more elegant than the ones we saw further back. Even with an occupant in them, they draw no more than eight inches of water and stir barely a ripple on the surface. The paddler seats himself—though just as often it is the women paddling them—on a soft sheet of bark with legs tucked under, arse on heels and bony knees employed in steadying the sides. They use wooden paddles that look like cooking spoons, one in each hand. To see them in motion is to watch the progress of a delicate insect.

We discover the extent of the natives' skill—and the lack of our own—when we reach the third of the rivers, having covered twelve miles. This time the riverbank bears no sign of our friends. Thompson evidently expects them to be standing there like Thames boatmen. *Can't rely on 'em*, he mutters. *They's boats'll be 'ere somewhere*, he mutters. He goes off searching through the undergrowth. Sure enough, ten minutes later he's procured himself a canoe. *Not so fuckin smart then are they*, and he slides the thing into the shallows. You can feel the lascars settling in for the show, and probably the natives, somewhere back in the deep forest, because what happens next is not unexpected.

Thompson gives the craft a shove with his hands on both the gunwales and tries to swing his legs in as the flow of the river gets a hold of it. He lands with half his arse in and the other half out: the canoe continues into the stream and he's left hanging sideways for a second before the whole thing flips and deposits him in the drink. He's already a good fifty yards downstream from us and heading for the mouth, which is not that much further on. The canoe is picked up by the current in its swirls and spun towards an eddy that holds some branches and there it sticks fast, upside down.

Thompson resurfaces spluttering and cursing, hair all down over his face like a fool, and the lot of us bellowing with laughter. At first, he has his feet on sturdy ground and he stands chest-deep calling us arse-cocklings and sons of damned whores, but then the river gets to work on him and he's much too busy for abuse. He starts tilting backwards, pushing against the current, but it's a good deal stronger than a half-starved Englishman so he employs his arms in frantic paddling, trying to stay upright.

Laughter dies in throats and Clark orders the lascars to

extend him a branch. He's only a few yards from the edge, and a good bough would reach him, but something has changed in them. For a moment it's more transfixing than the drowning fool, the sight of these twelve standing stony-faced.

Thompson's pleading now. Clark's screaming at them: *if you won't get a branch then get in the fucking water and pull him out.* Nobody moves. Plainly this is their common design, and it brooks no discussion. So Clark blusters forward, aiming a fist at the nearest brown face. He misses and staggers to stay upright in front of the intended victim, who stares contempt down on him.

And all the while Thompson is disappearing. He's sucked in some water, and the river has him: he's off his feet and borne fast by it, a good eighty yards from us, his head a lump of pallid meat in boiling water, bobbing and vanishing and lacking only the accompanying turnips. We move along the bank to follow his progress, though it's clear this won't involve any kind of help from the lascars.

Clark's on his feet, storming around them as they walk downstream on the pebbles of the bank. *Get him*, he screams at me, noting my relaxed saunter. I shrug. It is diverting, the impotent rage of a man with nothing to command.

Throughout these dramas, I'm watching Kennedy, and past him to the drowning wretch, when very suddenly the carpenter leaps in fright away from the scrub and towards the water's edge. For two of the Walbanja have now arrived, and by their focused movement it's clear they've assessed it all: us quickstepping along the bank, the overturned canoe wedged in the timbers and Thompson face-down and stuck now by the shreds of his clothes in the same snag.

They are young men, not painted, carrying nothing in hand.

They run featherlight over the shallows and splash in deeper, not fighting the current but riding it so that one spin takes them this way and another the opposite. In seconds one of them reaches Thompson and rights him; the other does likewise for the canoe. Then begins the tricky operation of manoeuvring him onto the delicate craft, which, with some effort, they achieve.

Thompson's a sorry sight on the bank, laid out so he drapes on the stones like wet washing. The natives have him face-down, and they press on his back while they speak their lingo over him. For a time, he fails to respond: then he stirs and starts heaving his guts onto the pebbles, yielding little of course but water and bile. I study his feet: the holes and abscesses soaked white, the long cuts revealing pink slashes of his flesh. His entire body is racked by shivers he cannot control: he shakes as if possessed. The river's done nine-tenths of my work.

The natives lean back from Thompson's slumped form and look to the rest of us, faces unmarked. If they feel any resentment over the theft of their canoe, they give no sign of it. And if they're confused to see we did not rush to him, that's disguised too.

Long moments he lies there, unattended by anyone, and I feel the urge deep within me to take up a river stone and deliver the last tenth. Crush his skull and splatter his brains on the sunlit rock for the flies to carry off. He's been a liability all along, and now he'll be a further impediment while he recovers from his riverpickling.

The sun must have dried out his innards, for at length he begins to moan. The natives produce a small kangaroo they'd been carrying and had left on the bank during Clark's rescue. Now a strange ceremony ensues, the younger man shaking the thing with its tongue lolling dead from its furry snout, then grinning and dropping it by the front of the canoe. I can see that the only reason they were late arriving at the riverbank, giving Thompson the opportunity to thieve the canoe and almost bringing about his end, was that they were obtaining the meat for us. Oh, what ungracious swine we are!

The two of them sit there, regarding us in silence. Deep judgments in the making, I suppose. Have they read what passes between the lascars and us? I wonder if they have any sense of their own endangerment at the hands of our chums in Sydney, whose civic aims blandly require their extermination? More specifically, can they read the plans in my heart, the nefarious intent visible only and even then only partially—to Clark?

Thompson raises himself to a lopsided crouch. Seeing he's up, we indicate to the natives that we wish to be on our way. North draws us inexorably towards itself, no doubt a subject of some curiosity to the Walbanja. Clark stands and studies the compass and his sodden watch: I doubt either remains operable but he clutches them like regalia, fooling only himself with his pomposity. A child could see what is required here: Sydney lies to the north-east: provided we keep the ocean on our right, and provided the sun rises each day more or less in the middle of it, we cannot lose our way.

The Walbanja men empty the water from the canoe and I watch one of them, the older of the two, making some minor repairs with a ball of tinted gum that comes from his purse. He's humming to himself as he works on the bark, his back turned to me, trusting no harm could come. From me, of all people.

These craft are well capable of carrying two men, and our friends spend the next hour ferrying us one by one, chattering happily as they paddle. Never once does an accident occur: not a drop of water is suffered to land on us or our measly belongings.

Arranged on the other side, we sit awhile, making what passes for conversation—you can get a fair bit done with gestures—until eventually, seeing that the two Walbanja men aren't about to leave us, I gather a small pile of firewood and gesture that we might cook the *walabee*. The lascars have somehow damaged the flint that was keeping us alive, fucking silly bastards, and now we must undertake a pantomime for the natives, rubbing our hands and making shivering noises to indicate our need for a spark. They know full well what the problem is—a tinderbox that works when it fucking well pleases—but they wait for the entire display so they can laugh and produce the sticks.

The younger one sits on his arse and points his knees outwards with the soles of his feet together, so the frontal viewer receives an unobscured view to his chop and bags. He places a long stick end-first in a slot on a flatter stick which he has laid on the ground, as though stepping a mast in a tiny model ship. Then he rubs the tall stick between his palms so it rotates fast in the groove, steadying the whole operation with his feet. The older one watches all this with evident satisfaction: then he cradles a handful of dry fibres just near the end of the stick. The spinning produces hot dust, which he scoops into his ball of tinder, blowing gently on it.

This trick captivated us each time we saw it: at first nothing much occurs, then a puff of smoke appears and increases, building to a magical point when a little *whoomf* issues forth, and the ball of fibre bursts into flame. This time, to reduce the need for puffing, the older man stands and whirls the fibre-ball around in his extended hand so the breeze does the work. Or perhaps he merely does this for theatre: everything is a performance.

The natives depart in their mysterious way once the fire's going. Kennedy and Clark have been out since we landed on this side of the river; the former without notice to anyone, sly

❦ 200

cur, and the latter surveying a route for the following day. By the time Clark returns, slouched and limping, we've built the fire up and allowed it to burn back down again, making a bed of good coals. We've got the little kangaroo on it, filling the air with the foody stink of singeing fur, its little dark eyes shrunk in like raisins dried by the cleansing heat, the puppydog nose perished and shrivelled to leather. I confess by now I want to rip the thing from the embers and gnaw on it, but I am on my best behaviour.

And in wanders this ridiculous twat, shrinks in horror from the bubbling rat on the fire and declares that we can't eat it.

Fucking watch me, I reply.

It's Friday, he says. *Sixteen April by my reckoning.*

So? says someone.

Good Friday. No matter our straitened circumstances, I will not have us reduced to the state of these—he waves at the bush—*people*. With but three fingers I could lay waste to the pious look on his dial, but I'm struck dumb with disbelief. Clark starts trying to drag the roast from the fire. The spectacle's unpopular enough with Thompson, who's protesting feebly between fits of coughing, but the lascars can't believe it. Whatever god or gods they worship, seems they'd not deny a feed to men slowly starving. Their ribs are starker than the ones on the charring rodent, and Clark has sorely tested the bounds of their tolerance with this display. It takes the endless forbearance of the old man, Prasad, to keep them in order. It's a feat of no little skill. Some of them are plant-eaters, on account of their religion, but the majority are most definitely not. He speaks in some Indostani patter: they respond quietly in assent.

At which point Kennedy turns up.

What's going on? he inquires, sensing the mood.

Fuckhead here's holding a conventicle, I tell him.

It's Good Friday and we will observe a short fast from the taking of meat. It won't kill anyone, says the newly appointed bishop.

Well I'm not wi' the kirk, laughs Thompson, *and I doubt these darkies are neither*. He takes a step towards the smoking meat, now lying in the grass, and grabs it by one paw. And then things get interesting. Clark takes up the tomahawk and gets himself between the man and the meat. *I'll thank you to step back, Mr Kennedy*, he says. There's a part of me watching this charade that thinks *you didn't look so lively in defence of the girl*, but he gets his way and Kennedy backs off, looking thunder at old Clarkey.

But while the two of them are locking horns the roast is unattended, so I lean over and tear off a leg. It's delicious. By the time Clark looks back I'm having difficulty gnawing on the thing because the chuckling's got me. He summons all his little fury into a glare that only makes me laugh harder. I wave the bone at him.

'Come on, reverend. Have a go. It's delicious.'

He raises the tomahawk again but I don't believe his heart's in it. Is he angry on his Lord's behalf, or because I've defied him? Just in case, I stand up while I eat.

He swings it, fuck him. Level with my eyeballs.

I have to take the thing by its handle as it comes round. I can hold his eyes there and he lacks the steel, of course, to stare me down; a little more pressure and he has to concede the weapon. I smack him halfweight with the back of the blade and drop it at his feet.

It takes the poor idiot long minutes to regain his composure, holding his jaw where I clocked him. Then he sends the crew off to gather roots as we have seen the natives do, leaving only me and the deathly looking Thompson there beside the fire.

Scruffy ruminants they are, grumbling and cracking their way through the undergrowth. I sit myself back down by the warm glow, chewing on the *walabee* leg as Thompson's glazed eyes watch me. He is pale, maybe near expiring. *Please*, he says. But his wants are none of my concern.

Eventually they all return clutching their daft handfuls of greenery which they proceed to chew and spit. I've ripped the leg down to the bone and tossed it and Clark fixes me with a furious stare. Thompson sleeps now; the rest are out of earshot. I speak even and quiet to Clark.

Which of them dies, then?

He feigns horror, the hypocrite.

You know how it is to go. It's you and me reaches Sydney. I didn't invite any of these.

He looks at his mangled feet.

Why don't you set us underway, Clarkey? Take Thompson in his sleep. I'm talking soft, making a lullaby for Mr Pious with his bunch of spinach. *No match for you in his condition. Just pinch his wee nose and clamp his mouth. Two or three twitches and your good lord's taken him. Hmm?*

Nothing.

You do that and I'll do the next three.

He's still fascinated by his feet. I need to do the talk again.

If any of them makes it to Sydney, I sigh, *they will tell of the state of that ship. The one* you *bought, suicidal fucking tub of a thing. The company will never darken the doors of New South Wales again. And oh—if Hamilton gets there, first thing he says to save his own skin? 'Clarkey made me do it.' They know about your debts. They'll tell the company.*

It delights me, the panic inside him.

The deal holds: the insurance money's yours, every penny, and you can forget me and disown me, and once those brave idiots on the rock are dead and rotting, I'll tend to the casks. What do you say, hm?

He finally looks up. *Go to the fucking devil, Mr Figge.*

Don't be like that, now. These all are going to die out here regardless. You and I, we're merely hastening the process. No harm enriching ourselves at the same time.

I swear his lip quivers. *Well if they're going to die, they're not going to tell. There's no need for me in the thing.*

Fine, I shrug. *I'll start it then. But I'm telling you I'm starting it, see? So you best stop me somehow if you don't want it to start.*

He neither moves nor speaks.

Just as I thought.

⁂

The fire died and the bush went quiet, and the shufflers and the yippers were done with their chorus.

Then a new sound began: moaning, and the gurgling of bowels. It started with either Thompson or, more likely, Kennedy, for the one who still lay there was coughing. The other one rose and groaned a little, took himself ten yards aside and sprayed his guts on the undergrowth. He made no attendance to his arse but hitched the remnants of his strides and lay down again.

Within minutes, the lascars were moving likewise. One by one they stood and bolted to the cover of the bush to squirt and spew their poor choice of victuals from both ends. The kangaroo sat well in my guts, and no more than contented wind had escaped me all evening. I lay with my head on a small nest of leaves I'd gathered, hands under one cheek as I'd become accustomed to do. Any man with two hands has a pillow.

I pondered deeply as the shitters came and went, and before long I came to realise that the old man was the answer. I saw what was clear about him: that the Bengalis loved him, that he was their quiet and unshifting lodestar, that rarest of men who knows what to do and how to act. Twelve lascars, him at their head. Christ, he was their Christ. And so I must be his Caiaphas. But I was a man like any other: I couldn't very well eliminate twelve of them simultaneously, nor even by gradual increments.

Then it came to me: that perhaps their very devotion was the key to it.

Oh babbling Babel and Barabbas, the bony Messiah with his knuckly old head and its wispy hair. He was down to the thin trousers that had once been white but were now stained with the earth and his body's oozings, nothing to cover his concave chest anymore. Let's be reasonable: his days were numbered. And so I decided it.

The next day, we were again in the forest country, heavy and dark even in the middle of the day. The air was warm and still, mist blurring the middle distance. It shouldn't have been so easy to cut him away from the herd but there was little involved. *I am taking Prasad to search for the natives*, I announced, and Clark merely shrugged. The old man was surprised—it was not something we had done in our wanderings thus far. I came in close to him, took his hand where others could not see it, and placed it over the hilt of the knife, lodged in my belt. Then I whispered soft: *Refuse me and I will drive this blade through your son's heart.*

Love. A most dependable lever over a good man.

He pulled back, fear and alarm in his brown eyes. From across the camp, the boy was craning to see what was afoot. He looked torn, as one would expect: love of his father, fealty to Clark, which really was love of his father as well. He made a small move in the old man's direction and was called back by Clark: His Indolent Excellency required his midday victuals. The boy looked from me to his father, who made some tiny expression of resignation. He went to the boy, placed a hand on his shoulder and lowered his head. For a long moment his nose almost touched his fingers and the bone of the boy's shoulder. When he turned away, the boy stayed.

We walked through the giant trees, following a contour in the undergrowth that may have been a track, or perhaps just a string of coincidence. Upwards it wound and we followed it, both of us struggling on wounded feet. After an hour or more the path led to an open space that gave a view down: over the folding swells of the forested hills, out to the coast and the ocean beyond. The sky was vast and placid over the sea. Far below, a curl of smoke revealed the location of our fellows, the boy no doubt tending to that fire as he wrestled with the pot and the now-permissible remains of the kangaroo. The boy would be in turmoil; he sensed something.

I looked to the old man and found he was looking directly back at me. His eyes spoke of a clear understanding. Even as they darted to either side of me, seeking any available means of escape, they indicated his comprehension of what was happening.

I took Kennedy's knife from my belt.

You will care for the boy? he asked simply.

You have my word.

What now?

We need to walk further.

He pointed behind himself, deeper into the bush. Eyed the knife. *That way?*

His head never turned but once, when he reacted to the shouting of the yellerwhite birds that hung upside down by their claws, biffing one another. He eyed them with what might have been fear.

Never mind them. They's herbivores, I said. *'Twon't be them as takes you.*

There were faint shuffles and whispers in the undergrowth; the passage of unseen creatures.

Interesting though. Where are the predators on this land? Must be some. Wolves, maybe? Bears? I made a paw in the air but he didn't laugh.

I corrected him occasionally, to set him back on the path I wanted as the land tilted down, shadowed now, the darkness not far away. A chill had descended. Presently the trees gave way to an opening and I could hear water. We were passing along the side of a gigantic tree that had fallen across a creek, the rills of it now licking our feet. I cannot say for sure what place I was seeking, but this seemed about right. I thought to ask him if he was right with the Lord; but likely his gods were more complex than that.

At the point where the giant trunk crossed the creek bed, I took him by the shoulder—no force was required—and had him kneel in the damp hollow where the trunk met the ground. Rocks and small rushes and wet moss lined that final place. Such was his fear now that he was nearly all eyes. His breaths were short and urgent, an aspect of these moments I'd not been able to savour the last time, in Fort William, because I'd taken Figge—the previous Figge—by surprise.

The idea occurred to him, as it was always going to, that a chance might still be open. I saw his eyes move before his body reacted: he dashed left of me but I was on him. I clubbed him twice with the knife's hilt: the first one buckled him senseless and the second laid him out on the mat of soft humus.

I sat athwart him and thought about what could be done. His left hand had ended up between my feet, and I picked it up and took the knife to it, thinking of taking it off. I had watched the old boy and I knew him to be left-handed: this hand therefore responsible for both the highest and the lowest functions in his life. Were I to discommode him thus, it might be interesting: stuck out here he would eventually have to eat the hand. Such sweet paradox, struggling with one hand to eat the other. Here, in the whispering gully under the giant trees I might have struck upon a metaphor for life's futility.

But then I chided myself for making art of business. I took the old man by the chin and placed the knife to open him from ear to ear when a better idea came to me with remarkable clarity.

I had to lift him myself—his strength had deserted him. What had caught my attention was the jagged stumps of two branches, one of which had poked me painfully as I lowered him into his position. Some tempest, some flood or roaring of the unsound earth had rammed this great tree into the riverbank and in doing so had torn away its limbs. The broken-off boughs, each as thick as the human thigh, formed a set of steps. I threw the old man upon my shoulder and climbed them; then, standing atop the broad ancient timber, I laid him down once more. The chorus of the forest fell silent: the chippering, the rawks, the rhythmic thuds of the departing kangaroos—all subsided as I laid my offering on the altar.

Such peace he radiated there! Prepared for one thing, bless him, but not the other.

I knelt astride his chest, looking over his feet. I rolled his left foot over so that its arch and its inner curve looked up at me; felt along his ankle till I had the bone in my fingers. Then I took the knife and forced it down into the dip between that bone and the big tendon. The tip went through and stuck in the wood beneath. I wiggled it free of the wood but left the blade in him, turned the tip slightly and whipped it outwards to sever the tendon. There was a snapping sound from within the leg, the release of a taut rope. Then the blood started to run freely from the slice I had created, a dark spreading pool on the ancient timber, sticky in the dim light.

He screamed of course, bellowed fit to wake his ancestors, and that was the aim of the exercise. There was weeping in among the screaming, and I couldn't say to what it referred, but I could make out just enough to wonder if the clenching of his eyes spoke of more than agony. Perhaps, belatedly, he understood my plan: for now he was not just sacrifice but bait.

∿

I reported late to the camp, having first washed in the creek. Clark was still up, standing watch while the others slept, his face restless and fearful.

Seeing I was alone, he inquired as to the fate of my companion. I told him that we had been set upon, and that the natives had carried away the old man. *He was brave*, I said loudly, so my words could be heard by his countrymen. *It was very hard to say what their intentions were but the last I saw of him he was alive. We were over the first hill, down in a gully.*

You're wet, Clark observed, and I responded that there had been a struggle, and in fleeing from the evildoers I had fallen in a creek. That seemed enough to lay the scent.

Meanwhile, the lascars were waking up one by one, and someone woke the boy, who was sleeping next to Clark. I saw his face struck by the shock, and then the great wave of grief. He stood resolute, small man, while the tears rolled down his cheeks. The other Indians gathered around him, consoled him with embraces and a stream of their gibberish. I must credit their fidelity, these people, how they cleave to one another in such times.

The boy burst forth from among them—he was having none of my story—and raced at me, flailing at my chest with his fists. I swatted him off, catching his eye with the back of my hand: the lascars snarled and leapt to his aid but there was little intent in it.

I dried myself as best I could and lay down to sleep, covered with enough leaves and branches to hold some of the warmth against my body. I rolled onto my side so that the knife was under my hip: uncomfortable, but better than having it stuck into me during the night. The others, the lascars at least, would have slept little. Their leader was gone, and they had decisions to make. A watch was posted against the remorseless savages I had described.

By the time dawn glowed through the trees, they were resolved. One of the Javanese claimed he had heard a cry of distress up the hill, and it unified them in their decision. They wanted us all to stay where we were and begin a search for their leader.

I told them we could not waste a day on the fallen, and any confrontation with the natives could cost us dearly. The ones I had met with Prasad were fierce individuals, warlike and intent on mayhem. It would not do to come into conflict with them in larger numbers. If the lascars wished to bargain or to fight for his return, then that was their choice. But the rest of us must keep moving.

I could see I had convinced them before I finished talking, but one aspect of the response I hadn't anticipated. Clark spoke up, spoke collectively to the remaining lascars. *Well hello*, I thought, *a show of authority*. They were not to take the boy, said Clark. His duty was with him, Clark, and he would not be allowed to desert his post. The boy was crushed anew, and the others were plunged into another round of agonised debate. It came to pushing at one stage—such demonstrative folk—but their decision was presented by the oldest remaining among them, the Mussulman. It pained them to be without the boy, especially as it was his father who had gone missing, but they would remain and try to rescue the old man; the boy would be released to Mr Clark.

Here the lad surprised me again. The news was delivered to him in their language and he accepted it with his chin high and the tears still gleaming in their tracks.

And thus, unburdened of the dozen, we prepared to resume the journey.

28

Charlotte had walked at dawn, but had not gone far. These were the terms of a compromise they'd struck. Joshua was resigned to her walking, and asked only that she did so early in the day, and stayed within the bounds of the cleared land.

She had abided by the request, mostly. At the bluff where the sandstone projected over a short escarpment, she'd pushed on into the tree-line. The angling sun here glowed on the damp trunks of the eucalypts, and the birds—the heavy, loud ones she was still trying to understand—swept between their haunts, paying her no heed.

She was careful to keep the hem of her dress dry as she passed through the undergrowth. She stopped and listened to her heartbeat and her breath slowing; to the smaller birds in secret conversation; to the dripping and the barksounds. It was all she needed.

As she returned over the loose stones on the paths of the

settlement, she pictured him alone in the small house, measuring the minutes of her absence. She scoffed too much at his worry: it was love speaking as fear.

Passing the well in the small front yard she sensed a movement to her right, under the wide eave that formed the skillion roof.

The girl was back.

⸭

When Charlotte came in the door, Joshua was at the table, sitting a teacup in the palm of his left hand, as was his habit. She glanced sideways, in the direction of the skillion.

'Boorigul returned overnight.'

Joshua placed the cup carefully on the saucer. 'I didn't hear anything. How does she appear?'

'Oh,' now Charlotte could feel the sadness she hadn't allowed herself when she spoke to the girl. 'Someone has struck her, I think. She has a cut up here, at her hairline. A bruise too.'

She took a cloth and adjusted the chain so the pot hung closer to the coals, her back turned to him as he spoke. There was an edge of frustration in his voice.

'It puzzles me, this coming and going. If the girl's presence at our house is causing disharmony somewhere else, why does she keep coming back?'

Charlotte said nothing. She had no answer.

'Who did it, do you think?'

'I don't know. I offered to wash it but she wouldn't let me near. I feel so sad for her. She watches me in a way…she wants help but she will not accept it.'

'You spoke to her?'

'I tried just then, but she has so few words. She said she was out past the Cowpasture, on the flats where the yams are. With the women. That was all.'

'She was gone a week. Good lord—did you tell her you were worried?'

'Yes I did, and...' she turned and smiled a little. 'She looked at me as if I was mad. I don't think she can understand that we worry for her.' She heard herself, heard the irony in it, but Joshua appeared not to have noticed.

'We put her up in our home! Of course we worry for her. I would have thought that was obvious.'

'She leaves things in there sometimes. Little...pouches. Fishing lines.'

'I've seen.'

'I looked in one of them a while ago.' Charlotte had wondered as she picked it up whether the girl left it there as a small experiment in permanence. 'I felt like a busybody but...the things in there, I couldn't understand them. Just stones and shells.'

'I'm sure they have value to her. Here we are, trading food and promissory notes and rum because none of us have any currency. It might be something like that.' He smiled a little. 'She means a lot to you.'

That may have been what stirred in Charlotte's heart. But more, it was the unspoken exchange of freedoms between them: the girl feeling her way towards domesticity, and Charlotte absconding from it at every opportunity.

'Heavens, a girl takes up residence in our skillion and I start mothering her all of a sudden.' She did not want to disown the feeling, not entirely. She lowered her eyes, and he held her and kissed her on the mouth. She stayed there long enough to feel the warmth of him.

'Go and bother the governor,' she said eventually.

He kissed her forehead, a dry peck at the edge of her hair, and swept out of the house. As she watched him go she felt a wave of shame. She was already planning to confound him again.

⚜

An hour later, Charlotte Grayling knocked uncertainly at the main door of the guesthouse and found it ajar. It swung back under faint pressure—the frame was not quite square, because that was the way of this place. Nothing submitting to order; nothing quite square. Mr Clark was not inside. His room was neat, the bed carefully made, a small pile of clothes folded on the chair. He'd been provided with his every want, she knew, and yet it seemed he wanted little. Perhaps the wants had died in him somewhere out there.

She thought her husband might be with Mr Figge, though she wasn't sure enough to keep a shiver at bay: the shiver she knew in the bush. The one that belonged to being lost. This was faithless in some way she couldn't define. And so soon after his horror and fury at finding she'd been out there again.

She wanted to help, she told herself. That was all. She looked once over her shoulder, out into the bleaching sun. The natives there who waited for something nobody knew, and the rigid upright English, weaving to avoid them. Then she closed the door.

That first room wrapped her in its silence, its scent of warm timber. She placed a hand on the bedclothes as she passed, traced her fingers over the weave of the blanket and moved quietly to the second door. She knocked once more and in answer she heard the legs of a chair slide back over floorboards. Five light footsteps, the door opened and the lascar boy stood there.

He seemed mildly surprised by her presence: his expression passed through shades of confusion and came to rest at deference.

'*Memsahib*,' he breathed.

He stood nearly as tall as her, thin and delicate. Were it not for the shape of his face she thought he might pass for one of the natives. But his cheekbones were softer, just swells under his dark eyes, and his nose as short and finely tapered as her husband's. There was a healing wound near his hairline, a jagged scabbed split in the centre of a bruise that suggested he'd been hit with something heavy. A dark fuzz shaded his upper lip, and long lashes filtered his gaze. The curve of one ear was torn across its outer margin; not cut but ripped somehow. It looked angry and painful. He lowered his gaze to the floor when he could no longer meet her eyes.

They had dressed him in the clothes of a domestic serv-ant: a neat white tunic that opened to show the meeting of his collarbones and the delicate curve of his throat, but otherwise passed over him straight and square. His hands searched for a role in the awkwardness of their meeting: he settled on clasping his long fingers just below his sternum. His feet, dusted white at their creases, protruded bare from cotton trousers. His toes were still healing from where the landscape had punished them. The toenails were paler than his skin and in the places where they hadn't split, they were as fine and pink as tiny seashells.

She gestured back into the room behind him and he stepped aside. She drew the wooden chair, presumably the one he'd been sitting on, towards the bedside and sat on it.

'Do sit down, please,' she said to him, hearing her own station in her accent. He planted himself, with excruciating formality, on the edge of the bed. She drew her chair a little closer.

'I'm Mrs Grayling. I believe you have met my husband, the lieutenant.' She smiled at him and waited for an answer but there was none. The lascar boy only watched her.

'Would you like to tell me your name?' She looked up and into the dark pools under the lashes. He did not respond. In the stillness of the room she could discern that he was trembling. She was aware of his breathing, then of her own. She dusted at something imaginary in her lap and studied her feet now, in their battered satin shoes. 'You have been through so much, you poor boy. I know a little about life at sea, you might appreciate, as my husband describes it to me. And of course,' she smiled, 'the journey out. Though we had a reasonable passage.'

The boy had not moved, other than in constant, tiny shudders.

'And you had the wreck...the wrecks. My, to go through that twice! And then you walked all that way, and you, obliged to attend to Mr Clark as well as fend for yourself...ward off whatever other dangers were out there. Perhaps these men...I don't know about these men. I have met Mr Figge—'

He looked up at her suddenly, horror in his eyes. In full daylight, that name had rung like a bell in the night.

'Please. I can assure you Mr Figge does not know I am here.'

She waited a little. 'Strange surroundings, strange food. It seems the natives have been good to you and also...hostile.' She was watching him carefully now, measuring his reaction to each sentence, to ensure her instinct was right.

'You must have thought all was lost, and yet'—she looked around the room—'here you are! A remarkable achievement. No, I wonder if that is the word, *achievement*. You will have a story to tell your children one day, at any rate.'

His eyes roved left and right, always hidden by the lashes. He would not look at her. She was nearing him now, she knew.

'How did you come to be at sea, young man? How does a boy farewell his family and board a vessel, never knowing when he will return, or what will become of him? Or them? What

217

did your parents say when you told them you would go?'

She could see him grappling, struggling.

'I don't have children of my own. Yet.' She laughed a little, blushed; composed herself. 'But I think I can imagine how it would have been for them. We left our own parents behind, the lieutenant and I.'

The square light of the window formed a glint on his left eye, on its lower lid. The glint curved and lengthened, swelled into a tear.

'You can tell me,' she whispered. The tear rolled, then hung near his chin. 'You can tell me everything.'

The sudden intake of air startled her: his face broken by forceful sobs. She kept her voice to a murmur. 'I think you speak English as well as I do. You've been silent because that was safest.'

The sobbing was overtaking him now. His hands came over his face as his shoulders rocked. A strange wail escaped him and he strangled it, the effort only increasing his physical distress. She felt that she would cry, too: she no longer knew what to say. She had found out what she suspected, and now she had no idea what to do with the knowledge. Moving from the chair to the bed, she sat beside the boy and took him to her, an arm over his shoulders and a hand somewhere over his tear-stained hands and his hair. The grief moved through him like sickness; waves of constriction and release. He collapsed onto her breast and her hand fell to his ribs, which squeezed and expanded as if working to force something vile from his body. She stroked his hair and rocked him softly, though she did not understand her own actions.

From somewhere deep in her bosom his voice rose as if it was her own, a sentence formed in momentary control of his weeping.

218

'I no longer wish to hide.'

She clutched at his hair and he trembled on and on under her hands. He was not a settler, this grief-stricken thing she held; had not been invited to the grand project of civilising. But he was not a native, nor a miscreant. Not entitled to be called a sailor, certainly not a soldier.

He was neither man nor boy. He was something adrift and overlooked.

29

The governor's kitchen had been a source of many favours to Charlotte Grayling and her husband. In a hungry township they were among a privileged few.

The favour they cherished most was the new bread and eggs on a Sunday morning. At first it had been Joshua who would make the short journey to the servants' entrance on the north side of Government House, but more recently Charlotte had made the errand a part of her morning walks, returning with the basket draped in muslin and smelling wonderfully of the warm loaf as she made her way back to their cottage. The walk was a display: her best dress and a chance to launch combative smiles at the neighbours.

Sunday's dawn had brought rain, bright droplets shaking from the limbs of the throwing trees. The natives had scrambled under bark shelters in the grounds of the houses. She'd had to increase her pace to a run, boots slipping in the quickly forming mud.

On the way inside she found Boorigul nestled warm and dry under the skillion. She smiled at the wary eyes and tore off a hunk of the warm bread for her. The girl nodded and took the bread but did not speak.

Inside the house, in the room that was the house, Charlotte fried the eggs in a heavy iron pan and sat down to breakfast across the table from her husband. He saw the distance in her eyes.

'Church is at ten this week,' he started. 'Then I thought we could walk in the town?'

A bland, obliging smile as she took another forkful.

'What is it?' he asked gently. She did not look up.

'I didn't have the chance to speak to you last night,' she began. 'You were out in the afternoon. I believe you might have been walking with Mr Clark. Anyway, an idea came over me and I...'

'What?' Joshua Grayling's face began to darken.

'Please don't be upset with me.'

He waited.

'I went to visit the lascar boy, Srinivas.'

His face passed through shock to confusion.

'Charlotte, *why*? That's...' he looked up in exasperation; found a drip coming through the rafters. 'You can't just take a hand in this because it *interests* you. It's a delicate situation. And what might people think? You, going and visiting upon a young man without me?'

They were the arguments she had expected him to make, but she was not entirely contrite.

'Do you want to know what I found out?'

He sighed, ran a hand through his hair as another droplet landed there. 'What?'

'He speaks English. Perfectly. And he wants to talk about what happened out there.'

Grayling recoiled in shock. '*Talk*? Talk to whom?' He studied her. 'You're not suggesting that you meet him again?'

She swung her napkin into a fold. 'I don't believe he will do it any other way. I have his confidence.'

'But how would I know you've accurately conveyed to me what he says? I'd be left with…with your hearsay!'

'Darling, please. I'm not *hearsay*.' She watched him calmly. 'You have the commission from the governor, my love, but we both know that's not how this place works. Our interests are shared: everyone must contribute what they can.'

'For God's sake, Charlotte! There's expertise involved here. You don't just—I am *experienced* at this…'

She fixed him with a sceptical look but he blustered on.

'Don't pretend this is about the greater good of the colony! This is about you wanting to involve yourself in a confidential matter. One that is of the utmost importance.' He stood and swept his coat from a chair, then took up the journal and his writing materials. 'Please convey my apologies to the reverend. I will be gone for the morning.'

She had stood as well now, a mischievous smile forming. 'You didn't forbid me.'

He grunted and slammed the flimsy door behind himself.

30

When the *memsahib* returns, Mr Clark, I will tell her everything. What follows from that, I cannot say. But I will have to bear it.

⁂

We were five now, broken and walking apart.

Sleep was the only escape from my grief. My father, who was everything, had been taken from me. I had no doubt at whose hand.

That first night, I felt Mr Figge's eyes upon me in the dark. There was no fire: the damaged tinderbox could be made to work, but not often. There were no natives at hand who could make us a fire. But his eyes burned in the dark: they glittered like shattered glass and never left me.

He stood that night, walked towards me, to where I slept. The horror arrived before he did: I woke as he loomed over me and cried out, knowing no help would come. *You*, Mr Clark: you could hear my cries. But I knew enough of you by now to know you would take no steps. Even as he came like a shadow to close the space between us I heard you, maybe even saw you, roll over to turn your back. And Mr Thompson was half-dead. And Mr Kennedy never cared.

I thought of my father, my countrymen.

And then his hands were on me.

His knee pressed into my back, forced my belly hard against the earth. And he took me by the hair, his fingernails biting into my scalp, and he twisted my head to one side. *Hush now*, he whispered, though silence was no real concern of his. His face came down close to the side of mine and his rotting breath spoke from a place inside him where things decayed in darkness. And I prayed to the birds that were silent, and to the Kurnai, and the Thaua, the Walbanja and the mother I'd left grieving and my father wherever he might be—I prayed to them all but none of them answered, and he brought his mouth down to my ear and his lips were hot and wet on it and the noise of it was loud and sudden like a thunderstorm in close somehow and his tongue was in my ear, squirming and exploring in there, his breath making animal sounds and grunts behind the sticking noises of his mouth. Then his teeth bit down hard on my ear and I cried out again as a giant force struck the back of my head—like mercy, because for an instant I had no idea where I was. He had hit me only with his fist but the blow had power and it was hard as iron.

The teeth closed again harder now and I felt gristle tearing, his jaw moving as it chewed, blood mixed with slobber, matting my hair. The screams in me were crushed as I made them, and his other hand, the one not holding my hair, reached down and

I knew where it was going and he dragged down his tattered breeches and mine and now he was climbing further over me. He took my legs, easy as the bones of a finished meal, and he got them apart. I forced them back and he hit me again, this time in the side of the throat so that I choked, then coughed. I felt sure my belly would push out every trace of the food in me but he'd pinned me so hard even my retching was crushed still.

He was over me now and he'd rammed his knees up the insides of my thighs so I had nowhere left to move and I feared my hips would come apart but then the feeling of that was nothing at all because the world became a rod of bright red pain driven through the centre of me and I could not believe the whole world had room for so much pain. He rammed into me harder and harder, a barbed pike hammered into soft earth. A body has no instinct for this, to be impaled against its will: every muscle a riot of resistance and pain, and the demon above me had summoned such force that no response could have any effect.

A hand now came up to take hold of my throat, and there it gripped, the fingers gouging into the sides of my windpipe. With each shove he made into me the hand took it also, deep into the cords of my neck, leaving only whistles of breath to squeak through. He grunted fierce and quick now, loud enough to wake those who slept and to shame those who pretended. My cheek slid back and forth along a rough carpet of leaves—the beautiful sawtooth leaves I have never seen the same way again.

Then he collapsed, his forearms over my shoulders, and he took himself from me leaving a scalding trail of sticky fluid—part of him or some part of me he'd torn free, I had no way of knowing.

The heavens spun above me uncaring and the pain left in its own time. The horror I sucked deep down into myself; I buried it there. I told myself it was better my father was gone, for he would have died trying to stop it.

We had our answer now: the bush hid its monsters, but they were not the kind we expected. Thompson and Kennedy would go on fearing and hating the natives despite their own crimes, and despite seeing with their very own eyes the act of this man in their midst.

Mr Figge went back to the rough bed he'd dug at sunset with the end of a stick. Within minutes he was snoring and I thought to take up the knife that I knew was somewhere beside him and drive it through him. What stopped me—it makes no sense now—was the fear that the others might step in. So I lay there and watched him curled and smiling and I thought about what I would do and when that would happen.

When the morning came it was calm and still once again. The trees rang with the calls of unseen birds. I took myself down to the beach and its shining dawn water and I eased myself in, and washed the spit and dried blood from my ear. Attended to worse damage below the water. As I stood chest-deep amid the yellows and greens of that new light I looked back at the land and wondered if I could forget. Knew that I could not.

We walked. We had walked. We would always walk, or so it seemed.

I was slow, torn worse than I had thought. A trickle of blood worked its way down my leg throughout the morning, like something melted by a fire above it. I could not draw one leg after the other without the burning.

Thompson was slow, too. Coughing all the time: staggering when the coughing made him dizzy.

No one spoke anymore. All five of us looking forward and

down into a small parcel of space in front of our feet. Your back ahead of me, Mr Figge's eyes on me from behind. And further back, heard only in their cursing and the cracks of twigs, Mr Thompson and Mr Kennedy.

At some point you told us to stop. The coastline had been taking us straight east for hours and the land sloped up sharply behind. You said we must be walking out on a long headland; that we might be able to save time by going over the top of it. The same argument with every headland: whether to climb over it or press on to the east.

This time you walked off, intending to find a view, and Mr Figge smiled as you went. I wondered what would happen if you failed to return.

Then the bush closed around your back, and I thought of nothing for a while but the sense, the old sense, that we were being watched. It did not seem important.

By the time you returned in the mid-afternoon the sun was weak. You were pleased: you'd found a pass over the ridge and a vast and beautiful bay beyond it. We had been indeed walking out on a long headland; we would save many dozens of miles by going over the hill.

And so we turned, and we walked again. Uphill this time, following a narrow gully that made a snake's progress up the hill, brushing sticks and softer branches away from our faces.

My thoughts were a bloody list: Mr Figge had one knife. You had the other, the one that was more like a short sword. The second short sword was gone. The pistols were ruined by the seawater. I had no object, no plan for these weapons. Only they circled in my thoughts: knife, sword, drowned guns...

A stop for water. You crouched by the stream that flowed down the gully and tore a handful of bright stems from a ferny plant. The stems were fine like cress and they broke above the roots so they were clean of soil. You pushed a few into your cracked mouth and began to chew. You seemed pleased with the flavour, and handed another bunch to me. I ate, and the leaves were agreeable so I lay down where I was, on a mat of small ferns, and ate a few more handfuls. The others, as they joined us, did likewise.

When the four of you set off once more I waited and then I sat in the water and once more washed the injuries Mr Figge had left me. My neck was tight from the choking and it hurt to move my jaw to eat the leaves.

I caught up a little further on. You were all struggling to climb a rounded face of granite. It took a while but eventually we all stood on the tall boulder and looked out through the roof of trees. Below us was the coast we had walked: beaches weaving the headlands together, the sea a deep blue made darker, almost purple, by large spreading shadows near the shore. The sun was just about to hide itself behind the crest of the great hill we had been climbing. The gully and its stream had disappeared and there was little more climbing before we would reach the peak and see this great spreading bay you had spoken of, and—

I wobbled and fell where I was.

Felt…surprise.

You stooped to peer at me, then shrugged and walked away. I looked around me in confusion. Picked at the torn edge of my ear until my fingers were sticky with blood.

One tree on the hill above captured my gaze; I stared at the bark, formed with deep creases that ran straight up. Not a single branch until it was perhaps sixty feet tall, and then the branches spread like wings beyond a hundred feet. The edges of the leaves, the branches, the trunk, the edges of all were blurred by a faint rainbow that mixed the outlines of the tree and the light behind it. I blinked but the colours stayed. It was not my eyes. The tree was making them.

A tilted head in my vision blocked the trees: someone had bent to check on me and—oh!—it was my father, his kindly face full of worry. He looked in, smiled and then his eyes went dark and became holes in the day and his features drifted off into nothing, like the mist from the hills and I was staring at the bright unending sky that had no sorrow for wrecked mariners and no time for a poor broken boy. I stood, unsteady, and ran as best I could after the others and I found Mr Kennedy on his knees praying and Mr Thompson not much further on, flat on his face crying into the ground.

Beyond them the rocks and the pillars of the trees beat and swelled like they were painted on a sail that billowed in the wind. I saw you up ahead, Mr Clark, and I felt a wave of relief. But when I caught up with you, you were singing. Some grinding dirge, flat words blurring into each other so none could be heard clear. The sound of it terrified me, and I looked around again for comfort in a world that had gone mad.

The trees. They were different here. Or perhaps I hadn't noticed before but now my senses were whipped and I could see trunks of a beautiful shining clear white, dotted with thousands of small dark divots. It was as if the children of centuries had tossed stones at them and each strike had left an imprint. Closer to the ground the trunks bore round patches of yellows and greys, and even the pale green of the strange hard mosses we had seen on the granite. The blurring colours I had seen a moment before were gone now but the world was fixed somehow in the white spears that carried the holy green canopy across the sky.

My mind was working against me but I understood the

crowding undergrowth was gone from here, as if it had been cleared. It was grass, the going easy upon it, and it was trees, openly arranged. Soft sunlight fell on me, and the wind still carried your rudderless song as I walked onwards, wishing my father would appear from behind one of the great growing columns and this time not as a ghost.

You stopped.

You stood before a different tree.

A darker trunk, a thick coat of bark that cracked into long plates, dark needles on its twigs like a pine, instead of leaves. But none of this was what had stopped you.

You were staring, Mr Clark, at the trunk of the tree. There, at exactly your eye level, a little over my head, the bark had been cut away in a great sheet, leaving a diamond-shaped scar. The wood beneath had been cut over and over again into patterns of short angled lines like the meat of a fish. The cuts were new: so new that the sliced flesh of the tree bled sap from its wounds. The cuts were intended and they were not made to remove the bark. They were a message to any who passed. I felt their meaning in my body—a cold dread flowing through me, and I knew it as the direst warning.

You seemed astir, Mr Clark, but in no great panic.

There's a saltire, you said to yourself in the oddest voice. *In the tree. Andrew's cross.*

Mr Figge had his fingers on the cuts in the bark, walking them slow over the sticky sap. He held his palm up so it faced you like a sign of its own, and his eyes just then were not of our world. *'Tis a sign of some sort, Clark,* he said. *We're being told to go another way.*

And you turned slow round to face him, sir, and looked him over as though you'd never met the man.

It's a forest, Mr Figge. Doesn't belong to anyone. If I want to go there, I'll go there. If I want to go over there—you were pointing east now—*then that's where I shall go.* You stood and started forward again, spoke over your shoulder. *These people are wandering over it just the same as us. They're simply too stupid to realise what could be made of it.*

You left us at odds behind you. Mr Kennedy moved to follow, then Mr Thompson, slower. Mr Figge moved last and I was left alone with my fear. A fat grey bird sat on a lower branch of one of the great white trees and watched me. Then it told me I was a bright and attentive boy and I hissed at it until it flew off.

When I caught up, the three of you were standing in a shady place on the grass. Before you, a series of trees had been taken down to make a small clearing. It had the air of a temple; walled by trees and filled with quiet power.

You turned in a slow circle, then sat yourself down, dropped the small calico-wrapped bundle of your possessions, and got out your journal and pencil. Without regard to us, you began writing your business there, stopping now and again to parley with your compass.

What're ye doin, ye dottle-heided wandocht? That was Mr Figge, mocking your Scots.

You looked left and right. *Me? I am recording our journey, Mr Figge. Others will want to know what transpired.*

The heat rose up in Mr Figge. He stood over you, no mockery now. *You're lying on dangerous ground, little man.*

Again, you looked around yourself. *This? I think not. Now if you'll excuse me—*

I looked to the bush, out wider. The day was darkening now, the shadows less certain. Mr Thompson and Mr Kennedy sniffed the tension like they smelled food. Poking sly fun at you, Mr Clark, even as they laughed at Mr Figge's anger. What had happened to us all? Why were we so untied? I hated the shadows all of a sudden. I wanted to rush through them and sweep them away to see what secrets lay behind.

You ignored us; you continued to write.

The others had sat down now.

The bush.

I turned a circle as you had just done, and a gasp got away from me. The others looked and I pointed: the patterns were cut in the trees all round us, facing in at us. Circles, spirals, squares. One was the outline of a huge lizard.

The air changed and you stopped writing. Another round of dispute seemed about to start. Then the shadows moved.

I was looking at Mr Kennedy when I saw him open his mouth to shout. I followed his gaze and a man stepped from the trees at the edge of the clearing: tall, thin and naked but for the twine belt around his waist. He had a spear raised, lying in a *wumera*.

Pointed straight at you, Mr Clark.

He had no expression on his face at all. Not the welcome smile we had seen so often nor any other. He was watching you as though the rest of us were not there. And from behind and around the man came more and more, painted in the white streaks we had seen before, but this time also stripes of a red clay. Their eyes were changed by the painting. These were not the Walbanja: all were naked but none the same; some carrying the sacred scars and some unmarked. None talking to the other, nor to us.

I was not myself. The trees were turning into more and more warriors. Dozens now, slipping forward by inches. More spears than I had ever yet seen, and every lethal point trained on you.

I dug my fingernails into my thigh to feel the pain and know for certain this was real. Trees becoming men, and yet I felt the fingernails telling me this was no dream. The other three stood now, slow. Hands out, not a twitch.

More of them, and more. Not a woman, not one. Not a scrap of clothing. Clubs, axes and spears and the quiet like a thin layer of oil coating everything. I wanted to cut it open with a scream. But the minutes were passing without me in them.

The one who'd come furthest forward, the one who was the first from the tree-line—now he began to speak. Not to us, but to his fellows, without ever taking his eyes off you. Soft words. Their effect was that the spear carriers divided their aim: five or six now covered each of us. Even then, the bulk of the weapons still focused on your beating heart.

Now see here, you began, but the warriors showed no sign of hearing you, other than to take several steps forward. Your eyes darted about, desperate now: they fell on Kennedy and lit up.

*This is the man you seek. Yes! Him, and the other here…*You extended a hand towards Kennedy, then Thompson, who looked back at you with disgust. That hand stayed there, accusing him: the white palm bright against the gloom. *If you'll spare us, you may—*

There was a flash of movement, a blur in the air and you fell, clutching at the hand. Your screams tore open the silence and bodies moved in every direction. Thompson had fallen. There were arms raised, sounds of shouting and timber snapping. Mr Figge I could not see. One of the natives stepped swiftly to you, ripped your good hand away from its grip on the wounded one. He yanked it out at arm's length; drove his long spear through it and into the earth.

The spear stood there, quivering, while you twisted and

wept in pain. The man who did it stood back tall and watched you. I was watching him, then there was a blow and a terrible pain I did not understand. I remember falling in the soft grass and wishing it was all there was in the world.

31

 The man appeared in Joshua Grayling's doorway that afternoon.

Grayling had been reading at the table. The man did not knock. He did not call out. It happened that the door was open to bring air through the house; his form in the doorway altered the light, so Grayling looked up.

He was naked, which was nothing remarkable among the Eora. It was clothing, not nudity, that stood out in Sydney. The familiar strings draped over the taut drum of his chest, which was latticed with straight scars.

He was not an old man. His beard was thick, the skin pulled tight over his cheekbones, but Grayling reckoned him to be no older than twenty. His hair was matted with a reddish mud, and other things caught Grayling's eye in odd sequence: the sleek roping of his arms, the cracked traces of old paint in his skin, a scar over his right forearm that looked not ceremonial but riven by trauma. His eyes were clear and dark and level. They did not defer to him nor offer any hint of good humour.

He opened his mouth and uttered just one word: *Boorigul*.

Come in, sit down, Grayling ventured, trying to make time in which to sift through his growing dread. The man did not move from where he stood but lifted one hand to chest level and made a sign with it that Grayling did not understand: it was quick and emphatic and with it came the girl's name again. His intonation hadn't changed; if he was impatient, it did not show.

Grayling was alone in the house. Charlotte had persuaded the girl to walk with her to the Rocks to bargain for new clothes. He was not going to tell the man that they'd gone to *tallawolladah*, to the wattle and daub and twisting alleys growing rudely on a meeting place.

He turned side on and gestured at the interior of the house. *She is not here*, he said.

The man glanced into the space without moving from the doorway. Grayling found himself staring at the splay of long, bony feet on the cut sandstone block he had ordered and laid himself as a front step. The feet bore authority, as the stone did. Together, the meat of them and the cold block of cut stone spoke of death and interment.

The man turned and left without another word, and Grayling was surprised to find his heart racing in his chest.

⁜

Later that afternoon, Grayling walked to Government House for the meeting he had promised he would attend.

He watched as William Clark settled himself in the chair that faced the governor's desk. To Grayling's eye, his movements looked freer now, and the wounds around his face had cleared into a faint matrix of pink lines. His hair was cut neatly and his jaw again clean shaven. He wore a dark coat and trousers, not new but hastily acquired by someone from the governor's office for the purpose. His hands, still bandaged, rested in his lap.

The governor had stood as Clark entered: he seemed unsure how to formalise his greeting, given the state of Clark's hands. He settled on a solemn nod before he resumed his seat. The customary notebook lay open in front of him, the quill to its side. To his left, pushed back towards the bookshelves, an easel had been covered with a dark cloth. It stood, along with the violin in its case there by the wall, as a mark of the private John Hunter, the one the Corps loved to pursue and to mock.

Here and now he presented only his public self. He spoke to his guest with diplomatic ease.

'Mr Clark, thank you for coming to see me. I have followed your progress closely through Lieutenant Grayling here. I trust you have been well looked after?'

Clark's face resumed the stiff reluctance Grayling recalled from their first meeting.

'Thank you, excellency. The care has been impeccable.'

'Good, good.' The passage of a cloud somewhere over Sydney changed the light. The fire crackled behind them. Nothing about the governor's face revealed the slightest clue to his thoughts.

'And your hands?'

Clark lifted them, looked at the bandages. 'The doctor says they are free from infection, which is most important. It will be a slow process.'

'Do they hurt?'

'No. No, very little. An inconvenience, mostly.'

'Of course.' The sunlight strengthened again, picking up

the straggling silver hairs that stood from the governor's scalp.

'Mr Clark, there is nothing unusual about this meeting, I want firstly to assure you of that. Lieutenant Grayling here has told me that he is reaching a critical passage in your story, and I thought it would be of benefit if I listened. Does that cause you any concern?'

Hunter leaned forward slightly, studying Clark closely.

'No, sir. None at all. It's a pleasure to be in Your Excellency's company.' Clark's eyes roved over the desk, the drapes behind it, the squared timbers of the window frames. The wood smoke mingled with timber smells and rosin and turpentine and all of it offered a seductive feeling of civilisation.

The governor smiled brightly. He retreated behind his desk, sat down and took up a quill.

'Fine, then! Lieutenant Grayling, would you proceed? And just pretend I'm not here...' he smiled again and Clark tried wanly to respond.

Grayling opened the journal at the page he'd bookmarked with a length of twine. The bookmark was unnecessary: the book fell open there because of the weight of the page, stained and smeared in old brown blood.

'Forgive me, Mr Clark,' Grayling began. 'This is probably not material you will wish to revisit, but what I wanted to examine is the twenty-sixth of April. I will read your entry back to you, perhaps, before I ask you about it.'

Clark watched him and said nothing.

'*At 9 a.m. observed several natives on the top of a high bluff, who came down to us as we approached and remained with us for some time.*

'Now firstly, my understanding was that you were attempting

to cut off a headland by walking north over a range of hills here, is that right?'

'Yes.' Clark chewed his lip pensively.

'Was the going steep?'

'Yes, it was. We were quite exhausted by the time we reached the ridge. I think we had stopped to recover from the climb.'

'I see. Then you encounter the natives. And then you write this—

> *'When we had made signs to them that we were hungry and much exhausted, they brought us plenty of fish and treated us very kindly.*

'Why—I'm just a little confused. How far inland were you at this point?'

'Some hours' walk, though we did not cover the ground with any great haste.'

'Fish?' The governor put the goose quill down. 'Are these river or sea fish?'

Clark looked perplexed. 'Why I—I don't…I cannot say. I assumed they were sea fish, Your Excellency.'

A look of irritation creased the governor's face. 'It is my experience, Mr Clark, that these people travel light. Why would they have carried fish up onto a high ridge, several hours' walk inland, on the off chance that you might ask them for a meal?'

'I—I don't know, sir.'

'Were they stored somewhere? Were they carrying the fish on their persons?'

'I really could not say, sir. It is just, just…I think we had fish there.'

'You think…' The governor looked sceptical. 'Very well. I am sorry, lieutenant.'

Grayling looked for the point in the scrawl where he had left off. The governor took up his quill once more.

> 'After we had refreshed ourselves and put up some fish to carry with us, we were preparing to proceed, when about fifty strong natives made their appearance, of whom we soon took leave, giving them such little presents as we could afford, and with which they were apparently well satisfied.'

Grayling stopped there and thought for a moment. 'Mr Clark, do you recall what you gave these people?'

'No.' Clark's mood had soured. 'No I don't, but the usual things were calico and the knives, the axe. We handed them most all of our belongings by the end.'

'You couldn't have had much left to hand over by this stage, surely,' contributed the governor.

'No. Very little, I would think.'

Grayling did not want his witness to turn sullen. 'I only ask because I wonder whether the gift could have inadvertently caused offence.'

Clark sighed. 'That is not how these people work. They are entirely unpredictable from one encounter to the next, one moment to the next.' His voice was rising. 'Surely you can see it outside this very window?'

'Yes of course. Allow me to continue.

> 'We had not parted more than twenty or thirty minutes when a hundred more approached us, shouting and hallowing in a most hideous manner, at which we were all exceedingly alarmed. In a short time a few of them began throwing their spears, upon which we made signs to them to desist, giving them some presents, and appearing

no ways dismayed at their conduct—

'Now here, I—'

'You *what*? What troubles you *here*, lieutenant?' Clark's voice was shrill now. He had lifted himself slightly in his seat by leaning his forearms on the arms of the chair, his physical discomfort ratcheting his anger higher.

Grayling waited a moment. 'Here, Mr Clark, I—'

The governor interrupted. 'I imagine the lieutenant merely wanted to ask you what were these further presents?'

'I don't know! I've said I don't know. Maybe it was something Mr Figge was carrying. Maybe it was Mr Kennedy's tools, or one of the pistols. Maybe we sang them a bloody song.'

Once again, the governor dropped the pen. 'You wouldn't have handed them *weapons*, Mr Clark, surely?'

'We'd already given them a short sword. Besides, the pistols didn't work.'

'Let me continue, Mr Clark,' said Grayling. 'I realise this is distressing, but it is important that we understand it all.

'No sooner had we turned our backs on this savage mob
than they renewed hostilities and wounded three of us,
viz., Mr. Hugh Thompson, myself, and my servant.'

'Yes. I had instructed the others to retreat from them and we had turned around when I saw a spear strike Mr Thompson in his side. He fell and I, I turned around and raised a hand to command them to desist, and one of their spears passed clean through it. The treacherous fiends had launched their salvo behind our retreating backs. That's the measure of their character.'

The governor was writing furiously to keep up, but now he paused. 'The spears that I've seen are nine or ten feet long, Mr

Clark. Are you saying the *whole thing* passed through your hand?'

'Yes. It was launched from a *wumera,* so fast I could not see it in flight.'

'And the other hand, Mr Clark?'

Clark sighed and looked at the other bandaged hand as though the answer was written on it. 'There was a fusillade of spears by this time. The natives charged forward: they were shouting, howling in a most terrifying manner. The lascar boy was struck a tremendous blow with a club and he fell down: I immediately assumed he was dead.' Clark paused.

The governor looked up, annoyed. 'But the other hand?'

'*I am getting to the other hand.* I reached down to the small bundle of my belongings, intending to grasp the pistol and wave it at them in hopes its terror might be known to them. But when I had my hand on the bundle, my other hand'—Clark held up his left—'I was speared. It went through the hand and the bundle, pinning both to the ground. And the one who did it—I can still smell him—he came right up to me, bold as day and he stood on my forearm and pulled the spear free. Not, I hasten to add, out of any concern for me, but in order to retrieve his weapon.'

'So you were speared—' The governor placed his own hand on the desk, trying to visualise it. 'You were speared through the back of your left hand?'

'Yes.' Clark looked slightly confused for a moment, then nodded vigorously. 'Yes, the left.' He shook his head in exasperation, then added: 'Really, do you people not believe there is a hole there?'

'Mm.' The governor resumed his patient longhand.

Grayling had long since lost the intended route of his questioning. He thought hard now. 'Did you ever ascertain who these people were, Mr Clark? Are they just the Sydney natives?'

'Mr Figge had tried to exchange pleasantries with them during the exchange of the fish and the gifts. They were called the *Wandandean*.'

'Wan-dan-de-an,' the governor repeated slowly. 'These ones here are Eora, as you know. They're not the same people, are they?'

Clark shrugged. 'They are of a species, sir.'

'All right. It's just—Lieutenant Grayling was explaining to me about there being, perhaps, a kind of sub-set. Could the Wandandean have been Guyangal people?'

Another shrug. 'I think not. I heard the term *Kurial*, but...'

'And this incident: it took place on a high ridge just south of a very large bay that you next encountered?'

'Yes. And deep, sir.' Clark seemed happier on this subject. 'An excellent anchorage, I would think.'

'What became of you next?' the governor asked. *The old man's not to be diverted*, thought Grayling.

'We were helpless there. Only Mr Figge and Mr Kennedy had been spared—I do not know why. Mr Thompson was bleeding quite freely and I was in wretched pain. We remained where we were and—'

'—and the boy? What was his condition? You said you mistook him for dead?'

'The boy, yes. I believe he had come to his senses by then. It is in the nature of the Bengalis, you understand, to feign unconsciousness in such extremity. He may well have been playing dead in the hope the natives would not finish him off.'

The governor hurried his notes towards an end, as Grayling and Clark watched him. Something was exercising his mind. A maid advanced into the room, looking hesitant. She was elderly, worn. She placed a tray of tea on a side table near the desk and retreated; the dust swirled lazily in the light where she'd been.

'Mr Clark, can I ask you this: you say you were struck deliberately in both hands. That seems to me to be a feat of extremely fine marksmanship. Yet Mr Thompson, who I can't imagine was much nearer to or further from their lines, from the way you describe it, was struck non-lethally in the side.'

'Indeed. It passed through him completely, but only in the flesh above his hipbone.'

'Do you think that was a deliberate aim or a poor one?'

'Well, these spears were launched by different people…'

'Yes, yes. I understand that, but do you think these people were trying to kill you or not? You were unable to take any evasive action as far as I understand it, and yet all five of you emerged alive from a volley of spears.'

'I am, as you know, reluctant to credit the savages with undue skill. I think it is possible that they intended to wound us, perhaps just for the sport of watching us make our way under even greater duress.' He stopped, thought for a moment. 'Or they were marking us for others further up the coast.'

'That would explain them not completing their assaults by killing you.'

'Yes, but nor did they offer us any succour. They simply vanished back into the forest. We spent that night in mortal terror that they would return.'

'What had you done about Mr Thompson?'

'You might wish to ask Mr Figge about that. He took charge of the operation: he lay Thompson on his other side and spent some time notching the spear shaft with a knife, then snapped off the lengths on both sides of his body so that only a small shaft remained in him. The thing had such a terrible barb on it—made of little shards of sea shells. So there was no prospect of pulling it back out—it had to go through in the direction it arrived. He worked away at it for some time and Mr Thompson was setting up an awful hollering, and when he had wriggled it enough in the wound he was able to pull it free. The pain was such that we had to restrain Thompson, and by the time Mr Figge had got the thing out of him, he had lost consciousness.'

'You must have thought he would not survive the night.'

'As I say, you would have to ask Mr Figge about that.' Clark stared resolutely ahead.

The governor did not write any of this down. He looked at the page in front of himself, apparently lost in thought. The silence was an awkward one, tinged with something incomplete. Eventually he broke it.

'Mr Clark, you've been very helpful. I do not wish to tire you unnecessarily. Lieutenant, I take it you are done?'

Grayling nodded. He wasn't, but the governor's intent was clear.

'Very well, then. Mr Clark, I'll finish up with the lieutenant here. Do you require an escort back to your quarters?'

Clark eyed him with open suspicion. 'No, thank you, Your Excellency.' He stood, took his coat from the stand by the door and left. Grayling watched the governor, who watched the door as they both listened to Clark's footsteps fading over the hallway planks outside.

'Tell me what you thought, lieutenant.'

'A little discordant, if I may be so bold, sir.'

Governor Hunter arched a silver eyebrow. 'Thoroughly unconvincing, you mean?'

'Yes.'

'You know, I had a discussion with Ewing about Clark's hand wounds. I have my reservations about the surgeon and his efficacy generally, but he did say an interesting thing.' He held up his hands palm-outwards and considered them. 'Mr Clark has two broken bones in his left hand and one in the right, as far as Ewing can tell. When he was first brought in, the ends of those bones were visible. They were spiked from front to back. Both hands.'

'Sir?'

'Mr Clark just told us he had his left hand on the bundle, and the spear went through the back of it and pinned it to the ground. Yet the bones broke the other way, lieutenant. Both hands were pierced through the palm, according to Ewing.'

'As you intimated, sir, Ewing is not—'

'Nor, I suggest, is Clark.'

'Through both palms says what, sir? Abject surrender?'

The governor ran the vane of the quill over his cheek. 'Mr Clark may have been on the right track with his comment about the Wandandean marking them. But what if they weren't just marking them for others of the native race?'

Grayling looked at him blankly.

'What if they were passing their judgment generally? What if they wanted to leave visible signs on these men that they had transgressed—the ritual ground they entered, or some other misdeed we haven't been told about?'

Grayling hesitated a moment. 'Sir, there is one other matter that might be relevant here. It's Charlotte.'

'Yes.' The governor's face brightened. 'I hear she has improved dramatically.'

'She has sir. She's been…she's been out and about.'

'Oh?'

'She went to visit the lascar boy. Without asking me.'

The brows came down over those sea-green eyes. 'Why?'

'I'm given to understand it was merely concern for his welfare. But she has made a discovery in the process, sir.'

'And?'

'The boy speaks English. He *understands* English. Perfectly.'

'Oh.' The governor considered this for a long moment. 'He's been privy to some interesting conversations, then.'

'Exactly, sir. Their exchange was only very brief, but it holds great import for us. I believe the way through our…reservations might be for me to talk to the boy.'

The governor had steepled his fingers and he frowned into them. 'No,' he said from behind the fingers. He picked up a piece of rosin from a corner of the desk blotter; rolled it over in his hand so it glowed amber in the light. 'The boy hasn't wanted to speak to authority. He may be under duress. If Mrs Grayling has found a way in, let her try again.'

32

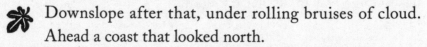 Downslope after that, under rolling bruises of cloud.
Ahead a coast that looked north.

The bay that Clark had promised us was indeed a thing
of beauty. In the small intervals when the sun lit it up we saw
curves of glorious white beach below us, water that was turquoise
in the shallows and a crescent bay of the most exquisite blue.

Clark and Thompson were imprisoned in their own agonies,
neither taking it well. Clark had discovered that if he slung his
burden over his shoulder and kept his hands raised they did
not bleed so much but cooled to a deathly white as the blood
drained from them. Thompson, on the other hand, was bleeding
well. His wound was over to one side, straight through him. No
imminent danger to his vital organs, but the seepage might yet
do him in. And how he groaned, the feeble wretch. The two of
them were a diptych Christ: stigmata and lance. Had the natives
been got at by the missionaries, they might have been tempted

to crown the boy in brambles and send them off a trinity.

I was a little knocked and chipped by the journey but mostly whole, and the walking was mine to enjoy. The prospects were good for Thompson's demise, and Kennedy had a talent for his own undoing; there'd be time for that. Clark and his boy were the most useful to me as walking companions: the boy was a mouse to paw. Later for them.

When we reached the sand, the bush surrendered to it with a carpet of succulent little shoots that were pocked with purple flowers. The shoots were edible, I quickly discovered. These I devoured, sitting on the sand, along with a fine lizard I had found in a scatter of loose bark. Once I tore the guts out and the scaly jacket off, the meat was tender enough. I waggled him at the others, slumped nearby, knowing that the swinging tail would be enough to offend their delicate tastes. Clark, with his Hebridean insistence on meal times and foods he understood, had missed countless opportunities for sustenance.

When I'd eaten my fill I walked across the perfect beach again and disrobed at the water's edge. Naked in the rain, four steps into the sea, scooping handfuls of the grainy sand from the bottom and using them to scour my tatty vestments. Then I took the clothes to the nearest ledge of flat rock and laid them out in the rain. Back into the shallows, and I stood there, listening with a pleasing sensation of melancholy to the rush of the heavy droplets on the surface. I took handfuls of sand again and scrubbed out the stinking parts of me, stepping away from the discarded clouds of sand into clean water as I worked. Behind me I could see a scum forming—flakes of skin, dried food and the various emissions of my body—disappearing as the heavy rain pounded them through the surface. I felt some small alarm at the bumps of my ribs under my hands, and the two points that now revealed my hips like those of a child. I'd become accustomed to the sight of my scrawny companions, but the nourishment I'd extracted from the bush I'd thought would keep me fat and jolly. No matter: sustenance was near at hand.

Up at the high tide line, the others showed no inclination to take advantage of this marvellous laundry. Fitting, then, that I should be the odyssey's sole survivor. That day exemplified like no other that the pleasures of this place were well within reach of those who would embrace them.

The days that followed were unexceptional for the most part. Only late on the second day of our curve around the crescent bay we rested, under another downpour, on a sheet of sandstone that sloped up from the shallows. I sat near the lascar boy, watching what my proximity did to his eyes. He shied in terror, perhaps mistaking our recent moment for an ongoing romance. He shifted, I shifted. The game moved us all over the rock.

As the rain became a little steadier, the contours in the wet stone began to reveal themselves, much the way a human body looks different after immersion: superficial defects disappearing to reveal the truth in shapes.

I was peering thus at the boy—entertainment among us by now having run rather thin—when beyond his slender shoulder I saw a fine cleft in the rock. An inch deep and bent to a curve that instinct said was not the work of nature. I stood and my eyes followed the line. A fork, an angle, a straight line. *Stand up*, I roared at the boy and he did so.

And there, carved in the sandstone, was a ship-rigged vessel resting eternally at anchor.

It had a foresail, three masts and a square stern. I squatted and ran a finger along the lines, cut clean and deep as the scars in the trees. For a people working with stone tools it must have been a long project. *This is a wonderful sign*, Kennedy squawked. *There is a rescue about.* But the last sentence was curled up at the end and became half a question and in answer to it I pointed to the lichen that had grown slow and steady in the wells of the lines.

Being no more a seafarer than a tea merchant, I deferred to poor old Thompson as he studied the carving. *It's a bark*, he said eventually. *They even got her boxy beams right. That there is Mr Cook's ship, thirty years back.* He looked up and out at the hooked headland that made half the horizon, the low island just off the tip of it. *And that would be Cape St George.*

There was some desultory conversation about what that meant: how many miles, how many days. Kennedy was greatly anguished that the ship wasn't the work of his imaginary rescue party. *Fuck me if I ain't killin' the next one we meet* he muttered. Clark ignored the fool and tried to write in his diary, pencil flapping uselessly in his holey hands. Thompson lay flat and sucked water out of the carved ship's keel while his weeping flank stained the rock. For seconds the blood was bright and alive and then it faded and washed away with the trickles.

None of it mattered to me. They would all be dead soon enough. And I could walk like this for another year, if pressed.

33

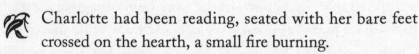Charlotte had been reading, seated with her bare feet crossed on the hearth, a small fire burning.

She smelled the bread and slammed the book down on its face. *The Mysteries of Udolpho*: a gift from the governor. Not, she thought, a book he'd choose to read himself, and she worried what he'd discerned in her that made him choose it for her. But she loved it anyway.

Joshua smiled as she rushed to pluck the tin from the coals in towelled hands, and flipped the loaf onto the table to cool. The soup she ladled into a smaller pot and found a lid for it. Her husband took in the aroma of the bread, drew a finger through the flour on its upper surface. Between his wife and the governor, he was outflanked and he knew it.

'I can't talk you out of this, can I?'

Charlotte stopped, closed her hands in the warmth of the towel.

'No.' She kissed him. 'It needs to happen this way. Is the old man still in favour?'

'His Excellency? I've told you, he thinks it's a good idea. I just…you know my reservations. You being drawn into… something is very wrong here, I can feel it. And I don't know that it is wise to bring a woman into it.'

She arched an eyebrow at him and said nothing, but added a bowl, a plate and a spoon to the basket.

'The fishermen should be back today,' he said.

'Fishermen?'

'The ones who went down the coast to find whatever's left of Thompson and Kennedy.'

'That's a bleak prediction. They might just be sitting around a fire waiting for them.'

'These are dangerous people, Charlotte. Figge's a dangerous man. The Wandandean, Pemulwuy and Goam-Boak, any number of escapees out there…I can't imagine a situation in which those men are fine.'

'And if you're right about that? What then?'

'We have three survivors from seventeen. And according to Clark's journal, another thirty-two awaiting rescue on this rock island.' He was drumming his fingers on the table now. 'I believe I ought to post a watch outside Clark's quarters. And Figge's.'

'Not a guard?'

'No, just a watch. There is no reason to detain either of them, but I feel considerable relief now that we elected to keep them apart.'

A towel over the top of the basket and she was done. She pressed against him, feeling a strange reluctance to leave, then she broke the embrace and hurried out.

The Sydney morning crowded her immediately, the sounds of a place making itself: pounding hammers, livestock protesting, human voices and a faraway ringing of iron on stone. She passed down the paths and laneways as one of a busy throng; a tilted cap here and there from a soldier, averted eyes from a lag.

It had been agreed in advance that William Clark would be summoned to the governor's office to discuss geography so that Charlotte would have time and privacy to talk to the boy. At Clark's quarters she found things as she had hoped: the front door open, the room empty and the connecting door swung back. A convict maid scuttled out as she entered.

She called cheerfully from the main room but Srinivas did not respond. She found him sitting formally on the bed, in much the same position as she had left him last time. Something like embarrassment threatened to rise in her but she ignored it. She placed the basket on the floor, removed its contents and set out the meal for him. His dark eyes were wide with apprehension, but also something else. Resolve, she thought.

He thanked her, again with the formal *memsahib*, and ate with a delicacy that surprised her, using the cutlery correctly and dabbing his mouth with the cloth she had included. Every now and then he would raise the spoon to his mouth and his eyelids would come up as he did so, his eyes fixing on hers. She saw an eclipse in them, a light obscured.

'Do you still want to talk?' she asked gently.

He nodded, arranged the spoon carefully on the plate under the bowl.

'I'm not going to write it down or anything,' she smiled. She raised her hands, fingers spread: unarmed.

'That is all right,' he answered.

She leant forward, clasped her hands together and looked into his eyes again. 'Tell me what happened on that beach. When they found you.'

He looked momentarily unsettled, confused maybe.

'Tell me why you were crawling.'

And so he began, haltingly at first, until his speech gained strength and purpose.

⸙

'Mr Thompson was speared late in April, and he had a hole through his side that would not heal. Through the front and out the back, ma'am. I would walk at times behind him, watching it bleed. The stain spread over his breeches, went brown and grew again from the top where the blood was still coming.

'We walked a long way around a beautiful harbour. The place was marked by the natives, a ship they had carved into the stone, and Mr Kennedy was angry because he thought it was made by a rescue party, a signal for us, and Mr Figge made fun of him.

'The land was good north of the harbour: the walking was easy and the days were warm. Little wind, just the rain sometimes but never cold. Only the dawn was cool.

'Every day I cried for my father, empty inside. He was our guide and he had answers to all the questions. Every hour of every day was filled with questions and when there were thirteen of us he knew how to answer. But now it was just me and I did not feel able.'

Charlotte's eyes wandered the room as the boy spoke. He had taken the coat that someone had brought him and placed it on the chest of drawers, folded so that the lapels faced symmetrically upwards. The slippers were on his feet and he had placed the boots precisely side by side under the edge of the bed. He was making tiny order from the chaos.

'What do you think became of your father?'

'I do not think the natives killed him. They knew he was our *serang*, our senior man. They had no reason.'

'Maybe some didn't, but some others did?'

'I am sure, ma'am, that they spoke to each other. I think such things passed ahead of us as we went.'

Charlotte found herself thinking about reasons. About Pemulwuy, and Goam-Boak, the so-called cannibal of the south. Was the boy thinking wishfully about his father's death? The natives she'd seen had no need to kill a man for food; the food was all around them. But that didn't stem the terrified whisperings of Sydney. It only focused them upon the notion that the cannibalism in which they wished so fervently to believe was gratuitous ritual: a pagan lust.

The boy had fallen silent, deep in thought. He looked up eventually.

'Mr Figge went into the bush with him. He came back without him. That man'—his jaw clenched and flexed—'he is a great deal stronger than my father.'

'Only his body.'

Almost a smile. 'Only his body, yes.'

An image came to her, unwelcome, of a small man who could be the father of this boy. Sorrowful, broken. At the mercy of Figge's powerful hands. She shuddered. 'I am sorry, Srinivas. I interrupted you. Keep going.'

The boy waited until the anger had subsided. He muttered to himself—Charlotte assumed it was Hindi—until he was composed.

'Two days on from walking the bay we were going north

again. Mr Clark said we might be only a week from reaching Sydney, but we were tired. Mr Thompson was in a terrible state. I did not like him, you understand, ma'am. But he was suffering, and he fell behind us all the time, even though we were slow. Mr Figge made fun of him, did cruel things like hide behind trees and leap out at him shouting, and Mr Thompson would fall to the ground and cry out or weep. It only made him slower.'

'Why was there a need to hurry?'

The boy paused as though the question had never occurred to him, then shrugged. 'Faster would end the misery sooner; but it also made it worse.'

'Keep telling me,' Charlotte said. She took the loaf and tore an end off it. 'Excuse me. I'm starving.' She heard herself, and blushed. 'You were walking north after the bay you described...'

'Yes, it was a dark time now. The way was clear but Mr Figge and Mr Clark were at each other now and I still had my duties to Mr Clark. Make his meals, carry water for him. Some days wash his clothes, if that was his order. Mr Thompson was dying, I think, by then. The carpenter was close to him.'

He paused, pointed in the air at the walkers in his haunted eyes. 'One, one, two, one. Very slow, wide apart.'

'Srinivas, there is something I have not asked you. Which of these people knew you could speak English?'

'None of them. Something my father taught me. He did it as a young man at sea until he could do it no longer.'

'But they must have been giving you orders, and you were carrying them out? Even back on the ship...'

'Yes. But ma'am, forgive me: the gentlemen do not stop to wonder whether you speak the King's English. They think as far as the order: *is the lascar doing as I say?* If not, a fist or a boot. A lascar on a ship is a...a turnbuckle or a binnacle. They no more think a lascar will talk back than a pump. My father taught me: you keep your world and you are its king. It is the place you go to.'

He stopped, smiled carefully. 'And you hear things.'

'Of course,' said Charlotte. She took another mouthful of the bread, wondering as she chewed if the eating was disconcerting to the boy. He showed no indication that it was. 'Keep going, please.'

'So those days, bad days. We met more natives. Not the ones who had attacked us. We had an eye for them by then: different markings, different things they carried. And when we tried our words, the ones we had learnt, we could see they knew some but not others. The words were new again.

'They came to us, out in the middle of this long beach, just after we made two rivers. The coast there was hard: lakes and sand spits and creeks. At one time we followed a spit, the ocean to our right and a lake full of swans to our left and the land ahead of us was, oh, less than thirty yards across. We were tired. Our feet sank deep with each step in the soft sand and each step we would pull them out and...It took...*work* to find the line that was the hardest sand and made the walking lighter. Mr Thompson was past that now: he just dropped his feet wherever they fell.

'There were mountains ahead of us to the north, or—you are Scottish, ma'am? Big hills, I should say then. Mr Clark would not have called them mountains. I could hear him talking low to Mr Figge—if the spit ended, we would have to double back so far that it might be the end of us.

'Then these men came. Four native men, painted, no spears. Smiling and showing great care for Mr Thompson and Mr Clark.'

'And you?'

'They were kind with me but the cut on my head had dried and the blood had stopped.' He touched the old bruise at his hairline, with the crust of scab in its centre. 'I was lame like the others, that was all. They wanted us to go with them. At first the men did not trust them, but we had to. They led us back off the sand spit, into the low ground behind the beach, and we came into a clearing as the sun was coming down through the trees in the smoke of their fires.

'A family was there; not so many of them but women and children, and we knew by now that if the women and children were shown to us it was a good thing, a sign of trust.

'We sat about their fire and they made a great fuss of us. This was not their village, no houses, just somewhere they had stopped to camp. They sat on logs they had brought up, and they touched our wounds; they made much of Mr Clark's hands: *maramal*, they said, over and over. But we were apart from each other and they must have seen this. The women tried to use herbs on Mr Thompson's wound, but he would not let them. He slapped them away, weak as he was, when they came near, and Mr Kennedy shouted and made fists to protect him. Mr Thompson's face was, oh it was ash by now. His breath very small and quiet.

'But they took the food. We all did. The natives gave us good fish they called *mara mara*, but Mr Kennedy was angry, wanting more. He took one off a small girl and she cried, and the natives saw it, but they did not act.

'We tried to talk, we drew in the earth with sticks and we pointed, like always. They were Tharawal, or Dharawal'—the boy's mouth made the sound several more times as he grappled with it—'and this land was theirs for many more miles, they said. They would protect us, they said. *Gaba*, they called us and they made like to embrace us. I wanted to stay with them and recover. I did not trust that Mr Clark had reckoned it right and we were within reach of Port Jackson.

'But Mr Figge was set on it. We go on, he said. And Mr Kennedy argued with him, in front of the natives. You could see they were shocked. Mr Kennedy was in two minds, you could see that too: he hated the natives and did not trust them. *Where are their spears?* he kept asking, out loud. *Prob'ly in the grass all round us, waitin' for a chance*, for that was how he talked. But he knew Mr Thompson was near finished; Mr Thompson himself could not speak on it. Mr Figge still insisted. I had a dark feeling that he did not want others around us.

'And so we went. Mr Kennedy was talking rough, pushing the native men, though they could have blown him over with a strong breath. He was like a drunk, and they stepped away from him with much grace.

'So we walked on and the sky cleared after the rain, the day was hot, the sweat burned in the places where my arms rubbed against my sides, itches from biting bugs. If the others had not yet thought about what we faced as our strength fell away... Well, there it was, miles of it in front of us.

'We had no eats for a long time after the fish that the Tharawal gave us. They stayed away, I think shy of Mr Kennedy. We looked for things to feed us: anything our teeth could crush up. At the creeks we took water in our hands, but it was often salty.

'Mr Clark tried to keep his hands clean by washing them in the ocean. I went to a rock pool one day—he asked me to go with him—and I saw him on his knees by the water's edge so he could put his hands in. And this is the—this is how we were: he watched me before he bent to it, as if I would attack him. He looked over both shoulders. When he finally put his hands in the pool he was watching the water, the reflection, to make sure nobody was behind him. We were animals now, wary of everything.

'There were bones broken in Mr Clark's hands, white splinters I could see. But no one was brave or not brave about any of it; there was no one to talk to and nothing to say. We each carried our ills. Mr Thompson had not spoken in days—he was no man anymore, but a corpse that still walked. The wound in his side had mortified, and it was clear he would not live.

'And so the days. Over the little headlands and crashing through the bush, weaving around strange squatting palms everywhere. Mr Figge went mad one morning: he saw a seal on a rock shelf and he chased the thing and it roared at him and stood tall and there they were: man and seal, up and screaming each at the other like they knew only hell and pain. Mr Figge took a stout branch and he swung it at the seal and it howled and went to bite him like a great fat dog but it missed, and he clubbed its head. I heard the crack when it hit and it broke the stick he was using. He got his senses back and he ran, with the seal behind him, so fast over those rocks with its big—'

He made a desperate flapping motion with his flat hands. Charlotte laughed, and it felt like releasing something.

'Flippers?'

'*Flippers*. Yes, ma'am. Slapping. But Mr Figge went like he'd stole something and the seal gave up. He was laughing ma'am, hard as you are, when he came back to us, but the fight had slowed him and he rested in the sun, and so we all did.

'I watched his head resting on the bundle of his things, ma'am, and it shames me but I thought of doing him in. I would just take a rock, just *take a rock*—'

Charlotte looked at the boy holding an imaginary rock between his outstretched hands. He seemed too delicate for the deed he had contemplated.

'—and break his head with it. In a world that had my father in it, I would not have thought this thing. This is what the walk had done to us all. I looked at Mr Clark and I knew his thoughts were the same.

'Mr Figge woke after the sun had come round to afternoon. Mr Kennedy had been out looking for food and he came back tired just as Mr Figge was waking. Mr Kennedy was looking to settle down for a bit, and Mr Thompson had already laid himself out in a gap between two rocks. He had pulled a branch over him, to stay warm; or maybe Mr Kennedy had done it. From one of those big bushes with the bark like paper, a dead part. Mr Thompson was under there, shivering.

'Mr Figge woke up to this and he was in a strange temper, very hard to read. Something in him had changed while he slept. He walked around a little. Looked at Mr Kennedy, who'd laid himself down on the open rocks. Oh and he—'

'Go on, Srinivas. You must.'

'—looked at Mr Thompson in his place under the branch. And he looked at me, and I was wishing he didn't. I was sitting like this with my chin on my hand, resting my head there. So tired. And he bent down and he looked into me, cold knife in my heart and he said, *A head is a heavy thing*.

'He did not look at Mr Clark. My bones ached that something was not right. Mr Figge did a little walk around where we were. He found some old bark and he sat down with it, took it apart in his fingers until it was all just…bits?'

'Fibres?'

'When his hands were full of the fibres he went to his things in their cloth and he found his little tinderbox. He worked the tinder and he got a spark up in the fibres and he crowed, happy he'd got it to work this time, and blew on the fibres and they caught nice, and then he got up. He took the ball of burning tinder and he dropped the bundle on the branch that was covering Thompson.'

'What? *No...*'

'I'm sorry ma'am. It might be best for you if I stop there.'

Charlotte Grayling steadied herself and thought of what she'd been entrusted with. 'Please continue,' she said, as formally as she could.

'It all happened very quickly. The branch lit up—*whoosh*—and Mr Thompson began to scream. And he fought, ma'am, he shook for all he was worth trying to get that branch off him. But Mr Figge walked away like he had already thought of this; he picked up a rock nearby, a good-sized one, and he walked back and dropped it on the burning branch and he just stood there. Mr Thompson was screaming and screaming and begging, and by now Mr Kennedy had got up and he tried to lift the rock but while he was bent over Mr Figge kicked him so hard he nearly fell into the fire.

'I tried to run forward too, ma'am, but Mr Clark...He held me. He got me around my middle and he said I should stay back. I was duty bound to do as he told me but I was watching a man die...we were both very weak anyways and I don't know how it would have gone if I had broken free but the screaming had become crying that was not like a man but an animal and there was a hissing sound that, maybe boiling...I don't know what.

'Mr Kennedy then, he was back on his feet and he took a branch and swung it at Mr Figge and it got him over the ear, knocked him sideways. But the second one was too slow and Mr

Figge got the end of it and took it from his hands and hit him with it. Mr Kennedy fell down and now it was getting darker but things were lit up awful by the fire over Mr Thompson, and he was no good for sounds but a groan or two.

'It was clear enough that Mr Thompson was done for but the fight went on—slow for a fight. Every time one of them moved you could see it cost him. I remember Mr Kennedy took a stone about this big and he threw it at Mr Figge and it caught him on the chin. It hurt him, there was blood. But he kept coming at Mr Kennedy and took a hold of him and took him to the ground. Not too hard for him, because he is plenty bigger.

'Mr Kennedy was shouting at Mr Figge, ma'am, foulest curses I've ever heard, and I've been at sea. I was thinking *you'd best use your air for the fight*, and Mr Figge just kept coming like he couldn't even hear it. He hit Mr Kennedy's face hard enough to kill a man. It was straight and it took him right between the eyes.'

Srinivas mimed the fist in front of his own face, looked at his knuckles like they were Figge's again.

'He fell *crack* with his head on the rock but he started getting back up again and it weren't on our account I can be fairly sure or even to save his own skin but he just hated the man so much I think it kept him going.'

The boy was wide-eyed now and his voice had risen in pitch, his breathing shallow. Charlotte stood and stepped to the window; was about to place her fingertips on the sill when she saw marks in the dust there: the shapes of fingertips. The boy had been standing there in lonely vigil. His sorrow filled her completely now.

'What happened to him?' she asked. 'To Mr Kennedy.'

'Mr Clark was still holding me but I had given up, really. The smoke from Mr Thompson and the branch was on the air and now it was blowing between us and the other two and the smell was so bad. The smuts got in the sweat on our faces, sticking there.

'There was…tumbling, times where everything happened and nothing happened. More fighting. Then Mr Kennedy was down, propped against a tree, eyes maybe open, maybe not. Mr Figge went back to the bundle of his belongings and I was just sure he was looking for that big knife to finish him. But his hand came out holding the gun. It felt like years ago that I'd watched him try out that gun, on the beach when we first started walking. It hadn't worked because of the seawater. I thought to myself, well why would you go and get that?

'He went over to Mr Kennedy ma'am and I need to say again it's no pleasant business but he put the gun up against the man's chin and moved his head up that way, and Mr Kennedy was just there enough to look evil at him and Mr Figge, who was much busted up himself, was singing or maybe chanting low sounds and I could not say for sure what it was. Nothing I ever heard on board.

'Mr Kennedy showed his teeth at him like a mad dog, even though the gun was up under his chin and if it worked it would make a big hole in his head from there. Mr Figge had his foot on him so he could not move and Mr Kennedy said to him clear as day, and forgive me cursing ma'am, he said *Ye cannae kill a man wi' a gun that doesnae fuckin' work.*

The boy sighed and gathered himself. Charlotte felt his disgust, his reluctance to go on. But they shared a hateful desire that this thing be said, and be heard.

'Mr Figge took him by the hair, ma'am, and pulled his head back hard and he said *oh it works all right* and he opened Mr Kennedy's jaw with his fingers until we could see the teeth he had and his tongue and a funny sound came out of him and I started pulling away from Mr Clark again—I'm not sure if it was to help Mr Kennedy or whether just because of the smoke—and the thing he was doing was…well, he had got the gun. He had his fingers pulling the mouth open and he took the gun, ma'am, and he rammed the barrel down the man's throat until it was five, maybe six inches down there all the way to the trigger guard and Kennedy's eyes went huge and Mr Figge struck the butt of the gun a couple of times with his fist and stuff shook out like spit and…and it went even further down and Mr Kennedy turned a bad shade of dark and the blood started to come up round the edge where his lips were round the metal and it was spillin' around the gun and Mr Figge was laughing and slapping his legs like he'd never seen a thing so funny. Like he were a child and the pedlar's monkey had danced for him, but the blood was bubbling in the poor man's throat and the veins in his neck and all bursting flesh and spots that came from bleeding inside and when he got tired of laughing, and it had been quite a long time now that the man had been in these torments, Mr Figge just pinched his nose and held it. He looked back at us with this empty, smiling face and the poor man went even darker and the part of his eyes that was white went red as blood. And then he stopped.'

'Oh, dear God.'

'I'm sorry, ma'am.'

Charlotte nodded; swallowed hard. Her task. The end of this saga, these awful men. 'Go on, Srinivas.'

The boy studied her for a moment.

'Mr Clark let me go then. Mr Figge stood up and Mr Kennedy stayed sitting as he was but he was dead as the rock under him. The foul smoke was over us and in us and I made to be sick, but I'd not eaten a thing for days by then. It was more just a sound.

'*The goin' should be easier now*, Mr Figge said to us like it never happened. Then he went back and he pulled the gun out of Mr Kennedy's mouth and wiped it on the leg of his breeches and put it back in his bundle. And there were other words on his breath as he did so. *Taking those as none shall miss*, he said. *Small lives go unmourned*.

'I couldn't take my eyes from Mr Kennedy because his mouth and his eyes were wide open and there were two of his teeth that the gun had broken off and they were stuck to his lip in the blood.'

The boy slumped a little where he sat. 'That was all that happened there. As I said, ma'am, I'm sorry.

'It is a fearful thing to be told. But that is the man you have here.'

34

Joshua Grayling had been admitted to Governor Hunter's office but not invited to sit. In the clear bright light of the room, William Clark had brought a chair around to the same side of the desk as Hunter, and neither appeared to register his presence.

He watched the two of them, deep in discussion and shoulder to shoulder, the merchant explaining to the governor how the escarpment ran closer to the coast as it stretched north, until it was a straight line of cliffs rising almost vertically from the sea.

It was obvious to Grayling that Clark's confidence surged when he got on to the commercial opportunities he felt he'd uncovered. The prevarication, the evasions he practised when asked about his companions: they were gone, and in their place was a condescending ease that infuriated Grayling. Why would the governor not push him harder?

'It was mostly just rock platform through there,' Clark

explained as he pointed to a drawing he had made with the governor's assistance. 'The platform was big flat stretches of sandstone, good on the feet, although the oysters could deliver a cut. Some boulders at the foot of the cliff, little pebbly cove here and there but no harbour, no landings. And the land, as I said, was narrow between sea and cliff, and so thick as to be nearly jungle.'

'But what was so very interesting here,' Clark continued, 'is that I wandered the beach in search of driftwood to make a fire and to my amazement, I found a block of the purest black coal.' He looked at them both like he had produced a rabbit from somewhere under his coat. 'Yes. Black coal, of a fine enough grade that I was able to burn it in a small campfire.'

An eyebrow betrayed the governor's interest. 'Did you find the source of the block?'

'Yes, Your Excellency, a seam running back into the cliff. A rich reserve, at least to my untrained eye. I believe it might be amenable to quarrying.'

The governor made careful note of this.

'Now I take it that Mr Figge and the lascar boy joined you at this coal fire you'd made...'

'Indeed they did, sir.'

'And they were still in reasonable health at this stage,' the governor said, as much to himself as to the room. The quill made its swirls over the page. Grayling saw now how his impatience had blinded him to Hunter's strategy. He'd seduced Clark, imperceptibly, into dropping his guard. 'But you and the two crewmen? Had your pace fallen by now?'

'Ah,' said Clark. 'I neglected to explain. As you will have seen from the journal, we had been forced to leave Mr Thompson and Mr Kennedy behind by this stage.'

'You referred to him only as "the carpenter" in your journal, I think,' Grayling said.

'I did, sir. I did not know him well to begin with, and once I had reached this sorry pass, what with my hands and all, I didn't find detail to be a priority.'

The governor frowned but did not look up from his work. 'Tell me a little about that parting. When you left the two of them.'

'Well now,' Clark rolled his eyes towards the ceiling. 'What do I remember? Late afternoon. As the day wore on, I'd made several entreaties to them to get up and move before dark. We held grave reservations regarding the attitude of the savages in those parts. But despite my pleas, Thompson was lying down and could not get up. Mr Figge made a fire, and there was an argument—Kennedy became quite vocal in his defence—then Mr Figge intervened and the matter was settled. We were forced to leave them there.

'Where *exactly*, Mr Clark?' The governor held his quill ready again, quivering over the page.

'The cliff country, but north of where we found the coal. There were about ten miles between the coal and the beach where we were rescued, and I would estimate it was the day before…the place must be two or three miles south of the rescue site. Yes, yes—I am satisfied that is it.'

'Mr Clark,' said the governor, 'you seem less sure of this than other matters, yet it is quite recent.' The governor looked up and spoke to Grayling as though Clark wasn't there. 'Is that where we've sent the boat on the basis of this man's journal?'

'Yes, sir. I think it is, more or less.'

He turned back to Clark, and Grayling could see, from having watched him over the years, that the governor was closing in.

'Mr Clark, the fishing vessel that picked you up on the sixteenth went back out again on the seventeenth, after the lieutenant and I had read your journal. I expect they will be back later today. I had asked them to make urgent searches and to inquire of the natives if they could. So we may hope'—he watched Clark as he formed the words—'that they will have news of your abandoned companions.'

The governor's pale eyes never left Clark. His weathered face betrayed no judgment, nothing but a calm expectation.

'Yes,' Clark replied eventually, looking down at the wounded hands resting on his lap. 'We can only hope. But I fear the natives will have done them harm by now.'

⊪

After the meeting was over, Grayling sat with Clark's journal in a small anteroom off the governor's office, studying the book with his head in his hands. The morning light made squares on the desk, framed by the window panes.

> *Our disagreeable and treacherous companions continued with us on our journey until mid-morning, when they betook themselves to the woods, leaving us extremely happy at their departure.*

He had always assumed it was Clark's disdainful reference to the Wandandean, or the other natives that Charlotte said the boy had mentioned, the Tharawal. Now it seemed loaded with meaning.

He was lost in the words, so that the knock at the door made him jump. Mrs Butcher, the governor's head maid. She stood with a hand on the doorhandle, which for her meant reaching up to eye level.

'Forgive me,' she said. 'Your wife, lieutenant.'

Charlotte peered around the doorway behind the maid. She had never come to this part of the building, never encroached on his working life in this way. Her face betrayed no worry, but he knew better than to make assumptions. He dismissed the maid and Charlotte closed the door behind herself.

'What is it?' he asked.

'I'm sorry—' she stammered. 'I wouldn't have come here, of course, but I...'

'What's happened?'

'The man, the one you described to me. He's come back.' Her hands rose nervously to her face. 'He's taken Boorigul.' She began to cry.

Grayling rushed around the desk to her and held her. She plunged her head into his chest and sobbed. With his fingers in her hair and the rise and fall of her breath close against him, he felt again that chaos she brought: steadying him and flustering him by turns. The girl was not their child. She was not even their lodger. She was someone who had sought refuge near them. Not even in their home, but near them. Charlotte's face, her whole body, was focused down into his heart.

The man no doubt had some business with the girl. An intended husband, he thought, or a tribal relationship—they seemed as complex and unending as the weather. It was beyond him and Charlotte to stop such a thing, or to interfere in it.

She raised her head. 'I had her inside the house,' she began. 'I wanted her to try some of the things I'd bought at the Rocks. He came in and he just started to shout and wave his arms, he came in and...'—she wiped tears from her eyes—'and she screamed back at him and he took the chair and...and he tried to strike her with it and I got between them and the chair hit me and...'

'Charlotte! What were you *thinking*? Are you hurt?'

'...and then he did, he struck her with it and it broke apart and no, I'm fine, but she fell and he took her up by the hair and the arm and he dragged her out and she was crying, Joshua, she was crying and I have never heard her utter such sounds. Dear God.'

The rage inside him made him quieter. 'He *hit* you with the chair?'

'Well, yes, but it was because...'

'I cannot let that stand.'

'Please.' She took him by the lapels and looked deep into his eyes. 'Please, Joshua, understand it's not that which grieves me. It is the poor girl. She did not want to go. She might...come and go from our house, but she did *not* want to go with that man.'

'Maybe she had to. Maybe she had done the wrong thing, being with us.'

'*Had* to? He dragged her out by the hair! Why must you always be so...so...'

She broke free from him and turned away, wrenched open the door and paused, then closed it behind herself with composure. Because, he knew, she would be thinking of him and the dignity of his place of work even now. He hated himself, and perhaps her too, for that consideration.

He followed her downstairs, through the hall. She crossed the orchard without looking up at the colourful violence of a mob of parrots attacking an apple tree, and swept through the gate that marked the end of the Government House gardens, where the kangaroo grass began. He realised he did not know what he would say if he caught up with her. He couldn't descend to shouting at her in the street. People were already turning and looking: eager for a fresh feed of gossip.

She was striding, determined now, away from the houses of the administrators, their foolish fences and their walls. Her head was down, and though he could only see the angry slant of her back, he knew the grim line in which her mouth was set. Her white dress, so bright in the clean sunlight, beat across the dun-coloured land like a tiny sail. She was aiming herself at the bush. Past the Eora, circling their small fires; towards some mystery in the trees that would always beckon her.

35

In the afternoon, Charlotte took off the clothes she had walked in, wrestled them through a cask of water then hung them to dry behind the house. Obscured from the street by the heavy foliage of the peach tree, she stood barefoot in a shift, the sun on her shoulders and chest. The ground was littered with the large woody nuts that the wind threw down from the big trees. The sun and the wind coming over from inland would dry everything by the time he returned in the evening, but she cared less now. What she did for herself, she would keep to herself.

The washing done, she sent for the boy.

She tidied the house and broke flowers from the garden, spiked and strange. She stuffed them in a jug on the table; threw open the sash windows so the clear air swept through the two rooms. She swept the floor and took a rag to the spiderwebs in the corners that held the dry husks of enormous flies.

By the time the private returned with the boy, she'd wrestled the cottage into a satisfactory state. The soldier was tall, the red sleeve of his coat extended with disdain to where he had the boy's upper arm in a painful grip. She had no idea whether Srinivas was in custody, or this was merely one of the small acts of bullying that made up a private's busy day.

'You may release him,' she said firmly, and the soldier shoved the boy forward. She thought to tell her husband about the brute; but she knew he had no sway with the Corps. She would only make it worse for him and the governor. Srinivas shook himself loose with a flash of anger and gave her a nod that might have been a shallow bow, but without words. The soldier shuffled a few paces back and stood to smirking attention. Charlotte glared at him as she retreated inside and shut the door.

She turned and gestured to the boy to sit. Studied his face as he did so. She found shades there of wariness, and the glimmer of something illicit.

'You didn't speak to the soldier?'

He smiled faintly. Now they were conspirators. 'No, ma'am.'

'I should have come for you myself. It's just…I was worried for you.' *Shut up*, said an inner voice.

He accepted a cup of tea, some bread. She waited through the slow clearing of his hesitance, busying herself with trivial things around them. Re-closing the windows, poking the fire. The last discussion had shaken her deeply: curdled her misgivings about the tea merchant into deep loathing. But of Joshua's motivations she was less sure. She knew he also hated the man, but perhaps in his case it was that Figge had handled her, had laid his hands on her body and—as ugly as the reality was—had cured her.

Her back was turned, the boy slurping loudly on the rim of the teacup, when she abruptly began.

'Can you tell me what happened afterwards? After the two men...'

He put the cup down, watchful. 'Ma'am,' he said softly, 'I hope I am not impolite, but I have a question.'

She nodded eagerly. 'Of course, dear. Go ahead.' *Dear*. It echoed falsely in her mind.

'What will you do with what I tell you?'

She had considered this. She had spoken to her husband, told him the shape of her thinking. 'We must go to the governor. He needs to know, Srinivas. He needs to know what happened, and to take appropriate measures.'

He did not seem agitated by this. 'My safety...?'

This she had worried about. She knew no firm answer but the need to reassure was the greater thing. 'You will be safe.'

And when he nodded calmly she had the sense that he had accepted it on that basis: good intentions—nothing more.

⚓

'We walked all that night, ma'am. I don't know why. Mr Clark's no longer in charge—it's all Mr Figge, but he's not saying much. We're following him, I suppose. He acts as if he knows where to go. Cliffs, and we're high on the edge of them, then beaches then cliffs again. North-east, not straight north anymore. And every cliff I wonder if he will catch us off guard, just throw us to our deaths.

'By dawn we're on that long line of high rocks with the sun coming up below us, weak and grey. A fever dawn, you understand, ma'am? I think Mr Figge had walked us through the night because he was in fear of the natives. But by then I've forgotten what to be scared of. We're walking so we can watch each other. Sometimes we walk into things: trees, or holes in the ground, because we're watching each other.

'Someone falls down, I can't remember who. It could have been me. Never have I felt the pull of sleep so strong as that morning. There we are ma'am, the middle of the morning, the three of us capsized in the grasses by a swamp, a pool that reflects the light, filled with reeds and things moving. Turtles, maybe. Ducks. So bright there it makes a great weight on my eyes.

'There is some time there, hours. When I wake up I've got the sense to keep my eyes closed, to look without being seen looking. I can see Mr Figge and Mr Clark sitting. Awake, talking. They've made a small fire and they're talking quiet. Talking about their plans. And then they're talking about killing me.

'Mr Figge has a rock in his hand, ma'am. The rock is the size of that loaf, and he's pushing it towards Mr Clark, saying *do it*. Mr Clark's upset, saying he doesn't have the stomach—*stomach*?'

'Yes,' Charlotte replied.

'And Mr Figge's laughing at him. *How many more must I do for you, Clarkey?* he says.

'Mr Clark's cursing Mr Figge, words I don't wish to repeat, and still Mr Figge laughs. And Mr Clark, he says *Give me the rock then*, and Mr Figge hands it over and I can feel such a fear in me, I'm choosing a moment to find my feet and run. If Mr Clark had the rock he would be slow, but Mr Figge would run me down quick.

'Of course it will be me next. I can see it then. And the chance to run has been closed off, as Mr Clark's already on his feet with the rock in his hand. I close my eyes and think once of my father, praying that this blow would join me to him once again.

'But instead ma'am there's a noise, a thud, and I open my eyes to find that Mr Clark has struck Mr Figge with the rock, hit him right between the eyes. His nose is broke, that is clear, and there's a great deal of blood coming down through his beard and over his chest, making drops on the rock as he falls back. He goes back on the rock on his arm, like this'—the boy demonstrated with his elbow on the table—'and Mr Clark's quick on him and hits him again. This time over his head.'

Again, the boy demonstrated by pointing at his own scalp.

'Both times, ma'am, they are enough to kill anyone else. And I cannot say, I do not know what's in his mind, but Mr Clark, he just drops the rock and runs. He has the bag over his shoulder, the one where he keeps his diary and his instruments. But he doesn't stop to pick up anything else. He doesn't speak to me. He just goes.'

'Perhaps he couldn't finish it. Kill him, I mean,' offered Charlotte.

'Maybe. But before long Mr Figge's moving about. Making sounds of pain. And he reaches a hand for the rock and there is such terror in me, I cannot say. A man may have to take up a rock against another one day and with good reason, but Mr Clark had raised a hand against the devil himself. I could not imagine what terrible fate he had opened for us by doing it.

'So I go too, ma'am. I get to my feet and go blind into the scrub as fast as I can run. It makes a lot of noise—a lot of cracking branches and my *breathing*—so I cannot be sure what's happening behind. Only that he's coming. I know he's coming.

'Ahead of me I see Mr Clark and I'm calling to him. He doesn't look back, just head-down running, and that is what I got for all my good service. We're on a path—sometimes in the thick places there's a path that's clear and it goes where you're going—and this one followed the cliff top. Always close to the edge so you could see out to the sea, but far enough back so you would not fall.

'Mr Clark's running ahead and I'm chasing him, calling, and Mr Figge's coming behind. I look back at him and I can see him at the bottom of a rise in the path, carrying his bundle as he always does. That means he has a knife, the gun and the tinderbox and I do not know what else. There is much blood on him and he roars like a beast. I try to keep looking ahead because it's hard not to trip, even though the path is good. On both sides are the trees, the ones with the big flowers that become cones.'

'Banksias. After Mr Banks.'

'Oh. Yes. They make roots across the path sometimes. Easy to trip on them, is the thing I was saying. Many times I fall, and each time I get up Mr Figge is closer.

'After that last beach, we run the length of it, heavy, deep, and then the cliffs are high and straight and there's no break for maybe, I don't know, three or four miles. I'm staying with Mr Clark though he's not helping me at all or even looking at me, ma'am, but we've both lost the path. It just comes to a point…some thin trees had fallen, and we just crash through and go straight ahead and we're in the bush. I'm thinking at any minute we'll come through blind and fall and die on the rocks below.

'As we're running I'm shaking again, thinking only let me lie down and allow what comes. Perhaps the reason I am still going is the fear it would not be a quick death. I'm calling out to Mr Clark, just loose words, but saying I can no longer hear Mr Figge, that we could stop and hide and he won't find us in the thick bush. Mr Clark must have heard me because one skip left and he throws himself down a little ditch and behind a heavy log and lies still. There's time for me to do the same, then we both lie there. Breathing hard but trying to make no sound.

'And soon Mr Figge comes by, moving fast, breaking

everything in his path. I can see his eyes ma'am and they're...
There is no man living in there.

'Then I press my face into the earth and in front of my eyes
is one of the holes that the ants make, the big ones...?'

'Yes, I know the ones.'

'They're coming out, many dozens and fast. I have been stung
by them before, so I know how much it's going to hurt and I
can see them coming, so I might not cry out. But Mr Clark's
facing the other way. If they sting him he'll cry out and we will
be discovered. I'm pinching them, stopping them as best I can
but there's more and more coming out, and I'm looking at Mr
Figge and he's moving about, searching. Almost *smelling*, his
face close to the ground and not so far from us. The slightest
noise and he will know. I cannot understand how he hasn't
seen—we'd torn the ground in our rush to hide ourselves.

'But it doesn't matter, the ants I mean, because then Mr
Clark does the most surprising thing. He was next to me under
the log, safe there, but he gets up and stands, only six or seven
feet from Mr Figge. I can see the whole thing: Mr Clark's legs
all covered in sores and the ragged ends of his trousers, but past
him, Mr Figge, with the blood stuck like tar in his whiskers and
on his shirt. And those eyes. The broke-up nose just making
them burn worse than ever.

'He drops the bag off his shoulder and out comes the knife.
Just holds it low like there's a snarl in a buntline. Steps forward
at Mr Clark and says *Where is the boy?* And Mr Clark just says
I'd got away, gone running off into the bush. *We don't need to
worry about him now*, he says, but any fool can see there's no
we for them anymore. Mr Figge's got a bone come out under
his eye that says so.

'They've still got the log between them, and they're both

shouting and I see that Mr Figge doesn't have the strength to get past the log, to stick the knife in Mr Clark and end it. His hand hangs like the knife is a great weight to him. Mr Clark steps back, keeps the log in the way. Little steps, watching Mr Figge close, like you might a wild beast. Once he's back a little he stands on open ground, and Mr Figge comes around the log. Mr Clark backs away some more and the shouting stops. Now they just watch to see what the other will do.

'So Mr Clark goes on walking backwards into the bushes with his eyes on Mr Figge and then there is a noise and he cries out and…he's gone. Just thumps and breaking sticks and such.'

'Where did he go?'

'The cliff. The land just ended and he was gone. Do you understand? When you are in the bushes everything is so close and scratching you and then it just stops: just air. It always felt to me like someone was going to go over.'

'What's Mr Figge doing when this happens?'

'Coming for him, like I said. To where Mr Clark disappeared and he's looking down—I can't see from where I'm hiding—and then he puts himself on his arse, sorry ma'am, like a child and pushes with his hands and he slides a bit and then a bit more. Then, same as Mr Clark, he's gone. I come out and I'm glad to be away from those ants but there's very little left in me, just this shaking in my knees.

'I hold on to a tree for a time. There's no sound. The noise from the two of them going down the cliff has stopped and it's just the wind and some birds.

'I'm still thinking Mr Figge will come from somewhere like this is a game and he's won it. I'm stepping forward in the scrub to where they went down and I can see it's very steep. *Maybe they died*, I'm thinking, *and now it's just me*. But it's not a great height like I had thought. Only yards, I don't know, maybe twenty yards through the little trees to the beach.'

His brow furrowed in concentration. 'I can see them. They are moving all broken over the rocks, then they are trying to walk across a creek mouth. Up to their knees, but it's nearly enough water to knock them over. The water goes down, they take a step and then a wave comes up the creek and hits them. Mr Figge nearly has him now, but a wave gets him and he falls down and Mr Clark gets out onto the sand and starts off across the beach. Mr Figge, he's swept back with the wave to where the seawater is, and he's rolled over by another wave and he looks like a bundle of rags in that wave rolling over and by the time he's got his feet again Mr Clark is quite a way up the beach. But then he stops and falls and I think maybe it is the end of him.

'Do I want him to get away from Mr Figge? I can no longer say. The world unfolds now and I can only watch. Duty is nothing: I cannot send loyalty down the cliff. My father would let it be so, whatever it is. That is how I think. Anyway, I have no strength left. I have been several days now without food, and the ground is clean where I lie. Just a soft mat of leaves between the trees, some shoots of the tough grass. The light is kind—it does not burn.

'There is a time when I recall nothing at all. Perhaps I'm sleeping. When I open my eyes, I can see the world as it is for the smallest creatures. In front of me is an arch in the grass, maybe ten inches high. Bent together, I don't know how. Maybe they grow like that. Something is moving behind it. Not clear; then it becomes so: there is a bird inside the arch. I've been still so long the bird is not worried by me. A heavy, fat bird, its feathers a bright black that is…what do you call that colour ma'am, the jug?'

283

Charlotte regarded it. The glass jug she had placed on the table: thick and dark, but where it had been chipped on one shoulder it refracted light.

'Indigo.'

'Yes. That. And oh! An *eye*. An eye I've not seen on a bird, or on any other animal. A jewel, deepest blue. Like a glass bead, shining on those black feathers. Fixed on me now—'

He turned his head to one side and it became the bird's head: cocked, considering. Charlotte almost laughed.

'I don't move, and it minds its business, pecks at all the dried stuff around it. I can see now that the things did not just fall so: they were put there by the bird, and there it is, tending them with its beak: moving, putting, moving again. And all through the soft mound it's made, put very delicate round the arch of grasses, are all manner of…feathers, flower petals and berries, flakes of mussel shells—each of them as blue as that eye. Blues that—' He absently raised a finger in the air. 'Can you have… when you say "blue", more than one blue?'

She smiled. 'Yes.'

'They would not be other colours, then?'

'They can all be blue. The sky and the sea.'

'Yes. So many blues I never knew to be out there in the world. My poor eyes see the strange collection, so neat that at first I think the natives have put it there. But the way the bird *tends* to its blue things…'

Again, his hands worked at providing the meanings that his speech lacked: they patiently shuffled imaginary blue objects, each in turn, so the spaces between them appeared uniform. *There is a man close by who brings a passage to hell with him*, Charlotte thought, *and here you are—you and the bird…*

'I watch as the bird picks up a thing from its collection and

I stare at the thing in its beak. I reach out a hand and the bird drops it, struts off very cross as I pick it up. A tiny pin of bone, ma'am, polished. Snapped off at one end. Some words in English, carved like scrimshaw. On the end that was not broken there's a little brass chain, and on it the thing that caused the bird to want it: four beads of lapis lazuli: bright blue like the bird's eye.

'A lost bobbin. A token of love, ma'am. And the moment I see it I know the fat bird has not flown far.'

A fat bird worried the ground in Charlotte's mind, drawn to both its collection and the sky, but she couldn't grasp its significance. 'I'm not sure I follow, Srinivas.'

'The bobbin could come from only one place, you see. Very close by.'

Charlotte smiled and he nodded furiously.

'Sydney.'

〜

'So there I am lying, bobbin in my hand. So close to harbour; too weak to get up and walk there.

'The bird returns to its work, and I shuffle myself down low on the edge of the cliff where I can look over the beach. At first nothing is out of place. You do not see what you are not looking for. You see sand, blue water and rock. Just as any other day.

'And then…Then there is the boat. It has come around the headland from the north, just small but under full sail in a light breeze. Heeling over as if it will pass the back of those two reefs and keep going south. I cannot believe my eyes. I can see men on her decks working and it feels like they have come with their boat from a different world, we have been so long in the bush. I am supposed to know boats, of course, my whole life. But this is like something that has fallen from the skies.

'I'm waving and jumping and I no longer care that this will reveal me to Mr Clark and Mr Figge. They are far below and halfway across the beach by now, too spent to come back up the hill. I think, too, that they are too low down to see the boat. They do not change their positions: at first, they look dead. Perhaps sleep has taken them too. But Mr Clark starts to crawl along the sand and Mr Figge starts after him, also on his hands and knees. The most pitiful sight.

'Then the boat changes course and tacks between the two reefs, and a new hope comes to me. It is safe now, I think, to go down there—they cannot kill me in front of other men—and I cannot afford to be missed by being up there on the bluff.

'I start down the rocky parts between the trees, sideways, like I had seen walabees do. I fall anyway, once or twice; yards only, not the full distance. Maybe it's seeing the boat, or maybe I have come to the end of everything and death is approaching, but my body is giving up. My eyes, my legs are…I let myself fall, just lie down and slide over the loose rocks at the bottom, pulling with my arms when my legs will not do the work. I can still feel the shells on the rocks: they tear at my skin and I no longer care for the pain. The joy at the sight of the boat, the power gone from inside me, all at once.

'I fall to the creek mouth and I am bleeding—these are the cuts ma'am, here and here—and the blood's going out in clouds in the water. I drag myself across on my hands and knees, a hopeless turtle in the sand, sand stuck in my wounds and stinging eyes, sand in my mouth like a helpless infant. I breathe and it tears my throat.

'Ahead I can see the other two and now I feel I could laugh if only I can remember how: all three of us on our hands and knees, each lost to the world. The boat luffs its sails there off the beach and they drop an anchor and a jollyboat and two sailors row it to shore and call out to us but I cannot hear what they are calling and we are saved, we are saved and they could be the angels or just ordinary men but the difference comes to naught because nothing matters any longer.'

III

36

Grayling generally took pains to avoid the Brickfields.

There was a hunger about the place, away down the South Head Road and far from judgment's eye.

Seeing as the colony provided no formal entertainment, the people gathered there on a Saturday and found their own. The Contests, they called it, or the Fighting.

As they would loiter and stare at a corpse in the street or the stop-swing snap of a hanging, so the people would mill about the gruesome spectacle of two natives going at each other. They lit upon an intersection of language; it came to be understood that the fighting was payback. And it was not always the Eora who sated the lust. Sometimes it was white men—and if no one could find a human grudge to settle there was always cockfighting or dogs to fall back on.

Of the four thousand colonists and as many Eora, a fair majority would throng the dusty flats of the Brickfields for the Fighting. Weapons might be used—the rules of an Eora contest were beyond the control of the audience—and there was no predicting the age or sex of the combatants, or the terms of the dispute. The crowd came for the skill of it, the sweat and the open wounds and the ultimate collapse of the vanquished. It mattered not whether the Eora had organised the fight to take place there on the open ground in order to accommodate onlookers or whether the place had come to be used because the traditional places were now seized: nobody involved in watching the Contests gave any thought to their deeper meaning. The point was simply to have a place to drink openly, something on which to wager—and unthinking release.

A girl had died in the dust there, late in the summer. Entirely innocent, it turned out, of the thing being litigated, but positioned in the family such that she must answer for it. The governor had asked Grayling to be present that day out of concern for the public order. The young woman gasping on the ground, her bright, ghastly wounds under the roar and the smashing of bottles and the pitiless sun: it paralysed Grayling with horror. He could not describe it when Charlotte later asked him what had happened. He had no words, no way of knowing whether the scene represented the workings of another society or a mutation of those workings: changes wrought by the pox and the land taken and the slavering hordes.

Now he found himself part of that disturbing crowd once again. A leaflet had gone around the town.

The Much-Celebrated Shipwreck Survivor and Businessman Mr William Clark is to be Farewelled, Upon the Occasion of His Departure for Calcutta, at the Brickfields after the Contests.

Senior members of the New South Wales Corps would be in attendance, the flyer promised.

Grayling left his arrival as late as he could. He placed himself on the rise above the contest ground where the crowding trees offered swift escape as the sun softened in the west. It was women and children this far out: the men were concentrated closer in and thoroughly drunk by now. All that remained of the preceding violence was a patch of scuffed ground and a large bloodstain. He had no desire to know whose blood it was: the body from which it had run was now the concern of Dr Ewing, or the sexton.

A group of troopers entered the open ground and deposited a small wooden stage there. More of them came forward with a podium and a weary flag, St George and the saltire, on a small pole.

A delegation pushed forward, the soldiers swinging freely at the drunks to clear a way. In their midst was a stallion; as they neared, Grayling recognised the rider perched high above the fray. Thin and disdainful, John Donald Macarthur had chosen an immaculate uniform jacket for the occasion, though no one had seen him engaged in soldierly duties for months. Grayling felt a deep surge of the enmity that the governor knew, but unmediated by the governor's measured character. The man was a tyrant in the making: a grasper made powerful by influential friends.

Their posse rumbled forward, taken off course at times by the weight of the crowd. Macarthur dismounted and handed the reins to a soldier. Elizabeth, normally a fixture at her husband's appearances, had had the sense to stay away. The horse shied and baulked, its eyes big with fear as it was led off. Standing a head taller on the podium, Macarthur surveyed the crowd.

Grayling searched the faces near the stage and found William Clark, partially visible behind the gold-encrusted shoulder of Macarthur's jacket. His face showed only confusion.

Macarthur lifted his chin high and aimed a glare at the crowd down his long, thin nose. He held it as silence descended, then abruptly smiled at the melee before him: these were his friends now, eager to hear from him. They cheered at the feint, because they didn't know what else to do. Two dogs broke into a vicious tangle of teeth and fur before they were kicked apart.

'I hope you have enjoyed your day,' Macarthur began. 'Not something I would ordinarily be a part of'—he smirked—'but having a commercial interest in intemperance, I wish you well.'

The crowd took a moment to disentangle the language, then cheered again and raised their bottles. He waved, dismissive.

'Now as a Scotsman, it falls to me to farewell a countryman of mine. I know'—he raised a hand to refute a protest that had not occurred—'I know your esteemed governor is also a Scot, but it seems he was too busy to come and discharge this responsibility'—widespread booing—'busy playing his fiddle and painting his birds. His time will come, I assure you.'

Grayling could scarcely believe what he was hearing. The brazenness of it.

'But for today,' Macarthur continued, 'it is my duty to pay tribute to Mr William Clark'—he swept a hand in Clark's direction and Clark made a gesture at doffing his hat—'a good man and true, who not only survived the worst ravages of the sea but led seventeen men on a trek that will surely become famous in this colony's history.'

Fourteen of them dead, Grayling muttered to himself. A small drunkard with a matted beard was stroking the leg of Macarthur's trousers, apparently entranced by the quality of the fabric. Macarthur slapped him away and droned on.

'Mr Clark was pursuing business for this colony, gentlemen. Business. He wanted us to have rum, so that we might enjoy some means of commerce—*commerce*! The good Lord doesn't want us idle here, but productive, turning this wild place into a model of harmonious society and a great trading port of the Pacific. Aye, that He does.'

Dust; the restless stirring of the crowd.

'Yet Mr Clark's treatment upon arriving here has been, sadly, less than civil. His account called into question—disbelieved, even—by those at Government House who might struggle to take a long walk in their garden, let alone survive the manifold horrors of the bush.'

Macarthur looked around himself, out into the crowd, as though searching. The faces of the men formed a collective snarl and some of them looked back to the south-west, towards Government House.

'A hero, ladies and gentlemen. Cross-examined and hectored by the self-appointed gentry. How *dare* they.'

Grayling felt a surge of fear. The man had an instinct for this: he had the crowd baying. If Macarthur pointed him out now, he would have to answer to the mob. They knew he was Hunter's aide: it would be as good as lynching the governor. But Macarthur showed no awareness of Grayling's presence.

'I want tae thank Mr Clark on your behalf; for his part in the bold expedition to bring consumer goods and aye, spirituous liquors'—much hooting and laughter at this—'to our humble colony. For his bravery in surviving the natives and all the other privations of that long journey. And for his good grace in tolerating the excesses of our bureaucracy. We wish him all the best for his return to Calcutta, and we ask that perhaps one day he will consider returning to us, when conditions are more…receptive.'

Clark looked up gratefully at Macarthur from his station behind the podium, declining, with a modest wave of his bandaged hands, to make a speech in reply. The crowd raised three cheers to his health and more brandishing of bottles followed. And then a curious spectacle ensued: the men surrounding the podium ushered Clark onto it and induced him to sit. They then produced two long poles, which they slotted into iron rings on the sides of it. On a signal, they raised the podium aloft with Clark on it, supported by six or eight of the largest men. The cheering began again and Clark waved feebly. When the crowd continued to call his name he took off his hat and threw it to them.

The platform was rotated now and pointed downhill towards the shore at Rose Bay. The crowd followed, the men leading and the women bringing the children along behind. The Eora divided themselves: some were happy enough to join the procession, clapping arms around each other and even the convicts. Others walked off, indifferent.

Grayling remained still, feeling the energy of the mob dissipating as it poured downhill. A ship waited at anchor just off the bay, a rowboat on the beach. Bottles, bones and the gnawed remains of fish littered the ground. Gulls massed over the empty ground for scraps: human shit glistened here and there, coiled and smeared underfoot.

Clark was gone: and at his going remained as much of an enigma to Grayling as the day he arrived. Was he a bad man? Or just an ordinary one, taken to extremity? Grayling had no idea, and no measure, either, of his complicity with Figge. Perhaps he was a simple opportunist—it put him in company with just about every resident of the town.

Of one thing he was absolutely sure: Clark was no hero. He had evaded the capricious version of justice on offer here. Now, somewhere out at sea, he would prepare his explanations for others, brandishing the bloodied diary in defence of his curious tale.

37

 Grayling made his way to the governor's residence in the last light of evening, his mind alive with ideas.

The man who had taken Boorigul had a name. It had been made known to him in the same way so much else was passed to him: in reports, filed for the governor. Reports about the settlers' complaints and fears; about armed soldiers pushing deep into hostile country, successfully and unsuccessfully; about their bodies returning to Sydney in carts, studded with spear-ends snapped off by their desperate comrades. About intelligence gleaned from Eora with a score to settle—or a family to save, with diversionary information, from someone else's score-settling.

There was enough corroboration between the accounts that a picture was emerging.

Boorigul had been taken by a young warrior who went by the name of Warrander. The man was said to be Cadigal and did not reside within the limits of the township. She was betrothed to him and had left to seek shelter in the town because of his involvement with another woman. Over the same period that Boorigul had been coming and going, Warrander had been implicated in a number of maize fires around Toongabbie and Parramatta, unrelated to her presence in Sydney—but possibly motivated by a loyalty to Pemulwuy. To date he was not known to have killed anyone.

These matters came to Grayling and he recorded them. Names and dates and incidents and reports—the passage of lives themselves—were the victuals that nourished the growing administration. It did not have to be a personal matter that Grayling collected such things. It was one of the subjects that occupied him, nothing more.

Another was Figge. He knew enough of him now, enough to pounce. Pemulwuy, out there in the darkness somewhere, was the fire that threatened them from without. But ultimately he would flicker and die. The greater danger was the malignancies within: Macarthur and the Corps. And this man Figge. Wherever it was that he had come from, Figge had attached himself to the colony through the demise of the *Sydney Cove*, and now Grayling would be the one to put an end to it. He needed only an order.

His footfalls rang on the flagstones of the entryway and he heard the familiar music from upstairs. The melancholy strains of the governor's violin, leaking from the study and into the night: the sequence of long, mournful bowing; a faster, skipping passage, another long note.

Grayling's knock at the door was answered by Mrs Butcher, still crisply attired in cap and apron, despite the late hour. She regarded him evenly, and led him into the hallway.

'You may wish to take a seat, lieutenant,' she said, gesturing to the alcove by the stairs and a pew that had the look of convict work. The music curled carefully onwards, resonating in the timbers of the big house. As he sat, placing himself more or less in the centre of the short bench, he saw that the old woman was turning to do the same. He scurried to one end before her backside came to weary rest. She straightened her back and folded her hands on her lap and they listened in silence. There was a gravity about her, a quiet authority. He had no doubt she was a tyrant in the back rooms—the young girls would live in terror of her silences. She would rule by inference, he thought, not by rage.

Grayling had never learnt an instrument but, turning his mind to the sound from upstairs, he sensed a tiredness in the bowing, little cracks at the edges like the faintly slurring speech of a man on watch in the deep hours.

'What is the music?' he asked, turning his head finally to Mrs Butcher. She did not look back at him but down at her hands.

'Geminiani. His Excellency has been working on it for many weeks.'

'Oh. Splendid.' Grayling took out his watch and examined it. 'Will he perform it for us, do you think?'

'No,' she said firmly. 'He will perfect it, then move to another piece.' The knots in her knuckles. The worn nails. The liver spots on the backs of those hands, the abrasions from scrubbing.

'Why do it then?' It felt like something he would wonder privately; but he had asked out loud.

She looked at him now. 'With the utmost respect, lieutenant, why do anything?' There was no censure in her expression. She took a fold of the fabric in her lap; rearranged it under her hands. 'It's the largo from the *Sonata in D*. The final bars. He will put the instrument aside momentarily.'

'How can you tell?'

'I taught him when he was a boy. Impatient, like you. Will you take tea, lieutenant?'

⚜

The violin had been returned to its case and removed from sight. The easel was still shrouded; these were planes of other existences in the man. The governor had opened a chiffonier and was stooping into it uncomfortably. Grayling had heard stories about the wounded leg, but the governor never spoke of it.

'I have brandy,' he said, his back turned to the lieutenant as he searched among bottles. Receiving no answer, he turned to look at Grayling.

'I'm sorry sir, I thought...'

'You thought I'd banned it? Public example must give way occasionally to private necessity, lieutenant.' He smiled gently. 'I'm having one. Won't you join me?'

Grayling nodded assent. The governor poured them two rummers and took a seat in the armchair that faced Grayling's. He heaved a deep sigh.

'I have to find someone to replace the sails on the windmill.' He laughed at himself. 'My great edifice. My two-hundred-year windmill.'

'You don't need to concern yourself with the details of it, sir.'

'I know. I know. It's just...there's so much. This place so strongly resists civilisation.'

'The natives, you mean?'

'Not just them. The land...the bush, good lord. Snakes and insects. The wind. Much of what I've done seems undone already. The windmill's a sort of public demonstration of the futility of it all. Why did I have to go and say it had two hundred years in it?'

He laughed again; Grayling smiled with him.

'You brought the place up out of lawlessness, sir. Now it's a society, isn't it? It might be rough, but it bends to the rule of law. A few more years and we'll—'

'There won't be a few more years. The home secretary has me singled out. I brought the convicts back in from the farms to appease him and now I'm culpable for the farmers' anger.' A shadow crossed the lined face, where Grayling had only ever seen kindness. 'Can you imagine Westminster from here? I can't. But they're speaking my name in Westminster, speaking it with derision.'

Grayling sipped silently from the brandy. He had never heard the governor speak this way; had become accustomed to the man's dry practicality, his caution.

'There is much at stake for the Corps.' The governor motioned towards the dark window. 'Fortunes. And these men who've come in from the wreck: if there are seals down south in the numbers they say, if this new strait takes days off the voyage from the west, if there is, indeed, coal to be found...if all of these things come to pass, the commercial pressures will be significant. Civil administration like this, it only works when it has support from home. And I don't have it.'

The governor placed his glass on the desk.

'This place won't be ruled,' he continued. A wry chuckle escaped him: 'Remember that herd of Afrikanders we brought over? Wonderful beasts. Hardy; docile, usually. Then they go and break out of their enclosures like something's possessed them, wander inland—and now we have a herd of ten dozen minotaurs somewhere out there in the bush. They were just bloody cows until we brought them here.' He shook his head. 'Terrors without and thieves within.'

'The Corps?'

Hunter shrugged faintly. 'Well, we're stuck with them. Maybe the presence of parasites tells us there's some worth in the host. But Macarthur is already moving against me. He tells the Home Office we've had forty-six escapes this year and they conclude it's my inattention. Perhaps it is.'

'Some have escaped. On the other hand, there's been three hundred births. Doesn't your measure of success depend on what you think the experiment is?'

'I'm tired, lad.' He considered the glass in his hand, tilted it. 'Well. You came here for a purpose, I am sure.'

Grayling was no longer convinced his proposal was a good idea. He hadn't expected such pessimism. 'I do not wish to delay you with long-winded explanations, excellency, but—'

'*Excellency*, now?' A hint of amusement in his voice.

'But I believe you must order the arrest of John Figge.'

One of the silver eyebrows shot upwards. The humour vanished from his face. Grayling pressed on quickly.

'The lascar boy, Srinivas, has spoken extensively to Mrs Grayling, as you know. He describes a plot between Mr Clark and Mr Figge to ensure it was only them that reached Sydney.'

'You mean by murdering the others?'

'In relation to the carpenter and the first mate, yes. In other cases, I mean ensuring they didn't survive.'

'*Ensuring they didn't survive.* How does one prosecute such a thing?'

'It is enough that we proceed on Thompson and Kennedy.'

The governor considered this for a moment. 'What value was there to the two of them in doing that?'

'I cannot say. It depends on the financial circumstances of the voyage, I suppose. Salvage, maybe, or insurance.'

'This rests upon the testimony of the boy?'

'Yes.'

'He's reliable?'

'He's alone. He has no reason to lie.'

'Isn't there an immediate problem with your idea about a conspiracy? Figge and Clark started telling us about the other survivors almost as soon as they arrived. Why would they do so if they did not want to set in motion the rescue of those people?'

Grayling hesitated. He'd argued this endlessly with Charlotte. 'I can only conclude, sir, that it was not intended that the three of them would make it here. I believe Figge aimed to have no companions, and that the sudden arrival of the fishing boat at Wattamolla upended his plan. With the first story in ruins, they're competing to tell us a new one.'

'In which they feature as heroes.' The governor stared into his glass again, lost in thought. 'Clark was lucky, wasn't he? Managed to evade Figge and then us, and when he gets back to Calcutta he'll have the protection of his family. No complicity on the part of the boy?'

'He appears innocent. And from my observations he has been in mortal terror of the other two throughout.'

'Charlotte confirms this from her conversations with him?'

'Entirely. The boy had enough wit to conceal his understanding of English. I feel sure he would have been killed, had they known.'

'Very well. Take the boy in and hold him until we can have him testify. You will have to make him understand it is for his own protection. What do you want to do about Mr Figge then? You want to *arrest* him? The whole place is enraptured by his heroic story.'

'I'm told he's in Parramatta, giving audiences in the taverns. Yes, I want to go and bring him in.'

The governor recoiled slightly in his chair. 'If you're right, then...he's a dangerous man.'

'I am right. And he is. It doesn't sway me at all.'

'Drink the brandy, lieutenant.' The governor watched him stiffly take the glass to his mouth and sip from it.

'Sir?'

'I was young once, Joshua. So was Phillip before me, and so was...whoever comes after me. I felt that frantic kicking at fate that you feel. It falls to old fools like me to counsel against it, even though young fools like you will do it anyway. I'm so fond of Charlotte. I'm so grateful that the two of you came here with me and gave me the benefit of your youthful energy. I wish, I suppose, that I was dealing with subordinates who were nothing more than machine parts. But you two are...I'm so tired, forgive me. You two are close to my heart.'

Grayling listened in churning silence. The governor had never spoken this way, even in private.

'Just let the thing take its course,' Hunter continued. 'Why do you need to go? Why can I not just authorise a detachment of marines and leave you out of it?'

The answer had been lodged in Grayling's heart for days. The evil bastard had touched Charlotte: *handled* her. Posed as a faith healer and, worse still, succeeded where Ewing had failed. The man had openly defied him. That alone should not have mattered. It was the bigger things: the lies, the deceptions; the fact that he had very possibly murdered his companions. And somewhere deeper, the matter of his identity. It worked on Grayling like slowly creeping nausea. Figge was not what he said he was.

'You gave me this work, sir. You asked me to find out what led to these men turning up on the beach. The last part is to go to Parramatta. Let me bring him to you and put at least this worry aside.'

The governor tried to scoff. 'You think I'm beset with worries?'

'I would never presume to comment, sir.'

'Tell me—do you think the Cadigal are out there burning the scrub because that's the season? Or to send us a message? I've heard it said that it flushes out the animals, you know.'

Grayling knew the governor was trying to move the conversation away from harder realities. 'Sir, the people out there can deal with Pemulwuy. They know what he fights for, much as he terrifies them. But *this* man, Figge, he poisons from within. He's no more a tea merchant than I am. I've spent time in his company and I tell you sir, he's a devil. He'll sow mistrust, and from mistrust comes division. He is dangerous in a way the plain enemy is not.'

Seeing the governor had not contradicted him, Grayling hurried on. 'And then, and *then*, sir, you can send Mr Bass, Mr Flinders; make an industry down there in the seals. Find that coal on the beach, find the passage west through the strait…'

The governor smiled at the mention of it. 'Aye, the bloody strait. I'll tell you lad, I don't miss having command of those voyages one little bit.'

'Give the order, sir. I beg of you.'

The governor raised his weary eyes to Grayling's once more and saw nothing there but determination. He sighed. Tipped the rummer, only to find it empty. 'You have my order.'

Grayling clapped and stood instantly to go.

'But lieutenant,' the old eyes flamed briefly with wry humour. 'If Charlotte says no, I'm overruled.'

38

Grayling made his preparations. Two days selecting men and armaments and devising an approach to Parramatta. It was a distasteful but necessary aspect of the work that he had to confer with informers, men trading flecks of information for other advantages. The exchanges occurred in their places of work or their homes or favourite taverns because it was in no one's interest for them to be seen visiting Government House. He hated taking his uniform into such places.

He waited to tell Charlotte of his plans: the one task he dreaded. And then, on the afternoon of the second day, just as he felt he had everything in place, Boorigul returned. She was sullen and downcast. Grayling could elicit no greeting from her, though he had never built the intimacy that Charlotte had. Charlotte herself was overjoyed, and cared little that the girl wouldn't communicate. She fussed about, undeterred by Boorigul's refusal to enter the house, and guided her to a seat on the narrow verandah. Inside, she set about making food for her, looking brightly at Grayling and mouthing the words *She seems fine*, as though her optimism alone would make it so.

Grayling smiled back at his wife; tried to enjoy the moment on its uncomplicated surface. They stood at the verge of a hard winter, the governor under pressure from the ascendant Macarthurs and the machinations of the Corps. But Charlotte was healthy and she was smiling, and the dark thoughts that had assailed him over previous weeks, his anger at her wandering; all of it he felt he could put aside. She was happy.

He went to the washbasin while Charlotte headed outside with bread and stew. The birds were in raucous voice, and across the slope above the Tank Stream he could hear the Eora in their usual exchanges. As they displayed their bodies without shame, so too, it seemed to him, they had no use for discreet conversation. There was a private realm somewhere in them, but it grew in different ground. Over the sounds of the hillside he could hear Charlotte murmuring to Boorigul, just beyond the doorway. *Where have you been?* she was asking.

There was a whispered reply. Sibilant, too soft for him to catch.

Are you hurt? The flat *plink* of spoon on bowl; a reply in the negative.

He splashed water over his face and it trickled loudly back into the basin, so that he missed a moment of their exchange.

…Warrander come for you again? Charlotte was asking.

Grayling blotted the droplets with his towel to make a perfect silence. He knew the answer to the question.

The silence lasted a long time, and he thought even the birds had hushed to listen. Then he heard Boorigul's gentle voice.

No missus, she said. *Warrander finish.*

After they'd eaten, Charlotte walked out of the house and into the darkness, head bowed in thought. Grayling had let her go, understanding her need to take stock of Warrander's death.

Outside, as her eyes left the lantern behind, the path became clear, pale grass underfoot between darker borders of bracken. Then the harbour lay before her, the water she had heard the women calling *warrane*, gleaming with the moon and the stars and the fine speckled lines of reflected fires on other shores.

The air smelled of an agreeable meeting of humans and nature: wood smoke that may have curled around the boots of the settlers but more likely came from the endless burning projects of the Eora. Eucalyptus, dry grass, old ash and the pungency of exposed reef. Some other scent she could not define, herbaceous and reassuring. For all the endless discussion of the ways in which the land was forbidding, this was a welcoming air. If she thought back, the remembered smells of Leith were not so kind.

The land was marked out as areas of soft blackness against the sky and the living gleam of the water. In places it threw sharp corners at the sky; in others it was rounded or stretching a bent finger into the bays, a picture made of silver and black and the faint profound traces of blue. The trees bent in filigrees over the water; only the first trees or the last, for those deeper in had given over their individual shapes to the darkness. The birds were silent now. A dog barked here or there. The only human voices that continued at this hour were those of drunks arguing further along the shore. The fireside laughter of the Eora, like the birds, was in repose. She imagined fathers curled protectively around their sleeping children.

The women were not there in the sleep-warm shelters, not now as the moon worked its beauty over the water. They were out in front of her, part of the night. Two women in each *nowie*, a fire between them, fishing. Calling to each other, softly, as though they held sacred the peace of the night. They paddled in a straight-backed kneel, balancing the fragile craft with their knees. Her eye followed one of them, an infant clutched to her breast and lit warm by the small flame in front of her as she manoeuvred the craft with the paddle in her other hand.

The flames flickered when they moved, made burnished glows in the coin of the surface when they were still. They were lamps adrift on the pond of a temple; more so when the women began to sing together, a song that passed from one *nowie* to the next, moving around the harbour like something with physical form—a food, perhaps—that could be handed and shared.

When one of them raised a fish into the little craft, Charlotte could hear its splashing all the way up to where she stood on the promontory, high above them; the small thudders of its last struggle on the *nowie*'s bark floor.

Then the splashes sounded at regular intervals, spaced in time and between the boats; the waters surrendering fish one by one. She had seen the convicts bring in nets so full they couldn't lift them onto the beach; had been compelled to wait for the tide to empty them. A day they had claimed they took four thousand fish: vulgar beside this, this delicate singularity.

When she closed her eyes the tracks of the moving lights were there on the insides of her eyelids, maps of an unknowable world. The eyes of the women down there, she thought, might see through the ink of the night-time sea; a sense—*sight* but not seeing—that belonged to the slow passage of generations.

In the morning the men would have fish for sale, but soon

enough the winter would close in and there would be no more fishing. The winter would be different.

It was time that she told her husband.

Here at the end of the world and in the heart of the night, the voices and the tiny lights and the thing she must tell him; all of them were more mystery than fact. Only one clear certainty held: she had never seen such a beautiful night.

⚬

Charlotte knew that something was troubling Joshua too. She thought it was the return of Boorigul, the odd and abrupt end to the girl's troubles with Warrander. Charlotte had worked patiently to extract the story from her: even then she had only parts of it.

A detachment had come to their camp on the flats beyond the Cowpasture. Redcoats, not patrolling but looking specifically for Warrander. Boorigul wasn't there at the time—she was out fishing—but she was told a short conversation had turned to shouts, and the shouting to gunfire. The soldiers had shot Warrander, and shortly afterwards two women and a child. They insisted they were attacked when they approached the camp, and were forced to fire in self-defence. Boorigul thought this was unlikely—Warrander had been asleep when she left. Charlotte recognised the euphemisms: she'd heard them often enough.

And Joshua had been spending long days at Government House. He was distant and unsmiling. It seemed most logical to put it down to the soldiers and the raid and the four more human lives that had been taken without reason or process. But it could be something else entirely. And unlike with Boorigul, there would be no coaxing the story from him. She waited, and finally he spoke.

She listened with horror as they lay in bed and he explained the Parramatta mission to her. Nothing to do with Boorigul and Warrander after all; and yet this was worse. Matters were closing in, he said. He had to act against Figge, and she had to understand.

But there in the dark with the words making terrible pictures in her mind, his explanation brought only foreboding. His hip and a length of his thigh were touching hers, and their fingers were interlaced. That vicious man and all the trouble that came with him. He had made a little empire of his own up there in Parramatta, she had no doubt. He would be waiting for Joshua, ready to harm him. And Joshua's usual caution had deserted him: he was rattled, vengeful. He would act in haste.

'I need you here,' she said simply.

'No you don't.' He tried laughing but nothing came. 'It is a small matter, and I will have a detachment with me anyway.'

'It's not small. He frightens me.'

'Surely that's a reason to go and bring him in?'

The wind picked up outside the small house, and the loose whipping of the lone eucalypt above sent a scatter of debris down to their roof, each falling twig on the shingles puncturing the darkness. She imagined the girl outside, listening to the same sounds; understanding them to mean different things.

'I can't lose you,' she said. 'I mustn't lose you.'

'You're the woman who walks the bush alone, the one who can speak to the Cadigal. You'd cope without me.' Again, he tried to chuckle in defiance of harder things.

'*Do not make light of it,*' she said, fiercely now. In the darkness she couldn't tell if her vehemence had changed his expression, but his hand squeezed hers more tightly. 'I cannot have you gone. Imagine this night without me here, because I am imagining it without you.' She shook his hand away, traced her fingers urgently upwards to his face and over the light beard he had grown. The fingertips found his brow and brushed gently down over his eyes. One finger stopped on his mouth.

'What of all this emptiness? If there was nothing more than all of that and just one of us alone?'

'The governor,' he said.

'What?'

'He lives that way.'

'He's old, Joshua. You're loyal to him, but he's old and we are not.'

He made a small sound of assent.

'Feel me here,' she said and took his hand and placed it on her belly. 'I can't tell you...the love and the fear and all these things in my heart.' She began to cry, and it shook her. 'Our child is in here.'

Her hand was on his, on the warmth of her skin, when she became aware he too was crying. Quietly at first, so she only knew by the faint shaking in his body. But then she could hear it in his breathing, tiny moans in the night among the wind-clatter and the restless trees.

A cold stake of fear had been driven between them and her joy was washed away.

39

Grayling didn't want to go.

He could no sooner imagine himself a father than he could imagine the prospect of leaving Charlotte widowed. But this was all foolishness: no one was going to kill him. The light of day washed the doubts from his mind and returned him to pragmatism.

He wanted to believe that a malign presence had absented itself from the township; that in any case feinting at dark things was a fool's errand for those with such scant resources to devote to keeping order. Figge was gone, and with him a shadow and a taint that covered everything.

But he saw the settlement with different eyes as he made the familiar walk to Government House. He saw a camp that had overreached, and clung fearfully to the cleared spaces in the bush. Looking outward for spectres, for Black Caesar and Goam-Boak and Pemulwuy, and inward for traitors. The Rum

Corps and the civil classes eyeing each other for evidence of open revolt and the Cadigal and the Gweagal watching them all for further moves to despoil their world. The farmers and the traders watching their convicts and the convicts watching each other and it was a wonder anyone got anything done for all their compiling and cataloguing of paranoid visions.

He found the governor alert and clear eyed. Gone were the doubt and worry that seemed increasingly to shadow the old man. He had the lascar boy, Srinivas, waiting in an anteroom. He had satisfied himself that the reports were consistent: since his disappearance from Sydney, Mr Figge had been observed over several nights in the taverns of Parramatta.

He'd ordered the *Eliza* and the *Francis* to head south under ballast and bring back all of the *Sydney Cove*'s survivors and cargo, or as much of the latter as they could carry. They would leave within days. He would impound the cursed rum and sell it off in rations: if he couldn't stem the tide of spirits he could at least turn that tide to the colony's financial benefit. With Clark gone back to Calcutta, profiting from some unspoken brand of immunity that attached itself to the merchant classes, all that remained in conclusion of the strange episode was to bring in Mr Figge.

What worried the governor most was the mythology that was building up around the story, a scandal that had set the malcontents gossiping. *I have no wish to make heroes of rum speculators*, he'd said in front of the Macarthurs—apparently in reference to Captain Hamilton, who still waited on Preservation Island. The two of them had glared at the governor in malevolent silence.

In the previous week, a group of convicts had absconded with the avowed intention of finding and commandeering the wreck. It was no more or less ambitious than any other fantasy the lags had cooked up, like walking to China; but public order was a thin veneer, and excitement could lead to anarchy. A fortune in rum, wedged between boulders to the south, with no sentry other than a straggle of bony survivors to be clubbed like seals. It was only geography, not governance, that prevented it.

They agreed that Clark's departure was a blessing of sorts. The Corps were already suggesting that his evasive journal left room to place blame for the loss of fourteen men at the feet of the natives. 'It is ugly but useful,' the governor told Grayling, 'that the only surviving account of the episode is one which says *Go out there and this is your fate*.' It rang false to Grayling, but of course the old man was right. The people would rush to reinforce their own fears.

Hunter marked Grayling's mission with his signature caution: in addition to the earlier stipulation that he take an escort, he was to approach the town by river to avoid the convict stopover on the road at Longbottom. This, the governor reasoned, would lessen the chances of an ambush. Lastly, most crucially, he was to ensure the thing was done without bloodshed.

When he had received Grayling's nod of assent, he looked to the door of the anteroom. 'You'd best bring in the boy.'

Srinivas appeared different from how Grayling had seen him previously. His chin was up now: he looked angry and defiant. Older, somehow. Over his shoulder Grayling could see that a sentry had been posted by the door: this must have been a jarring change of circumstance for the boy.

'It is a pleasure finally to meet you,' said the governor, once Srinivas was seated. 'I'm told that you speak good English.'

'I do,' he said calmly. No trace of his earlier deference to authority.

'I hope you understand my reasons for detaining you.'

There was no response. The boy's gaze travelled vaguely over the braided shoulder towards the window.

'You have suffered, I know,' the governor continued. 'I was shipwrecked once, too.' He laughed unexpectedly. 'In fact I was shipwrecked several times. But I refer to a time when I was very young, smaller than you, sailing aboard a naval vessel with my father. We were separated in the wreck. I don't remember being distressed by it, but I am told my father was beside himself. I suppose in youth it is hard to know the sorrows you inflict on your parents.'

From the tilt of the boy's head, his lowered brow, it was clear he was listening intently. 'I wish to go to him,' he said, unexpectedly.

'Pardon?' said Grayling.

'I wish to go and find him. In the bush. I do not believe he is dead.'

The governor paused. He folded one hand over the other on the surface of the desk. 'My lad, it sorrows me greatly to say it, but the likelihood is that your father is long deceased. You have the opportunity to make a life here now. We will assist you until you are able—'

'No.' The governor recoiled from the interruption. 'I wish to go and find him. And the other lascars.' The boy levelled his gaze at the two of them. 'This is your place. It is not mine. I am as likely to prosper on that coast as I am to do so here. Perhaps more so.'

Grayling and the governor looked at each other briefly before the older man spoke. 'You showed great sense in keeping your counsel throughout the shipwreck, and along the walk. In hiding your English, I mean. You would be wasting all that effort.'

317

'No, sir, I was mistaken to come here. I should have gone with my companions to look for my father when the chance was there. I chose duty at the time, but duty is worth nothing. I wish to make it right.' The boy sat back in his chair, but made no attempt to leave.

The governor sighed. 'I am sorry lad. I am truly sorry, but that cannot happen just now. Lieutenant,' he said quietly, looking away, 'will you have the corporal come in here and take the lad into custody? I cannot risk that man's proximity to him. When Mr Figge is tried and convicted—and only then—we will release the lad to do as he pleases.'

He turned to Srinivas as the corporal entered the room and stood heavily behind him. 'I am sorry, boy. I do this solely for your protection.'

40

Now the night slipped past the longboat, north from Cockle Bay then west. Silent eucalypts framed the evening lives of those on the bank: convicts drinking around fires, families in their dimly lit cottages and Cadigal on the ground in huddles of six or eight. It was cold, a breeze bringing the ocean over the river from behind them, clouds obscuring the stars. Grayling stood while the company of six redcoats rowed. He could smell food cooking on fires that were visible only as a glow. He could smell the slime and the oysters, the smoke and the night. He felt wary of the places that glowed and the ones that didn't, in equal measure but for different reasons. The shadowy mangroves. He was a target for any whistling bottle the drunks cared to hurl as much as a silent spear.

Pemulwuy was out there in the night. Maybe seated in a rock shelter somewhere on the south side of the river: Wangal country. A tall man folded in thought. Nursing his grudges, ruminating. Perhaps hidden close by, watching and waiting and flanked by warriors bent on mayhem. Such was the nature of their campaign—no one could tell, and the warriors aimed to keep the settlers in a state of constant, exhausting suspense.

Grayling felt relief when he saw the lights of Parramatta ahead, the rowers dipping their oars so the stern swung round and the beam of the slender boat lay alongside the wharf. Their faces did not reveal what they thought of this expedition. Anything to relieve the monotony, he supposed. They threw lines over the bollards, on the quiet orders of the provost marshal who'd sat his considerable frame in the centre of the boat.

The party worked their way up the ladder, standing to loose attention under the oil lights of the wharf in a small forest of bayoneted muskets. A dipped knee, a hand on a hip, approximations of discipline. How much use would they be in a crisis? Figge's fame was already spreading in the colony—this man who had defied shipwreck and distance and the terrors of the natives at close quarters enjoyed a rare prestige among those confined to the cleared acres of civilisation. Grayling, by comparison, represented little more than the constraints upon excess. Regulations, boundaries. No one would be going to any lengths to ensure his safety out here.

The township rose from the bank, its bulk concealed by the night. He gestured to the provost marshal to have the men follow him across the open square to the tavern, cutting a path around a drunken trooper flailing at a taptoo drum by a bonfire. The King's Birthday: he had forgotten. He was about to look away when he recognised a man half-lit by the firelight. Barrington, the convict Macarthur had raised to chief constable in Parramatta on the promise of his useful violence. He was seated on an upturned cask on the far side of the flames, the dull, flattened face turned towards Grayling, assessing him with rum-washed eyes. Barrington had been told by letter of the expedition. His assistance had been requested. There had been no answer. The man made no move to stand.

They walked on, and found the place Grayling had been told about. At the door he told the detachment to wait outside and entered, stooping under the heavy lintel.

A waft of grease and beer and noise struck him. Lamplight, a fiddler on a table, wheeling about as though his body was strung to the instrument. The floor was hard earth built up with planks to make a platform where the bar was. The place neither stopped nor even paused for his entrance, despite the uniform.

A crowd gathered around him, roaring and swaying, the room more shadow than light. There were a handful of women in the room, each clutched in the embrace of a male, leering, groping, laughing: the approaches differed but the intent did not. Grayling saw a man's whiskered face buried in the creamy downslope of a woman's bosom, two men in sweaty embrace, lost in sentiment as they howled a song—possibly not the same song—at the fiddler. Others clutched spilling fistfuls of ale or wooden cups of rum. Some sat among the handful of chairs, drinking determinedly with glazed eyes, or they stared into the fire or did none of these things but merely occupied space. It was Tuesday, or possibly Thursday or Friday to them all. It was of no significance. It was oblivion.

Grayling stepped delicately through the crowd, struck once or twice by an insensible body until he reached a man who looked, because he wasn't swaying, as if he might be the innkeeper. He inquired after Figge and received only a stare in return. Tried describing him: a tall man with a broken nose and pale eyes. The barman scrunched his veiny face and broke his silence only to scoff. *Good many broken noses in 'ere, lieutenant.*

Grayling could see every corner of the room from where he stood. And Figge, he knew, was not one for hiding in the shadows. He stepped outside, found the soldiers wandering off from their posting at the door, two of them talking to convict women, one pissing, the others deep in conversation. He took them along the waterfront, tried a different tavern and this time was told to go up the hill. The detachment was straggling again. These latest directions might have drawn him closer to his quarry, but might also have reflected nothing more than a desire to keep the armed posse moving down the road. Arrayed on the boat with their rifles stood, the detachment had represented order. Here on the street they were a rabble. He pressed ahead of them, disgusted.

The last tavern was on the far side of the rise, a growth in the dip between hills. The streets out here were wreathed in wood smoke, the building visible as a patch of spilled firelight in the gloom, a dark timber structure that stood beyond a pen holding goats and swine. A worn path led to its door, weaving around the mud and laid with a few planks. Somewhere beyond sight a mule cried out its soul to the sky.

He approached the building in a kind of haze, feeling strongly now that he was drawing close. He gave no thought to whether the soldiers had bothered to follow. Or half a thought: *You walked recklessly, Charlotte, and I chastised you.* He pushed through the door and its corner dragged on the compacted ground within. And now he remembered he was unarmed.

It could have been the same people as he'd seen in the last place. Carousers, drunks, trollops: forlorn and forgotten. They had no cause for celebration; their desperate revelry only mimicked it. The attire of traders, farmers, convict slops, even, to Grayling's disgust, military uniforms. Bodies that heaved and collided. The tables in the centre of the room had been pushed haphazardly aside to allow space for dancing, or staggering. Beneath a table, a yellow dog fucked a bald one, tongue lolling. A row of small benches projected from the far wall, lit only by a greasy lamp overhead. The reek in here was rancid tallow and piss.

A woman tended the bar, her face a sack of wrinkles under a stained bonnet. Her eyebrows curled in front of her eyes, compelling her to squint as though through fog. Grayling edged his way towards her, but was intercepted by a younger woman, short and strong. She took hold of his lapels, swung from them a little and made a face that mocked seduction. There were words about him, how handsome he was, a promise to suck him dry for a silver coin. He reeled back and threw her off and she disappeared, cursing, into the crowd.

'I'm looking for a man named Figge,' he said to the old woman at the bar and she looked over his right shoulder. Before he could turn, a hand clamped itself on that shoulder.

Figge smiled down on him. Heavier and stronger than he'd been in Sydney, and quite unlike anyone else in the room. A man in confident command of himself. Days ago, though it felt like an eternity, he had insisted he was not much older than Grayling. But the pale eyes belonged to another age.

'Rum,' he said, without taking his eyes from Grayling's. The woman busied herself with a bottle and two cups. 'Have you come alone?' Figge's tone indicated no surprise that he was there. On the contrary, he sounded as though this was a social engagement fulfilled. Grayling's throat tightened. The hand hadn't moved from his shoulder. He was seized by a desperation closing in on panic.

'There are redcoats outside,' he said. 'Half-a-dozen. And a provost.'

Figge laughed mildly. 'Expecting trouble, then.' He took the bottle and cups and motioned towards the far wall. When they sat either side of the narrow bench Figge had indicated, Grayling found that their knees were touching. He wasn't sure where to begin. Figge was watching him with a look of sly anticipation.

'You left town unexpectedly, Mr Figge.'

'I was bored,' he smiled. 'I am fully recovered. A man senses opportunity in a place like this. Can't blame me for getting out and pursuing it.'

'It seems you left just as the most interesting questions were starting to arise.'

'Whatever can you mean?'

'You don't know a great deal about tea, do you, for someone in the trade?'

'Bah.' He grinned again. 'I wasn't at my best those early days.'

'You got the leaf wrong.'

'Easy mistake.'

'Three times.'

He shrugged. 'Three easy mistakes.'

'How did you come to be on the *Sydney Cove*?'

Figge looked up at the beams of the low ceiling. He ran a hand over the timber surface of the bench, dug the ends of his fingers into the smooth join where two boards met. 'The lags make fine furniture, don't they? Poor old Kennedy would've approved.'

If he was trying to look bored, he had missed the mark by just enough that Grayling sensed a sudden advantage. 'What were you doing on that ship?'

'I told you, lieutenant, I was accompanying the tea consigned to the vessel by Sumpter & Co., traders of Calcutta, where I am employed as a merchant. You will not have seen, but I provided a letter of introduction to Captain Hamilton when I boarded the vessel on the Hooghly.'

Grayling sipped at the rum and the raw spirit burned in his throat. It was no example to set, the drink and the uniform.

'Do you want to take any of that back, sir? Do you want to take your opportunity again, and this time tell me the truth?'

Figge watched him carefully. After a long while he spoke. 'I don't care to be interrogated, lieutenant. Perhaps you should explain whatever concern it is you're harbouring.'

'Very well. A ship came in. You might be unaware of it, holed up here. The *Reliance*. Usual speculative stuff aboard: rum, of course; textiles, shoes. Guinea fowl in cages, oddly enough. But you see, sir, there were two representatives of Sumpters on board and they carried rather alarming news. It seems their agent, a Mr John Figge, was found murdered at Fort William several days after the *Sydney Cove* sailed last November. Head stove in, letter of introduction stolen, along with a sum of money.'

Grayling looked directly into the man's eyes. 'So who are you?'

Nothing, not even the tiniest muscle, altered the man's stare. 'No, no, go back a moment. Are you accusing me of murder?'

Grayling knew the circling and feinting was over.

'*They* are, sir. You will have to reckon with them.' This imposter, whoever he was, had his hands under the table and his body had taken on a faint attitude of readiness. Where in the name of Christ were the fucking redcoats?

'And you, lieutenant? What reckoning do I have with you?'

'With me the matter is of a different nature. Your true identity, for one. But you have more than that to answer to.'

'Yes?'

'It turns out that the lascar boy, Srinivas, speaks very good English.'

If this surprised the man, he showed no sign of it.

'And it follows, of course, that he *understands* English. Perfectly.'

Grayling was waiting for a movement now, some outburst of violence that would break open the standoff. He pressed his fingers on the sticky surface of the bench to stifle their trembling.

'He overheard, sir, and he relayed to us, your discussions with Mr Clark about the *Sydney Cove*.'

The man's face took an ugly turn towards aggression. 'What *about* the *Sydney Cove*?'

'About you having persuaded Captain Hamilton to beach her in a place where no shipping could lend assistance. Having deliberately scuttled the longboat in an attempt to cause more casualties. Having done away with the boy's father, Prasad, in the knowledge that the other lascars would remove themselves from the party out of loyalty to him.'

'My, the lad has me busy.'

'He witnessed with his own eyes the murders of Kennedy and Thompson. I anticipate that when the current search party finds their remains his version of events will be corroborated.' The tiniest echo of his shaking had started now to infect his voice.

The man sensed it. He leaned forward confidently. 'You don't do this very often, do you? This weak excuse for a confrontation. You're all over the place because you're *scared*, lieutenant. This is what you give me after I saved your lovely fainting wife. You give me *this*—this cheap attempt at intimidation executed without any plan, without even a vestige of style or substance. Nothing, just this'—he waved a dismissive hand—'play acting.'

'I am doing as the law requires me to do.'

The man laughed. 'Really.' He leaned forward, both hands still concealed. 'I did what I had to do also, lieutenant. You've not been in the bush, have you? Maybe a timorous peek in at the fringes. Maybe you wondered, some days, what it holds? Days like the ones when your wife betook herself to the wilds on those lovely long legs of hers. I *know* it, you understand. I've slept the nights and walked the days that were the same as the other days and heard the sounds and fought the temptation to sob like a frightened child and the other temptation to jump at the shadows and to see a cannibal in every native because it is nigh impossible to accept that such spreading immensity could still be part of God's creation. Clark and his ilk, they want the place to behave like the woods of Midlothian, all gentle glades and fucking robins in the trees. Deluded, and cowards with it. If I seem a little *raw* to you, lieutenant, it might be a response to five hundred miles of traipsing a godless waste with no fucking shoes.'

'Doesn't explain the man with the crushed head in Fort William. Or what you did to Kennedy and Thompson.'

'Your people will find their bodies stripped and violated and the blame will naturally fall on the natives.'

'You reckon without the Bengali boy.'

'Really? You want to try my version against the word of a lascar?' He drank, wiped his mouth under the bend of the shattered nose. The whore who had earlier approached Grayling now staggered free of the crowd and draped herself over the man in a clumsy embrace. He pushed her away without a glance.

'He is being held as we speak, in anticipation of giving that evidence. He wishes to walk back into the bush in search of his father. Perhaps you know what he will find.'

The man looked around himself, took in the tumbling packs of drunks and the wreckage about them. 'If you want a confession, go to Clark.'

'He was staunch for you to the last. Still saying it was the Tharawal that did it. What did you have over him?'

'The last? What's happened to him?'

'Clark has left. He sailed on the *Reliance* when it left harbour. In doing so it seems he's relinquished any claim on the salvage that you and he might have cooked up.'

'You think that's what this was about? You'd arrest me if you had any proof.'

'I'd arrest you but for the small chance I want to extend to you.' The words he had to say were like bile, but he forced them out. 'My debt to you…after…my wife. I could call the redcoats in, but I want to let you walk out of here without duress.'

'Just surrender myself to your redcoats and sign a confession for the governor?'

'Yes. That is all.'

The man laughed and shuffled forward again, so close now. His eyes darted around the room as if seeking escape from his thoughts.

'You,' he breathed, with an air of resignation, 'have a very poor sense of obligation. No sooner had I saved your wife's life than you reneged on your promises to me.'

'Promises?'

'I'll read you the journal,' he hissed. 'I *won't* read you the journal. I'll put you on the rescue ship to Preservation. Actually, no, I won't.'

Grayling said nothing. He was watching, tensed for violence.

'I wanted a pretty uniform too, but that was a flourish.' The man's face curled once more into a smile, pulling the skin taut over the broken bone in his nose. 'I'll tell you a thing I learned out there. All these people are taken with a morbid loathing of the spear. More so even than the natives fear the gun. Not—I don't know—not snakes, or poisonous plants or falling trees. The spears fucking terrify them.

'Elemental, I suppose, the fear of having something thrust through you. *Impaled*. Mouth filling with blood, eyes like a landed fish. The *doulls* they use, the Cadigal, they're lined with sharp stones, tiny slivers of shell. They come away in the wound so the more some friend helps you by pulling out the shaft, the more horribly they are killing you. The malignant will of the thrower, lodged there like a curse. When Pemulwuy put one through McIntyre, they say it took him weeks to die. He screamed himself to death, lieutenant. For *weeks*. Impressive, no? How many generations did it take for that idea to perfect itself? For the hunters to realise that the mortal damage might be done in the extraction as much as in the insertion? This is the thing, isn't it? You cause more harm by trying to help.'

His face never altered as he moved and the sudden pain shocked Grayling. Robbed him of the opportunity to understand what had been done; a pinpoint of fire burning ferociously from the base of his scrotum.

The man was leaning in now, breathing hard on his face. Grayling didn't want to look down but he couldn't help himself. The steel of the knife glinted just faintly in the shadows of his lap: blood was spreading warm already under the creases of his thighs and onto the seat.

The man looked quickly from one side to the other. 'Now, where are your companions?'

Grayling held a tight breath, pressing down against the pain. 'Supposed to be here. Out the front.'

'Good. None in here I trust?' He pushed the knife just a little. Grayling couldn't tell how much of it had been thrust into him.

The man's face was close, the tombstone teeth bared with

malevolent intent. 'I crossed a fucking ocean only to fall a couple of islands short. Walked hundreds of miles only to get picked up with Sydney in sight. And now I have you on a pike, lieutenant, and the obvious thing to do is finish the *job*.' He pushed again. Grayling wanted to howl.

'But I won't. It's the incomplete that lights our dreams, don't you think?' The faintest chuckle. 'So here's how we're going to do this: I can cut the balls clean out of you if you make just one squeak. Last thing you will ever see is the two of 'em and their bloody coils lying here on the table. I am going to stand and walk out. You are going to sit there and...' He turned the blade. 'Let me.'

The tip of the knife came free and the blood flowed warm. He lifted it to the level of the table and wiped its edge across the timber; they both watched the red smear it left. He secreted the blade somewhere in his coat and stood, looking at Grayling but also through him or past him, a thing now dealt with; immaterial to a racing mind. He walked past the fireplace to where a small doorway was closed off by a curtain of hessian sacks. The curtain billowed slightly: the flow of air told Grayling the doorway led outside, behind the building. The man was gone then, the curtain swirling after him. The fire blew sparks. Someone near him cursed the rush of cold air, but there was no one in the doorway to accost. Grayling wanted to stand and give chase, but he was slow and cold. He thought to pick up the cup and drink more of the rum, but his hand wouldn't cooperate. His fingers fell from the bench and dabbed sticky in the pool of blood that was collecting under him.

He saw the runs and swirls of the grain in the benchtop. They came alive and spilled around each other like slicks of oil, turning and curling but never meeting and his head fell and smashed heavily against the timber. The troopers were pouring through the door now, peering through the haze and the tumbling fools to find him. A face turned from the crowd and registered without surprise the man sliding from his stool. The room churned relentlessly on.

He spilled almost to the ground. Found his feet and careened towards the doorway where the man had vanished. His shoulder punched into an unyielding hip and someone swore, then he swept the curtain aside and fell forward into a small stable. In the gloom, three or four horses were tied and stamping restlessly as though a sudden wind had thrown dust in their soft eyes.

Outside in the night, further away, a chestnut mare turned as a rider worked its reins. The man cast one look at Grayling and was gone, clatters fading into the night.

41

Charlotte had walked beside Srinivas for a long time before she felt she could speak. So many thoughts troubled her that it was hard to know where to start. But one thought returned most often: a sorrow that stayed with her and could not be shifted. What the boy wanted to do was impossible.

'Have they taken everything ahead for you?'

His head was down. He spoke distractedly. 'Yes ma'am.'

There were cut walls of sandstone along the bridle trail that led to the wharf. They'd gone the long way, though it wasn't discussed. The boy's shadow passed along the old rock, swallowing the sunshine and being replaced by it. He was walking fast, pulling away from her so that she was left watching his shoulders: their width hinted now at the man emerging from within him.

'Have they given you enough food?'

'Of course.'

'What else? A flint? Blankets?'

'Yes ma'am. There is nothing I need.' Faint exasperation in his voice.

She hurried along until she was beside him again. Sunlight fell through the loose cover of the banksias and wrapped over his cheeks. 'You're angry, Srinivas, I know. You're angry that the governor took you into custody.'

'It did not need to be that way.'

'But can't you see? Mr Clark has gone. Mr Figge has disappeared. It was necessary for him to hold you while there was a chance that Mr Figge might be arrested. You're the only one who can tell the whole story.'

'I am the only one who is a Bengali, ma'am. No one locked up the Scotsman.' He stopped walking and eyed her with an unfamiliar bitterness. 'I trusted you.'

'And we, my husband, managed to get you out,' she answered. 'You struck a fine deal. Provisions and a passage south on Mr Bass's boat. You did well out of a grim situation.'

'Mr Bass will be wealthy, ma'am. We did the suffering and he gets the strait. Those seals that Mr Clark had in his journal: I saw them too. Thousands, ma'am, millions, perhaps. And the coal, and the timber and the land for clearing. Good water. All those things. All those fortunes coming. There will be a rescue and Captain Hamilton will be a hero. None of that counts for me. I will be fine. But I did not "do well".'

'No, I suppose not,' Charlotte offered meekly. 'But you are free now.'

Birds overhead, whips and piercing whistles. The metal and timber sounds of people working, the cove a shimmering blue below. The place made beauty despite itself, despite the intentions of almost everyone in it. The boy had stopped walking and was

333

staring out over the harbour to the folds of the drowned valley that formed its points. The flash of anger in him was gone.

'What is that rock out there, off the cove?' He pointed and she followed the line of his finger.

'With the timberwork on it? They call it Pinchgut. The previous governor had the convicts cut it into that flat shape.'

An object was faintly visible on the high point of the rock island they were looking at: a short mast, or a flagpole. Neither of those things.

'Why does the man's body hang there?' he asked.

'His name was Morgan, an Irishman. He murdered a man and they executed him there last year. They gibbeted his body as a lesson to others.'

'Gibbeted?'

'Strung it up. In chains.' She studied him closely, and found he was lost in thought. 'Can you see that from here?'

'No ma'am. When they brought us in, on the fishing boat. I was…sometimes awake, sometimes not. But I remember the boat tacked off that island to come into the cove and I looked out over the gunwale and saw the skeleton. It swung in the wind, and there was the metal sound from the chains. You arrive at this place, and a rotting man greets you.'

They both stared over the blue distance at the faint black mark that disfigured it.

'How long will it stay there?'

'Until the chains break, I imagine.'

'Then what will they do to caution us?'

They will hang another one, she thought. But she did not answer him.

He started walking again and she stayed close by him. He seemed forlorn.

'Where will you have them take you?'

'Moruya. That is the last name the Walbanja gave us, before...'

'You must be careful. There was a native man from the south who came to Sydney. Goam-Boak, they called him. They said he was a cannibal.'

'Ma'am, if there were cannibals to the south I would not be talking to you now.' Silence again as they walked. Then: 'You think my father is dead, don't you?'

She said nothing.

'The Walbanja were good people,' Srinivas insisted. 'They carried us over rivers. They fed us.'

'And Mr Figge? There was nothing good about him.'

'No. But I think his plan was to leave my father alive. A trap, of sorts. His'—the boy swallowed—'his cries in the dark. If he was dead he would be of no use. And Mr Figge wants people for their *use*.'

Charlotte kept her counsel. For just a moment she saw the endless vanishing cliffs of the boy's pain. What Mr Figge, whoever he was, had done to her husband; what he must have done to Thompson and Kennedy and to the man in Calcutta; even if the ultimate goal was financial gain, he had gone about it in the cruellest way he could devise.

'I hope you are right,' she said eventually. 'How will you find him?'

'Those people talk across the bush. Walbanja, Tharawal, even the Cadigal. If one knows, someone else knows, they all know. It is a big place, but I do not think it can hide a dozen Bengalis.' He smiled a little. They were stepping down now, following a shallow cutting the convicts had made the previous summer.

'Something I don't understand, Srinivas,' she said. 'How

could you struggle as you did for safety, then turn your back on it? That distance you walked, no man has even contemplated it before. You survived all these terrors I can barely imagine—you survived Mr Figge. And now you have found refuge. You don't want it anymore?'

He stopped again. 'You have your home here, ma'am. The lieutenant, and you will have your child…' He gestured faintly towards her body and then let his hands hang awkwardly at his sides as they both blushed.

They'd reached the timbers of the wharf. The weather was coming in and the breeze that had picked up was slapping a light chop into the hulls of the moored boats.

'Anyway,' he said absently, 'Sydney is not an end, nor an answer.'

He looked down the row of vessels, some forming the focus of movement and activity, others patiently waiting. 'This one,' said Srinivas, gesturing to a small sloop roped to the windward side of the wharf. 'They showed me yesterday.'

The men working on its decks, occupied in tiny ways, were unaware of the boy. She watched him step through the gunwale and across the deck to the hatch, at home in his surrounds but a guest now rather than a lackey. Either way, she knew, he would adapt to his surroundings by effacing himself.

She stepped forward to the edge of the wharf and watched as they prepared the vessel for sea. She could feel the gaps between the boards under the thin soles of her shoes. Srinivas reappeared from below, having deposited the few possessions he was carrying. He was staring out over the wide harbour, the blue and the sun, disappearing fast now behind lowering clouds. The interrupting dark sentinel over Pinchgut and its column of birds, framed on the far side by the slopes of Cremorne.

He turned back to her, found her eyes and waved. She tried desperately to read the small gesture, then simply returned the wave. She left him there and stepped onto the path. She would depart from it halfway home; walk into the bush once more and think of him. The passage of time and the vast silence of the land would soon erase his name so completely that no one else would remember him at all.

42

Joshua Grayling let his eyes fall closed in the sun's narcotic warmth. Alone in a chair that had been brought out from the house and placed on the lawn, he could see down over the cleared ground and the remaining trees to the cove, to the sun glittering on the water, so bright it hurt his eyes.

In the west, above the rise where Parramatta would be, a storm was gathering, building a wall at its advancing edge: a fortress mounting across the sky. It was dark beneath the ramparts of cloud, and the darkness devoured even the tallest trees in its path. The breeze had dropped to nothing. The cove and the headlands waited.

Still the blessed sun lit everything in the near distance, as though it didn't care: as though there would be time later for the rest of it. It lit the water and the headlands, the front edge of the cloud-wall and the gulls that passed before it. It lit his hands where he had placed them on the blanket on his lap.

The storm was headed directly for the cove, but its progress was imperceptible—it was only by looking away and looking again that Grayling could sense its advance. The Eora were gone: he could not see a human anywhere on the downslope before him.

A sail hurried its way towards the heads, eager to make open sea before the change. It would be the sloop, carrying the lascar boy to his dreams. The last of the three survivors to leave, and the only one of whom it could be said that his freedom was well earnt. If Figge was out there in the bush, then he was only one among the dozens of escapees, the warriors and crazed visionaries. The land would absorb his malevolence, and ultimately it would do him in. Sooner or later, the land did everyone in.

From behind him, in the house, he could hear Ewing working at a bowl with a spoon, mixing something. One of his improbable poultices. Grayling couldn't look around: some connection in his body from his neck down to the wound would not allow it. The sound of stirring ceased and Ewing approached behind him. Puffing, muttering greetings and something about the day and its weather, the concoction in the bowl. His crippling lack of confidence meant every word of it was directed at the ground.

He arrived before Grayling now in a waft of booze, the bowl clutched like treasure before his round belly. 'A balm, lieutenant, an emollient. It will aid the healing.'

The substance in the bowl was thick and murky. A smile threatened to break across Grayling's face. He hadn't smiled in so long.

'From what have you made this balm, Doctor Ewing?'

'Kidneys, sir. The kidney of any large mammal is said to have curative properties. If...correctly prepared.'

'And what is the large mammal in this instance, doctor?'

'The badger, lieutenant. Badgers. A male and a female, to ensure unity of the essences.' He was slurring, and an odd obsequious gesture escaped him, the gist of which was that Grayling would be required to lower his trousers. The doctor held the spoon at the ready.

'I see this is a topical ointment.'

Ewing was wrapping his glasses onto his nose with his free hand. He nodded vigorously and his jowls wobbled. Grayling looked away to suppress his laughter, looked down towards the wharf on the near side of the cove. There was still activity there, despite the building storm, convicts and merchants packing and stowing, preparing for the rain.

A tiny white speck separated itself down there, curled away like a dust mote. It wound slowly up the path and became a human figure, a woman in a dress. Grayling squinted against the light: the sun was now at the verge of the giant cloudbank, ferocious in its last instants. The hill was ablaze in light but the cove was plunged in darkness. The woman stopped, turned to the sky and for a moment was no different from the birds at rest, white against the dun-coloured ground.

'Why don't you go home, Doctor Ewing?'

Ewing looked at his patient with undisguised horror. 'Lieutenant Grayling, you are at a very delicate stage of your recovery.'

'I do believe I will be fine. The day is about to turn: you ought to reward yourself with a drink.' It took so little; such was the compulsion.

'Yes, well…of course. I could come by tomorrow.'

'I don't think that will be necessary, Doctor Ewing. You may leave me alone from here on.'

A shadow of offence touched the doctor's face before the more powerful impulse took over and he picked up his bag, returned the bowl to the kitchen and hurried off. The last of the sun warmed Grayling's clothes and the blanket. The aching had a symmetry about it: it came from the centre of him, a place he could draw every sinew towards. It could be held and contained. But to be stilled like this, to be an invalid, was not his nature.

The giant eruption in the sky extinguished the light, sudden as a snuffed lantern. But not a drop had yet fallen. A thing he hadn't understood, and it came to him like a flood: how fortunate he was. It was Charlotte on the path—of course it was. Her steps, the sway of her hands and the tilt of her chin. She'd taken him to the end of his patience, had near enough outwitted him. She saw him now, shipwrecked on the grass, and she looked puzzled, then amused. Something about the light, the preternatural gloom and Charlotte the only bright point in it. He would turn a blind eye to a thousand of her ill-advised walks.

She'd picked up her skirts, was running now. Grayling saw the flash of light on the moving fabric of her dress and felt a quickening in his body as he waited for the thunder. A smell rose from the earth, a vapour that was of neither the ground nor the sky but deeply both.

In the time it took for him to breathe in and out the troubled heavens erupted: a flat, percussive wave that rumbled over the town from the south, rippling at its edges, a deep detonation at its centre. Birds rose and scattered in response to the sound. Had it always been so violent, so majestic here, before they came?

It felt like the thunder had broken over Botany Bay, well to the south: it was from there that the rain now swept in. He wondered what the Eora did when the heavens opened like this.

341

He had seen them under sandstone overhangs at night. Maybe the storm didn't bother them. Thunderstorms were something they could explain to their children like the stars and the wind. Men in ships were not.

She reached him, held him, laughed and kissed him. The first large drops smacked into them both.

Over her shoulder, through her hair, he watched the rain beating down on the roofs of the downhill houses, the pulverised droplets raising a spray. The sound was vast and it overwhelmed everything else: if the Eora were still calling to each other, and the lags and the lorikeets, the dogs and the swine and the fowl, all of it was consumed by the rushing of the rain.

43

❋ The chestnut mare slowed to a walk at the new chandlery on the southern side of the quay. Sydney still slept, lit only by an occasional oil lamp yellowing the windows of the larger houses. The waters of *warrane* were calm, the masts of the waiting vessels standing still. Dawn was still two hours away; the wind and all human activity had died with the moon.

The rider stepped down and tied off the bridle at a post by the wall. He searched the silent wharf a moment until a low whistle caught his attention. A man in sailor's clothes, beckoning from the wharf's edge.

'Conrad,' said the rider, approaching him with a hand extended.

The sailor lifted his face into the light: bearded like the rider but slightly younger. He was the right size. Boils on his neck, but it mattered none.

'Connor, sir. Connor Mailon.'

'Yes, of course.' The man smiled and shook his hand warmly. 'Can you take me to her?'

The younger man hesitated. 'You haven't told me your name.'

'I am Manfred.' A curl of amusement under the misshapen nose.

'Very well,' said the other man, though his face betrayed disquiet. He led them along the wharf for some distance until he came to a small sloop. The man could see the vessel was rigged and fully provisioned, and a small cluster of crewmen slept forward of the mast under rough blankets.

'This is the *Eliza*?'

'Yes sir,' whispered Connor Mailon.

'Not much of her. Still sailing at dawn, as planned?'

'Far as I know. Can we address the money please, if you don't mind?' He glanced at the sleeping crew. 'The other half?'

'Of course. Forgive me.' The man produced a small leather pouch from inside his coat and raised it before the sailor's eyes, then withdrew it. 'But there's a few small things before we do business.'

The sailor crossed his arms, and a look of wariness came over him. 'Well?'

'What county?'

'Sligo.'

'Town?'

'Mullaghmore.'

'Parents?'

'Mary and fuckin' Joseph.'

'Don't be impatient with me.'

The sailor sighed. 'William and Constance.'

The man studied the rigging sceptically. 'How's she sail?'

'Masthead rigged, genoa jib.' He pointed. 'Forestay, backstay and shrouds. Simple.'

'Fuck-all of it. This tub's supposed to carry survivors and cargo? She's barely a longboat.'

The sailor shrugged. 'Ten tons burthen. She'll get there.'

'Might not get back.' The man thought a moment. 'This is only the escort, right? Where's the leading lady?'

'Aye, the *Francis*. Over there.' The sailor nodded over the water to a schooner waiting on the far side of the cove.

'Ah, that's more like it.'

The man stepped down from the wharf onto the deck of the *Eliza;* it rocked faintly against its hawsers.

The sailor raised his voice now to an urgent hiss. 'What're ye fuckin doing? Get orf.'

'Just looking.' The man peered about, unconcerned. He took in the slumbering crew, the stores and the furled sails, then leaned back against the pinrail as the sailor climbed down to prevent him wandering further over the deck.

'None o' these men have met you, you say?'

'No,' said Connor Mailon. 'Got the job with the stevedore yesterday.'

'Hmm; aye. Have ye brothers or sisters, Conrad?' The man had his hands on the pinrail behind his hips, resting idly on the heads of the belaying pins.

The sailor's face turned to a scowl in the dark. This man was making no attempt to lower his voice. He seemed to revel in the risk of being challenged.

'A brother. Tommy. Younger, all right? Ye've got enough now, so be done with questionin' me. Told yeh. None of 'em knows me anyways.'

The man smiled broadly and clapped the sailor on the back.

'You're right,' he beamed. 'Come. I'll buy you a drink and we'll settle the money.'

He gestured for the sailor to climb off the gunwale ahead of him and then followed behind, leaving an empty bracket in the pinrail where one of the belaying pins had been.

⚓

The cut stone steps led up a short embankment and through a dark glade that followed the coast between the wharves and the town. The sailor was complaining louder now, arguing that the tavern would never serve them at this hour, that he had no cause to trust some Manfred if that's yer real name, that for the love of God his name was Connor not Conrad.

The man followed behind. The whining did not trouble him at all, though he felt tempted to hurry things along as they passed under the secretive canopy of the scrub. He curled his hand around the heavy head of the pin under his coat. An instinct counselled patience.

As the trees opened into a laneway with the glittering water on one side, they passed a row of timber yards. The first was filled with sheep, strange-looking beasts with heavy rolled coats and curling horns. *Now there's a slow road to a fortune,* thought the man. There were perhaps twenty of them pressed tightly together, flank to flank. Silent and quite still, as though they were mere depictions in a painting, not living things. The absence of movement, their flat stupid eyes. The sole thing that made them corporeal was the inescapable stink of shit.

Next came a sty fenced with lengths of rough-cut timber. As they came level with the fence at shoulder height, the man heard a hog snuffling in response to their passing. It was up now and moving their way, a fine beast of maybe five hundred pounds, trotters squelching under its weight as it approached through the mud. The shit-stink again, sourer, filling the curl of his nose.

Onward; and now he saw why he'd waited. The faint light of the stars was glowing on the place where the convicts had cut away the embankment above a small beach, revealing the cut face of a great pile of seashells. He knew the place; had considered it at length on his walks. Seashells, ashes and flakes of stone. The hand of man here, the ghosts of families and the deep burial of time. The convicts had arranged bricks to form a kiln—the ashes of the day's work still smouldered faintly in the great hearth they'd constructed. They were un-making in mere days that great aggregation of years, like sifting out the stars from the sky.

A whiter patch where the lime was heaped and the barrels stood in rows, filled and sealed, half-filled, empty. Wooden shovels, flat-bladed. And he saw it all perfectly. Poor Connor still walked ahead in hope of his rum, mumbling about something.

The man slid the pin from his coat, hefted it once in his hands and brought it down swiftly. Connor Mailon slumped facedown on the path, dead before he came to rest. It took the man some minutes to get all the clothes off him and to arrange them on himself. Although the singular blow had been sufficient, the sight of him naked awoke something else in the man and he gave him another and another until the vault of his skull had yielded and the egg-wobble brains jellied his blood. The man drew the pin several times over the leg of his discarded trousers, wiping the muck from it, then returned it to its place under his—Connor Mailon's—coat. It would still serve perfectly on the *Eliza*. Would perhaps whisper this memory to him once or twice.

He lifted Connor Mailon by his legs and dragged him to the barrel rows, further spillages stringing from his skull as it bumped over the rough ground. He found a barrel that was yet to receive its load and made Connor Mailon its contents, folding him arse-first into the darkness. The body wedged there for a moment, and the man took out the pin and struck the knees once each, hard, so the feet went in against his belly and the knees were inverted and topmost alongside the staring eyes.

It was a generous cask: there was room still for a dozen shovels of the lime. The dusted sailor looked back at him as he worked, until the powder covered his eyes and soon enough his wrongful knees as well.

The man searched the site and found a timber bucket. He took it down to the gleaming cove, where he filled it. He stood over the barrel, poured the water in and stepped back. Nothing happened for a moment, then the slaking took its course; bubbling, smoking and sputtering. A horrible stink rose from the tub and the man found himself laughing that he'd rather go back past the pig shit.

When the reaction had slowed he found himself a lid and tapped it in place with a stone. Then he rolled the barrel on its edge into the row where the completed ones stood.

And thus was interred Connor Mailon. Boils on his neck, but it mattered none.

The *Francis* and the *Eliza* reached Preservation Island on 10 June 1797. The majority of the survivors and the bulk of the cargo were loaded onto the two vessels, leaving behind a small complement of volunteers to guard whatever could not be carried.

On their return voyage, the vessels were separated in a storm. The *Francis,* carrying Captain Guy Hamilton, continued on to Sydney. There he began the long process of negotiating salvage rights and sale of the cargo. In all, three voyages were required, over nearly a year, to remove the remaining humans and cargo from the island. The rum was purchased by the New South Wales government at a generous price.

The wreck of the *Sydney Cove* lay slowly disintegrating on a shallow sandbank for one hundred and eighty years, before its eventual rediscovery on New Year's Day 1977.

No trace of the *Eliza* has ever been found.

Acknowledgments

Preservation was written as part of a PhD in Creative Writing at La Trobe University, Melbourne. I'm indebted to La Trobe's School of Humanities and Social Sciences for their financial support, and especially to my supervisors, Alison Ravenscroft and Juliane Roemhild, for their ideas, their patience and their faith in this story from the very beginning.

A circle of trusted sceptics including Damien Newton Brown, Lilly Serong, Jo Canham, Robert Gott, Matt Ryan, Dom Serong, Chris McDonald, Ed Prendergast and Nick Batzias read the manuscript at various stages and gave me valuable feedback.

My thanks also to Simon Barnard for the bobbin and the maps, Jarrod Ritchie for the ride to Preservation, Emma Viskic for Geminiani, Kate Grenville, Rebe Taylor and Mark McKenna for their wisdom, and Ben Wilkie for the Scots. For their gracious advice about Aboriginal culture, I'm grateful to the Gunaikurnai Land and Waters Corporation, Graham Moore of the Bega Local Aboriginal Land Council and Monaro-Ngarigo woman Lynette Solomon-Dent, all of whom offered friendship and support, not just information.

Books…there are so many books. On the wreck of the *Sydney Cove*, I was greatly assisted by Mark McKenna's *From the Edge: Australia's Lost Histories*, and *Sydney Cove*, by Michael Nash. On historical fiction writing, Tom Griffiths' *The Art of Time Travel*. On lascars, Aaron Jaffer's *Lascars and Indian Ocean Seafaring*. On Governor Hunter, I read *A Steady Hand* by Linda Groom, and on Pemulwuy, Eric Willmott's neglected but wonderful novel, *Pemulwuy*.

Two books that are essential reading for anyone interested in pre-contact Aboriginal life and agriculture are Bruce Pascoe's *Dark Emu* and Bill Gammage's *The Biggest Estate*. And soaring over all the reading I did, Grace Karskens' excellent history of early Sydney, *The Colony*.

I wish to thank Michael Heyward and the smart and dedicated team at Text; Chong Weng Ho for his cover and in particular Mandy Brett who, like all great editors, brings both the highwire and the net.

And lastly, my love and gratitude to my family, and especially my wife Lilly, for all the sacrifices—large and small—they have made during the writing of this book.